BEOWULF

To Professor Michael Drout, who taught me Old English and gave me the confidence to translate
Beowulf. And to Professor Tom Shippey, who helped me to swim in the dark mere of *Beowulf* studies.
And also to the late Professor J.R.R. Tolkien, who first kindled my love of all things Anglo-Saxon.
Wæs þú hál!

TABLE OF CONTENTS

BEOWULF
TRANSLATION & ORIGINAL TEXT

PART 1
DEFENDER OF THE DANES

PART II
THE LORD OF GEATLAND

COMMENTARY

Introduction

HISTORY OF *BEOWULF*

Beowulf is one of the most famous poems in the English language. It has inspired myriad writers, from J.R.R. Tolkien to Michael Crichton to Neil Gaiman. It is the longest poem in Old English, the language of the Anglo-Saxons, at 3,182 lines long, written in alliterative verse, running from folios 129r to 198v in the so-called 'Nowell Codex', a medieval manuscript containing a poetic version of *Judith*, a prose version of the *Life of St. Christopher*, *The Wonders of the East*, and *Alexander's Letter to Aristotle*, as well as *Beowulf*. *Beowulf* concerns the exploits of Beowulf, a 6th century Scandinavian prince, and later king, and his battles against the monster, Grendel, his mother and a dragon.

The Nowell Codex was privately owned first by Laurence Nowell in the 1560s, and then Sir Robert Bruce Cotton, his son and his grandson, who gifted the entire Cotton Library to the British Museum in 1753, before it was moved to the British Library in 1973. On October 23, 1731 a fire broke out in Ashburnham House, where the Cotton Library was held. The fire destroyed the binding of Cotton Vitellius A. XV (the volume that held the Nowell Codex) but the pages remained mostly intact. However, the codex was later partially damaged by handling, until it was put in paper frames in 1845. (Orchard, 2003) In 1787, the Icelandic scholar, Grímur Thorkelín transcribed *Beowulf* and in 1815, he published the first translation of the poem, albeit in Latin. In 1833, John Mitchell Kemble improved upon Thorkelín's transcription with his new edition of the poem. Many editions were released in the ensuing years, until in 1922, Freidrich Klaeber released a definitive scholarly edition. (Meyer, 2012)

Modern *Beowulf* scholarship really started in London on November 25, 1936. Professor J.R.R. Tolkien, later of *The Lord of the Rings* fame, presented the 1936 Sir Israel Gollancz Memorial Lecture to the British Academy. His lecture was titled *Beowulf- The Monsters and the Critics*. Not only is this considered perhaps the greatest essay on Beowulf scholarship ever written, by many scholars, but "possibl[y] ... the single most influential essay in the history of literary studies in the twentieth century." (Drout, 2010)

AUTHORSHIP OF *BEOWULF*

The *Beowulf* Manuscript was most likely written down in early 11th century Wessex, probably during the reign of Æthelred the Unready, but seems to have been a copy of an older manuscript.

For many years, it was debated whether or not *Beowulf* was the work of a single author. Many, including Professor Tolkien, argued that the poem was written down as a single whole. Some of these scholars thought that it had been authored by Cynewulf, a late 8th and early 9th Century poet who wrote poems such as *Christ II* and *The Fate of the Apostles* and possibly poems like *Andreas* and *The Dream of the Rood*. Others, including Francis P. Magoun, argued that *Beowulf* consisted of several poems stitched together. Modern analysis of the poem, however, suggests that *Beowulf* is almost certainly the work of a single author, but probably not Cynewulf. (Neidorf, et al, 2019)

Most scholars believe that *Beowulf* was written during the 7th or 8th Centuries, a time when England was firmly Christian, but Paganism was well remembered. It is usually thought to have a clerical authorship, but was written for a secular audience. Based on the dialect of various words used in the poem, it is thought to have first been written in one of the Anglian kingdoms, probably

n either Mercia or Northumbria, before being translated to the Wessex dialect by the scribes. (Bjork, 1998)

I suggest that the original poet of *Beowulf* was a Northumbrian monk, writing during the Age of Bede, the late 7th or early 8th Centuries. Professor Tom Shippey suggests that *Beowulf* was composed at a monastery within the triangle between Ripon, Whitby and Hartlepool, with evidence ranging from local folklore (like the Hart Hall Hob, relating to Grendel at Heorot, or Peg Powler, relating to Grendel's Mother) to places and place-names (Hell's Kettles, relating to Grendel's Mere, or Hartlepool, relating to the stag who will not enter the Mere) to similarities in manuscripts from the area (similar views on virtuous pagans, an uncommon view in the rest of Anglo-Saxon England) to local history (this area being possibly an area of Geatish settlement). (Shippey, 2015) More in written on this throughout the Commentary.

BEOWULF — CHRISTIAN OR PAGAN?

Perhaps the greatest and longest running controversy surrounding *Beowulf* concerns religion. Was the poem originally Christian or pagan? Myriad articles and books have been written on this subject. Of course, the real 6th Century Scandinavia was pagan and there are no records of any attempts to Christianize Scandinavia before the 9th Century, so some argue that the poem used to be pagan and the Christian elements were extrapolations made by the monkish scribes. Others argue that Christian Anglo-Saxons composed the poem (perhaps based in part on earlier legends,) and that the pagan elements were artificially added. While this argument is still ongoing, the most widely accepted belief is that *Beowulf* is of Christian origin. "The Christian elements are almost without exception so deeply ingrained in the very fabric of the poem that they cannot be explained away as the work of a revisor or a later interpolator." (Klaeber, 2008)

Beowulf, contrary to popular belief, actually has very few pagan elements. The characters, by and large, if not 'Christian' per se, are monotheists. While God is often mentioned in the poem, pagan gods are not. The only 'pagan elements' in the poem, like cremation, are rather more secular in nature, than pagan. "Christianity is part of the very fabric of Beowulf; the pagan elements are not. When we examine those elements that are actually secular rather than pagan, references to practices that ceased altogether or became criminal with the introduction of Christianity... we find that they are few in number and easily insoluble. Their removal would harm but not destroy the poem... but one can easily conceive of it without its few touches of paganism." (Benson, 1967)

POETRY OF *BEOWULF*

There are a few notes that should be made about the Anglo-Saxon style of poetry, before I begin my translation. Anglo-Saxon poetry, and Germanic poetry in general, does not use rhyming; it uses alliteration, Each line is broken into two half-lines, and two or three words that begin with the same sound are used in that line. Mind you, the sounds that alliterate are not necessarily the same letter, i.e. a hard *C* alliterates with *K*. Vowels, however, are Wild Cards. Therefore, an *E* can alliterate with an *A* or an *O*, as well as with another *E*. Old English also did not use the letter *J*, but several other Germanic languages did. However, it is used as a vowel; a *J* gives the sound of a *Y* (as in *yogurt* or *yes*), rather than a *Dg* sound (as in *edge* or *James)*. Occasionally, *Beowulf* will refer to things that originally began with a *J* (like *Jute*, which was transliterated as *Éote*). In these cases the *J* is retained and should be pronounced as *Y* in order for the alliteration to work. Other rules for pronunciation are provided in Notes on Language and Pronunciation.

Notes on Language and Pronunciation

Beowulf is primarily written in the West Saxon dialect of Old English, with some Mercian and Northumbrian words.

Unless otherwise stated, pronunciations are in the General American dialect. IPA stands for International Phonetic Alphabet.

A is pronounced like the *o* in *stop*, (/a/ in IPA).

Ã is pronounced like the *a* in *law*, (/aː/ in IPA).

Æ is pronounced like the *a* in *cat*, (/æ/ in IPA).

Ǣ is pronounced like the *a* in *care*, (/æː/ in IPA).

C is pronounced like the *k* in *king*, (/k/ in IPA).

Ċ (a C behind an *I, E* or *Æ*) is pronounced like the *ch* in *child*, (/tʃ/ in IPA).

Cg is pronounced like the *dg* in *ledge*, (/dʒ/ in IPA).

E is pronounced like the *e* in *bet*, (/ɛ/ in IPA).

Ē is pronounced like the *a* in *save*, (/eː/ in IPA).

F is pronounced like the *v* in *vine*, (/v/ in IPA), except when it is the first letter in a word, in which case its pronounced like the *f* in *father*, (/f/ in IPA).

G is pronounced like the *g* in *good* (/g/ in IPA).

Ġ (usually a G before an *I, E* or *Æ*) is pronounced like the *y* in *yes*, (/j/ in IPA).

H is pronounced like the *ch* in German *nicht*, (/ç/ in IPA), except when it is the first letter in a word, in which case its pronounced like the *h* in *hat*, (/h/ in IPA).

I is pronounced like the *i* in *hit*, (/i/in IPA).

Ī is pronounced like the *ee* in *eel*, (/iː/ in IPA).

Ng is pronounced like the *ng* in *henge*, (/ŋ/ in IPA).

O is pronounced like the *o* in *pond*, (/o/ in IPA).

Ō is pronounced like the *o* in *hope*, (/oː/ in IPA).

R is slightly trilled, as in Scots, but not as much as in Spanish.

Sc is pronounced like the *sh* in *she*, (/ʃ/ in IPA).

Both *Þ* and *Ð* are both pronounced like the *th* in *this*, (/θ/ in IPA).

U is pronounced like the *u* in *dull*, (/u/ in IPA).

Ū is pronounced like the *oo* in *moon*, (/uː/ in IPA).

Y is pronounced like the *u* in *dune*, (/y/ in IPA).

Ȳ is pronounced like *ew*, (/yː/ in IPA).

In Old English, every letter is pronounced. Other letters are pronounced as they are in Modern English. All emendations are enclosed in brackets (())

This is a simplified pronunciation guide, and does not show all of the complexities of the language. Anyone wanting to learn more about Old English is encouraged to buy *Drout's Quick and Easy Old English*.

Map

Scandinavia in Beowulf's day (from Andy Orchard's *Beowulf: A Critical Companion*)

Geneologies

GEATS

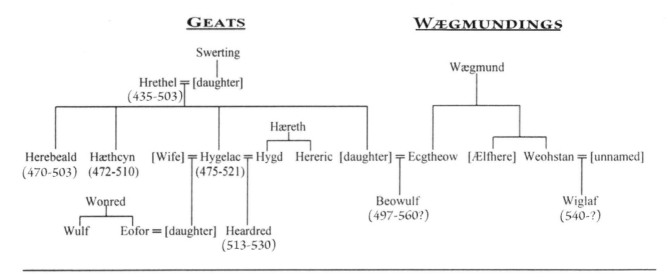

Swerting

Hrethel = [daughter]
(435-503)

Herebeald (470-503) Hæthcyn (472-510) [Wife] = Hygelac = Hygd Hæreth Hereric [daughter]

Wonred

Wulf Eofor = [daughter] Heardred (513-530)

WÆGMUNDINGS

Wægmund

Ecgtheow [Ælfhere] Weohstan = [unnamed]

Beowulf (497-560?) Wiglaf (540-?)

DANES

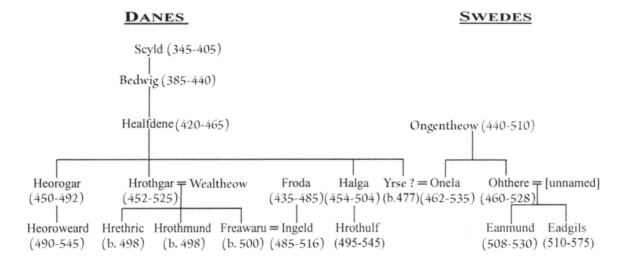

Scyld (345-405)

Bedwig (385-440)

Healfdene (420-465)

Heorogar (450-492) Hrothgar = Wealtheow (452-525) Froda (435-485) Halga (454-504) Yrse ? = Onela (b.477)(462-535)

Heoroweard (490-545) Hrethric (b. 498) Hrothmund (b. 498) Freawaru = Ingeld (b. 500)(485-516) Hrothulf (495-545)

SWEDES

Ongentheow (440-510)

Ohthere = [unnamed] (460-528)

Eanmund (508-530) Eadgils (510-575)

FRISIANS   HALF-DANES

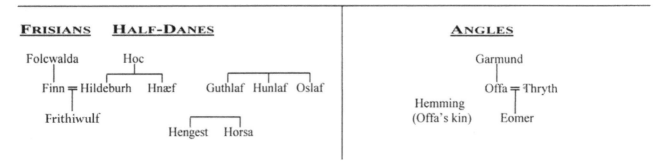

Folcwalda Hoc

Finn = Hildeburh Hnæf Guthlaf Hunlaf Oslaf

Frithiwulf

Hengest Horsa

ANGLES

Garmund

Offa = Thryth

Hemming (Offa's kin) Eomer

* For more on the proposed birth and death dates, refer to the Timeline at the end of the Commentary

BEOWULF

Prologue
Song of the Scyldings

How we have heard* of the glory   of the Spear-Danes*,
of the people's kings   in ages past;
we have been told of the deeds   the athelings* did!

       Oft did Scyld Scefing*   seize the mead-benches
5   of frightened foes   from many clans.
He brought terror to the Eorlas*   ere he was first found
forlorn and friendless.   He lived to see comfort,
waxed under welkin,   worthy of honor,
'til to him,   each of the neighboring nations
10   o'er the whale's road*   should yield
and give tribute.   That was a good king!

       Afterwards, an heir   was born to him,
young in the yard.   God sent him
to favor the folk.   He saw the great distress
15   that they had ere endured*,   without a leader
for a long time.   Then the Lord of Life,
the Wielder of Glory,   granted them worldly honor.
Bedwig* was renowned,   his fame spread far,
the son of Scyld   in the Scandian lands*.
20   So should a young man   do good deeds,
give gifts of land,   while in his father's bosom,
so that in old age,   when war comes,
those steadfast retainers   will stand with him,
willing warriors.   Thus by worthy deeds shall
25   a man earn honor   among the folk.

       Scyld then departed   at his appointed hour*;
very strong, he passed   into the protection of the Lord.
Then they bore him   to the sea's billows,
his hearth-companions   as he himself bade,
30   while he yet wielded words,   the friend of the Scyldings;
belovèd land-holder,   he had ruled for a long time.

Hwæt wé Gár-Dena   in ġeár-dagum,
þéod-cyninga   þrym ġefrúnon;
hú ðá æðelingas   ellen fremedon!

Oft Scyld Scéfing   sceaþena þréatum
5   monegum mǽġþum   meodo-setla oftéah.
Eġsode Eorl(e)   syððan ǽrest wearð
féasceaft funden.   Hé þæs frófre ġebád,
wéox under wolcnum,   weorð-myndum þáh,
oð þæt him ǽghwylċ   þára ymb-sittendra
10   ofer hron-ráde   hýran scolde,
gomban ġyldan.   Þæt wæs gód cyning!

Ðǽm eafera wæs   æfter cenned,
ġeong in ġeardum.   Þone God sende
folce tó frófre.   Fyren-ðearfe onġeat
15   þæt híe ǽr drugon,   aldor-léase
lange hwíle.   Him þæs Líf-Fréa,
Wuldres Wealdend,   worold-áre forġeaf;
Béo(w) wæs bréme,   blǽd wíde sprang,
Scyldes eafera   Scedelandum in.
20   Swá sceal ġeong guma   góde ġewyrċean,
fromum feoh-ġiftum,   on fæder bearme,
þæt hine on ylde,   eft ġewuniġen
wil-ġesíþas,   þonne wíg cume,
léode ġelǽsten.   Lof-dǽdum sceal
25   in mǽġþa ġehwǽre   man ġeþéon.

Him ðá Scyld ġewát   tó ġescæp-hwíle;
fela-hrór féran   on Fréan wǽre.
Hí hyne þá ætbǽron   tó brimes faroðe,
swǽse ġesíþas   swá hé selfa bæd,
30   þenden wordum wéold,   wine Scyldinga;
léof land-fruma,   lange áhte.

There in the haven stood   the ring-stemmed ship,
icy and outbound,   the atheling's vessel.
They laid out   their belovéd king,
35   the glorious giver of rings*   in the bosom of the ship,
the mighty one by the mast.   There were many mathoms*;
they brought gold and gems   from far-off lands.
Ne'er have I heard tell   of a more splendid ship,
adorned with battle-weapons   and war-armor,
40   blades and byrnies!*   On his bosom lay
many mathoms,   which must
float far   o'er the flood with him.
No less the gifts   they loaded on him,
the king's treasure,   than those who
45   first had him   sent forth,
alone upon the waves,   only a child.
Then they set   a golden standard
high above his head   and let the waters bear him away,
gave him to the sea.   Their souls were saddened,
50   mournful in mind.   Men cannot
truly say,   neither hall-counselors,
nor heroes under the heavens,   who collected that cargo.*

Then did Bedwig Scylding   rule in the burg*,
belovèd king of the people.   For a long time
55   was he well known among the folk,   after his father had passed on,
an ealdorman o'er the earth,   'til to him was born
high Healfdene*.   He held life for a time,
old and battle-grim,   the glad Scylding.
He was father   to four bairns,
60   born in this world,   the leader of the war-band,
Heorogar and Hrothgar   and Halga the Good,
and, I have heard, Yrse,   who was Onela's queen,
the Battle-Scylfing's   bed-fellow.

Then was Hrothgar   given glory in war,
65   such honor in battle   that his belovèd kinsmen
eagerly obeyed,   'til the young warriors grew
into a mighty host.   It then came to his mind
that he would bid   a bright hall,
a great mead-hall   to be built by men,
70   mightier than any man   had ever known,
and there within   he would allot all things,
to the young and the old,   such as God gave him,
except the common land   or the lives of men.

14

Þǽr æt hýðe stód   hringed-stefna,
ísiġ ond útfús,   æþelinges fær.
Álédon þá   léofne þéoden,
35   béaga bryttan,   on bearm scipes,
mǽrne be mæste.   Þǽr wæs mádma fela;
of feor-wegum   frætwa ġelǽded.
Ne hýrde iċ ċýmlicor   ċéol ġeġyrwan,
hilde-wǽpnum   ond heaðo-wǽdum,
40   billum ond byrnum!   Him on bearme læġ
mádma mæniġo,   þá him mid scoldon
on flódes ǽht   feor ġewítan.
Nalæs hí hine lǽssan   lácum téodan,
þéod-ġestréonum,   þon(ne) þá dydon
45   þé hine æt frumsceafte   forð onsendon,
ǽnne ofer ýðe   umborwesende.
Þá ġýt híe him ásetton   seġen gyldenne
héah ofer héafod,   léton holm beran,
ġéafon on gár-secg.   Him wæs ġéomor sefa,
50   murnende mód.   Men ne cunnon
secgan tó soðe,   sele-rǽden(d)e,
hæleð under heofenum,   hwá þǽm hlæste onféng.

I

Ðá wæs on burgum   Béo(w) Scyldinga,
léof léod-cyning.   Longe þráge
55   folcum ġefrǽġe,   fæder ellor hwearf,
aldor of earde,   oþ þæt him eft onwóc
héah Healfdene.   Héold þenden lifde
gamol ond gúð-réouw,   glæde Scyldin(g).
Ðǽm féower bearn   forð-ġerímed,
60   in worold wócun,   weoroda rǽswa(n),
Heorogár ond Hróðgár   ond Hálga Til,
hýrde iċ, þæt (Ýrse   wæs On)elan cwén.
Heaðo-Scilfingas   heals-ġebedde.

Þá wæs Hróðgáre   here-spéd ġyfen,
65   wíġes weorð-mynd,   þæt him his wine-mágas
ġeorne hýrdon,   oðð þæt séo ġeogoð ġewéox
mago-driht miċel.   Him on mód bearn
þæt heal-reċed   hátan wolde,
medo-ærn miċel   men ġewyrċean,
70   þon(n)e yldo bearn   ǽfre ġefrúnon,
ond þǽr on innan   eall ġedǽlan
ġeongum ond ealdum,   swylċ him God sealde,
búton folc-scare   ond feorum gumena.

I have heard then   that the work was widely proclaimed,
75   to many men   across Middle-Earth*,
to furnish the folk-stead.   In a while it passed for him
and swiftly for the men,   that it stood ready,
the greatest of halls.   Heorot he named it*,
he whose words   had wide worth.
80   He made not empty boasts,   but bestowed rings freely,
treasures at the table.   The hall loomed
high and horn-gabled,   awaiting the cruel fire,
those loathly flames.   The time was not far off
when the feud   'twixt father and son-in-law,
85   born of enmity,   would reawaken warfare.*

Ðá iċ wíde ġefræġn   weorc ġebannan,
75 maniġre mǽġþe   ġeond þisne Middan-Ġeard,
folc-stede frætwan.   Him on fyrste ġelomp
ǽdre mid yldum,   þæt hit wearð eal ġearo,
heal-ærna mǽst.   Scóp him Heort naman,
sé þe his wordes ġeweald   wíde hæfde.
80 Hé béot ne áléh,   béagas dǽlde,
sinc æt symle.   Sele hlífade
héah ond horn-ġéap,   heaðo-wylma bád,
láðan líġes.   Ne wæs hit lenge þá ġén
þæt se (e)cg-hete   áþum-swé(or)an
85 æfter wæl-níðe   wæcnan scolde.

Part I
Defender of the Danes

Chapter I
The Curse of Cain

Then a mighty Demon,   who lived in the moors,
suffered some time,   he who lived in the shadows
heard each day   the din of revelry,
loud from the hall.   There was harp music,
90   sweetly sang the scop*;   he who knew spake
of the making of Men.   He told from afar,
quoth he that the Almighty   wrought this world,
wide fields   by water encircled,
and victoriously set   the sun and moon
95   as lamps to illumine   the paths of land-dwellers.
He bedecked   the bosom of the earth
with limbs and leaves;   life also He created,
each and ev'ry race that breathes   and moves.

Thus, the retainers   dwelt in delight,
100   'til finally one night,   a fiend from Hell*
began to deal   death to the Danes.
This grim gast*   hight Grendel*,
notorious mark-stepper,   he who held the moors,
fens and fastnesses,   the country of the Giant-race*;
105   that wretched being   ruled a while
since the Shaper   had judged
the clan of Cain*   and avenged that murder,
the eternal Lord,   in which Abel was slain.
He was not fain of that feud,   for He banished him far,
110   the Architect, for this sin,   from the sight of Man.
From him, all broods   of evil were born,
Ettins and Dark Elves   and spirits of Hell,
and also the Giants,   who warred with God
for many long years.   For that, He dealt them their due.

Ðá se ellen-gǽst   earfoðlíċe
þráge ġeþolode,   sé þe in þýstrum bád,
þæt hé dógora ġehwám   dréam ġehýrde,
hlúdne in healle.   Þǽr wæs hearpan swéġ,
90   swutol sang scopes;   sǽġde sé þe cúþe
frum-sceaft fíra.   Feorran reċċan,
cwæð þæt se Ælmihtiga   eorðan worh(te),
wlite-beorhtne wang   swá wæter bebúgeð,
ġesette siġe-hréþiġ   sunnan ond mónan
95   léoman tó léohte   land-búendum
ond ġefrætwade   foldan scéatas
leomum ond léafum;   líf éac ġesceóp,
cynna ġehwylcum   þára ðe cwice hwyrfaþ.

Swá ðá driht-guman   dréamum lifdon,
100   éadiġlíċe,   oð ðæt án ongan
fyrene fre(m)man,   féond on Helle.
Wæs se grimma gǽst   Grendel háten,
mǽre mearc-stapa,   sé þe móras héold,
fen ond fæsten,   Fífel-cynnes eard;
105   won-sǽlí wer   weardode hwíle,
siþðan him Scyppend   forscrifen hæfde
in Cáines cynne,   þone cwealm ġewræc,
éċe Drihten,   þæs þe hé Ábel slóg.
Ne ġefeah Hé þǽre fǽhðe,   ac Hé hine feor forwræc,
110   Metod, for þý máne,   Man-cynne fram.
Þanon untýdras   ealle onwócon,
Eotenas ond Ylfe   ond Orc-néas,
swylċe Ġígantas,   þá wið Gode wunnon
lange þráge.   Hé him ðæs léan forġeald.

115   When night had fallen,   Grendel found
        the high house   where the Ring-Danes
        dozed off   after their beer drinking.
        He found there inside   the atheling's people
        asleep after symbel*;   they had known not sorrow,
120   misery of men.   That unsound wight,
        grim and greedy,   soon was ready.
        Wild and wicked,   he took from their rest
        thirty thegns*,   thence he went back,
        pleased with his plunder,   fared home
125   and with the bodies of the dead,   his dwelling sought.

        Then it was,   in the darkness 'afore the dawn,
        Grendel's war-strength   manifested itself unto men.
        Thus after plenty,   weeping went up,
        great sorrow that morning.   That mighty king,
130   the old and good atheling   unblithely* sat.
        The mighty one suffered sorrow   for his fallen thegns,
        when he looked   upon the loathly tracks
        of the wicked gast;   the struggle was strong,
        evil and overlong.   Nor was it a long time,
135   but after one night,   that again he carried out
        more murderous deeds.   He did not mourn;
        feud and ferocity,   he stood fast in these!
        Then was it easy   to find a few men
        who would seek someplace   further to rest,
140   a bed among the bowers,   when it was pointed out to them,
        truly told   by a clear sign,
        his hatred for the hall-thegns.   They must go
        farther and faster   to escape that fiend.

        And so it was that he ruled   and wrestled with justice,
145   one with all,   'till idle stood
        that high house.   For a great while,
        twelve winters' time,   the friend of the Scyldings,
        endured suffering   and sorrow,
        wide-spread woe.   Therefore to men it was,
150   children of men,   clearly sung
        in sad songs   that Grendel worked
        long against Hrothgar,   carrying out his cruel attacks,
        fear and feud   for many seasons,
        constant sacks.   He did not desire peace
155   with any man   of Danish might
        to withhold murder,   or wergild* pay.

115 Ġewát ðá néosian,   syþðan niht becóm,
     héan húses   hú hit Hring-Dene
     æfter béor-þeġe,   ġebún hæfdon.
     Fand þá ðǽr inne   æþelinga ġedriht
     swefan æfter symble;   sorge ne cúðon,
120 won-sceaft wera.   Wiht unhǽlo,
     grim ond grǽdiġ,   ġearo sóna wæs.
     Réoc ond réþe,   ond on ræste ġenam
     þrítiġ þeġna,   þanon eft ġewát,
     húðe hrémiġ,   tó hám faran
125 mid þǽre wæl-fylle   wíca néosan.

     Ðá wæs, on úhtan   mid ǽr-dæġe,
     Grendles gúð-cræft   gumum undyrne.
     Þá wæs æfter wiste,   wóp up áhafen,
     miċel morgen-swéġ.   Mǽre þéoden,
130 æþeling ǽr-gód,   unblíðe sæt.
     Þolode ðrýð-swýð   þeġn-sorge dréah,
     syðþan híe þæs láðan   lást scéawedon
     werġan gástes;   wæs þæt ġewin tó strang,
     láð ond longsum.   Næs hit lengra fyrst,
135 ac ymb áne niht,   eft ġefremede
     morð-beala máre   ond nó mearn fore.
     Fǽhðe ond fyrene,   wæs tó fæst on þám.
     Þá wæs éað-fynde,   þé him elles hwǽr
     ġerúmlícor   ræste (sóhte),
140 bed æfter búrum,   ðá him ġebéacnod wæs,
     ġesæġd sóðlíċe,   sweotolan tácne,
     heal-ðeġnes hete.   Héold hyne syðþan
     fyr ond fæstor   sé þǽm féonde ætwand.

     Swá ríxode   ond wið rihte wan,
145 ána wið eallum,   oð þæt ídel stód
     húsa sélest.   Wæs séo hwíl miċel,
     twelf wintra tíd,   torn ġeþolode
     wine Scyld(ing)a,   wéana ġehwelċne,
     sídra sorga.   Forðám (secgum) wearð,
150 ylda bearnum,   undyrne cúð
     ġyddum ġéomore   þætte Grendel wan
     hwíle wið Hróþgár,   hete-níðas wæġ,
     fyrene ond fǽhðe,   fela missera,
     singále sæce.   Sibbe ne wolde
155 wið manna hwone   mæġenes Deniġa,
     feorh-bealo feorran,   féa þingian.

None of the witan* had need for
a bright boon from their bane's hands.
Still, that awful fighter attacked,
160 that dark death-shadow. Veterans and youths
he stayed and snared. He held the deepest night
on the misty moors, for men ken not
where necromancers* wander in their wakes!

Thus, many sins 'gainst Mankind,
165 the loathly lone-walker oft committed,
hard humiliation. In Heorot he ruled,
the bright hall in the black night.
He would not greet the Gift-Seat*,
the Maker's mathom, nor did he hold Him in repute.

170 Great was the wretchedness of the Scyldings' ward,
his heart was heavy. Many oft were seated,
the councilors considered their redes,
what strong-minded men thought best
to do against the sudden assault.
175 They prayed at heathen harrows*,
and offered to idols; they bade in words
that they would find comfort from the Slayer of Souls,
for the pain of the people. Such was their habit,
the hope of heathens; they remembered Hell
180 in their hearts, but remembered not the Creator,
the Judge of Deeds. They knew not the Lord God,
nor did they praise Heaven's Helm,
the Glory-Wielder. Woe be to they who must,
through savage oppression, shove their souls
185 into the fire's embrace, where they can expect no relief
or alter anything; but well is it for they who are able,
after their death-day, to seek the Lord
and find peace in the Father's embrace!

24

Né þǽr nǽniġ witena   wénan þorfte
beorhtre bóte   tó ban(an) folmum.
(Ac se,) ǽġlǽċa   éhtende wæs,
160   deorc déaþ-scua.   Duguþe ond ġeogoþe,
seomade ond syrede.   Sin-nihte héold,
mistiġe móras;   men ne cunnon
hwyder helrúnan   hwyrftum scríþað!

Swá fela fyrena   féond Mancynnes,
165   atol án-gengea   oft ġefremede,
heardra hýnða.   Heorot eardode,
sinc-fáge sel   sweartum nihtum.
Nó hé þone ġif-stól   grétan móste,
máþðum for Metode,   né his myne wisse.

170   Þæt wæs wræc miċel   wine Scyldinga,
módes brecða.   Moniġ oft ġesæt,
ríċe tó rúne   rǽd eahtedon,
hwæt swíðferhðum   sélest wǽre
wið fǽr-gryrum   tó ġefremmanne.
175   Hwílum híe ġehéton   æt h(æ)rg-trafum,
wíġ-weorþunga;   wordum bǽdon,
þæt him Gást-Bona   ġéoce ġefremede,
wið þéod-þréaum.   Swylċ wæs þéaw hyra,
hǽþenra hyht;   Helle ġemundon
180   in mód-sefan.   Metod híe ne cúþon,
Dǽda Démend;   ne wiston híe Drihten God,
né híe húru Heofena Helm   herian ne cúþon,
Wuldres Waldend.   Wá bið þǽm ðe sceal,
þurh slíðne níð,   sáwle bescúfan
185   in fýres fæþm,   frófre ne wénan
wihte ġewendan;   wél bið þǽm þe mót,
æfter déað-dæġe,   Drihten séċean
ond tó Fæder fæþmum   freoðo wilnian!

Chapter II
Beowulf's Welcome

So then during this time's trouble,   Healfdene's son
190   ceaselessly seethed.   Nor could the wise hero
reject woe;   the struggle was strong,
loathly and overlong,   which befell the people,
enforcing dire distress,   the greatest of night-evils!

Then, Hygelac's thegn   heard from his home
195   of Grendel's deeds,   he who was good among the Geats.*
Of the might of Mankind,   he was the strongest
and the doughtiest   in those days,
noble and tall.   Then, he bade to be built
a wave-runner.   The war-lord, quoth he,
200   that o'er the swan-road   he wished to seek,
that famèd lord,   for he was in need of men.
Of his journey,   mindful men
found little fault,*   for he was dear to them.
They encouraged the strong-minded one,   and observed the omens.*
205   The good one had   from the Geatish people
chosen companions,   those who were keenest
that he could find.   Fifteen in number,
they sought the sea-wood.   He guided the men,
he who was wise in ship-craft,   to the shore.

210   Time went on.   The floater was on the waves,
the boat under the berg.   The men made ready;
they mounted the prow   o'er the wild waves,
the sea churned with sand.   The sailors bore
from the ship's bosom,   bright trappings,
215   wondrous war-gear;   the men pushed out
on their willing way   in the well-braced ship.
Then they traveled o'er the waves,   the wind urged them on,
that foamy-necked floater,   most like unto a bird,
until the appointed time,   on the second day,
220   the curvèd prow   that had carried them far,

III

Swá ðá mǽl-ċeare,   maga Healfdenes
190   singála séað.   Ne mihte snotor hæleð
wéan onwendan,   wæs þæt ġewin tó swýð,
láþ ond longsum,   þé on ðá léode becóm,
nýd-wracu níþ-grim,   niht-bealwa mǽst!

Þæt fram hám ġefræġn   Hiġeláces þeġn
195   gód mid Ġéatum,   Grendles dǽda.
Sé wæs Moncynnes   mæġenes strengest
on þǽm dæġe   þysses lífes,
æþele ond éacen.   Hét him ýðlidan
gódne ġeġyrwan.   Cwæð, hé gúðcyning,
200   ofer swan-ráde   séċean wolde,
mǽrne þéoden,   þá him wæs manna þearf.
Ðone síðfæt him,   snotere ċeorlas
lýt-hwón lógon,   þéah hé him léof wǽre.
Hwetton hiġe(r)ófne,   hǽl sċéawedon.
205   Hæfde se góda   Ġéata léoda
cempan ġecorone,   þára þe hé ċénoste
findan mihte.   Fíftýna sum,
sund-wudu sóhte.   Secg wísade,
lagu-cræftiġ mon,   land-ġemyrċu.

210   Fyrst forð ġewát.   Flota wæs on ýðum,
bát under beorge.   Beornas ġearwe;
on stefn stigon   stréamas wundon,
sund wið sande.   Secgas bǽron
on bearm nacan,   beorhte frætwe,
215   gúð-searo ġeatolíċ;   guman út scufon
weras on wil-síð   wudu bundenne.
Ġewát þá ofer wǽġ-holm,   winde ġefýsed
flota fámí-heals,   fugle ġelícost,
oð þæt ymb ántíd,   óþres dógores,
220   wunden-stefna   ġewaden hæfde,

that the seafarers   sighted land,
shining sea-cliffs,   steep hills
and broad headlands.   Then was the sea sailed,
their voyage was at an end.   Then up quickly
225   the Weder-folk fared forth   onto the strand,
moored the sea-wood.   They shook their mail-shirts,
their war-gear,   and thanked God,
that the sea-voyage   had been easy.

Then from the walls,   a Scylding ward saw them,
230   he who held   the sea-cliffs.
They bore bright shields   o'er the gangplank,
ready war-gear.   Curiosity arose in him
to know who   these warriors were.
Forth he rode,   his steed to the strand,
235   Hrothgar's thegn.   With strength, he shook
his mighty wood-shaft,   and in formal words spake,

"Who art thou,   ye armor possessors,
wearing byrnies,   who thus in thy broad ship
over the sea-road,   sailing came
240   hither o'er the waves?   I am the
sea-warden.   I hold the watch o'er the shore,
so that no foe   may fare to Danemark
with a fleet   to harry the folk.
Ne'er more openly   have approached
245   bearers of linden,   nor hath ye the leave-word
from the war-makers.   Clearly, ye ken not,
our kinsman's consent.   Nor have I seen a mightier
earl on this earth   than thee,
a warrior in armor.   Thou art no mere retainer,
250   by weapons made worthy,   'less thy splendor deceives me,
a peerless visage!   Now, I must know your
folk and forbearers,   ere ye go further hence,
lest ye be spies   to scout out Danemark.
Now, ye far-farers,   I ask thee again,
255   strangers from across the sea,   and hear my
plain thought-   haste is best,
to confess   from whence ye came."

þæt ðá líðende   land ġesáwon,
brim-clifu blícan,   beorgas stéape,
síde sǽ-næssas.   Þá wæs sund liden,
eoletes æt ende.   Þanon up hraðe
225 Wedera léode   on wang stigon,
sǽ-wudu sǽldon.   Syrċan hrysedon,
gúð-ġewǽdo;   Gode þancedon
þæs þe him ýþláde   éaðe wurdon.

Þá of wealle ġeseah   weard Scildinga,
230 sé þe holm-clifu   healdan scolde.
Beran ofer bolcan   beorhte randas,
fyrd-searu fúslícu.   Hine fyrwyt bræc
mód-ġehyġdum   hwæt þá men wǽron.
Ġewát him þá tó waroðe   wicge rídan,
235 þeġn Hróðgáres.   Þrymmum cwehte
mæġen-wudu mundum,   meþel-wordum fræġn,

"Hwæt syndon ġé,   searo-hæbbendra,
byrnum werede,   þé þus brontne ċéol
ofer lagu-strǽte,   lǽdan cwómon
240 hider ofer holmas?   (Iċ hwí)le wæs
ende-sǽta,   ǽġ-wearde héold,
þé on land Dena   láðra nǽniġ
mid scip-herġe   sceðþan ne meahte.
Nó hér cúðlícor   cuman ongunnon
245 lind-hæbbende,   né ġé léafnes-word
gúð-fremmendra.   Ġearwe ne wisson,
mága ġemédu.   Nǽfre iċ máran ġeseah
eorla ofer eorþan   ðonne is éower sum,
secg on searwum.   Nis þæt seld-guma,
250 wǽpnum ġeweorðad,   næf(n)e him his wlite léoge,
ǽnliċ ansýn!   Nú, iċ éower sceal
frumcyn witan,   ǽr ġé fyr heonan,
léasescéaweras   on land Dena
furþur féran.   Nú ġé feor-búend,
255 mere-líðende,   mín(n)e ġehýrað
ánfealdne ġeþóht-   ofost is sélest,
tó ġecýðanne   hwanan éowre cyme syndon."

Then, the foremost one   gave answer,
the captain of the company   unlocked his word-hoard,
260 "As to our kindred,   we are of the Geatish kingdom
and hearth-companions   of Hygelac's.
My father was   well-known to your folk,
a noble earl,   hight Ecgtheow;*
he enjoyed many winters,   ere he went on his way,
265 old on the earth;   he is well remembered
by all wisemen   throughout the wide world.
We, with loyal minds,   your liege lord,
Healfdene's son,   have come to seek,
guardian of the folk.   Be a good guide to us!
270 To that glorious one,   on a great mission, we come
to the lord of the Danes.   There should be no deceit
in this, methinks.   You surely must know if it is
indeed true   what we heard tell,
that among the Scyldings,   a scathing creature,
275 an unknown enemy   in the dark of night
shows awesome   his inhuman malice
in savagery and slaughter.   To Hrothgar, if I may,
in spacious spirit,   give my rede
on how he may, wise and good,   overcome this enemy,
280 if ever   any change should
from this baleful business,   come to pass,
and the care-surges   grow cool,
or else endure   a time of trouble.
He shall suffer dire despair,   as long as he should dwell there,
285 the best of houses   on that high place!"

Upon his steed,   the sea-ward spake,
the resolute warrior,   "He will, every
sharp shield-bearer,   discern the truth
in both words and works,   if he intends well.
290 I understand thou art   to be a company faithful
to the friend of the Scyldings.   Go forth then,
bearing arms and armor.   I shall guide thee.
Likewise, I shall order   mine own kin-thegns
to guard your   floater from foes,
295 newly-tarred ship   on the shore,
to hold in honor,   'til it glides again,
o'er the sea-streams,   belovèd man,
wound-neck'd wood   to Wedermark;
those who do good,   it shall be granted,
300 that they come back hale   from the battle-rush."

Him se yldesta   andswarode,
werodes wísa   word-hord onléac,
260 "Wé synt gum-cynnes   Ġéata léode
ond Hiġeláces   heorð-ġenéatas.
Wæs mín fæder   folcum ġecýþed,
æþele ord-fruma,   Ecgþéow háten;
ġebád wintra worn,   ǽr hé on weġ hwurfe,
265 gamol of ġeardum;   hine ġearwe ġeman
witena wél-hwylċ   wíde ġeond eorþan.
Wé þurh holdne hiġe,   hláford þinne,
sunu Healfdenes,   séċean cwómon,
léod-ġebyrġean.   Wes þú ús lárena gód!
270 Habbað wé tó þǽm mǽran,   miċel ǽrende
Deniġa fréan.   Ne sceal þǽr dyrne sum
wesan, þæs iċ wéne.   Þú wást ġif hit is
swá wé sóþliċe   secgan hýrdon,
þæt mid Scyldingum,   sceaðona iċ nát hwylċ,
275 déogol dǽd-hata,   deorcum nihtum
éaweð þurh eġsan   uncúðne níð,
hýnðu ond hrá-fyl.   Iċ þæs Hróðgár mæġ,
þurh rúmne sefan,   rǽd ġelǽran,
hú hé, fród ond gód,   féond oferswýðeþ,
280 ġyf him edwenden   ǽfre scolde,
bealuwa bisigu,   bót eft cuman,
ond þá ċear-wylmas   cólran wurðaþ,
oððe á syþðan   earfoð-þráge.
Þréa-nýd þolað,   þenden þǽr wunað
285 on héah-stede   húsa sélest!"

Weard maþelode,   ðǽr on wicge sæt,
ombeht unforht,   "Ǽġhwæþres sceal
scearp scyld-wiga,   ġescád witan,
worda ond worca,   sé þe wél þenċeð.
290 Iċ þæt ġehýre   þæt þis is hold weorod
fréan Scyldinga.   Ġewítaþ forð, beran
wǽpen ond ġewǽdu.   Iċ éow wísiġe.
Swylċe, iċ magu-þeġnas   míne háte,
wið féonda ġehwone   flotan éowerne,
295 níw-tyrwedne   nacan on sande,
árum healdan,   oþ ðæt eft byreð,
ofer lagu-stréamas,   léofne mannan,
wudu wundenhals   tó Wedermearce;
gód-fremmendra,   swylcum ġifeþe bið,
300 þæt þone hilde-rǽs   hál ġedíġeð."

Then they fared forth;   the floater lay still,
the broad-beamed ship   held fast by its anchor
and by cables bound.   The likenesses of boars* shone
above cheek-guards,   adorned with gold;
305   fierce and fire-hardened;   defense they gave,
the war-like masks.*   The men marched on,
moving together,   'til they saw the timbered hall,
gleaming and gilded   atop the hill.
Among earth-dwellers,   that was the foremost
310   of halls under the heavens,   wherein the mighty one dwelt;
its light shone   o'er many lands.

Then he, brave in battle,   lead them to that mighty house,
and bade them go forth   to that bright burg.
Then the worthy warrior
315   wheeled his horse about,   and quoth these words,
"'Tis now the time   for me to fare from you.
May the Father Almighty   keep thee in His kindness
and show you favor in your fate.   To the sea, I must away,
against wroth warriors,   to hold my watch."

Ġewiton him þá féran; flota stille bád,
seomode on s(á)le síd-fæþmed scip,
on ancre fæst. Eofor-líċ scionon
ofer hléor-beran ġehroden golde;
305 fáh ond fýr-heard, ferhwearde héold,
gúþmód gr(í)mmon. Guman ónetton,
sigon ætsomne, oþ þæt hý (s)æl timbred,
ġeatolíċ ond gold-fáh onġytan mihton.
Þæt wæs fore-mǽrost, fold-búendum,
310 reċeda under roderum, on þǽm se ríċa bád;
líxte se léoma ofer landa fela.

Him þá, hilde-déor, (h)of módiġra,
torht ġetǽhte þæt híe him tó mihton
ġeġnum gangan. Gúð-beorna sum
315 wicg ġewende, word æfter cwæð,
"Mǽl is mé tó féran. Fæder Alwalda
mid ár-stafum éowiċ ġehealde
síða ġesunde. Iċ tó sǽ wille,
wið wráð werod, wearde healdan."

Chapter III
In the hall of heopot

320 The street was stone-paved, the road led
    the men together. Battle-byrnies shone,
    hard and hand-linked, ring-mail gleamed,
    steel sang as they strode to the hall,
    in their grim gear they marched.
325 Sea-weary, they set down their shields,
    resilient round-shields, against the palace walls
    and bowed to the bench. Byrnies rang,
    the men's war-trappings; spears stood
    and seamen's swords all together,
330 grey tipped ash-wood.* The iron troop was
    worthy of those weapons! Then, a proud hero
    asked of the origin of the warriors,

    "Whence do you go, with gilded shields,
    in grey mail and maskèd helms,
335 and a host of battle-hafts? I am Hrothgar's
    messenger and herald. Ne'er have I seen
    this many proud men from a foreign land.
    I take you for worthy men, not wretches,
    seeking Hrothgar with high hearts."

340 To him, the renowned one replied,
    proud lord of the Weders, he spake in words,
    hard 'neath his helm, "We are Hygelac's
    table companions; Beowulf is my name.*
    I wish to herald Healfdene's son,
345 that famed monarch, about my mission,
    if your glorious lord will grant to us
    the grace to greet that good one."

    Wulfgar spake, he of the Wendel tribe;*
    his mind by many was known,
350 skilled in warcraft and wisdom.

V

320   Strǽt wæs stán-fáh,   stíġ wísode
    gumum ætgædere.   Gúð-byrne scán,
    heard, hond-locen,   hring-íren scír,
    song in searwum   þá híe tó sele furðum,
    in hyra gryre-ġeatwum   gangan cwómon.
325   Setton, sǽ-méþe,   síde scyldas,
    rondas reġn-hearde,   wið þæs reċedes weal,
    bugon þá tó benċe.   Byrnan hringdon,
    gúð-searo gumena,   gáras stódon,
    sǽ-manna searo   samod ætgædere,
330   æsc-holt ufan grǽġ;   wæs se íren-þréat
    wǽpnum ġewurþad!   Þá ðǽr wlonc hæleð
    óret-mecgas   æfter hæleþum fræġn:

    "Hwanon feriġeað ġé,   fǽtte scyldas,
    grǽġe syrċan   ond grím-helmas,
335   here-sceafta héap?   Iċ eom Hróðgáres
    ár ond ombiht.   Ne seah iċ el-þéodiġe
    þus maniġe men   módiġlícran.
    Wén iċ þæt ġé for wlenċo,   nalles for wræc-síðum,
    ac for hiġe-þrymmum   Hróðgár sóhton."

340   Him þá ellen-róf   andswarode,
    wlanc Wedera léod,   word æfter spræc,
    heard under helme: "Wé synt Hiġeláces
    béod-ġenéatas;   Béowulf is mín nama.
    Wille iċ ásecgan   suna Healfdenes,
345   mǽrum þéodne,   mín ǽrende,
    aldre þínum   ġif hé ús ġeunnan wile
    þæt wé hine swá gódne   grétan móton."

    Wulfgár maþelode,   þæt wæs Wendla léod;
    wæs his mód-sefa   manegum ġecýðed,
350   wíġ ond wísdóm: "Iċ, þæs wine Deniġa,

"I, as a friend of the Danes,   will draw nigh to ask
the giver of gifts,   as you are petitioners to that
excellent lord,   of your journey,
and to you,   give the answer anon.
355   that the good one   grants you."

Then, he hastened hence   to where Hrothgar sat,
old and hoary amidst   his band of earls;
he stoutly strode,   'til he stood by the shoulder
of the Danish king;   he knew the customs.
360   Wulfgar spake   to his winsome lord,
"Men from afar   have fared hither,
o'er the wide sea,   from Wedermark.
The foremost   of those fighters,
is called Beowulf.   This boon he asks,
365   that they, my lord,   with you may
exchange words.   I pray, do not deny them
your answer,   high Hrothgar!
They seem worthy   in their war-gear,
esteemed earls;   indeed their leader seems valorous,
370   the hero who   hither led them!"

Hrothgar spake,   helm of the Scyldings,
"I knew him   when he was but a boy.
His old-father   hight Ecgtheow,
whom at home,   Hrethel of the Geats gave
375   his only daughter.   Now, his heir has
firmly come,   seeking a faithful friend.
Also, sea-farers   have said to me,
those who carried   our gifts to the Geats,
thither in thanks,   that he has the strength
380   of thirty men   in his mighty grasp,*
he who is brave in battle!   Holy God
in sympathy   has sent
to the West-Danes,   as I ween,
against Grendel's wroth!   I hope to give
385   the good man   gold for his courage.
Be in haste   and bid them hither,
that I may see   that band of brothers together.
Tell them these words also-   they are welcome indeed
to the land of the Danes!"

fréan Scildinga   frínan wille,
béaga bryttan,   swá þú béna eart
þéoden mǽrne,   ymb þínne síð,
ond þé þá andsware,   ǽdre ġecýðan
355   ðé mé se góda   áġifan þenċeð."

Hwearf þá hrædlíċe   þǽr Hróðgár sæt,
eald ond (a)nhár   mid his eorla ġedriht;
éode ellen-róf,   þæt hé for eaxlum ġestód
Deniġa fréan,   cúþe hé duguðe þéaw.
360   Wulfgár maðelode   tó his wine-drihtne,
"Hér syndon ġeferede,   feorran cumene,
ofer ġeofenes begang   Ġéata léode.
Þone yldestan   óret-mecgas,
Béowulf nemnað.   Hý bénan synt
365   þæt híe, þéoden mín,   wið þé móton
wordum wrixlan.   Nó ðú him wearne ġetéoh
ðínra ġeġn-cwida,   glædman Hróðgár!
Hý on wíġ-ġeatwum   wyrðe þinċeað,
eorla ġeæhtlan;   húru se aldor déah,
370   sé þǽm heaðo-rincum   hider wísade!"

VI

Hróðgár maþelode,   helm Scyldinga,
"Iċ hine cúðe   cniht-wesende.
Wæs his eald-fæder   Ecgþéo háten,
ðǽm tó hám forġeaf   Hréþel Ġéata
375   ángan dohtor.   Is his eaforan nú
heard hér cumen,   sóhte holdne wine.
Ðonne sæġdon þæt   sǽ-líþende,
þá ðe ġif-sceattas   Ġéata fyredon,
þyder tó þance,   þæt hé þrítiġes
380   manna mæġen-cræft   on his mund-gripe,
heaþo-róf hæbbe!   Hine háliġ God
for ár-stafum   ús onsende
tó West-Denum,   þæs iċ wén hæbbe,
wið Grendles gryre!   Iċ þǽm gódan sceal
385   for his mód-þræce   mádmas béodan.
Béo ðú on ofeste,   hát in gán,
séon sibbe-ġedriht   samod ætgædere.
Ġesaga him éac wordum-   þæt híe sint wilcuman
Deniġa léodum!"   . . . .

[To Heorot's door

390   Wulfgar then went]   and these words declared,
"My victorious master   sends you this message,
East-Danish king,   that he kens your nobility,
and you are to him,   o'er the sea surge,
hardy heroes,   hither welcome!
395   Now, you may walk inside,   wearing your war-gear,
under masked helms,   to see Hrothgar,
but let your battle-boards   stay here,
and wooden slaughter-shafts   to await the end of words."

Arose then that stalwart one,   about him his many men,
400   a multitude of mighty thegns,   but some stayed behind,
to hold their war-gear,   as their hardy leader bade.
Then, they hurried   to where the herald led,
under Heorot's roof;   the hero strode,
hard under helm,   'til he stood at the hearth.

405   Beowulf spake,   his byrnie shone,
the metal net sewn   by the skill of smiths,
"Be thou, Hrothgar, hail!*   I am Hygelac's
thegn and kinsman.   Much fame have I
gained in my youth.   Grendel's deeds
410   in mine homeland   have been heard.
It is said by sea-farers   that this stead stands,
the best of buildings,   to all warriors,
idle and empty,   after the sun
in the high heavens,   goes to hide.
415   I was prompted   by my people,
the best of people,   mindful men,
to seek you here,   Hrothgar King,
for my main and might   they knew well.
They had seen me   come back from battle,
420   stained with the gore of fiends   after five I slew,
ended the Ettin kin.

Amidst the waves, I slew
Nicors* by night.   I suffered dismay,
avenging the evil they caused the Weders,   whose woe they sought.
I destroyed those grim ones,   and now against Grendel I shall,
425   with the fierce one,   overcome alone
and gain everlasting glory.   Now, I
ask of you,   elder of the Bright-Danes,
the Scyldings' bulwark,   for this one boon.
Do not deny me,   defender of warriors,

38

390   . . . . . .   word inne ábéad,
"Ēow hét secgan   siġe-drihten mín,
aldor Ēast-Dena,   þæt hé éower æþelu can,
ond ġé him syndon,   ofer sǽ-wylmas,
heard-hicgende,   hider wilcuman!
395   Nú, ġé móton gangan,   in éowrum guð-ġetawum,
under here-gríman,   Hróðgár ġeséon,
lǽtað hilde-bord   hér (on)bíd(i)an,
wudu wæl-sceaftas   worda ġeþinges."

Árás þá se ríċa,   ymb hine rinc maniġ,
400   þrýðlíċ þeġna héap;   sume þǽr bidon,
heaðo-réaf héoldon,   swá him se hearda bebéad.
Snyredon ætsomne   þá secg wísode,
under Heorotes hróf;   (éode hilde-déor,)
heard under helme,   þæt hé on heorðe ġestód.

405   Béowulf maðelode,   on him byrne scán,
searo-net seowed   smiþes or-þancum,
"Wæs þú, Hróðgár, hál!   Iċ eom Hiġeláces
mǽġ and mago-ðeġn.   Hæbbe iċ mǽrða fela
ongunnen on ġeogoþe.   Mé wearð Grendles þing
410   on mínre éþel-tyrf   undyrne cúð.
Secgað sǽ-líðend   þæt þes sele stande,
reċed sélesta,   rinca ġehwylcum,
ídel ond unnyt,   siððan ǽfen-léoht,
under heofenes háðor,   beholen weorþeð.
415   Þá mé þæt ġelǽrdon   léode míne,
þá sélestan,   snotere ċeorlas,
þéoden Hróðgár,   þæt iċ þé sóhte,
forþan híe mæġenes cræft   mínne cúþon.
Selfe ofersáwon   ðá iċ of searwum cwóm,
420   fáh from féondum   þǽr iċ fífe ġeband,
ýðde Eotena cyn,   ond on ýðum slóg
Niceras nihtes.

Nearo-þearfe dréah,
wræc Wedera níð,   wéan áhsodon.
Forgrand gramum,   ond nú wið Grendel sceal,
425   wið þám áglǽċan,   ána ġeheġan
ðing wið þyrse.   Iċ þé núðá,
brego Beorht-Dena,   biddan wille,
eodor Scyldinga,   ánre béne.
Þæt ðú mé ne forwyrne,   wíġendra hléo,

430   friend of the folk,   since I came thus far,
         that I alone,   with my band of earls,
         this hardy host,   to cleanse Heorot.
         I have heard   that the fearsome fighter
         in his haughtiness,   heeds not weapons.
435   I too shall eschew   -so that my lord,
         Hygelac may stay   blithe in spirit for me-
         sword or broad shield   to bear in battle,
         gold-rimmed linden,   but with my gripe alone
         shall I fight with the fiend   and struggle for life,
440   foe against foe,   and have faith in
         the doom the Lord deemed   of who death should take.
         I expect he will,   if he is able,
         in the hall of battle,   my band of Goths,
         fearlessly eat,   as he oft did,
445   my mighty Hrethmen*.   Nor will you have need to
         hide mine head,   for he shall have me
         gore-drenched,   if death should take me.
         He shall bear   my bloody body away as prey,
         the lone walker shall   inhumanly eat me
450   and mark his moor-lair with my blood.   Nor must you
         the preparation of my lich*   any longer worry!
         Send to Hygelac,   if I am bested in battle,
         this best of battle-armor   that protects my breast,
         my splendid corselet,   'tis Hrethel's heirloom,
455   Weyland's* work.   Wyrd* goes ever as it must!"

         Hrothgar spake,   helm of the Scyldings,
         "For past favors,   my friend Beowulf,
         and for our support,   you have sought us.
         A great feud   your father began,
460   when by his hand,   he slew Heatholaf
         of the Wulfings*.   Then, for fear of war,
         his people would   not protect him.
         Thence, he sought   the South-Danish folk,
         o'er the sea-swell,   the Honor-Scyldings.
465   When first I ruled   o'er the Danish folk,
         full of youth,   wielded this wide realm,
         hoard-burg of heroes,   after Heorogar's death,
         mine elder brother,   unliving,
         Healfdene's bairn-   he was better than I!
470   I settled the feud   with fees;
         sent to the Wulfings   o'er the water's ridge,

430   fréo-wine folca,   nú iċ þus feorran cóm,
        þæt iċ móte ána,   mínra eorla ġedryht,
        ond þes hearda héap,   Heorot fǽlsian.
        Hæbbe iċ éac ġeáhsod   þæt se ǽġlǽċa
        for his won-hýdum,   wǽpna ne reċċeð.

435   Iċ þæt þonne forhicge   -swá mé Hiġelác síe,
        mín mon-drihten,   módes blíðe-
        þæt iċ sweord bere   oþðe sídne scyld,
        ġeolo-rand, tó gúþe,   ac iċ mid grápe sceal
        fón wið féonde   ond ymb feorh sacan,

440   láð wið láþum,   ðǽr ġelýfan sceal
        dryhtnes dóme   sé þe hine déað nimeð.
        Wén iċ þæt hé wille,   ġif hé wealdan mót,
        in þǽm gúð-sele,   Ġéatena léode
        etan unforhte,   swá hé oft dyde,

445   mæġen Hréðmanna.   Ná þú mínne þearft
        hafalan hýdan,   ac hé mé habban wile
        d(r)éo(re) fáhne,   ġif meċ déað nimeð.
        Byreð blódiġ wæl   byrġean þenċeð,
        eteð án-genga   unmurnlíċe,

450   mearcað mór-hopu.   Nó ðú ymb mínes ne þearft
        líċes feorme   leng sorgian!
        Onsend Hiġeláce,   ġif meċ hild nime,
        beadu-scrúda betst   þæt míne bréost wereð,
        hræġla sélest;   þæt is Hr(éð)lan láf,

455   Wélandes ġeweorc.   Gǽð á Wyrd swá hío scel!"

                  VII

        Hróðgár maþelode,   helm Scyldinga,
        "Fere fyhtum þú,   wine mín Béowulf,
        ond for ár-stafum,   úsiċ sóhtest.
        Ġeslóh þin fæder   fǽhðe mǽste,

460   wearþ hé Heaþoláfe   tó hand-bonan
        mid Wilfingum.   Ðá hine (Wul)gara cyn,
        for here-brógan,   habban ne mihte.
        Þanon hé ġesóhte   Súð-Dena folc,
        ofer ýða ġewealc,   Ár-Scyldinga.

465   ðá iċ furþum wéold   folce Den(i)ġa,
        ond on ġeogoðe héold   ġinne ríċe,
        hord-burh hæleþa,   ðá wæs Heregár déad,
        mín yldra mǽġ,   unlifiġende,
        bearn Healfdenes-   sé wæs betera ðonne iċ!

470   Siððan þá fǽhðe   féo þingode;
        sende iċ Wylfingum   ofer wæteres hrycg

old mathoms.   He then swore oaths to me.

"It sorrows   my soul to say
to any man,   what grief Grendel has wrought,
475   humiliation in Heorot,   and with a hateful mind,
caused chaos.   Mine hall-troop has failed,
my war-band has waned;   Wyrd has swept them
into Grendel's grasp!   God could easily
prevent that deathly   defiler's deeds!
480   Oft, full of boasts   and drunk on beer,
have warriors   o'er their ale-cups,
sworn they would   bide in the beer-hall,
and fight Grendel   with grim edge.
Then, would the mead-hall   in the morn,
485   this noble hall, dyed with blood   as day lightened,
all the bench-boards   would be wet with blood,
gory the hall.   Fewer friends have I;
death had taken   my dear retainers.
But, now sit down at the symbel   and unbind your thoughts,
490   victorious hero,   as your heart urges you."

Then were the Geatish men   gathered together
in the beer-hall;   a bench was cleared
and those strong-spirited ones   sat down,
the hardy host.   A thegn attended them;
495   in his hands he bore   an ornate ale-cup
and served them bright mead.   The scop sang
resonantly in high Heorot.   The heroes were joyous,
no dearth of warriors,   Danes and Weders.

ealde mádmas,   hé mé áþas swór."

"Sorh is mé tó secganne   on sefan mínum
gumena ǽngum,   hwæt mé Grendel hafað,
475   hýnðo on Heorote,   mid his hete-þancum,
fǽr-níða ġefremed.   Is mín flet-werod,
wíġ-héap ġewanod;   híe Wyrd forswéop
on Grendles gryre!   God éaþe mæġ
þone dol-scaðan   dǽda ġetwǽfan!
480   Ful oft, ġebéotedon   béore druncne,
ofer ealo-wǽġe   óret-mecgas,
þæt híe in béor-sele   bídan woldon,
Grendles gúþe   mid gryrum ecga.
Ðonne wæs þéos medo-heal   on morgen-tíd,
485   driht-sele, dréor-fáh   þonne dæġ líxte,
eal benċ-þelu   blóde bestýmed,
heall heoru-dréore.   Áhte iċ holdra þý lǽs;
déorre duguðe   þé þá déað fornam.
Site nú tó symle   ond onsǽl meoto,
490   siġe-hréð secgum,   swá þín sefa hwette."

Þá wæs Ġéat-mæcgum   ġeador ætsomne
on béor-sele;   benċ ġerýmed,
þǽr swíþ-ferhðe   sittan éodon,
þrýðum dealle.   Þeġn nytte behéold;
495   sé þe on handa bær   hroden ealo-wǽġe
scencte scír wered.   Scop hwílum sang
hádor on Heorote.   Þǽr wæs hæleða dréam,
duguð unlýtel,   Dena ond Wedera.

43

Chapter IV
The Flyting of Unferth

Then, Unferth* spake,   the bairn of Ecglaf,*
500   he who sat at the feet   of the Scylding lord;
he unbound his battle-runes.   To him Beowulf's journey
caused the scornful sea-farer   great vexation,
for he would not   allow any other man
ever to win more fame   on this Middle-Earth,
505   or be more heeded   under the heavens than he.

"Are you the Beowulf,   who with Breca struggled
in conceit across   the wide sea?*
When in pride,   you proved the waves,
and foolishly dared   the deep waters,
510   risked losing your lives?   No man,
loved nor loathed,   could dissuade you
from your foolhardy contest,   when you swam across the sea.
The ocean current   with your arms embraced,
measured the mere-path,   with your hands wove,
515   glided o'er the waves,   the sea seethed
in winter's winds.   In the water's domain,
you struggled for seven nights.   He bested you on the sea,
he had more might!   Then he, on the morning-tide,
was heaved up on the land   of the Heatho-Reams*.
520   Thence he hurried   to seek his homeland,*
where he was loved by his liegemen,   the land of the Brondings,*
the fair fortress,   where he had folk,
burg and rings.   Beanstan's bairn,
his whole boast   had been achieved.
525   Then, I ween that worse   results await you,
though you are   brave in battle
and grim in war,   if Grendel's coming
you dare await   in darkest night!"

Beowulf spake,   the son of Ecgtheow,
530   "Lo! You have spoken a great deal,   my dear Unferth,

VIII

(Ú)nferð maþelode,   Ecgláfes bearn,
500   þé æt fótum sæt   fréan Scyldinga;
onband beadu-rúne.   Wæs him Béowulfes síð,
módġes mere-faran   miċel æf-þunca,
forþon þe hé ne úþe   þæt æniġ óðer man
æfre mærða þon má   Middan-Ġeardes,
505   ġehédde under heofenum   þonne hé sylfa.

"Eart þú se Béowulf,   sé þe wið Brecan wunne
on sídne sæ,   ymb sund flite?
Ðǽr ġit for wlenċe,   wada cunnedon,
ond for dol-ġilpe   on déop wæter,
510   aldrum néþdon?   Né inċ æniġ mon,
né léof né láð,   beléan mihte
sorh-fullne síð,   þá ġit on sund réon.
Þǽr ġit éagor-stréam   earmum þehton,
mǽton mere-strǽta,   mundum brugdon,
515   glidon ofer gár-secg,   ġeofon ýþum wéol
wintrys wylm(um).   Ġit on wæteres æht,
seofon-niht swuncon.   Hé þé, æt sunde oferflát,
hæfde máre mæġen.   Þá hine, on morgen-tíd,
on Heaþo-Rǽmas   holm up ætbær.
520   Ðonon hé ġesóhte   swǽsne (éþel),
léof his léodum,   lond Brondinga,
freoðo-burh fæġere,   þǽr hé folc áhte,
burh ond béagas.   Béot eal wið þé,
sunu Béanstánes,   sóðe ġelǽste.
525   Ðonne wéne iċ tó þé   wyrsan ġeþingea,
ðéah þú heaðo-rǽsa   ġehwær dohte
grimre gúðe,   ġif þú Grendles dearst
niht-longne fyrst   néan bídan!"

Béowulf maþelode,   bearn Ecgþéowes,
530   "Hwæt! Þú worn fela,   wine mín (Ú)nferð,

drunk on beer,   of Breca's boast,
told of his triumph!   But truth I claim,
that I had the   greater sea-strength,
more ocean-endurance   than any other man.

535 We both had said,   being boys,
and boasted   -both of us were still youths-
that we would,   out on the ocean
dare to risk our lives,   and thus we did.
We wielded naked swords,   as we swam the sea,

540 hard in hand,   so that we could defend
ourselves against whales.   Not a whit from me
could he float   afar on the flood,
swift o'er the sea,   nor would I leave him.
United, we were   on the waves

545 for five long nights,   'till a storm separated us;
the waters welled;   'twas the coldest of weathers.
The night deepened   and the north wind
turned fierce;   the waves were wild.
Then was awoken   the wrath of sea-fish.

550 My mail-coat,   against the monsters,
hard and hand-linked,   helped me;
the braided battle-garment   lay on my breast,
garnished with gold.   Then, was I dragged to the sea floor
by the fell fiend;   it held me fast,

555 grim in its grasp.   But, it was granted to me
that I pierced with the point,   the monster;
with my battle-blade,   I destroyed in the clash of battle
the mighty mere-beast   with mine hand!

"So, oft against   the fearsome foe,
560 I struggled with severely.   I served them
with my sword dear,   as was due.
They favored   not their fill,
what those evil ones   earned from me,
they sat at their symbel   on the sea-floor,

565 but by dawn,   they were dead by my sword,
their corpses strewn   upon the strand,
put to sleep by the sword.   Never again were
sea-farers along   the steep ocean paths
molested by monsters.   A light came from the east,

570 God's bright beacon.   The brine was stilled,
so that I saw   the sea-cliffs,
the windswept wall.   For Wyrd oft saves

béore druncen,   ymb Brecan spræce,
sæġdest from his síðe!   Sóð iċ taliġe,
þæt iċ mere-strengo   máran áhte,
earfeðo on ýþum,   ðonne æniġ óþer man.

535   Wit þæt ġecwædon,   cniht-wesende,
ond ġebéotedon   -wæron béġen þá ġít
on ġeogoð-feore-   þæt wit on gár-secg út
aldrum néðdon,   ond þæt ġeæfndon swá.
Hæfdon swurd nacod,   þá wit on sund réon,

540   heard on handa,   wit unc wið hron-fixas
werian þóhton.   Nó hé wiht fram mé
flód-ýþum feor   fléotan meahte,
hraþor on holme,   nó iċ fram him wolde.
Ðá wit ætsomne   on sæ wæron

545   fíf-nihta fyrst,   oþ þæt unc flód tódráf;
wado weallende,   wedera ċealdost.
Nípende niht   ond norþan wind
heaðo-grim ondhwearf;   hréo wæron ýþa.
Wæs mere-fixa   mód onhréred.

550   Þǽr mé wið láðum   líċs-yrċe mín,
heard hondlocen,   helpe ġefremede;
beado-hræġl bróden   on bréostum læġ,
golde ġeġyrwed.   Mé tó grunde téah,
fáh féond-scaða;   fæste hæfde

555   grim on grápe.   Hwæþre mé ġyfeþe wearð
þæt iċ áglæċan   orde ġeræhte;
hilde-bille,   heaþo-ræs fornam
mihtiġ mere-déor   þurh míne hand.

IX

"Swá, meċ ġelóme   láð-ġetéonan,
560   þréatedon þearle.   Iċ him þénode
déoran sweorde,   swá hit ġedéfe wæs.
Næs híe ðǽre fylle   ġeféan hæfdon,
mán-fordædlan,   þæt híe mé þégon
symbel ymb-sæton   sæ-grunde néah,

565   ac on merġenne,   méċum wunde,
be ýð-láfe   uppe lægon,
sweo(rdum) áswefede.   Þæt syðþan ná
ymb brontne ford   brim-líðende
láde ne letton.   Léoht éastan cóm,

570   beorht béacen Godes.   Brimu swaþredon,
þæt iċ sæ-næssas   ġeséon mihte,
windiġe weallas.   Wyrd oft nereð

47

one who is utterly doomed,   when his courage is good!
So it was,   that I slew with the sword
575 Nicors nine.   I have not heard of a night-battle
under the vault of Heaven   harder fought,
nor on the current   by a miserable man!
Yet, I overcame that cruel clasp   and escaped with my life,
weary from my struggle.   The sea carried me away,
580 the current of the flood   to Finnmark,*
the welling waters.   No wise of thee,
in such battle-strife,   before have I heard told,
of bloody battle.   Breca has not yet,
at battle-play,   nor either of you pair,
585 carried out   such daring deeds
with bright blade.   Of that, I do not boast!

"You, however were   the bane of your brothers,*
your closest kin.   For that, in the hall you shall
receive reproach,   though your wit is good.
590 In sooth, I say unto you,   son of Ecglaf,
so many grim deeds Grendel   would not have committed,
that terrible monster   on your master,
humiliation in Heorot,   if your heart
and soul was as stout   as you believe!
595 But he has found   that the feud he fears not,
that terrible storm of swords   from your people.
He thinks his victory   o'er the Scyldings is secure.
He forces tribute   and favors none
from the Danish people,   but with pleasure carried on,
600 slicing and slaying;   he expects no resistance
from the Spear Danes.   But I shall show him
the power and pride of the Geats   before long!
I shall bid him do battle with me,   so that men can return,
blithe in their mead,   when the morning light,
605 the sparkling sun   of a new day,
shines from the south*   on the sons of men!"

(a)nfǽġne eorl,   þonne his ellen déah!
Hwæþere mé ġesǽlde,   þæt iċ mid sweorde ofslóh
575   Niceras niġene.   Nó iċ on niht ġefrǽġn
under heofones hwealf   heardran feohtan,
né on éġ-stréamum   earmran mannan!
Hw(æ)þere iċ fára feng   féore ġedígde,
síþes wériġ.   Ðá meċ sǽ oþbær,
580   flód æfter faroðe   on Finnaland,
w(a)du weallendu.   Nó iċ wiht fram þé
swylcra searo-níða   secgan hýrde
billa brógan.   Breca nǽfre ġít
æt heaðo-láce,   né ġehwæþer inċer,
585   swá déorlíċe   dǽd ġefremede
fágum sweordum.   Nó iċ þæs (fela) ġylpe!

Þéah ðú þínum bróðrum   tó banan wurde,
héafod-mǽgum.   Þæs þú in (healle) scealt
werhðo dréogan,   þéah þín wit duge.
590   Secge iċ þé tó sóðe,   sunu Ecgláfes,
þæt nǽfre Gre(n)del swá fela   gryra ġefremede,
atol ǽġlǽċa   ealdre þínum,
hýnðo on Heorote,   ġif þín hiġe wǽre
sefa swá searo-grim   swá þú self talast!
595   Ac hé hafað onfunden   þæt hé þá fǽhðe ne þearf,
atole ecg-þræce   éower léode.
Swíðe onsittan   siġe Scyldinga.
Nymeð nýd-báde   nǽnegum árað
léode Deniġa,   ac hé lust wíġeð,
600   swefeð ond sendeþ;   seċċe ne wéneþ
tó Gár-Denum.   Ac iċ him Ġéata sceal
eafoð ond ellen   unġeára nú!
Gúþe ġebéodan,   gǽþ eft sé þe mót,
tó medo módiġ,   siþþan morgen-léoht
605   ofer ylda bearn   óþres dógores,
sunne sweġl-wered   súþan scíneð!"

Chapter V
Before the Battle

Glad then was   the giver of treasure,
hoary and battle-brave.   Beowulf heard,
that the lord of the Bright-Danes   believed in him,
610   guardian of the folk,   with fast resolve.
Heroes' laughter   loudly rang
and winsome words were spoken.   Wealhtheow* strode forth,
Hrothgar's queen,   mindful of manners.
Gold-adorned,   she greeted the hall-guests,
615   and then the glorious wife   gave the cup*
first to   the East-Danish elder,
bade him be blithe   at their beer-drinking,
belovèd by the people.   Lustily, he took
the symbel-cup,   that victorious king.
620   Then she went through the hall,   the Helming lady,
and offered to both   the old and the young,
carried that precious cup,   'till it came
to Beowulf;   the bejeweled queen,
thriving in mind,   bore the mead-cup.
625   She greeted the Geatish lord,   and thanked God
in wise words,   that He answered her prayer,
that she in this earl   could count on
for solace from sin.   He accepted that cup,
the war-brave one   from Wealhtheow,
630   and gave answer,   eager for battle.

Beowulf spake,   the son of Ecgtheow,
"I made up my mind   when I went out to sea,
sat in the sea-boat   with my company of men,
that I would work   the will of your people
635   or fall fighting   in battle,
fast in the fiend's grasp.   I shall do
this heroic deed,   or else I will end
the last of these days of mine   in this mead-hall."

Þá wæs on sálum   sinces brytta,
gamol-feax ond gúð-róf.   Ġéoce ġelýfde,
brego Beorht-Dena,   ġehýrde on Béowulfe,
610   folces hyrde,   fæst-rǽdne ġeþóht.
Ðǽr wæs hæleþa hleahtor,   hlyn swynsode,
word wǽron wynsume.   Ēode Wealhþéo forð,
cwén Hróðgáres,   cynna ġemyndiġ.
Grétte gold-hroden,   guman on healle,
615   ond þá fréolíċ wíf   ful ġesealde
ǽrest Ēast-Dena   éþel-wearde,
bæd hine blíðne   æt þǽre béor-þeġe,
léodum léofne.   Hé on lust ġeþeah
symbel ond sele-ful,   siġe-róf kyning.
620   Ymb-éode þá,   ides Helminga
duguþe ond ġeogoþe   dǽl ǽġhwylċne,
sinc-fato sealde,   oþ þæt sǽl álamp,
þæt hío Béowulfe;   béag-hroden cwén
móde ġeþungen,   medo-ful ætbær.
625   Grétte Ġéata léod,   Gode þancode
wís-fæst wordum,   þæs ðe hire se willa ġelamp,
þæt héo on ǽniġne   eorl ġelýfde
fyrena frófre.   Hé þæt ful ġeþeah,
wæl-réow wiga   æt Wealhþéon,
630   ond þá ġyddode,   gúþe ġefýsed.

Béowulf maðelode,   bearn Ecgþéowes,
"Iċ þæt hogode   þá iċ on holm ġestáh,
sǽ-bát ġesæt   mid mínra secga ġedriht,
þæt iċ ánunga   éowra léoda
635   willan ġeworhte   oþðe on wæl crunge,
féond-grápum fæst.   Iċ ġefremman sceal
eorliċ ellen,   oþðe onde-dæġ
on þisse meodu-healle   mínne ġebídan."

That wife liked   these words well,
640   the Geat's boast.   Adorned with gold,
the fair folk-queen   sat down by her lord.
Then again as there once was   in the hall,
bold speeches were spoken   and people were filled with joy,
singing of victorious-folk,   'till suddenly
645   Healfdene's son   sought his
evening-rest.   He knew that the fierce fighter
for the high hall   had planned his attack,
when they could no longer see   the sun's light,
and the gloaming   gathered o'er all;
650   when shadowy shapes   come slinking,
black 'neath the clouds.   The company all arose.

The good king   greeted the others,
Hrothgar bade   Beowulf be hail,
the wielder of the wine-hall   spake these words,
655   "Ne'er before have I   entrusted to any one man,
since I could raise my round shield   with mine hand,
this high hall of the Danes,   'till now, to you.
Have now and hold   this best of houses.
Be mindful of fame,   make your might known,
660   and keep your watch against Grendel's wroth!   You will not lack in reward,
if you can complete   this courage-work."

Then Hrothgar departed,   with a company of heroes,
the helm of the Scyldings,   from the mead-hall.
The war-leader wished   to seek Wealhtheow
665   and his queen's bed.   The glorious king
against Grendel   gave assignment
and set a hall-guard,   so men heard,
about the Danish elder,   to ward 'gainst the Ettin.
Truly, the Geatish lord   eagerly trusted
670   in the proud might   the Maker granted him!
Then he cast off   his iron corselet,
the helm from his head   and gave his ornamented sword,
forged from the finest iron,   to his retainer
and bid him bear   his battle-gear.

675   In bold boast   spake he then,
Beowulf the Geat,   ere he sought his bed,
"My battle-stature   I consider no less
in grim warcraft   than Grendel himself!
Therefore, I shall not   put him to sleep by my sword,

Ðám wífe þá word　　wél lícodon,
640　ġilp-cwide Ġéates.　　Éode gold-hroden,
fréolícu folc-cwén　　tó hire fréan sittan.
Þá wæs eft swá ǽr　　inne on healle,
þrýð-word sprecen　　ðéod on sǽlum,
siġe-folca swéġ,　　oþ þæt semninga
645　sunu Healfdenes　　séċean wolde
ǽfen-ræste.　　Wiste æt þǽm áhlǽcan
tó þǽm héah-sele　　hilde ġeþinged,
siððan híe sunnan léoht　　ġeséon (ne) meahton,
oþ ðe nípende　　niht ofer ealle;
650　scadu-helma ġesceapu　　scríðan cwóman,
wan under wolcnum.　　Werod eall árás.

(Ġe)grétte þá　　guma óþerne,
Hróðgár Béowulf,　　ond him hǽl ábéad,
wín-ærnes ġeweald　　ond þæt word ácwæð,
655　"Nǽfre iċ ǽnegum men　　ǽr álýfde,
siþðan iċ hond ond rond　　hebban mihte,
ðrýþ-ærn Dena;　　búton þé núðá.
Hafa nú ond ġeheald　　húsa sélest.
Ġemyne mǽrþo,　　mæġen-ellen cýð,
660　waca wið wráþum!　　Ne bið þé wilna gád,
ġif þú þæt ellen-weorc　　aldre ġedígest."

X

Ðá him Hróþgár ġewát　　mid his hæleþa ġedryht,
eodur Scyldinga,　　út of healle.
Wolde wíġ-fruma　　Wealhþéo séċan
665　cwén tó ġebeddan.　　Hæfde kyningwuldor
Grendle tó-ġéanes　　swá guman ġefrungon,
sele-weard áseted,　　sundor-nytte behéold,
ymb aldor Dena,　　Eotonweard ábéad.
Húru Ġéata léod　　ġeorne truwode
670　módgan mæġnes　　Metodes hyldo!
Ðá hé him of dyde　　ísern-byrnan,
helm of hafelan,　　sealde his hyrsted sweord,
írena cyst,　　ombiht-þeġne
ond ġehealdan hét　　hilde-ġeatwe.

675　Ġespræc þá se góda　　ġylp-worda sum,
Béowulf Ġéata,　　ǽr hé on bed stiġe,
"Nó iċ mé an here-wǽsmum　　hnágran taliġe
gúð-ġeweorca　　þonne Grendel hine!
Forþan, iċ hine sweorde　　swebban nelle,

680 deprive him of life, although I am fully able,
  for he does not know the skills to strike against me,
  to hew my round-shield, though he is renowned
  for nithing-work.* That night, both of us shall
  spurn the sword, if he dares to seek me,
685 in battle without weapons. Then our wise God,
  shall deem whose hand, holy Lord,
  grants mastery, as He feels fit."

  Then the battle-brave one lay down;
  the cushion cradled the earl's head,
690 while 'round him many brave seamen sank in hall-rest.
  None of them thought that he from there
  would ever again see his dear home,
  the folk and fair stronghold that had fostered them.
  They knew full well that far too many Danes already
695 in the wine-hall had been dealt death.
  But to the Weder-folk, the Lord wove
  a Wyrd of war-prowess,
  support and success, that they the fiend,
  through the skill of one, overcome all,
700 by single might. In sooth 'tis said,
  that mighty God o'er Mankind
  has ruled forever!

680   aldre benéotan,   þéah iċ eal mǽge,
        nát hé þára góda,   þæt hé mé on-ġéan sléa,
        rand ġehéawe,   þéah ðe hé róf síe
        níþ-ġeweorca.   Ac wit on niht sculon
        secge ofersittan,   ġif h(é) ġeséċean dear,
685   wíġ ofer wǽpen.   Ond siþðan wítiġ God,
        on swá hwæþere hond,   háliġ Dryhten,
        mǽrðo déme,   swá Him ġemet þinċe."

        Hylde hine þá heaþo-déor   hléor-bolster onféng;
        eorles andwlitan,   ond hine ymb moniġ
690   snellíċ sǽ-rinc   sele-reste ġebéah.
        Nǽniġ heora þóhte   þæt hé þanon scolde
        eft eard-lufan   ǽfre ġeséċean,
        folc oþðe fréo-burh   þǽr hé áféded wæs.
        Ac híe hæfdon ġefrúnen   þæt híe ǽr tó fela miċles
695   in þǽm wín-sele   wæl-déað fornam,
        Deniġea léode.   Ac him Dryhten forġeaf
        wíġ-spéda ġewiofu,   Wedera léodum
        frófor ond fultum,   þæt híe féond heora
        ðurh ánes cræft,   ealle ofercómon,
700   selfes mihtum.   Sóð is ġecýðed,
        þæt mihtiġ God   Manna cynnes
        wéold (w)íde-ferhð!

Chapter VI
The Grasp of Grendel

In the dark of dusk came
the shadow-walker, slinking.   The spearmen slept,
they that held   the horn-gabled hall,

705   all save one.   The men knew
that they must not,   against the Measurer's will,
by the deathly shade   be drawn under shadow,
but be wakeful   and full of fury,
bide in boldness   for the battle's end.

710   Then from the moors,   under the misty fells,
came Grendel stalking,   bearing God's wrath.
The monster meant   from Mankind,
to ensnare his prey   in the high hall.

Under the sky he strode   'til the wine-palace,
715   the gold-hall of men,   he in the gloom beheld,
the house gleaming like fire.   Nor was it the first time
that he had sought   Hrothgar's home,
although ne'er in his life,   afore or since,
found he such hard heroes   and hall-retainers!
720   To the house then   the wicked warrior went,
of delights deprived.   The door opened,
fast by fire-hardened iron,   when he struck it with his fist
and with baleful intent,   he burst in his rage
the mouth of the hall.   Hastily, then,
725   o'er the painted floor   the fiend trode,
in anger approached.   From his eyes shone
an unholy light,   most like unto flames.
In the hall, then, he saw   many warriors in slumber,
kith and kin,   sleeping together,
730   a warrior host.   His heart laughed,
he thought that,   ere the day dawned,
he could ensnare   from each and everyone,

        Cóm on wanre niht
scríðan, sceadu-genga.   Scéotend swǽfon,
þá þæt horn-reċed   healdan scoldon,
705   ealle búton ánum.   Þæt wæs yldum cúþ
þæt híe ne móste,   þá Metod nolde,
se s(c)yn-scaþa   under sceadu breġdan,
ac hé wæċċende   wráþum on andan,
bád bolgen-mód   beadwa ġeþinges.`

              XI
710   Ðá cóm of móre,   under mist-hleoþum,
Grendel gongan,   Godes yrre bær.
Mynte se mán-scaða   Manna cynnes,
sumne besyrwan   in sele þám héan.

Wód under wolcnum   tó þæs þe hé wínreċed,
715   gold-sele gumena,   ġearwost wisse,
fǽttum fáhne.   Ne wæs þæt forma síð
þæt hé Hróþgáres   hám ġesóhte,
nǽfre hé on aldor-dagum,   ǽr né siþðan,
heardran hæle,   heal-ðeġnas fand!
720   Cóm þá tó reċede,   rinc síðian,
dréamum bedǽled.   Duru sóna onarn,
fýr-bendum fæst,   syþðan hé hire folmum (ġe)hrán,
onbræd þá bealo-hýdiġ,   ðá hé ġebolgen wæs
reċedes múþan.   Raþe, æfter þon,
725   on fágne flór   féond treddode,
éode yrre-mód.   Him of éagum stód
líġġe ġelícost,   léoht unfǽġer.
Ġeseah hé in reċede   rinca maniġe,
swefan sibbe-ġedriht,   samod ætgædere,
730   mago-rinca héap.   Þá his mód áhlóg,
mynte þæt hé ġedǽlde,   ǽr þon dæġ cwóme,
atol áglǽċa,   ánra ġehwylċes

the life from their limbs;   he now thought he had
a full feast!   But it was not his Fate
735   to devour   any more of Mankind
after that night.   Those mighty men beheld,
the kinsman of Hygelac,   how that heinous monster
how he fared   in that fearful ambush.

Nor did the monster   deem to delay.
740   Suddenly he   grasped a guard*
and ruthlessly rent   the sleeping warrior,
bit into his bone-locks   and gulped down blood,
swallowed him whole.   Soon, he had
wholly engorged   the unliving one,
745   even the hands and feet!   Further then he strode,
and took in his hands   the high-hearted one,
the warrior from his rest.   He reached forward,
but the hero   grasped him in his gripe,
and with cunning,   clamped down on the fiend's arm.

750   Then, he found,   the Soul-Slayer's servent,
that ne'er had he met   in Middle-Earth,
on the surface of the Earth,   any other man
with a greater gripe.   In his heart he
felt fear take him.   None the sooner, he fought to escape.
755   It was in his mind to get away   and flee to the fens,
seek the company of Demons;   ne'er again would he do those deeds,
such as he had done   in former days!

Then Hygelac's good retainer   remembered
the boast he spake at eventide;   upright then he stood
760   and held Grendel fast.   His fingers burst.
The Ettin outward moved,   but the earl stepped closer.
The monster meant-   if he might-
to wider wend,   and on his way thence,
flee to the fens;   he knew the fingers' might
765   in the grim one's gripe.   That was a grievous venture
that the harmful scather   had to Heorot made.
The lordly hall was filled with din,   then all the Danes,
each burg-dweller,   bold men all,
the earls were stunned with fear*.   Ire then arose in both
770   of those harsh hall-wards.   The house resounded.
Then, it was a great wonder   that the wine-hall
withheld their war   and fell not to the ground,
fair fortress,   but stood fast;
bound inside   and out by iron,

　　　　　　líf wið líċe;　　þá him álumpen wæs
　　　　　　wist-fylle wén!　　Ne wæs þæt Wyrd þá ġén,
735　　þæt hé má móste　　Manna cynnes
　　　　　　ðicgean ofer þá niht.　　Þrýð-swýð behéold,
　　　　　　mǽġ Hiġeláces,　　hú se mán-sceaða
　　　　　　under fǽr-gripum　　ġefaran wolde.

　　　　　　Né þæt se áglǽċa　　yldan þóhte,
740　　ac hé ġeféng hraðe　　forman síðe
　　　　　　slǽpendne rinc　　slát unwearnum,
　　　　　　bát bán-locan,　　blód édrum dranc,
　　　　　　syn-snǽdum swealh.　　Sóna, hæfde
　　　　　　unlyfiġendes　　eal ġefeormod,
745　　fét and folma!　　Forð néar ætstóp,
　　　　　　nam þá mid handa　　hiġe-þíhtiġne,
　　　　　　rinc on ræste;　　rǽhte onġéan
　　　　　　féond mid folme,　　hé onféng hraþe
　　　　　　inwit-þancum,　　ond wið earm ġesæt.

750　　Sóna þæt onfunde,　　fyrena hyrde,
　　　　　　þæt hé ne métte　　Middan-Ġeardes
　　　　　　Eorþan scéata,　　on elran men
　　　　　　mund-gripe máran.　　Hé on móde wearð
　　　　　　forht on ferhðe.　　Nó þý ǽr fram meahte.
755　　Hyġe wæs him hin-fús,　　wolde on heolster fléon,
　　　　　　séċan Déofla ġedrǽġ:　　ne wæs his drohtoð þǽr,
　　　　　　swylċe hé on ealder-dagum　　ǽr ġemétte!

　　　　　　Ġemunde þá se góda　　mǽġ Hiġeláces
　　　　　　ǽfen-sprǽċep;　　up-lang ástód
760　　ond him fæste wiðféng.　　Fingras burston.
　　　　　　Eoten wæs út-weard,　　eorl furþur stóp.
　　　　　　Mynte se mǽra　　-(þ)ǽr hé meahte swá-
　　　　　　wídre ġewindan,　　ond on weġ þanon,
　　　　　　fléon on fen-hopu;　　wiste his fingra ġeweald
765　　on grames grápum.　　Þæt hé wæs ġeocor síð
　　　　　　þæt se hearm-sceaþa　　tó Heorute átéah.
　　　　　　Dryht-sele dynede,　　Denum eallum wearð,
　　　　　　ċeaster-búendum;　　cénra ġehwylcum,
　　　　　　eorlum ealu-scerwen.　　Yrre wǽron béġen
770　　réþe rén-weardas.　　Reċed hlynsode.
　　　　　　Þá wæs wundor miċel　　þæt se wín-sele
　　　　　　wiðhæfde heaþo-déorum,　　þæt hé on hrúsan ne féol,
　　　　　　fǽġer fold-bold　　ac hé þæs fæste wæs;
　　　　　　innan ond útan　　íren-bendum,

775   cunningly crafted.   From the floor, tore loose
        many a mead bench   -I have heard tell-
        adorned with gold;   the grim ones struggled.
        The Scylding witan   weened not
        that a man,   by any means
780   might break apart   that bone-decked hall,
        by any deed destroy,   but for fire's embrace,
        swallowed by smoke.   Then arose
        a new noise.   The North-Danes stood,
        petrified with awe,   each one
785   from the wall   heard the wailing,
        the ghastly shriek   from God's foe,
        a victoryless song*;   his sorrow he bewailed,
        the captive of Hell.   He held him fast,
        he who of Men   in might was strongest
790   on that day   in this life.

        The earls' ward   had no wish
        for the savage stranger   to escape with his life,
        nor did he deem his days,   to any people
        to be of any worth.   Then the warriors,
795   Beowulf's men,   brandished ancestral blades;
        they would protect   the life of their lord,
        the celebrated commander,   if they could.
        They knew not when   they entered the battle,
        those hard-hearted   heroes of war,
800   thinking to hew his hide   on every side
        and seek the soul   of that sinful enemy,
        that even the choicest   of earthly irons
        the stoutest of battle-blades   could not pierce his flesh,
        for by an enchantment   he was immune to weapons,
805   to iron edge.   Yet his end,
        on this day   in this life,
        would be anguishing,   and his unknown shade
        would flee far   to the solace of fiends.

        Then he found,   he who in former times
810   in his murderous heart,   on many of Mankind
        carried out his crimes   -he was God's foe-
        that his life   would not last,
        for Hygelac's   haughty kinsman
        had him by the hand;   each by the other was
815   loathed while they still lived.   Then he felt a pain,
        the terrible Troll;   on his shoulder

775   searo-þoncum besmiþod.   Þǽr fram sylle ábéag
        medu-benċ moniġ   -míne ġefrǽġe-
        golde ġereġnad;   þǽr þá graman wunnon.
        Þæs ne wéndon ǽr   witan Scyldinga
        þæt hit á mid ġemete   manna ǽniġ
780   (b)etlíċ ond bán-fág   tóbrecan meahte,
        listum tólúcan,   nymþe líġes fæþm,
        swulge on swaþule.   Swéġ up ástág
        níwe ġeneahhe.   Norð-Denum stód,
        atelíċ eġesa,   ánra ġehwylcum
785   þára þe of wealle   wóp ġehýrdon,
        gryre-léoð galan   Godes andsacan,
        siġe-léasne sang;   sár wániġean,
        Helle hæftan.   Héold hine fæste,
        sé þe manna wæs   mæġene strengest
790   on þǽm dæġe   þysses lífes.

XII

        Nolde eorla hléo   ǽniġe þinga
        þone cwealm-cuman   cwicne forlǽtan,
        né his líf-dagas   léoda ǽnigum
        nytte tealde.   Þǽr ġenehost brægd
795   eorl Béowulfes   ealde láfe,
        wolde fréa-drihtnes   feorh ealgian
        mǽres þéodnes,   ðǽr híe meahton swá.
        Híe þæt ne wiston   þá híe ġewin drugon,
        heard-hicgende   hilde-mecgas,
800   ond on healfa ġehwone   héawan þóhton,
        sáwle séċan   þone syn-scaðan
        ǽniġ ofer eorðan   írenna cyst,
        gúð-billa nán   grétan nolde,
        ac hé siġe-wǽpnum   forsworen hæfde,
805   ecga ġehwylċre.   Scolde his aldor-ġedál
        on ðǽm dæġe   þysses lífes,
        earmlíċ wurðan   ond se ellor-gást
        on féonda ġeweald   feor síðian.

        Ðá þæt onfunde,   sé þe fela ǽror
810   módes myrðe,   Manna cynne
        fyrene ġefremede   -hé wæs fág wið God-
        þæt him se líċ-homa   lǽstan nolde,
        ac hine se módega   mǽġ Hyġeláces
        hæfde be honda;   wæs ġehwæþer óðrum
815   lifiġende láð.   Líċ-sár ġebád,
        atol ǽġlǽċa;   him on eaxle wearð

a great wound showed,   the sinews snapped
and bone-locks burst.   To Beowulf was
glory granted,   but Grendel thence,

820   death-sick,   fled to the fens,
to his loathly lair.   He clearly knew
then, that his   life had ended,
the day of his doom   had come.

Then the Danes' desire   had passed.

825   He who had come   from afar had cleansed
Hrothgar's hall,   the clever and bold one,
defended from destruction.   He was delighted in his night-work,
that famèd feat.   To the East-Danes had
the Geatish leader   brought to bear his boast,

830   he had avenged   their anguish,
the evils they had   ere endured
and the dire distress,   they suffered
no small sadness.   That was a clear token,
when the battle-hard one   hung the hand,

835   shoulder and arm,   all of
Grendel's gripe   under the golden roof!

syn-dolh sweotol,   seonowe onsprungon
burston bán-locan.   Béowulfe wearð
gúð-hréð ġyfeþe,   scolde Grendel þonan.
820 feorh-séoc, fléon   under fen-hleoðu,
séċean wyn-léas wíċ.   Wiste þé ġeornor,
þæt his aldres wæs   ende ġegongen,
dógera dæġ-rím.

Denum eallum wearð
æfter þám wæl-ræse   willa ġelumpen.
825 Hæfde þá ġefælsod,   sé þe ǽr feorran cóm,
snotor ond swýð-ferhð,   sele Hróðgáres,
ġenered wið níðe.   Niht-weorce ġefeh,
ellen-mǽrþum.   Hæfde Ēast-Denum
Ġéat-mecga léod   ġilp ġelǽsted,
830 swylċe oncýþðe   ealle ġebétte,
inwid-sorge,   þe híe ǽr drugon
ond for þréa-nýdum   þolian scoldon,
torn unlýtel.   Þæt wæs tácen sweotol,
syþðan hilde-déor   hond áleġde,
835 earm ond eaxle   -þǽr wæs eal ġeador
Grendles grápe-   under ġéapne h(róf).

Chapter VII
The Hero of Heorot

Then in the morn,   men told me,
many warriors gathered   in the gift-hall.
Folk leaders fared   both far and near,
840   o'er wide ways to see   that wondrous sight,
those terrible tracks.   His death was not
mourned   by any man,
who saw that   honorless foe's footprints;
how he went,   weary-hearted,
845   overcome by enmity,   to the Demon's mere.
Wretched and accursèd,   the bloody tracks bore.
The tide   boiled with blood,
the swells seethed   and swirled together,
hot gore   welled in the water.
850   Doomed to die,   he hid in his joyless den
and in his fen fastness,   gave up his life.
There, Hell collected   his heathen soul.

Then returned   the agèd retainers,
and also many youths,   back from the hearty hunt,
855   winsome warriors   on white horses,
from the mere.   The might of Beowulf
was then announced.   Oft was it said,
that from north to south,   between the seas,
none other   o'er the wide Earth,
860   under the high heavens,   could be found
a shield-bearer   more worthy of wealth!
Of their lord and friend,   they found no fault,
for glorious Hrothgar   was a good king.

Sometimes,   stout-hearted men
865   would fare   on fallow horses,
holding races   when the roads seemed fair,
the way wide.   At other times, a thegn of the king,
a man who had   mastered song

XIII

Ðá wæs on morgen,   míne ġefræġe,
ymb þá ġif-healle   gúð-rinc moniġ.
Férdon folc-togan   feorran and néan,

840 ġeond wíd-wegas   wundor scéawian,
láþes lástas.   Nó his líf-ġedál
sárlíċ þúhte   secga ǽnegum,
þára þe tír-léases   trode scéawode;
hú hé wériġ-mód   on weġ þanon,

845 níða ofercumen,   on Nicera mere,
fǽge ond ġeflýmed,   feorh-lástas bær.
Ðǽr wæs on blóde   brim weallende,
atol ýða ġeswing   eal ġemenged
hátan heolfre,   heoro-dréore wéol.

850 Déað-fǽġe déog,   siððan dréama léas
in fen-freoðo   feorh áleġde.
Hǽþene sáwle,   þǽr him Hel onféng.

Þanon eft ġewiton   eald-ġesíðas,
swylċe ġeong maniġ   of gomen-wáþe,

855 fram mere módġe,   méarum rídan,
beornas on blancum.   Ðǽr wæs Béowulfes
mǽrðo mǽned.   Moniġ oft ġecwæð,
þætte súð né norð   be sǽm twéonum
ofer eormen-grund   óþer nǽniġ

860 under sweġles begong   sélra nǽre
rond-hæbbendra,   ríċes wyrðra.
Né híe húru wine-drihten   wiht ne lógon,
glædne Hróðgár,   ac þæt wæs gód cyning.

Hwílum heaþo-rófe   hléapan léton

865 on ġeflít faran   fealwe méaras,
ðǽr him fold-wegas   fæġere þúhton,
cystum cúðe.   Hwílum cyninges þeġn,
guma ġilp-hlæden   ġidda ġemyndiġ

and had studied   the sagas of yore,
870   would remember old lays   and tell new tales,
with words well bound.   Soon, the scop,
of Beowulf's valor,   skillfully sang
and recited   the remarkable story.

In verses of varied words,   he spake of all
875   that he had heard   said of Sigemund*;
of daring deeds   and eldritch happenings,
of the Wælsing's wanderings   and his struggles,
things not known   by the children of men,
feuds and feats,   but Fitela alone,
880   -of those things   he was wont to speak of-
uncle and nephew   as ever they were,
in every struggle,   constant companions.

"A great many   of monster kind
laid they low with swords.   Of Sigmund grew,
885   after his death-day,   no small fame,
since the hardy warrior   the Wyrm slew,
and won his hoard!   On the hoary rock,
the atheling,   alone dared,
the fell deed;   Fitela was not with him.
890   Yet it happened that   his sword hewed
the wicked Wyrm,   and its blade stood in the wall.
By that splendid iron,   the Dragon died.
Thus, the awe-inspiring one   ensured with his might,
that he might rule   o'er the ring-hoard
895   by his will.   They weighed down the sea-boat,
the bosom of the ship   bore the bright treasure,
the heir of Wæls.   The Wyrm was consumed by the flames.

"Of wanderers he had   the widest renown
among the people,   the protector of warriors,
900   for daring deeds   -he had, ere prospered in this-
since Heremod's* dominion   had dwindled,
his tyranny and might.   Among the Jutes was he exiled,
given up by his folk,   to the hands of his foes,
doomed to die.   Whelms of despair
905   they had suffered too long.   A sorrow he was to his earls,
he proved to be an oppressor   to his people.
Once it was,   that wise men mourned
the death of a doughty king,   from whom they could,
from baleful harm,   hope for retribution,
910   for they believed   the bairn of the king

sé þe eal fela   eald-ġeseġena,
870   worn ġemunde,   word óþer fand
sóðe ġebunden.   Secg eft ongan,
síð Béowulfes,   snyttrum styrian
ond on spéd wrecan   spel ġeráde.

Wordum wrixlan,   wél-hwylċ ġecwæð
875   þæt hé fram Siġemunde   secgan hýrde,
ellen-dǽdum,   uncúþes fela,
Wælsinges ġewin,   wíde síðas,
þára þe gumena bearn   ġearwe ne wiston,
fǽhðe ond fyrene,   búton Fitela mid hine,
880   -þonne hé swulċes hwæt   secgan wolde-
éam his nefan   swá híe á wǽron,
æt níða ġehwám   nýd-ġesteallan.

"Hæfdon eal-fela   Eotena cynnes
sweordum ġesǽġed.   Siġemunde ġesprong
885   æfter déað-dæġe,   dóm unlýtel,
syþðan wíġes heard   Wyrm ácwealde
hordes hyrde!   Hé under hárne stán,
æþelinges bearn,   ána ġenéðde
frécne dǽde;   né wæs him Fitela mid.
890   Hwæþre him ġesǽlde,   ðæt þæt swurd þurhwód
wrǽtlícne Wyrm,   þæt hit on wealle ætstód.
Dryhtliċ íren,   Draca morðre swealt.
Hæfde áglǽċa   elne ġegongen,
þæt hé béah-hordes   brúcan móste
895   selfes dóme.   Sǽ-bát ġehléod,
bær on bearm scipes   beorhte frætwa,
Wælses eafera.   Wyrm hát ġemealt.

"Sé wæs wreċċena   wíde mǽrost
ofer wer-þéode,   wíġendra hléo,
900   ellen-dǽdum   -hé þæs ǽr onðáh-
siðða Heremódes   hild sweðrode,
ea(r)foð ond ellen.   Hé mid Ēotenum wearð,
on féonda ġeweald   forð forlácen,
snúde forsended.   Hine sorh-wylmas
905   lemede tó lange.   Hé his léodum wearð,
eallum æþelingum,   tó aldor-ċeare.
Swylċe oft bemearn   ǽrran mǽlum
swíð-ferhþes síð   snotor ċeorl moniġ,
sé þe him bealwa tó   bóte ġelýfde,
910   þæt þæt ðéodnes bearn   ġeþéon scolde,

would triumph,   take up his father's title
and rule the folk,   hoard and hold,
the hero's realm,   the home of the Scyldings
All men thought   that Hygelac's kinsman was kinder
915 than he who was   wasted by his own wickedness!"

Meanwhile, horses flew   down the fair street,
measured by their sturdy mounts.   Then the morning-sun
rose in the heavens.   Many men came,
high-hearted folk,   to the mead-hall,
920 to see the strange sight.   Likewise, the king himself,
came from his wife's bower,   the warden of the ring-hoard,
triumphantly strode   at the head of his host,
his radiance renowned   and with his queen,
passed down the path   to the mead-hall.

925 At the hall,   Hrothgar spake,
on the steps he stood   and observed the steep roof,
adorned with gold   and Grendel's hand.
"For this sight,   I swiftly thank
the All-Ruler!   Many evils have I endured
930 from the hand of Grendel,   but God works still
wonder after wonder,   the Glory-Warden!
Not long ago,   I thought that ne'er
would I receive relief   from my woes
as long as I lived,   when stained with blood
935 stood that splendid house,   awash with sword gore;
woe widespread   for every wise man,
they harbored no hope   in their hearts that
the burg would ever   protect the people
from shucks* and shades.   Now a warrior has,
940 through the Lord's might,   done this deed
which we afore   could ne'er achieve,
by craft nor cunning.   Lo, they may say
that whatever woman   bore this warrior
among Mankind,   if she yet lives,
945 that the King of Ages   was kind to her
in that bairn's birth!   Now, Beowulf,
the best of men,   I, like mine own son
love you   with my whole heart,
keep this kinship new.   Ne'er shall you lack
950 in worldly wishes   while I rule.
Oft have I rewarded   fully for far less,
with mathoms honored   humbler men,

fæder-æþelum onfón,   folc ġehealdan,
hord ond hléo-burh,   hæleþa ríċe,
(éþel) Scyldinga.   Hé þǽr eallum wearð,
mǽġ Hiġeláces   Manna cynne,
915   fréondum ġefǽgra   hine fyren onwód!"

Hwílum flítende   fealwe strǽte,
méarum mǽton.   Ðá wæs morgen-léoht
scofen ond scynded.   Ēode scealc moniġ
swíð-hicgende   tó sele þám héan,
920   searo-wundor son.   Swylċe self cyning,
of brýd-búre,   béah-horda weard,
tryddode tír-fæst   ġetrume miċle,
cystum ġecýþed,   ond his cwén mid him.
medo-stíġġe mæt   mæġþa hóse.

XIV

925   Hróðgár maþelode   hé tó healle ġéong,
stód on stapole,   ġeseah stéapne hróf,
golde fáhne   ond Grendles hond.
"Ðisse ansýne   Al-Wealdan þanc
lungre ġelimpe!   Fela iċ láþes ġebád
930   grynna æt Grendle,   á mæġ God wyrċan
wunder æfter wundre,   Wuldres Hyrde!
Ðæt wæs unġeára,   þæt iċ ǽniġra mé
wéana ne wénde   tó wídan feore
bóte ġebídan   þonne blóde fáh
935   húsa sélest   heoro-dréoriġ stód;
wéa wíd-scofen   witena ġehwylcne
ðára þe ne wéndon,   þæt híe wíde-ferhð
léoda land-ġeweorc   láþum beweredon
scuccum ond scinnum.   Nú scealc hafað,
940   þurh Drihtnes miht   dǽd ġefremede,
ðé wé ealle   ǽr ne meahton,
snyttrum besyrwan.   Hwæt, þæt secgan mæġ
efne swá hwylċ mæġþa   swá ðone magan cende
æfter gum-cynnum,   ġyf héo ġýt lyfað,
945   þæt hyre Eald-Metod   éste wǽre
bearn-ġebyrdo!   Nú iċ Béowulf þeċ,
secg bet(o)sta,   mé for sunu wylle
fréogan on ferhþe,   heald forð tela
níwe sibbe.   Ne bið þé (n)ǽniġra gád
950   worolde wilna,   þé iċ ġeweald hæbbe.
Ful oft iċ for lǽssan   léan teohhode
hord-weorþunge   hnáhran rince,

weaker in war.   You have
these deeds fulfilled,   so that your fame will endure
955   through all ages!   May the All-Ruler
reward you well,   as He has now yet done!"

Beowulf spake,   the son of Ecgtheow,
"This courage-work   have we willingly
carried out,   and fearlessly fought
960   against the unknown enemy.   Rather would I
had, that you   had seen him yourself,
the fiend in his full gear,   wearied to death.
I, hastily   in mine hard clasp,
on his death-bed   thought to bind him,
965   that he,   in mine hand's gripe, should
lie, struggling for life,   but he broke away.
I might not,   for the Measurer did not will it,
impede his escape,   or grip him too eagerly,
the mortal-foe;   too mighty
970   and fast was the fiend.   So that he might
save his life,   he left his hand behind,
arm and shoulder.   There was not any
solace the pitiful creature   could procure.
The loathly beast   cannot have lived long,
975   sunk in sin,   but his wound holds him
greedily in it's gripe,   tightly ensnared
in baleful bonds.   There he must abide,
the murderous monster,   whatever terrible doom
the shining Measurer   meets out."

980   Silent then was   the son of Ecglaf,
in boastful speech   of war-works,
since all the earls,   at the atheling's craft
beheld the hand   that hung from the roof.
On each   of the fiend's fingers
985   were strong nails,   most like unto steel,
the hateful foe's   heathenish hand-spurs,
the Demon's cruel claw.   All the men now said
that no weapon   could hew his hide,
agèd iron,   of them, none
990   could harm   the beast's bloody hand.

sémran æt sǽċċe.   Þú þé self hafast
dǽdum ġefremed,   þæt þín (dóm) lyfað
955 áwa tó aldre!   Alwalda þeċ
góde forġylde,   swá Hé nú ġýt dyde!"

Béowulf maþelode,   bearn Ec(g)þéowes,
"Wé þæt ellen-weorc   éstum miċlum
feohtan fremedon,   frécne ġenéðdon
960 eafoð uncúþes.   Úþe iċ swíþor
þæt ðú hine selfne   ġeséon móste,
féond on frætewum.   fyl-wériġne.
Iċ hi(ne) hrædlíċe   heardan clammum,
on wæl-bedde   wríþan þóhte,
965 þæt hé for (mund)gripe   mínum scolde
licgean, líf-bysiġ,   bútan his líċ swice.
Iċ hine ne mihte,   þá Metod nolde,
ganges ġetwǽman,   nó iċ him þæs ġeorne ætfealh,
feorh-ġeníðlan;   wæs tó fore-mihtiġ
970 féond on féþe.   Hwæþere hé his folme forlét
tó líf-wraþe,   lást weardian,
earm ond eaxle.   Nó þǽr ǽniġe swá þéah
féa-sceaft guma   frófre ġebohte.
Nó þý leng leofað   láð-ġetéona,
975 synnum ġeswenċed,   ac hyne sár hafað
in (n)íðgripe   nearwe befongen,
balwon bendum.   Þǽr ábídan sceal,
maga máne fáh,   miċlan dómes,
hú him scír Metod   scrífan wille."

980 Ðá wæs swíġra secg   sunu Ec(g)láfes,
on ġylp-sprǽċe   gúð-ġeweorca,
siþðan æþelingas,   eorles cræfte
ofer héahne hróf   hand scéawedon,
féondes fingras,   foran ǽġhwylċ wæs,
985 steda næġla ġehwylċ,   stýle ġelícost,
hǽþenes hand-sporu   hilde-rinces
eġle unhéoru.   Ǽġ-hwylċ ġecwæð
þæt him heardra nán   hrínan wolde,
íren ǽr-gód,   þæt ðæs áhlǽċan
990 blódġe beadu-folme   onberan wolde.

Hastily was it commanded   that the Heorot Hall
by hands be managed.   Many there were
of men and women,   who the wine-hall made ready,
garnished the guest-hall.   Gold shone
995 the tapestries among the walls.   Many worldly wonders
the eyes   of each man beheld.
That bright house   was badly broken,
though 'twas fastened   all inside with iron-bands;
the hinges were burst,   alone the roof remained
1000 unbroken,   when the fearsome foe,
stained with sin,   turned in flight,
despairing of life.   'Tis no little thing
to flee to safety   -try it who will-
but, forced by fate,   they must seek
1005 the soul-bearers,   the sons of men,
the doom   of earth-dwellers,
his lich lying fast   on his death-bed,
asleep after the symbel.

Then came the hour
that Healfdene's son   went to the hall
1010 the king himself,   to sit at the symbel.
I have not heard   of a host so great,
graciously gathered   about a treasure-giver.
Those bearers of glory   bowed to the bench,
rejoicing at the feast.   Fain they accepted
1015 many a mead-cup;   the kinsmen
were hearty   in the high hall,
Hrothgar and Hrothulf.   Heorot was
filled with friends,   no treason
had the Scylding clan   yet committed.

1020 Then Healfdene's bairn   to Beowulf gave
a golden standard   to signal victory,
adornèd banner,   byrnie and helm,
and a splendid sword   many saw
brought before the warrior.   Beowulf received
1025 the cup in the hall;   of those generous gifts
he shouldered   no shame.
Ne'er have I heard of a hero,   four such mathoms,
glittering with gold,   receive more graciously,
honoring the others   on the ale-bench.

XV

Ðá wæs háten hreþe   Heort innan-weard
folmum ġefrætwod.   Fela þǽra wæs
wera ond wífa,   þe þæt wín-reċed,
ġest-sele ġyredon.   Gold-fág scinon
995   web æfter wágum.   Wundor-síona fela
secga ġehwylcum   þára þe on swylċ starað.
Wæs þæt beorhte bold   tóbrocen swíðe,
eal inne-weard   íren-bendum fæst;
heorras tóhlidene,   hróf ána ġenæs
1000   ealles ansund,   þ(á) se áglǽċa,
fyren-dǽdum fág   on fléam ġewand,
aldres or-wéna.   Nó þæt ýðe byð
tó befléonne   -fremme sé þe wille-
ac ġesaċan sceal   sáwl-berendra
1005   nýde ġenýdde   niþða bearna,
grund-búendra   ġearwe stówe,
þǽr his líċ-homa   leġer-bedde fæst,
swefeð æfter symle.

                    Þá wæs sǽl ond mǽl
þæt tó healle gang   Healfdenes sunu
1010   wolde self cyning   symbel þicgan.
Ne ġefræġen iċ þá mǽġþe   máran weorode
ymb hyra sinc-ġyfan   sél ġebǽran.
Bugon þá tó benċe,   blǽd-ágende,
fylle ġefǽgon.   Fæġere ġeþǽgon
1015   medo-ful maniġ;   mágas þára
swíð-hicgende   on sele þám héan,
Hróðgár ond Hróþulf.   Heorot innan wæs
fréondum áfylled,   nalles fácen-stafas
Þéod-Scyldingas   þenden fremedon.

1020   Forġeaf þá Béowulfe   b(earn) Healfdenes
seġen gyldenne   sigores tó léane,
hroden hilte-cumbor,   helm ond byrnan,
mǽre máðþum-sweord   maniġe ġesáwon
beforan beorn beran.   Béowulf ġeþáh
1025   ful on flette;   nó hé þǽre feoh-ġyfte
for sc(é)oten(d)um   scamiġan ðorfte.
Ne ġefræġn iċ fréondlicor,   féower mádmas,
golde ġeġyrede,   gum-manna fela,
in ealo-benċe   óðrum ġesellan.

73

1030   On the helm's roof   was a ridge,
        wound with wire   to protect without,
        that the leavings of files   could not fiercely
        scathe the shield-bearer   in the storm of battle,
        when he warred   with wrathful foes.

1035   Then the protector of earls   ordered eight horses
        with decorated head-gear,   hie to the hall-floor
        into the enclosure.   One of them stood,
        the saddle skillfully crafted,   and set with gems,
        the battle-seat   of the brave king,
1040   when in sword-play   the son of Healfdene
        wished to fight;   his valor in the vanguard
        never failed when men   were falling in the fight.
        And, then both of these to   Beowulf's possession,
        bestowed the bastion of   the Ingwines*,
1045   steeds and weapons;   he wished them to serve him well.
        Thus manfully,   the mighty king,
        hoard-ward of heroes,   repaid that onslaught
        with those mathoms.   Thus, no fault can be found,
        in he who wishes to say sooth   in what is right.

1050   Then, the lord   to each of the earls
        who traveled with Beowulf   o'er the briny sea,
        on the mead-benches,   mathoms gave,
        heirlooms, and for the   one man paid
        the gold-price   for he whom Grendel
1055   had killed;   he would have slain many more,
        had wise God   not his Wyrd hindered
        or for the courage of the man's.   But the Measurer
        rules o'er the race of Man,   now and always.
        Therefore, understanding   is always best,
1060   a heedful heart,   for he shall abide much,
        love and loathing,   if here he would long
        endure these days   of woe in this world!

1030   Ymb þæs helmes hróf   héafod-beorge,
          wírum bewunden   walan útan héold,
          þæt him féla láf   frécne ne meahton
          scúr-heard sceþðan   þonne scyld-freca,
          onġéan gramum   gangan scolde.

1035   Heht ðá eorla hléo   eahta méaras
          fǽted-hléore,   on flet téon
          in under eoderas.   Þára ánum stód,
          sadol searwum fáh   sinċe ġewurþad,
          þæt wæs hilde-setl   héah-cyninges,
1040   ðonne sweorda ġelác   sunu Healfdenes
          efnan wolde;   nǽfre on óre læġ
          wíd-cúþes wíġ   ðonne walu féollon.
          Ond ðá Béowulfe   béga ġehwæþres,
          eodor Ingwina   onweald ġetéah,
1045   wicga ond wǽpna;   hét hine wél brúcan.
          Swá manlíċe,   mǽre þéoden,
          hord-weard hæleþa,   heaþo-rǽsas ġeald
          méarum ond mádmum.   Swá hý nǽfre man lyhð,
          sé þe secgan wile   sóð æfter rihte.

XVI

1050   Ðá ġýt ǽghwylcum   eorla drihten
          þára þe mid Béowulfe   brim-l(á)de téah,
          on þǽre medu-benċe,   máþðum ġesealde,
          yrfe-láfe,   ond þone ǽnne heht
          golde forġyldan   þone ðe Grendel ǽr
1055   máne ácwealde;   swá hé hyra má wolde,
          nefne him wítiġ God   Wyrd forstóde
          ond ðæs mannes mód.   Metod eallum wéold
          gumena cynnes,   swá hé nú ġít déð.
          Forþan bið andġit   ǽghwǽr sélest,
1060   ferhðes fore-þanc;   fela sceal ġebídan
          léofes ond láþes,   sé þe longe hér
          on ðyssum win-dagum   worolde brúceð!

Chapter VIII
The Fight at Finnesburg

Then were the sounds of song   and music together
before Healdene's   battle-commander;
1065   the joy-wood was played,   a tale oft told
in the hall.   And so, Hrothgar's scop,
about the mead-benches   made his song,
concerning the fall   of Finnesburg*.

"The hero of the Half-Danes,   Hnæf the Scylding,
1070   was fated to fall   in the Frisian slaughter.
Hildeburh had no need   to praise
the Jute's honor.   Innocent, she was
of loved ones bereft   from the battle-play.
Bairn and brother   bowed to their fate,
1075   by spears felled;   a forlorn lady indeed!
Not without reason   did the daughter of Hoc
mourn the Measurer's judgement   with the coming of the morn.
That under the sun   she might see
her kin's baleful murder,   where most she had held
1080   joy in the world.   War had destroyed all
of Finn's thegns,   save a few only,
that he might not,   at the folk moot,
openly wage war   on Hengest,
or rescue   his wretched remnant
1085   from the atheling's thegn.

"So, he offered a truce-
that they should   hold the other house,
hall and high-seat,   and rule o'er half,
while the Jutish sons,   ruled the rest.
When Folcwald's son   gave gifts
1090   each day,   the Danes would honor him
and favor with rings,   Hengest's host,
even as truly,   with gleaming gems
and glittering gold,   as his Frisian kin

Þǽr wæs sang ond swéġ   samod ætgædere
fore Healfdenes   hilde-wísan;
1065 gomen-wudu gréted,   ġid oft wrecen,
ðonne heal-gamen   Hróþgáres scop
æfter medo-benċe   mǽnan scolde
Finnes eaferum,   ðá híe se fǽr beġeat.

"Hæleð Healf-Dena,   Hnæf Scyldinga,
1070 in Fréswæle   feallan scolde.
Né húru Hildeburh   herian þorfte
Ēotena tréowe.   Unsynnum wearð
beloren léofum   æt þám (l)i(n)d-plegan,
bearnum ond bróðrum,   híe on ġebyrd hruron,
1075 gáre wunde;   þæt wæs ġeómuru ides!
Nalles hólinga   Hóces dóhtor
Meotod-sceaft bemearn   syþðan morgen cóm,
Ðá héo under sweġle   ġeséon meahte
morþor-bealo mága,   þǽr hé(o) ǽr mǽste héold
1080 worolde wynne.   Wíġ ealle fornam
Finnes þeġnas,   nemne féaum ánum,
þæt hé ne mehte   on þǽm meðel-stede
wíġ Hengeste   wiht ġefeohtan,
né þá wéa-láfe   wíġe forþringan
1085 þéodnes ðeġne;

                    ac hiġ him ġeþingo budon-
þæt híe him óðer flet   eal ġerýmdon,
healle ond héah-setl,   þæt híe healfre ġeweald
wið Ēotena bearn   ágan móston,
ond æt feoh-ġyftum   Folcwaldan sunu
1090 dógra ġehwylċe,   Dene weorþode
Hengestes héap   hringum wenede,
efne swá swíðe,   sinc-ġestréonum
fǽttan goldes,   swá hé Frésena cyn

in the beer-hall   would embolden.
1095 Both sides   then pledged peace,
fast and firm.   Finn and Hengest
each in earnest,   swore an oath
to the wretched remnant,   by the witan's judgement,
that they would hold the others in honor   and that no man,
1100 by word or work   should break that pact,
nor of malice   bemoan
and take revenge   on their ring-giver's bane,
lordless men,   as they were lief to do.
And should any Frisian   speak with spite
1105 and make them mindful   of their murderous feud,
then they should, by sword-edge,   seal their fate.

"The bale-fire was built   and ancient gold
heaped from the hoard.   The Scylding's
best battle-man   lay on his bier.
1110 On the pyre   was he plainly seen,
his sark stained with blood,   and gilded swine crest,
the boar iron-hard.   The atheling by many
wounds fell,   surrendered to slaughter.
At the hest of Hildeburh,   on Hnæf's pyre
1115 her own son   was sent to the flames,
the bone-house to   burn on the balefire,
at his uncle's shoulder.   The lady lamented
a woeful dirge   as the warrior was laid out.
Smoke wound in the sky,   the greatest of death-fires
1120 roared before the barrow.   Heads were consumed,
wound-gates burst   and blood flowed
from the hate-bites of the body.   The fire consumed all,
-those greedy flames-   all those who fell in that battle,
from both folk;   their glory had faded.

1125 "Then those heroes   their homeland sought;
friendless,   they sought Frisia,
their houses and the high burg.   Yet Hengest,
that deathly winter   dwelt with Finn
in that foreign land,   but he did not forget home.

1130 "He could not   sail the sea,
his ring-prowed ship   o'er the welling waves,
wan under the wind,   for winter locked them
in bonds of ice.   Then came another
year in the yard,   as yet they do;

on béor-sele   byldan wolde.

1095   Ðá híe ġetruwedon   on twá healfa
fæste frioðu-wǽre.   Fin Hengeste
elne unflitme   áðum benemde
þæt hé þá wéa-láfe,   weotena dóme
árum héolde,   þæt ðǽr ǽniġ mon
1100   wordum né worcum   wǽre ne brǽce,
né þurh inwit-searo   ǽfre ġemǽnden,
þéah híe hira béag-ġyfan   banan folgedon
ðéoden-léase;   þá him swá ġeþearfod wæs,
ġyf þonne Frýsna hwylċ   frécnan sprǽce
1105   ðæs morþor-hetes   myndgiend wǽre,
þonne hit sweordes ecg   syððan scolde.

"Á(d) wæs ġeæfned   ond i(n)cge gold
áhæfen of horde.   Here-Scyldinga
betst beado-rinca   wæs on bǽl ġearu.
1110   Æt þǽm áde wæs   éþ-ġesýne,
swát-fáh syrċe,   swýn eal gylden,
eofer íren-heard.   Æþeling maniġ
wundum áwyrded,   sume on wæle crungon.
Hét ðá Hildeburh,   æt Hnæfes áde
1115   hire selfre sunu   sweoloðe befæstan,
bán-fatu bærnan   ond on bǽl dón,
earme on eaxle.   Ides gnornode
ġéomrode ġiddum   gúð-rinc ástáh.
Wand tó wolcnum,   wæl-fýra mǽst,
1120   hlynode for hláwe.   Hafelan multon,
ben-ġeato burston,   ðonne blód ætspranc
láð-bite líċes.   Líġ ealle forswealg,
-gǽsta ġífrost-   þára ðe þǽr gúð fornam,
béġa folces;   wæs hira blǽd scacen.

XVII

1125   "Ġewiton him ðá wíġend   wíca néosian;
fréondum befeallen   Frýsland ġeséon,
hámas ond héa-burh.   Hengest ðá ġýt
wæl-fágne winter   wunode mid Finne
(ea)l(le) unhlitme,   eard ġemunde.

1130   Þéah þe (ne) meahte   on mere drífan
hringedstefnan,   holm storme wéol,
won wið winde,   winter ýþe beléac
ísġebinde.   Oþ ðæt óþer cóm
ġéar in ġeardas,   swá nú ġýt déð,

1135   they continue to carry   out their seasons,
sun-bright weather.

               "Then was winter gone,
fair was the earth's bosom;   the exile was eager
to depart from those dwellings.   Of revenge he
pondered much   on the sea passage,
1140   of how he might   bring about that battle;
for that the Jutish bairn   remembered.
So it was that he did not deny   that worldly deed,
when to him, the son of Hunlaf   lay Hildeleoman,
the best of blades   on Hnæf's lap;
1145   its iron edge   was famed among the Jutes.
Thus Finn, his foe,   received his due,
slashed by swords   in his own home,
and of that grim battle,   Guthlaf and Oslaf
spoke of their sorrow   after the sea-voyage,
1150   mourning their misery;   their wandering moods
they could not hold in their hearts.   Then was the hall reddened
with the blood of foes.   Here Finn was slain,
the king with his companions,   and the queen was taken.
The Scylding shooters   fared to their ships
1155   with all that   earthly king's wealth,
whatever they could   find in Finn's home,
cunningly crafted brooches   and finely cut gems.
They carried the queen   back to her homeland,
o'er the deeps to Danemark,"

1135 þá ðe syngáles   séle bewitiað,
    wuldortorhtan weder.

                        Ðá wæs winter scacen,
    fæġer foldan bearm;   fundode wreċċa
    ġist of ġeardum.   Hé tó gyrn-wræce
    swíðor þóhte   þonne tó sǽ-láde,
1140 ġif hé torn-ġemót   þurhtéon mihte,
    þæt hé Ēotena bearn   inne ġemunde.
    Swá hé ne forwyrnde   woroldrǽdenne,
    þonne him Húnláfing   Hildeléoman,
    billa sélest,   on bearm dyde;
1145 þæs wǽron mid Ēotenum   ecge cúðe.
    Swylċe ferhð-frecan   Fin eft beġeat,
    sweord-bealo slíðen   æt his selfes hám,
    siþðan grimne gripe,   Gúðlaf ond Ósláf
    æfter sǽ-síðe   sorge mǽndon,
1150 ætwiton wéana dǽl;   ne meahte wǽfre mód
    forhabban in hreþre.   Ðá wæs heal hroden
    féonda féorum,   swilċe Fin slæġen,
    cyning on corþre,   ond séo cwén numen.
    Scéotend Scyldinga   tó scypum feredon
1155 eal in-ġesteald   eorð-cyninges,
    swylċe híe æt Finnes hám   findan meahton,
    siġla searo-ġimma.   Híe on sǽ-láde
    drihtlíċe wíf   tó Denum feredon,
    lǽddon tó léodum."

Chapter IX
The Bright Brisingamen

Then the song was done.
1160 the gleeman's lay. Gladness arose,
bench-joy brightened.   Cup-bearers served
wine from wondrous vats.   Then came Wealhtheow forth,
wearing a golden necklace,   to where the good pair sat;
uncle and nephew,   each to the other true,
1165 fast their friendship still.   Unferth the thyle* was also there,
seated at the Scylding lord's feet.   They both trusted his spirit;
he had cunning,   though to his kindred he was not
principled in sword-play.

Spake then the Scylding lady,
"Accept this cup,   my noble lord,
1170 treasure-giver,   and be glad,
gold-friend to men!   To the Geats, speak
mild words,   as men should.
Be glad with the Geats,   and mindful of gifts,
which, near or far,   you now have.
1175 Men tell me   that you wish for a son*
to lead the levies.   Heorot has been purged,
the bright beer-hall;   enjoy while you can
this boon,   but leave to your kin
the realm and folk,   when you go forth
1180 to meet your doom.   For I deem
that glad Hrothulf   wishes to hold
the youths in honor,   if you before he,
friend of the Scyldings,   should leave this world.
I ween that he   will well repay
1185 our offspring,   if he is mindful of all that,
what he   for his will and word-fame,
before, in his youth,   bestowed honor."

Then, she turned to the bench,   where her boys sat,
Hrethric and Hrothmund*   and heroes' sons,

               Léoð wæs ásungen,
1160   gléo-mannes ġyd.   Gamen eft ástáh
        beorhtode benċ-swéġ.   Byrelas sealdon
        wín of wunder-fatum.   Þá cwóm Wealhþéo forð,
        gán under gyldnum béage,   þǽr þá gódan twéġen
        sǽton suhter-ġefæderan;   þá ġýt wæs hiera sib ætgædere
1165   ǽġhwylċ óðrum trýwe.   Swylċe þǽr (Ú)nferð þyle,
        æt fótum sæt fréan Scyldinga,   ġehwylċ hiora his ferhþe tréowde;
        þæt hé hæfde mód miċel,   þéah þe hé his mágum nǽre
        árfæst æt ecga ġelácum.

               Spræc ðá ides Scyldinga,
        "Onfóh þissum fulle,   fréo-drihten mín,
1170   sinces brytta;   þú on sǽlum wes,
        gold-wine gumena!   Ond tó Ġéatum sprec
        mildum wordum,   swá sceal man dón.
        Béo wið Ġéatas glæd,   ġeofena ġemyndiġ,
        néan ond feorran,   þú nú hafast.
1175   Mé man sæġde,   þæt þú ðé for sunu wolde
        hereri(n)c habban.   Heorot is ġefælsod,
        béah-sele beorhta;   brúc þenden þú mót
        maniġra médo   ond þínum mágum lǽf
        folc ond ríċe,   þonne ðú forð scyle
1180   metod-sceaft séon.   Iċ mínne can
        glædne Hróþulf,   þæt hé þá ġeogoðe wile
        árum healdan,   ġyf þú ǽr þonne hé,
        wine Scildinga,   worold oflǽtest.
        Wéne iċ þæt hé mid góde   ġyldan wille
1185   uncran eaferan,   ġif hé þæt eal ġemon,
        hwæt wit tó willan   ond tó worð-myndum,
        umbor-wesendum ǽr,   árna ġefremedon."

        Hwearf þá bí benċe,   þǽr hyre byre wǽron,
        Hréðríċ ond Hróðmund   ond hæleþa bearn,

1190   the youths all together;   there too sat the good one,
        Beowulf of the Geats,   the two brothers between him.

        Then, Beowulf   was borne the cup.
        She offered him   friendly words and wound gold,
        honored him   with two armlets,
1195   robes and rings,   and the greatest of necklaces
        that I have heard of   on this Earth.
        Ne'er have I heard of better,   under the heavens,
        from a hero's hoard,   since Hama bore away
        Brisingamen*   to the bright burg.
1200   With the gem-encrusted necklace,   he fled from
        Eormenric's enmity,   and chose eternal reward.
        Hygelac the Geat,   grandson of Swerting*,
        wore that necklace   on his last raid*.
        Under his standard   he protected his plunder,
1205   guarded the war-spoils;   when his Wyrd o'er-whelmed him,
        when in his folly,   he started a feud,
        fought with the Frisians.   He wore that fair mathom,
        that wondrous arkenstone*   o'er the welling waves,
        the folk-king,   when he fell beneath his shield.
1210   Then did the king's corpse   come into the keeping of the Franks,
        both the byrnie   and the neck-ring together.
        Weaker warriors   looted the corpses
        after the assault.   The Geats were routed,
        corpses covered the battle-field.

        The hall resounded with cheers.
1215   Wealhtheow spake   to the warriors, then.
        "Accept this torc,   belovèd Beowulf,
        and take benefit   from these byrnies,
        treasure of the people,   and prosper!
        Make known your might,   and teach these lads,
1220   that they might learn litheness,   and I shall reward you.
        You have done deeds,   that for all time,
        men far and near   will know your name,
        even across   the wide seas,
        the windy walls.   Whilst you live,
1225   atheling, be affluent!   I wish you
        many wondrous treasures.   To my sons,
        do good deeds   and uphold their joy.
        Here, every earl   is true to the other,
        and with a mild mind,   in the defense of their lord,

1190 ġiogoð ætgædere;   þǽr se góda sæt
Béowulf Ġéata,   be þǽm ġebróðrum twǽm.

XVIII

Him wæs ful boren   ond fréond-laþu
wordum bewæġned   ond wunden gold,
éstum ġeéawed   earm-hréade twá,
1195 hræġl ond hringas,   heals-béaga mǽst
þára þe iċ on foldan   ġefræġen hæbbe.
Nǽniġne iċ under sweġle   sélran hýrde
hord-má(ðð)um hæleþa,   syþðan Háma ætwæġ
tó herebyrhtan byriġ   Brósinga-mene,
1200 siġle ond sinc-fæt,   searo-níðas fealh
Eormenríċes,   ġecéas éċne rǽd.
Þone hring hæfde   Hiġelác Ġéata,
nefa Swertinges,   nýhstan síðe.
Siðþan hé under seġne   sinc ealgode,
1205 wæl-réaf werede;   hyne Wyrd fornam,
syþðan hé for wlenċo   wéan áhsode,
fǽhðe tó Frýsum.   Hé þá frætwe wæġ
eorclan-stánas   ofer ýða ful,
ríċe þéoden   hé under rande ġecranc.
1210 Ġehwearf þá in Francna fæðm   feorh cyninges,
bréost-ġewǽdu   ond se béah somod.
Wyrsan wíġ-frecan   wæl réafedon
æfter gúð-sceare.   Ġéata léode
hreá-wíċ héoldon.

Heal swéġe onféng.
1215 Wealhðéo maþelode,   héo fore þǽm werede spræc;
"Brúc ðisses béages,   Béowulf léofa,
hyse mid hǽle   ond þisses hræġles néot,
þéo(d)-ġestréona,   ond ġeþéoh tela,
cen þeċ mid cræfte   ond þyssum cnyhtum wes
1220 lára líðe!   Iċ þé þæs léan ġeman.
Hafast þú ġeféred,   þæt ðé feor ond néah
ealne wíde-ferhþ   weras ehtiġað,
efne swá síde   swá sǽ bebúgeð,
windġeard weallas.   Wes, þenden þú lifiġe,
1225 æþeling éadiġ!   Iċ þé an tela
sinc-ġestréona.   Béo þú suna mínum
dǽdum ġedéfe   dréam healdende.
Hér is ǽġhwylċ eorl   óþrum ġetrýwe,
módes milde,   man-drihtne h(leo),

1230   the thegns are united,   the people prepared,
and men drunk on mead,   do as I bid!"

She then went to her seat.   'Twas the greatest of symbels,
the men drank wine.   They knew not their Wyrd,
the grim fate   that would befall
1235   one of the earls   when eventide came.

Hrothgar then went,   blithely to his bower,
the ruler to rest.   The hall was guarded
by many earls,   as they had oft done before.
The benches were bared   and over it was spread
1240   bedding and bolsters.   One of the beer-drinkers,
doomed to die,   lay down in the hall.
By their heads   they set battle-shields,
bright boards.   On the benches there were,
over each atheling,   easily seen,
1245   a high helm,   a ringèd byrnie,
and a splendid spear.   'Twas their custom to
always be ready   for war,
both at home   and while harrying,
for any time   their atheling
1250   had need.   Those were worthy warriors!

1230   þeġnas syndon ġeþwǽre,   þéod eal ġearo;
        druncne dryht-guman,   dóð swá iċ bidde!"

        Ēode þá tó setle.   Þǽr wæs symbla cyst,
        druncon wín weras.   Wyrd ne cúþon,
        ġeó-sceaft grim(m)e,   swá hit ágangen wearð
1235   eorla manegum   syþðan ǽfen cwóm.

        Ond him Hróþgár ġewát   tó hofe sínum,
        ríċe tó ræste.   Reċed weardode
        unrím eorla,   swá híe oft ǽr dydon.
        Benċ-þelu beredon   hit ġeond-brǽded wearð
1140   beddum ond bolstrum.   Béor-scealca sum,
        fús ond fǽġe,   flet-ræste ġebéag.
        Setton him tó héafdum   hilde-randas,
        bord-wudu beorhtan.   Þǽr on benċe wæs,
        ofer æþelinge,   ýþ-ġeséne,
1245   heaðþo-stéapa helm,   hringed byrne,
        þreċ-wudu þrymlíċ.   Wæs þéaw hyra
        þæt híe oft wǽron   an wíġ ġearwe,
        ġé æt hám ġé on herġe,   ġé ġehwæþer þára
        efne swylċe mǽla,   swylċe hira man-dryhtne
1250   þearf ġesǽlde.   Wæs séo þéod tilu!

Chapter X
The Malice of the Merewife

Then sank they to sleep.   One sorely paid
for his evening rest,   as had oft happened before,
when Grendel guarded   the golden hall
and wrought evil,   'til his end came,
1255 slaughtered for his sins.   'Twas widely known to men
that an avenger   still survived,
lived in loath   for a long time.
After the grim battle   Grendel's mother,
that she-monster   was mindful of her woes.
1260 She dwelt   in the deep waters,
in the cold currents,   since Cain slew
with the sword's edge,   his only brother,
his father's son;   exiled he fled,
marked for the murder,   from the joys of men
1265 and went into the wilderness.   From him awoke many
grim gasts;   Grendel was one of those,
that hateful battle-wolf,   who found at Heorot
a watching warrior   ready for war.
There the grim foe   grasped him,
1270 yet he was   mindful of his might,
that great gift that God   had given him.
He put his faith   in the Father,
and with His aid,   he overcame the fiend,
cast down the Hell-gast.   Forlorn, he fled,
1275 bereft of joy,   to his dwelling to die,
the foe of mankind.   His mother now,
greedy and gloomy,   would go
on a journey of sorrow,   her son's death to avenge.

To Heorot she hied,   where the Ring-Danes
1280 slept in the stead.   Then there came about
the earl's ills,   when in came Grendel's mother.
Less was the awe   she inspired,
by e'en so much   as is the might of a maid,

XIX

Sigon þá tó slǽpe.   Sum sáre anġeald
ǽfen-rǽste,   swá him ful-oft ġelamp,
siþðan gold-sele   Grendel warode,
unriht ǽfnde,   oþ þæt ende becwóm,
1255   swylt æfter synnum.   Þæt ġesýne wearþ,
wíd-cúþ werum,   þætte wrecend þá ġýt
lifde æfter láþum   lange þráge.
Æfter gúð-ċeare   Grendles módor,
ides áglǽċ-wíf   yrmþe ġemunde.
1260   Sé þe wæter-eġesan   wunian scolde,
ċealde stréamas,   siþðan Ca(in hím) wearð
tó ecg-banan,   ángan bréþer,
fæderen-mǽġe;   hé þá fág ġewát,
morþre ġemearcod,   man-dréam fléon,
1265   wésten warode.   Þanon wóc fela
ġeósceaft-gásta;   wæs þǽra Grendel sum,
heoro-wearh hetelíċ,   sé æt Heorote fand
wæċċendne wer   wíġes bídan.
Þǽr him áglǽċa   æt-grǽpe wearð,
1270   hwæþre hé ġemunde   mæġenes strenge,
ġim-fæste ġife,   ðé him God sealde.
Ond him tó Anwaldan   áre ġelýfde,
frófre ond fultum   ðý Hé þone féond ofercwóm,
ġehnǽġde Helle gást.   Þá hé héan ġewát,
1275   dréame bedǽled,   déaþ-wíċ séon,
Man-cynnes féond   ond his módor þá ġýt
ġífre ond galg-mód,   ġegán wolde
sorh-fulne síð,   sunu (d)éo(ð) wrecan.

Cóm þá tó Heorote,   ðǽr Hring-Dene
1280   ġeond þæt sæld swǽfun.   Þá ðǽr sóna wearð
ed-hwyrft eorlum,   siþðan inne fealh
Grendles módor.   Wæs se gryre lǽssa
efne swá miċle   swá bið mæġþa cræft,

a woman's war-fury   for an armed man,
1285   when an adorned blade,   hardened and hammer-forged,
stained with sword-sweat;   the boar-crest
of the foe's helm   is sheared by its sharp edge.

Then in the hall,   the hard edge was drawn,
a sword o'er the seats,   many a broad shield
1290   held fast in hand;   the helm was not minded,
nor bracing byrnie,   when the monster seized him.

She was in haste   and hurried away,
to save her life   when they saw her.
Suddenly, she seized   a sleeping thegn,
1295   grasped firmly,   and fled to the fen*.
He was first   among Hrothgar's friends,
a hero in his household   betwixt the seas,
a powerful shield-warrior,   whom she ripped at his rest,
s battle-brave thegn.   Beowulf was not there,
1300   another lodging had been   earlier assigned to him,
after the gift-giving,   to the mighty Geat.
An uproar arose in Heorot.   That well-known arm,
blood-stained, she took.   Sorrow was renewed,
when she returned to her lair.   Loathe was that trade,
1305   where both   parties paid
with the lives of loved ones.   Then the wise king,
the hoary warrior,   his heart grew heavy,
when he knew his oldest thegn   lived no longer;
his dearest friend   was dead.

1310   From his bower,   then was Beowulf brought,
the bold warrior.   At day break,
the winsome earl,   and his war-band went
to where   the wise one waited,
to see whether   the All-Wielder would ever
1315   turn this tale of woe   for the better.
Then the battle-brave man   strode o'er the floor
with his warriors;   the wooden hall resounded.
In words he spake   to the wise king,
he asked   the lord of the Ingwines
1320   if it had to him   been a pleasant night*.

wíġ-gryre wífes   be wǽpned-men,
1285 þonne heoru bunden,   hamere ġeþuren,
sweord swáte fáh;   swín ofer helme
ecgum (dyhttiġ)   andweard sireð.

Þá wæs on healle,   heard-ecg togen,
sweord ofer setlum,   síd-rand maniġ
1290 hafen handa fæst;   helm ne ġemunde,
byrnan síde,   þe hine se bróga anġeat.

Héo wæs on ofste   wolde út þanon
féore beorgan   þá héo onfunden wæs.
Haðe héo æþelinga   ánne hæfde,
1295 fæste befangen,   þá héo tó fenne gang.
Sé wæs Hróþgáre   hæleþa léofost,
on ġesíðes hád   be sǽm twéonum,
ríċe rand-wiga,   þone ðe héo on ræste ábréat,
blǽd-fæstne beorn.   Næs Béowulf ðǽr,
1300 ac wæs óþer in   ǽr ġeteohhod,
æfter máþðum-ġife,   mǽrum Ġéate.
Hréam wearð on Heorote.   Héo under heolfre ġenam
cúþe folme.   Ċearu wæs ġeníwod,
ġeworden in wícun.   Ne wæs þæt ġewrixle til,
1305 þæt híe on bá healfa   bicgan scoldon
fréonda féorum.   Þá wæs fród cyning,
hár hilde-rinc,   on hréon móde,
syðþan hé aldor-þeġn   unlyfiġendne;
þone déorestan   déadne wisse.

1310 Hraþe wæs tó búre   Béowulf fetod,
sigor-éadiġ secg.   Samod ǽr-dæġe.
éode eorla sum,   æþele cempa
self mid ġesíðum,   þǽr se snottra bád,
hwæþre him A(l)walda   ǽfre wille
1315 æfter wéa-spelle   wyrpe ġefremman.
Gang ðá æfter flóre   fyrd-wyrðe man
mid his hand-scale   -healwudu dynede-
þæt hé þone wísan   wordum hnǽġde
fréan Ingwina   fræġn ġif him wǽre
1320 æfter néod-laðu(m)   niht ġetǽse.

Hrothgar spake,   the Helm of the Scyldings,
"Ask me not of my pleasure!   Sorrow is renewed
among the Danish folk!   Dead is Æschere,
the elder brother   of Yrmenlaf*,
1325   my rune-reader   and chief counselor,
my shoulder-companion   when armies clashed;
he warded mine head   from the hateful foe,
and I their boar-helms hewed.   So should an earl,
be as noble and honorable   as Æschere was.

1330   "In Heorot   was his hand-slayer,
a wavering slaughter-spirit.   I know not whether
she was proud of her prey   when she returned,
fain with the feast.   She had avenged the feud,
in which you,   yestereen
1335   quelled Grendel   in your hard gripe.
For too long   had he my people
humbled and destroyed.   He fell in that fight,
gave up his ghost.   Now, another has come,
a mighty man-scather   who would avenge her kin,
1340   she has carried   this feud far.
Many a thegn   may think,
who for the gift-giver   weeps in his heart,
-hard heart-bale-   the hand is still,
that once was willing   to serve each wish.

1345   "I, land-dwellers   and hall retainers,
my people   have heard said
that such a pair   has been seen,
great mark-steppers   who held the moors,
eldritch gasts.   One of them was,
1350   as far as my folk   could discern,
of the likeness of a woman, and the other   was wretchedly formed
in a man's shape,   but both were bigger than ordinary men.
Both trode the path of exiles,   the misty moors.
In days long gone,   they gave him the name Grendel.
1355   Earth-dwellers knew   not of his father,
nor of any offspring   of his among
the strange spirits.   Secret was their land*,
they wandered o'er wolf-lairs   and windy nesses,
the dangerous fen-pass,   where flows a stream
1360   under the dark headlands;   it travels down
and floods beneath the earth.   'Tis not far hence
in mile-marks,   that the mere stands,

92

Hróðgár maþelode,   helm Scyldinga;
"Ne frín þú æfter sǽlum!   Sorh is ġeníwod
Deniġea léodum.   Déad is Æschere,
Yrmenláfes   yldra bróþor,
1325 mín rún-wita   ond mín rǽd-bora,
eaxl-ġestealla   ðonne wé on orleġe,
hafelan weredon   þonne hniton féþan,
eoferas cnysedan.   Swylċ eorl scode,
wesan ǽr-gód   swylċ Æschere wæs.

1330 "Wearð him on Heorote   tó hand-banan,
wæl-gǽst wǽfre.   Iċ ne wát hwæ(d)er
atol ǽse wlanc   eft-síðas téah,
fylle ġefrǽġnod.   Héo þá fǽhðe wræc,
þé þú ġystran niht   Grendel cwealdest
1335 þurh hǽstne hád   heardum clammum.
Forþan hé tó lange   léode míne
wanode ond wyrde.   Hé æt wíġe ġecrang,
ealdres scyldiġ,   ond nú óþer cwóm,
mihtiġ mán-scaða,   wolde hyre mǽġ wrecan,
1340 ġé feor hafað   fǽhðe ġestǽled.
Þæs þe þinċean mæġ   þeġne monegum,
sé þe æfter sinc-ġyfan   on sefan gréoteþ,
-hreþer-bealo hearde-   nú séo hand liġeð,
sé þe éow wél-hwylcra   wilna dohte.

1345 "Iċ þæt lond-búend,   léode míne
sele-rǽdende   secgan hýrde
þæt híe ġesáwon   swylċe twéġen,
miċle mearc-stapan   móras healdan,
ellor-gǽstas.   Ðǽra óðer wæs,
1350 þæs þe híe ġewislicost   ġewitan meahton,
idese onlícn(e)s,   óðer earm-sceapen
on weres wæstmum.   Wræc-lástas træd,
næfne hé wæs mára   þonne ǽniġ man óðer.
Þone on ġeár-dagum,   Grendel nemdo(n).
1355 Fold-búende   nó híe fæder cunnon,
hwæþer him ǽniġ wæs   ǽr ácenned
dyrnra gásta.   Híe dýġel lond,
wariġeað, wulf-hleoþu,   windiġe næssas,
frécne fen-ġelád,   ðǽr fyrġen-stréam
1360 under næssa ġenipu,   niþer ġewíteð
flód under foldan.   Nis þæt feor heonon
míl-ġemearces,   þæt se mere stan(d)eð;

and o'er it hangs   a frost-bound forest,
huge and rooted deep;   the trees hang over the water.
1365 There each night is seen   an awful wonder,
there is fire on the flood.   No wise one that lives
of the sons of men   have seen the bottom.
Even when the heath-stepper   is harassed by hounds,
the stout horned hart   seeks the holt,
1370 thus far driven,   will first give up his life,
ere he will leap   into those loathly waters,
with its head raised high.   'Tis not a happy place!
The roiling waters   rise up,
the sky darkens,   and the winds whip up
1375 evil storms,   'til the day darkens to night,
and the heavens weep."

                    "The only hope
is you alone!   You do not know these lands yet,
a fearful place   where you may find
the sin-stained mere-wife.   Seek if you dare!
1380 For finishing this feud,   I shall reward you with treasure,
with ancient heirlooms,   as erst I did,
and with wound gold,   if you come away alive."

ofer þǽm hongiað hrí(mġ)e bearwas,
wudu wyrtum fæst, wæter oferhelmað.

1365 Þǽr mæġ nihta ġehwǽm níð-wundor séon,
fýr on flóde. Nó þæs fród leofað
gumena bearna þæt þone grund wite.
Ðéah þe hǽð-stapa hundum ġeswenċed,
heorot hornum trum holt-wudu séċe,

1370 feorran ġeflýmed, ǽr hé feorh seleð,
aldor on ófre, ǽr hé in wille,
hafelan (hafene). Nis þæt héoru stów!
Þonon ýð-ġeblond up ástígeð,
won tó wolcnum, þonne wind styreþ

1375 láð ġewidru, oð þæt lyft drysmaþ,
roderas réotað.

Nú is rǽd ġelang
eft æt þé ánum! Eard ġít ne const,
frécne stówe, ðǽr þú findan miht
felasinniġne secg. Séċ ġif þú dyrre!

1380 Iċ þé þá fǽhðe, féo léaniġe,
eald-ġestréonum, swá iċ ǽr dyde,
wund(un) golde, ġyf þú on weġ cymest."

Chapter XI
The Trail to the Tarn

Beowulf spake,   the son of Ecgtheow,
"Do not be sorrowful, wise king!   'Tis more seemly
1385 for a man to avenge his friend   than mourn over-much.
Each of us must   abide the end
of our lives in this world.   We should win, while we may,
glory before death!   'Tis the best of dooms,
a worthy end   for a noble warrior!
1390 Arise, realm-warden,   and let us ride forth,
and seek the spoor   of Grendel's mother!
I swear, she   will not stay hidden to us,
not in the earth's embrace,   nor in mountain-woods,
nor on the sea's floor,   or wherever she flees!
1395 But, you must, with patience,   endure this day
in each of your woes,   as I ween you shall."

Leapt up then the agèd king,   and thanked God,
the mighty Lord,   for the man's wise words.
Then Hrothgar commanded   his horse to be saddled,
1400 a mount with braided mane.   The wise king
rode ahead   as his men marched,
linden-bearers.   They were led
along the wooded path;   widely seen
was the way   where she trode
1405 o'er the murky moors,   bearing that mighty thegn,
lacking life,   the best retainer
who had defended   Hrothgar's home.

Onward rode   the atheling's bairn
o'er stony slopes   and through tight paths,
1410 narrow passes   and unknown ways,
sheer headlands,   the home of Nicors.
He fared forth   with a few
wise men,   looking o'er the ways,
'til he found   the mountain forest,

XXI

Béowulf maþelode,　　bearn Ecgþéowes,
"Ne sorga, snotor guma!　　Sélre bið ǽghwǽm
1385　þæt hé his fréond wrece,　　þonne hé fela murne.
Úre ǽghwylċ sceal　　ende ġebídan
worolde lífes.　　Wyrċe sé þe móte
dómes ǽr déaþe!　　Þæt bið driht-guman
unlifġendum　　æfter sélest.
1390　Árís, ríċes weard,　　uton hraþe féran,
Grendles Mágan　　gan(g) scéawiġan!
Iċ hit þé ġeháte,　　nó hé on helm losaþ,
né on foldan fæþm,　　né on fyrġen-holt,
né on ġyfenes grund,　　gá þǽr hé wille!
1395　Ðýs dógor þú　　ġeþyld hafa
wéana ġehwylċes,　　swá iċ þé wéne tó."

Áhléop ðá se gomela,　　Gode þancode,
mihtigan drihtne,　　þæs se man ġespræc.
Þá wæs Hróðgáre　　hors ġebǽted,
1400　wicg wunden-feax.　　Wísa fengel
ġeatolíċ gende　　gum-féþa stóp,
lind-hæbbendra.　　Lástas wǽron
æfter wald-swaþum;　　wíde ġesýne
gang ofer grundas,　　ġeġnum (swa) fór
1405　ofer myrċan mór,　　mago-þeġna bær,
þone sélestan,　　sáwol-léasne,
þára þe mid Hróðgáre　　hám eahtode.

Ofer-éode þá　　æþelinga bearn
stéap stán-hliðo　　stíġe nearwe,
1410　enge án-paðas　　uncúð ġelád,
neowle nǽssas,　　Nicor-húsa fela.
Hé féara sum　　beforan gengde
wísra monna　　wong scéawian,
oþ þæt hé fǽringa　　fyrġen-béamas,

1415 hanging o'er   a hoary stone,
      a joyless wood;   the water below
      boiled with bloody waves.   All the Danes,
      friends of the Scyldings,   had heavy hearts.
      Many thegns   could not thole it;
1420 horror awoke   in the earls,
      when they found Æschere's head   at the foot of the cliff.

      The folk saw blood   flowing in the flood,
      hot gore.   The horn then sang
      a mournful note.   The men all sat.
1425 In the water they saw   many of the Wyrm-kind,
      strange Sea-Dragons   swam in the mere,
      and Nicors   slept on the strand;
      oft they would,   in the early morn,
      commit savage deeds   on the sail-road.
1430 Wyrms and wild-beasts   rushed away,
      bitter and enraged,   when they heard the clarion call,
      that war-horn ringing.   A Geatish warrior
      loosed an arrow,   and took the life of one.
      The wave-struggle stopped   as it stood in its heart,
1435 the hard war-shaft;   it swam slower
      in the depths,   when death took it.
      Swiftly on the swells   it was taken by boar-spears,
      stabbed and hooked;   it was hard pressed
      and dragged dead   onto the ness,
1440 terrible and wondrous   water-beast.
      The men looked upon   the grisly gast.

      Beowulf donned his mail,   he mourned not for his life.
      His war-byrnie, broad   and braided by hand,
      cunningly adorned,   should test the tarn,
1445 and ward   the warrior's bone-house,
      so that when battle broke,   her battle-gripe
      might not   harm his heart.
      A shining helm   protected his head,
      garnished with gold.   He would stir up the ground
1450 and seek the mingled waters   of the mere,
      bound in fine chain,   as in former days,
      wrought wondrously   by Wayland himself,
      and beset with swine-forms,   so that no
      blade in battle   would bite him.

1455 Not the meanest   of his mighty helps,

1415 ofer hárne stán hleonian funde,
    wyn-léasne wudu; wæter under stód
    dréoriġ ond ġedréfed. Denum eallum wæs,
    winum Scyldinga, w(æ)rce on móde.
    Tó ġeþolianne ðeġne monegum,
1420 oncýð eorla ġehwǽm, syðþan Æscheres
    on þám holm-clife hafelan métton.

    Flód blóde wéol folc tó sǽgon,
    hátan heolfre. Horn stundum song
    fúslíċ f(orð)léoð. Féþa eal ġesæt.
1425 Ġesáwon ðá æfter wætere Wyrm-cynnes fela,
    sellíċe Sǽ-Dracan sund cunnian,
    swylċe on næs-hleoðum Nicras licgean;
    ðá on undern-mǽl, oft bewitiġað,
    sorh-fulne síð on seġl-ráde.
1430 Wyrmas ond wil-déor híe on weġ hruron,
    bitere ond ġebolgne, bearhtm onġeáton,
    gúð-horn galan. Sumne Ġéata léod
    of flán-bogan féores ġetwǽfde.
    Ýð-ġewinnes, þæt him on aldre stód,
1435 here-strǽl hearda; hé on holme wæs
    sundes þé sǽnra, ðé hyne swylt fornam.
    Hræþe wearð on ýðum mid eofer-spréotum
    heoro-hócyhtum; hearde ġenearwod,
    níða ġenǽġed, ond on næs togen,
1440 wundorlíċ wǽġ-bora. Weras scéawedon
    gryrelícne ġist.

        Ġyrede hine Béowulf
    eorl-ġewǽdum, nalles for ealdre mearn.
    Scolde here-byrne, hondum ġebróden,
    síd ond searo-fáh, sund cunnian,
1445 séo ðe bán-cofan beorgan cúþe,
    þæt him hilde-gráp, hreþre ne mihte,
    eorres inwit-feng aldre ġesceþðan.
    Ac se hwíta helm hafelan werede,
    sé þe mere-grundas mengan scolde,
1450 séċan sund-ġebland since ġeweorðad,
    befongen fréa-wrásnum swá hine fyrn-dagum,
    worhte wǽpna smið wundrum téode,
    besette swín-lícum, þæt hine syðþan nó
    brond né beado-méċas bítan ne meahton.

1455 Næs þæt þonne mǽtost mæġen-fultuma

was what Hrothgar's thyle   lent him in his need.
That long-hilted sword   hight Hrunting*;
'twas the foremost   of ancient mathoms,
iron was it's edge   and serpents gleamed in a blade
1460   hardened by blood.   In fights, it ne'er failed
the hand of any man   that held it,
he who dared travel   perilous paths
to his foes' folk-stead.   'Twas not the first time
that it had been   called to do works or courage.

1465   Indeed, Ecglaf's son   remembered not
that before he had spoke   bold words to Beowulf,
drunk on wine.   Now, this weapon he lent
to a fiercer fighter.   He himself dared not
risk his life   in the welling waters
1470   to do heroic deeds;   so, he gave up his glory,
honor amongst the earls.   Not so with the other,
he who braced himself   for battle.

Beowulf spake,   the son of Ecgtheow,
"Be mindful,   illustrious offspring of Healfdene,
1475   wise ruler, now that   I am ready for this adventure,
gold-giver to men,   of what I said before;
if I, in your cause,   came to
lose my life,   that to me, you would,
though I had fallen,   take my father's place.
1480   Be a bulwark   to my thegns,
these brave companions,   if battle takes me,
and the gifts   you gave me,
belovèd Hrothgar,   send to Hygelac.
Then, by that gold,   will the Geatish lord know,
1485   when Hrethel's son   stares upon the hoard,
that I had found a goodly king,   for kindness known,
and enjoyed the ring-giver's generosity   while I could.

"And let Unferth   wield this old heirloom.
This widely-famed man shall have   mine own wondrous wave-sword,
1490   keen and hard-edged.   For with Hrunting shall I
gain glory,   or death shall take me!"

þæt him on ðearfe láh   ðyle Hróðgáres.
Wæs þǽm hæft-méċe   Hrunting nama;
þæt wæs án foran   eald-ġestréona,
ecg wæs íren,   áter-téarum fáh,
1460 áhyrded heaþo-swáte.   Nǽfre hit æt hilde ne swác
manna ǽngum   þára þe hit mid mundum bewand,
sé ðe gryre-síðas   ġegán dorste
folc-stede fára.   Næs þæt forma síð
þæt hit ellen-weorc   æfnan scolde.

1465 Húru ne ġemunde   mago Ecgláfes,
eafoþes cræftiġ,   þæt hé ǽr ġespræc
wíne druncen.   Þá hé þæs wǽpnes onláh
sélran sweord-frecan.   Selfa ne dorste
under ýða ġewin   aldre ġenéþan
1470 driht-scype dréogan;   þǽr hé dóme forléas,
ellen-mǽrðum.   Ne wæs þǽm óðrum swá,
syðþan hé hine tó gúðe   ġeġyred hæfde.

XXII

Béowulf maðelode,   bearn Ecgþéowes,
"Ġeþenċ nú, se mǽra   maga Healfdenes,
1475 snottra fengel,   nú iċ eom síðes fús,
gold-wine gumena,   hwæt wit ġeó sprǽcon;
ġif iċ æt þearfe   þínre scolde
aldre linnan,   þæt ðú mé á wǽre,
forð-ġewitenum   on fæder stǽle.
1480 Wes þú mund-bora   mínum mago-þeġnum,
hond-ġesellum,   ġif meċ hild nime,
swylċe þú ðá mádmas,   þé þú mé sealdest,
Hróðgár léofa,   Hiġeláce onsend.
Mæġ þonne on þǽm golde onġitan   Ġéata dryhten,
1485 ġeséon sunu Hr(éð)les,   þonne hé on þæt sinc starað,
þæt iċ gum-cystum   gódne funde,
béaga bryttan,   bréac þonne móste.

"Ond þú (Ú)nferð lǽt   ealde láfe.
Wrǽtlíċ wǽġ-sweord   wíd-cúðne man,
1490 heard-ecg habban.   Iċ mé mid Hruntinge
dóm ġewyrċe,   oþðe meċ déað nimeð!"

Chapter XII
The Old Work of Ettins

After these words,   the Weder lord
boldly went forth;   he awaited not for a reply.
The rush of water   about the warrior,
1495 encircled.   The sun had risen
by the time   that he touched the bottom.

Soon she found in the flood   the sword-hungry one*,
she who had held this mere   for more than a hundred years,
grim and greedy,   a man from above
1500 who had entered   her unnatural domain.
She groped forth   and grasped the warrior
in her cruel clasp.   Yet, she could not crush
his hale body,   for his mail-harness protected him.
She could not   break his war-byrnie,
1505 the linkèd sark   with her loathly fingers.

When the water-wolf   came to the bottom,
she whisked the ring-lord   to her lair,
so that he might not,   though he had a hero's heart,
wield his weapon   'gainst that terrible woman
1510 or the many sea-beasts   that beset him in the deep,
and tried to tear at his war-sark   with vicious tusks.
As they pursued him,   the earl perceived
that he was in an evil hall,   unknown to him,
where no whit of water   could harm him;
1515 through the hall's roof,   reached him not,
the fury of the flood.   He saw fire-light,
a ghostly blaze   brightly shone.

Then the good warrior saw   the wolf of the deep,
and struck at   the mighty mere-wife
1520 with his war-blade;   his hand withheld not the swing.
The ring-sword   sang on her head
a wailing war-song,   but the warrior found

Æfter þǽm wordum   Weder-Ġéata léod
efste mid elne;   nalas andsware
bídan wolde.   Brim-wylm onféng,
1495 hilde-rince.   Ðá wæs hwíl dæġes
ǽr hé þone grund-wong   onġytan mehte.

Sóna þæt onfunde,   sé ðe flóda begong
heoro-ġífre behéold   hund misséra,
grim ond grǽdiġ,   þæt þǽr gumena sum
1500 ǽl-wihta eard   ufan cunnode.
Gráp þá tóġéanes,   gúð-rinc ġeféng
atolan clommum.   Nó þý ǽr in ġescód
hálan líce;   hring útan ymb-bearh.
Þæt héo þone fyrd-hom   ðurh-fón ne mihte,
1505 locene leoðo-syrċan   láþan fingrum.

Bær þá séo brimwyl(f),   þá héo tó botme cóm,
hringa þengel   tó hofe sínum,
swá hé ne mihte,   nó hé þæ(s) módiġ wæs,
wǽpna ġewealdan   ac hine wundra þæs fela
1510 swe(n)cte on sunde   sǽ-déor moniġ,
hilde-túxum   here-syrċan bræc,
éhton áglǽcan.   Ðá se eorl onġeat,
þæt hé (in) niðsele,   nát-hwylcum wæs,
þǽr him nǽniġ wæter   wihte ne sceþede,
1515 né him for hróf-sele   hrínan ne mehte,
fǽr-gripe flódes.   Fýr-léoht ġeseah,
blácne léoman   beorhte scínan.

Onġeat þá se góda   grund-wyrġenne,
mere-wíf mihtiġ,   mæġen-rǽs forġeaf
1520 hildebille;   ho(n)d sweng ne oftéah.
Þæt hire on hafelan   hring-mǽl ágól
grǽdiġ gúð-léoð,   ðá se ġist onfan

that battle-light   would not bite
and end her life;   the edge failed
1525 the noble in need.   It had already seen
much hand-to-hand combat,   and clove many helms
and doomed men's fighting gear.   'Twas the first time
for that fair sword,   that its glory fell.

Again, he was stout-hearted   in strength he lacked not;
1530 mindful of fame   was the kinsman of Hygelac.
He tossed away that pattern-welded sword,   studded with gems,
the angry warrior;   on the earth it lay,
firm and steel-edged,   and trusted in his strength,
his mighty hand-gripe.   Such must a man do,
1535 when in war   he wishes to win
everlasting fame;   he fears not for his life!
By the shoulder he seized,   -he shunned not that feud-
the war-lord of the Geats,   Grendel's mother.
Heaved then the hard man of battle,   full of wrath,
1540 his dire foe,   so she fell onto the floor.
Readily then,   she repaid for that
with grim gripe   she clutched him.
The strong one,   weary in spirit, stumbled,
the champion   fell to the floor.
1545 Then, the hall-guest set upon him   and raised her seax*,
broad and brown-edged,   to avenge her bairn,
her only offspring.   On his shoulder lay
the braided breast-net   -it saved his life-
for it withstood entry   of edge or point.
1550 Then, Ecgtheow's son   would have surely perished,
deep under the earth,   the Geatish champion,
had not his battle-byrnie   given him aid,
battle-net hard,   and holy God
wielded not victory,   the wise Lord.
1555 Yet, the Ruler of Heaven   deemed it right,
that he should   easily stand.

Amidst the battle-gear,   he saw a victorious blade,
an old sword of Ettins,   doughty and keen of edge,
worthy in war,   the choicest of weapons.
1560 But it was more   than any other man
could bear   in battle-play,
keen and good,   the work of Giants.
He seized then the golden hilt,   the savior of the Scyldings,
fierce and battle-grim,   he swung the ringèd sword,

þæt se beado-léoma   bítan nolde,
aldre sceþðan;   ac séo ecg ġeswác

1525   ðéodne æt þearfe.   Ðolode ǽr fela
hond-ġemóta,   helm oft ġescær
fǽġes fyrd-hræġl,   Ðá wæs forma síð
déorum mádme,   þæt his dóm álæġ.

Eft wæs án-rǽd,   nalas elnes læt;
1530   mǽrða ġemyndiġ   mǽġ Hy(ġ)eláces.
Wearp ðá wunde(n)mǽl   wrǽttum ġebunden,
yrre óretta;   þæt hit on eorðan læġ,
stíð ond stýl-ecg,   strenge ġetruwode,
mund-gripe mæġenes.   Swá sceal man dón,

1535   þonne hé æt gúðe   ġegán þenċeð
longsumne lof;   ná ymb his líf cearað!
Ġeféng þá be eaxle,   -nalas for fǽhðe mearn-
Gúð-Ġéata léod,   Grendles módor.
Brægd þá beadwe heard,   þá hé ġebolgen wæs,

1540   feorh-ġeníðlan,   þæt héo on flet ġebéah.
Héo him eft hraþe   handléan forġeald,
grimman grápum   ond him tóġéanes féng.
Oferwearp þá wériġ-mód,   wiġena strengest,
féþe-cempa,   þæt hé on fylle wearð.

1545   Ofsæt þá þone sele-ġyst   ond hyre sea(x) ġetéah,
brád (ond) brún-ecg;   wolde hire bearn wrecan,
ángan eaferan.   Him on eaxle læġ
bréost-net bróden   -þæt ġebearh féore-
wið ord ond wið ecge,   ingang forstód.

1550   Hæfde ðá forsíðod   sunu Ecgþéowes.
under ġynne grund,   Ġéata cempa,
nemne him heaðo-byrne   helpe ġefremede,
here-net hearde,   ond háliġ God
ġewéold wíġ-sigor,   wítiġ Drihten.

1555   Rodera Rǽdend;   hit on ryht ġescéd
ýðelíċe,   syþðan hé eft ástód.

XXIII

Ġeseah ðá on searwum,   siġe-éadiġ bil,
eald sweord Eotenisc,   ecgum þýhtiġ,
wiġena weorð-mynd,   þæt (wæs) wǽpna cyst,-
1560   búton hit wæs máre   ðonne ǽniġ mon óðer
tó beadu-láce   ætberan meahte,
gód ond ġeatoliċ,   Ġíganta ġeweorc.
Hé ġeféng þá fetel-hilt,   freca Scildinga,
hréoh ond heoro-grim,   hring-mǽl ġebrægd,

1565   reckless of life,   savagely struck,
        so it hewed hard   through her neck,
        broke bone-rings.   The blade cut through
        the fated flesh-cloak   and she crumpled to the ground.
        The sword was stained with blood.   He was glad with his work!

1570   Brightness blazed forth*,   the light stood within,
        even as from behind the clouds   clearly shines
        the heaven's candle.   He looked about the hall.
        Along the wall he went,   weapon raised,
        hard by the hilt,   Hygelac's thegn,
1575   angry and one-minded.   Nor was the edge useless
        to the warrior.   He wished to hastily
        repay Grendel   for his many grisly raids,
        for the war   he waged on the West-Danes,
        -he had made more   than one journey-
1580   when he,   Hrothgar's hearth-companions
        slew in their slumber   and ate in their sleep
        fifteen sons.   from the Danish folk
        and again as many   bore away
        as loathly prey.   He paid him his reward for that,
1585   the wroth champion!   Then he saw where he rested,
        war-weary,   Grendel lying,
        of life bereft,   as before he had been wounded
        in the battle at Heorot.   The body burst open,
        when after death,   it suffered the stroke,
1590   a hard swing of the sword   that severed the head.

        Then, saw they,   the "clever" companions*,
        who, with Hrothgar   watched the waters,
        that the waves   began to well,
        blood boiled in the mere.   Together,
1595   the old men   mourned their champion,
        that the atheling,   again would not,
        in conquest,   come to seek
        their great king.   Many agreed
        that the water-wolf   had taken his life.
1600   When came the ninth hour*,   they left the ness.
        Homeward went the Scyldings,   heavy of heart,
        with the gold-friend of men,   but the guests stayed on.
        Despondent,   they watched the waves.
        They wished,   but did not ween
1605   that they would see   their belovèd lord again.

1565   aldres orwéna,   yrringa slóh,
        þæt hire wið halse   heard grápode,
        bán-hringas bræc.   Bil eal ðurh-wód
        fǽġne flǽsc-homan,   héo on flet ġecrong.
        Sweord wæs swátiġ.   Secg weorce ġefeh!

1570   Líxte se léoma,   léoht inne stód,
        efne swá of hefene   hádre scíneð
        rodores candel.   Hé æfter reċede wlát.
        Hwearf þá be wealle,   wǽpen hafenade,
        heard be hiltum,   Hiġeláces ðeġn,
1575   yrre ond án-rǽd.   Næs séo ecg fracod
        hilde-rince.   Ac hé hraþe wolde
        Grendle forġyldan   gúð-rǽsa fela,
        ðára þe hé ġeworhte   tó West-Denum,
        -oftor miċle   ðonne on ænne síð-
1580   þonne hé Hróðgáres   heorð-ġenéatas,
        slóh on sweofote   slǽpende fræt
        folces Deniġea   fýf-týne men
        ond óðer swylċ   út of-ferede
        láðlícu lác.   Hé him þæs léan forġeald,
1585   réþe cempa!   Tó ðæs þe hé on ræste ġeseah,
        gúð-wériġne   Grendel licgan,
        aldor-léasne,   swá him ǽr ġescód
        hild æt Heorote.   Hrá wíde sprong,
        syþðan hé æfter déaðe   drepe þrowade,
1590   heoro-sweng heardne   ond hine þá héafde beċearf.

        Sóna þæt ġesáwon   snottre ċeorlas,
        þá ðe mid Hróðgáre   on holm wliton,
        þæt wæs ýð-ġeblond   eal ġemenged,
        brim blóde fáh.   Blonden-feaxe,
1595   gomele ymb gódne   onġeador sprǽcon,
        þæt hiġ þæs æðelinges   eft ne wéndon,
        þæt hé siġe-hréðiġ   séċean cóme
        mǽrne þéoden.   Þá ðæs moniġe ġewearð
        þæt hine séo brim-wylf   ábr(e)oten hæfde.
1600   Ðá cóm nón dæġes;   næs ofġéafon.
        Hwate Scyldingas,   ġewát him hám þonon,
        gold-wine gumena.   ġistas sétan,
        módes séoce   ond on mere staredon.
        Wiston ond ne wéndon   þæt híe heora wine-drihten
1605   selfne ġesáwon.

Then that sword, from the blood began,   in battle-icicles,
the war-blade to wane.   'Twas a wonder to behold
that it melted,   like unto ice,
when the Father unfetters   the bonds of frost
1610   and unwinds the water-ropes,   wielding all
seasons and times.   He is the True Lord!

He did not take from those dwellings,   the Weder-Geat lord,
more mathoms,   though he saw many there,
only the head   and the hilt,
1615   the gold glittered.   The sword had already melted,
the patterned blade was all burnt up,   for the blood was so hot,
the poisonous gast   perished within.

Soon he was swimming,   he who knew strife in the battle,
the fall of his foe,   he dove through the flood.
1620   The welling waves   were all cleared now,
the underwater realm,   where the wandering gast
gave up her life   and this waning world.
To land then came the leader   of the sea-farers,
the stout-hearted one swam,   rejoicing in his loot,
1625   the heavy burdens   which he bore.
They went to greet him,   and thanked God,
the band of thegns   were blithe with their lord
when they saw him   sound again.
The hardy man   from helm and byrnie
1630   was quickly loosed.   The mere stilled under the skies,
the waters were stained   with war-blood.

They fared forth thence   along the foot-paths
with fain hearts,   they traveled the trail,
the well-known ways.   Bold as kings,
1635   they carried the head   along the cliff;
'twas trying   for them all.
With full hearts,   four had to
carry with difficulty,   on a slaughter-stave
the head of Grendel   to the golden hall.
1640   The men   hastened to the hall,
firm and faithful,   the fourteen Geats
went forth   with the Weder lord.
Proud in the throng,   they marched to the mead-hall.

The captain of the thegns   came inside,
1645   the daring man   of deeds renowned,

                              Þá þæt sweord ongan.
            æfter heaþo-swáte   hilde-ġiċelum,
            wíġ-bil wanian.   Þæt wæs wundra sum
            þæt hit eal ġemealt   íse ġelícost,
            ðonne forstes bend   Fæder onlǽteð,
1610   onwindeð wæl-rápas,   sé ġeweald hafað
            sǽla ond mǽla.   Þæt is Sóð Metod!

            Ne nóm hé in þǽm wícum,   Weder-Ġéata léod,
            máðm-ǽhta má,   þéh hé þǽr moniġe ġeseah,
            búton þone hafelan   ond þá hilt somod;
1615   since fáge.   Sweord ǽr ġemealt,
            forbarn bróden-mǽl,   wæs þæt blód tó þæs hát,
            ǽttren ellorgǽst,   sé þǽr inne swealt.

            Sóna wæs on sunde,   sé þe ǽr æt sæċċe ġebád,
            wíġ-hryre wráðra,   wæter up þurh-déaf.
1620   Wǽron ýð-ġebland   eal ġefǽlsod,
            éacne eardas,   þá se ellor-gást
            oflét líf-dagas   ond þás lǽnan ġesceaft.
            Cóm þá tó lande   lid-manna helm,
            swíð-mód swymman,   sǽ-láce ġefeah,
1625   mæġen-byrþenne   þára þe hé him mid hæfde.
            Ēodon him þá tóġéanes,   Gode þancodon,
            ðrýðlíċ þeġna héap   þéodnes ġefégon
            þæs þe hí hyne ġesundne   ġeséon móston.
            Ðá wæs of þǽm hróran   helm ond byrne
1630   lungre álýsed.   Lagu drúsade,
            wæter under wolcnum   wæl-dréore fág.

            Férdon forð þonon   féþe-lástum
            ferhþum fæġne,   fold-weġ mǽton,
            cúþe strǽte.   Cyningbalde men
1635   from þǽm holm-clife   hafelan bǽron;
            earfoðlíċe   heora ǽġhwæþrum.
            Fela-módiġra,   féower scoldon
            on þǽm wæl-stenge   w(æ)rcum ġeferian
            tó þǽm gold-sele   Grendles héafod.
1640   Oþ ðæt semninga   tó sele cómon,
            frome fyrd-hwate,   féower-týne
            Ġéata gongan   gum-dryhten mid.
            Módiġ on ġemonge,   meodo-wongas træd.

            Ðá cóm in gán   ealdor ðeġna,
1645   dǽd-céne mon   dóme ġewurþad,

the stouthearted hero,   to greet Hrothgar,
and by the hair,   he bore to the hall
Grendel's head,   to where heroes drank,
to the earls and their ladies,   a loathly sight,
1650 a dread display,   for all to see.

Beowulf spake,   the son of Ecgtheow,
"Lo! We, this lake-loot,   son of Healfdene,
lord of the Scyldings,   show you
these true tokens   which you see here.
1655 I did not   easily endure
that underwater war;   these deeds I worked
with great effort,   but eventually,
when I thought the battle had been lost,   the Lord shielded me.
Nor could I with Hrunting,   in the clash of battle,
1660 work a whit,   though the weapon is good.
However the Wielder of Ages   granted to me,
that on the wall hanging,   I beheld a beautiful,
Giant sword of old.   Oft He guides
those without friends!   Then I wielded that weapon,
1665 and slew her in that strife   when I could,
the house's warden.   Then that war-sword,
the wave-patterned blade   all burned up when sprang
hot battle-sweat.   Then I, that hilt brought hence
from the fiends.   Those fell deeds, I avenged,
1670 baleful death of the Danes,   as was seemly.
So, I say that in Heorot,   you may now
sleep without sorrow   with your band of soldiers,
each fellow   of all your folk,
veterans and youths,   need never dread,
1675 friend of the Scyldings,   from his hand again,
evil for the earls,   as ere you had!"

Then was the golden hilt   given to the old ruler,
to the hand   of the hoary battle-chieftain,
ancient work of Giants.   It had passed into the possession,
1680 after the downfall of Demons,   to the lord of the Danes,
the work of wonder-smiths,   when this world gave up
that grim-hearted gast,   the enemy of God,
guilty of murder,   and his mother also.
It passed into the power   of worldly kings,
1685 the best between   the two seas,
who in Scandia   gave out gold.

hæle hilde-déor,   Hróðgár grétan.
Þá wæs be feaxe,   on flet boren
Grendles héafod,   þǽr guman druncon,
eġeslíċ for eorlum   ond þǽre idese mid
1650 wlite-séon wrǽtlíċ,   weras onsáwon.

(XXIV)

Béowulf maþelode,   bearn Ecgþéowes,
"Hwæt! Wé þé þás sǽ-lác,   sunu Healfdenes,
léod Scyldinga,   lustum bróhton
tíres tó tácne   þé þú hér tó lócast.
1655 Iċ þæt unsófte   ealdre ġedíġde
wiġġe under wætere;   weorc ġenéþde
earfoðlíċe,   æt-rihte wæs
gúð ġetwǽfed,   nymðe meċ God scylde.
Ne meahte iċ æt hilde   mid Hruntinge
1660 wiht ġewyrċan,   þéah þæt wǽpen duge;
ac mé ġeúðe   Ylda Waldend,
þæt iċ on wáge ġeseah   wlitiġ hangian
eald-sweord éacen.   Oftost wísode
winiġea léasum!   Þæt iċ ðý wǽpne ġebrǽd
1665 ofslóh ðá æt þǽre sæċċe   þá mé sǽl áġeald,
húses hyrdas.   Þá þæt hilde-bil,
forbarn, brogden-mǽl,   swá þæt blód ġesprang,
hátost heaþo-swáta.   Iċ þæt hilt þanan
féondum ætferede.   Fyren-dǽda wræc,
1670 déað-cwealm Deniġea,   swá hit ġedéfe wæs.
Iċ hit þé þonne ġeháte,   þæt þú on Heorote móst
sorh-léas swefan   mid þínra secga ġedryht
ond þeġna ġehwylċ   þínra léoda,
duguðe ond iogoþe,   þæt þú him ondrǽdan ne þearft,
1675 þéoden Scyldinga,   on þá healfe,
aldor-bealu eorlum,   swá þú ǽr dydest."

Ðá wæs gylden hilt   gamelum rince,
hárum hild-fruman   on hand ġyfen,
Enta ǽr-ġeweorc.   Hit on ǽht ġehwearf,
1680 æfter Déofla hryre,   Deniġea fréan,
wundor-smiþa ġeweorc;   ond þá þás worold ofġeaf
grom-heort guma,   Godes andsaca,
morðres scyldiġ,   ond his módor éac.
On ġeweald ġehwearf   worold-cyninga,
1685 ðǽm sélestan   be sǽm twéonum,
ðára þe on Scedeniġġe   sceattas dǽlde.

Hrothgar spake,   as he handled the hilt*,
an heirloom of old.   On it was engraved
the tale of that ancient folk,   whom the Flood slew,
1690   the sea raged   against the race of Giants;
a fearful fate!   That was a people foreign
to the Everlasting Lord.   To them was their reward,
the Wielder paid them   with the welling waters.
On the guard   of shining gold
1695   were rune-staves   rightly marking the name
of he whom that sword   had first been forged,
the finest of irons   in former days,
with the hilt well wound   and a serpent in the blade.

Hróðgár maðelode,   hylt scéawode,
ealde láfe.   On ðǽm wæs ór writen
fyrn-ġewinnes;   syðþan Flód ofslóh,
1690 ġifen ġéotende,   Gíganta cyn;
frécne ġeférdon!   Þæt wæs fremde þéod
Éċean Dryhtne.   Him þæs ende-léan,
þurh wæteres wylm,   Waldend sealde.
Swá wæs on ðǽm scennum   scíran goldes
1695 þurh rún-stafas   rihte ġemearcod
ġeseted ond ġesǽd,   hwám þæt sweord ġeworht,
írena cyst   ǽrest wǽre,
wreoþen-hilt ond wyrm-fáh.

Chapter XIII
Leaving the Land of the Danes

The wise one spake,   the son of Healfdene,
1700   and all were silent,   "Lo! He may say
who is sooth and right   and follows the folk,
that is mindful of times far-off,   old warden of the estates,
that this earl   was born a better man!
Fame is established   in far-off domains!
1705   My friend Beowulf,   o'er each of those peoples,
you must with patience hold,   might with your mood's wisdom.
To you, I shall give riches,   as I ere said.

"A solace you must be,   long-lasting to your people,
a help to the heroes.   Not such was Heremod
1710   to Ecgwela's offspring,   the Honor-Scyldings;
he waxed not for their satisfaction,   but for slaughter
and plague on   the Danish people.
Seething, he slew   his shoulder-companions,
the men at his board!   Alone, he passed,
1715   a mighty king,   from men's joys.
Mighty God had gifted him   with battle prowess,
in awesome strength,   exalted o'er all men.
Yet secretly in his heart,   deep in his breast-hoard,
he grew blood-thirsty.   He gave not rings
1720   to the Danes for their deeds.   He dwelt joylessly,
and for the pain he wrought,   he suffered strife,
bale to the people for a long time.   Learn from this,
understand the morality of Men.   Be mindful of this tale that I,
old and wise in winters, have told you!   'Tis a wonder
1725   how mighty God   to Mankind,
in understanding   sends wisdom,
lands and lordships,   though he rules all.
At times, he in His love,   will let go
the mind of men   of a mighty race,
1730   give him earthly joy   in his estates,
to hold   the folk's fortress,

Ðá se wísa spræc.
sunu Healfdenes,   swígedon ealle,
1700   "Þæt lá mæġ secgan   sé þe sóð ond riht
fremeð on folce,   feor eal ġemon,
eald (éðel) weard,   þæt ðes eorl wǽre
ġeboren betera!   Blǽd is árǽred
ġeond wíd-wegas!   Wine mín Béowulf,
1705   ðín ofer þéoda ġehwylċe,   eal þú hit ġeþyldum healdest,
mæġen mid módes snyttrum.   Iċ þé sceal míne ġelǽstan
fréoðe, swá wit furðum sprǽcon.
      "Ðú scealt tó frófre weorþan
eal lang-twídiġ   léodum þínum,
hæleðum tó helpe.   Ne wearð Heremód swá
1710   eaforum Ecgwelan,   Ár-Scyldingum;
ne ġewéox hé him tó willan,   ac tó wæl-fealle
ond tó déað-cwalum   Deniġa léodum.
Bréat bolgen-mód   béod-ġenéatas,
eaxl-ġesteallan!   Oþ þæt hé ána hwearf,
1715   mǽre þéoden,   mon-dréamum from.
Ðéah þe hine mihtiġ God   mæġenes wynnum,
eafeþum stépte   ofer ealle men,
forð ġefremede,   hwæþere him on ferhþe gréow,
bréost-hord blód-réow.   Nallas béagas ġeaf
1720   Denum æfter dóme.   Dréam-léas ġebád,
þæt hé þæs ġewinnes   w(æ)rc þrowade,
léodbealo longsum.   Ðú þé lǽr be þon,
gum-cyste onġit   iċ þis ġid be þé
áwræc wintrum fród!   Wundor is tó secganne
1725   hú mihtiġ God   Manna cynne,
þurh sídne sefan   snyttru bryttað,
eard ond eorl-scipes,   hé áh ealra ġeweald.
Hwílum Hé on lufan,   lǽteð hworfan
monnes mód-ġeþonc   mǽran cynnes,
1730   seleð him on éþle   eorþan wynne,
tó healdanne   hléo-burh wera,

and wields   from the world's portion,
a wide kingdom,   that he cannot, himself,
in his unwisdom,   ween the end.

1735   "He abides in bounty,   believing none can harm him,
illness nor age;   no evil sorrow
shadows his soul,   nor strife anywhere.
Sword-hate appears,   but to him the whole world
wends to his will,   no worse does he know.

1740   "Until all   within his overconfidence
waxes while   the warden slumbers,
the soul's keeper.   Too fast is that sleep,
with troubles bound,   when his bane comes near
and looses a loathly arrow   from his bow!

1745   "Then he strikes his heart   'neath his harness*,
by the bitter shaft,   -no shelter can he find-
by a fell command   from the fiendish gast.
He thinks it too little   what he has held too long,
cruelly covets.   In his greed,
1750   he gives not golden rings,   and then his fate
forgets and ignores,   that which God gave him before,
the Glory-Wielder,   wealth and honor.
Yet in the end,   it ever comes about,
when the life   that was leant to him yields,
1755   fated to fall,   and another follows,
who without care,   gives out gifts,
ancient treasures of earls;   he thinks not of fear!

"Be wary of that baleful fate,   dear Beowulf,
best of men,   and the better part choose,
1760   eternal profit;   heed not your pride,
choicest of champions!   The blossom of your might
will last but a while,   and erelong it shall be
that sickness or sword-edge   shall take your strength,
or the embrace of fire,   or flood's billows,
1765   or bite of blade,   or flight of spear,
weakens and grows dim.   Death shall
one day o'ercome even you,   mighty warrior!

"For half a hundred years*,   the Ring-Danes I have
1770   held under the heavens   and sheltered from war,
from countless clans   across Middle-Earth,
from spear and sword,   'till it seemed for me

116

ġedéð him swá ġewealdene   worolde dǽlas,
síde ríċe,   þæt hé his selfa ne mæġ
for his un-snyttrum,   ende ġeþenċean.

1735 "Wunað hé on wiste   nó hine wiht dweleð,
ádl né yldo;   né him inwit-sorh
on sefa(n) sweorceð,   né ġesacu óhwǽr.
Ecg-hete éoweð,   ac him eal worold
wendeð on willan,   hé þæt wyrse ne con.

XXV

1740 "Oð þæt him on innan   ofer-hyġda dǽl
weaxeð ond wrídað   þonne se weard swefeð,
sáwele hyrde.   Bið se slǽp tó fæst,
bisġum ġebunden,   bona swíðe néah,
sé þe of flán-bogan   fyrenum scéoteð!

1745 "Þonne bið on hreþre   under helm drepen.
biteran strǽle,   -him bebeorgan ne con-
wóm wundor-bebodum   werġan gástes.
Þinċeð him tó lýtel   þæt hé tó lange héold,
ġýtsað grom-hýdiġ.   Nallas on ġylp seleð
1750 fǽ(tt)e béagas,   ond hé þá forð-ġesceaft
forġyteð ond forġýmeð,   þæs þe him ǽr God sealde,
Wuldres Waldend,   weorð-mynda dǽl.
Hit on ende-stæf   eft ġelimpeð,
þæt se líċ-homa   lǽne ġedréoseð,
1755 fǽġe ġefealleð,   féhð óþer tó,
sé þe unmurnlíċe   mádmas dǽleþ,
eorles ǽr-ġestréon;   eġesan ne ġýmeð!

"Bebeorh ðé þone bealo-níð,   Béowulf léofa,
secg se bet(o)sta,   ond þé þæt sélre ġeċéos,
1760 éċe rǽdas;   oferhýda ne ġým,
mǽre cempa!   Nú is þínes mæġnes blǽd
áne hwíle,   eft sóna bið
þæt þeċ ádl oððe ecg   eafoþes ġetwǽfeð,
oððe fýres feng,   oððe flódes wylm,
1765 oððe gripe méċes,   oððe gáres fliht,
oððe atol yldo,   oððe éagena bearhtm,
forsiteð ond forsworceð.   Semninga bið
þæt ðeċ, dryht-guma,   déað oferswýðeð!

"Swá iċ Hring-Dena,   hund missera
1770 wéold under wolcnum   ond hiġ wiġġe beléac,
manigum mǽġþa   ġeond þysne Middanġeard,

that no foes could I find   under the vault of heaven.
Lo! In the freehold,   my fortune was reversed,
1775   joy was followed by grief   when Grendel became,
the ancient enemy,   mine invader.
Those raids   I ever endured,
a great sorrow for my soul.   Thank the Measurer,
the Eternal Lord,   that I lived long enough
1780   so that on   that sword-hewn head,
after that old strife,   could with mine eyes behold!
Go now to the seats   and of the symbel be glad,
worthy warriors!   I will share
many mathoms   when morning dawns!"

1785   Glad was the Geat   as he went
to seek his seat,   as the wise one had said.
Again, as before,   for the battle-strong men,
for those in the hall,   a fair feast was served anew.

The night-helm darkened   o'er the hall.
1790   From their meal,   the men arose,
for the hoary haired one   wished to seek his bed,
the old Scylding.   Eager for bed was the Geat,
the stout shield-bearer   was ready for rest.
At once, the hall warrior,   weary from his adventure,
1795   went forth,   the far-traveler,
who by custom,   cared for all
the thegn's needs,   such as in those days
a sea-warrior   certainly had.
So rested the large-hearted one.   The looming hall,
1800   grand and gilt;   the guest slept inside,
'till the black raven,   the bliss of the heavens,
blithe of heart,   heralded the dawn.

Then came brightness.   The battle-men hastened.
Eagerly, the atheling   wished to return
1805   to his folk;   he wished far thence,
the great-hearted guest,   to guide his keel.

The hardy one then charged   for Hrunting to be brought,
he bade Ecglaf's son   that sword to take,
belovèd iron,   for the loan he thanked;
1810   quoth he, that he found it to   be a friend in battle,
in war 'twas skilled.   He slandered not

118

æscum ond ecgum,   þæt iċ mé ǽniġne
under sweġles begong   ġesacan ne tealde.
Hwæt! Mé þæs on éþle,   edwendan cwóm,
1775   gyrn æfter gomene   seoþðan Grendel wearð,
eald-ġewinna,   in-genga mín.
Iċ þǽre sócne   singáles wæġ,
mód-ċeare miċle.   Þæs siġ Metode þanc,
Éċean Drihtne,   þæs ðe iċ on aldre ġebád
1780   þæt iċ on þone hafelan   heoro-dréorigne,
ofer eald ġewin,   éagum stariġe!
Gá nú tó setle,   symbel-wynne dréoh,
wíġġe-weorþad!   Unc sceal worn fela
máþma ġemǽnra   siþðan morgen bið!"

1785   Ġéat wæs glæd-mód   ġéong sóna tó
setles néosan,   swá se snottra heht.
Þá wæs eft swá ǽr   ellen-rófum,
flet-sittendum,   fæġere ġereorded
níowan stefne.
                    Niht-helm ġeswearc
1790   deorc ofer dryht-gumum.   Duguð eal árás,
wolde blonden-feax   beddes néosan,
gamela Scylding.   Ġéat un(ġe)metes wél,
rófne rand-wigan   restan lyste.
Sóna him sele-þeġn,   síðes wérgum,
1795   feorrancundum,   forð wísade,
sé for andrysnum,   ealle beweo(d)e
þeġnes þearfe,   swylċe þý dógore
héaþo-líðende   habban scoldon.
Reste hine þá rúm-heort.   Reċed hlíuade,
1800   ġéap ond gold-fáh;   gæst inne swæf,
oþ þæt hrefn blaca,   heofones wynne,
blíð-heort, bodode.

                    Ðá cóm beorht (léoma)
(ofer sceadwa) scacan.   Scaþan ónetton
wǽron æþelingas   eft tó léodum
1805   fúse tó farenne;   wolde feor þanon
cuma collen-ferhð,   ċéoles néosan.

Heht þá se hearda   Hrunting beran,
sunu Ecgláfes   heht his sweord niman,
léoflíċ írenm,   sæġde him þæs léanes þanc;
1810   cwæð hé þone gúð-wine   gódne tealde,
wíġ-cræftiġne.   Nales wordum lóg

the blade's edge;   that was a worthy warrior!
Armed,   they was eager to leave,
the warriors waited.   Honored by the Danes,
1815 hastened to the high-seat,   where the other sat,
the battle-bold atheling   greeted Hrothgar.

Beowulf spake,   the son of Ecgtheow,
"Now, we seafarers   wish to say,
having come so far,   we are fain to
1820 seek Hygelac.   Here we have been
well received.   You are a respectable host!
If ever on this Earth   I can win
more of your love   than is already mine,
make it known to me,   lord of men,
1825 for in war-works   I am ready!
If I ever hear   o'er the flood's way,
that a neighboring tribe   torments the folk,
as your foes   have oft done before,
then I shall bring to you   a thousand thegns,
1830 heroes to help.   I know that Hygelac,
lord of the Geats,   though he is young,
the folk's shield,   would fain support me
with words and works,   so that I might serve you well
and bring a forest of spears   to fight for you
1835 and support in strength   the men who need it.
If Hrethric should ever   come to the court of the Geats*,
king's son,   he may there many
friends find.   Far-off lands are
best sought   by he who is brave himself."

1840 Hrothgar spake   to him in answer,
"These words, to you,   the wise Lord
has sent to your mind!   Ne'er have I wiser words
heard from a man   as young as you.
You are mighty in strength   and your spirit is wise,
1845 an astute giver of redes.   Rightly, I reckon that
if ever it should happen   that Hrethel's heir
was taken by a spear   in sword-slaughter,
an iron illness,   your elder,
the defender of the folk,   while you have life left,
1850 that the Sea-Geats   will find no one greater
to claim as their king,   keeper
of the hero's hoard,   if you will hold
that realm of men!   Your mind and soul

méċes ecge,   þæt wæs módiġ secg!
Ond þá síð-frome,   searwum ġearwe
wíġend wǽron.   Éode weorð Denum
1815 æþeling tó yppan,   þǽr se óþer wæs,
h(æl)e hilde-déor   Hróðgár grétte.

XXVI

Béowulf maþelode,   bearn Ecgþéowes,
"Nú wé sǽ-líðend   secgan wyllað,
feorran cumene,   þæt wé fundiaþ
1820 Hiġelác séċan.   Wǽron hér tela
willum bewenede.   Þú ús wél dohtest!
Ġif iċ þonne on Eorþan   ówihte mæġ
þínre mód-lufan   máran tilian,
gumena dryhten,   ðonne iċ ġýt dyde,
1825 gúð-ġeweorca,   iċ béo ġearo sóna!
Ġif iċ þæt ġefricge   ofer flóda begang
þæt þeċ ymbe-sittend   eġesan þýwað,
swá þeċ hetende   hwílum dydon,
iċ ðé þúsenda   þeġna bringe,
1830 hæleþa tó helpe.   Iċ on Hiġeláce wát,
Ġéata dryhten,   þéah ðe hé ġeong sý,
folces hyrde,   þæt hé meċ fremman wile
weordum ond w(e)orcum,   þæt iċ þé wél heriġe
ond þé tó ġéoce   gár-holt bere,
1835 mæġenes fultum   þǽr ðé bið manna þearf.
Ġif him þonne Hréþríċ   tó hofum Ġéata,
ġeþinge(ð) þéodnes bearn,   hé mæġ þǽr fela
fréonda findan.   Feor-cýþðe béoð
sélran ġesóhte   þǽm þe him selfa déah."

1840 Hróðgár maþelode   him on andsware,
"Þé þá word-cwydas,   wiġtiġ Drihten
on sefan sende!   Ne hýrde iċ snotorlícor
on swá ġeongum feore   guman þingian.
Þú eart mæġenes strang   ond on móde fród,
1845 wís word-cwida.   Wén iċ taliġe
ġif þæt ġegangeð   þæt ðe gár nymeð
hild heoru-grimme   Hréþles eaferan,
ádl oþðe íren,   ealdor ðínne,
folces hyrde,   ond þú þín feorh hafast,
1850 þæt þe Sǽ-Ġéatas   sélran næbben
tó ġeċéosenne   cyning ǽniġne,
hord-weard hæleþa,   ġyf þú healdan wylt
mága ríċe!   Mé þín mód-sefa

please me well,   belovèd Beowulf.
1855 For what feat you have done,   the folk—
the Geatish sons   and the Spear-Danes—
shall have mutual peace;   their strife shall slacken,
wars that they   had ere endured.
While I still this   wide realm rule,
1860 mine hoard I shall hold   in common with yours.
We shall greet each other with gold   o'er the gannet's bath
and ring-prowed ships   will bring across the brimming seas
tokens of friendship.   My folk,
towards friend and foe alike   are firmly disposed,
1865 and hold honor   in the old ways."

Then the earl's bulwark,   the bairn of Healfdene
gave to him   twelve treasures,
and to his belovèd folk   bid him farewell with the gifts
and seek safety at home   and return soon.
1870 Then the king kissed   the good atheling
and Scylding lord,   the belovèd thegn
and took him by the neck.   Tears fell
from his grey head.   Good and wise,
there were two odds,   but one was greater,
1875 that they should   ne'er see each other again,
high-spirited in the hall.   The man was so dear to him
that in his heart's fount   he could not forbear,
but in his bosom,   his heart bound fast
for the belovèd man;   a secret longing*
1880 burned in his blood.   Then strode Beowulf,
glad of his gold,   o'er the grass-mound,
the warrior went   to the sea-runner,
riding at anchor,   awaiting its master.
Along the way,   were Hrothgar's gifts
1885 oft praised.   That was a peerless king,
in every way blameless,   until age had taken away
his joys of might,   as it does to all.

They came to the flood   with full hearts;
the young warriors   wore ring-mail,
1890 woven war-sarks.   The land-ward beheld
the earl's return,   as ere he had.
He spake no harsh words   from the hill,
but greeted the guests   as he rode forward.
He gave welcome   to the Weder folk,
1895 the shining scathers   as they went to the ship.

lícað leng swá wél,   léofa Béowulf.
1855 Hafast þú ġeféred   þæt þám folcum sceal,
Ġéata léodum   ond Gár-Denum
sib ġemǽnum   ond sacu restan,
inwit-níþas   þe híe ǽr drugon.
Wesan þenden iċ wealde   wídan ríċes,
1860 máþmas ġemǽne,   maniġ óþerne.
Gódum ġegrétan   ofer ganotes bæð,
sceal hring-naca   ofer héaðu bringan
lác ond luf-tácen.   Iċ þá léode wát
ġé wið féond ġé wið fréond   fæste ġeworhte,
1865 ǽġhwæs untǽle   ealde wísan."

Ðá ġít him eorla hléo   (h)i(n)e ġesealde,
mago Healfdenes,   máþmas twelfe,
hét hine mid þǽm lácum   léode swǽse
séċean on ġesyntum,   snúde eft cuman.
1870 Ġecyste þá,   cyning æþelum gód
þéoden Scildinga,   ðeġn betstan
ond be healse ġenam.   Hruron him téaras
blonden-feaxum.   Him wæs béġa wén
ealdum infródum,   óþres swíðor,
1875 þæt h(í)e seoðða(n)   ġeséon móston,
módiġe on meþle.   Wæs him se man tó þon léof
þæt hé þone bréost-wylm   forberan ne mehte,
ac him on hreþre   hyġe-bendum fæst
æfter déorum men;   dyrne langað
1880 b(o)rn wið blóde.   Him Béowulf þanan,
gúð-rinc gold-wlanc,   græs-moldan træd
since hrémiġ   sǽ-genga bád,
áge(n)d-fréan,   sé þe on ancre rád.
Þá wæs on gange,   ġifu Hróðgáres
1885 oft ġeæhted.   Þæt wæs án cyning,
ǽġhwæs orleahtre,   oþ þæt hine yldo benam
mæġenes wynnum,   sé þe oft manegum scód.

XXVII
Cwóm þá tó flóde   fela-módiġra;
hæġstealdra (héap)   hring-net bǽron,
1890 locene leoðo-syrċan.   Land-weard onfand
eft-síð eorla,   swá hé ǽr dyde.
Nó hé mid hearme   of hlíðes nosan,
gæs(tas) grétte,   ac him tóġéanes rád.
Cwæð þæt wilcuman   Wedera léodum,
1895 scaþan scír-hame   tó scipe fóron.

They boarded the sea-craft   on the sand,
their arms and armor,   near the ringèd-prow,
they laid in heaps.   High stood the mast
o'er Hrothgar's   hoarded wealth.
1900   To the boat-guard,   Beowulf gave a sword,
garnished with gold,   so that henceforth
he might, on the mead-bench,   by that weapon
be made worthy.

124

Þá wæs on sande   sǽ-ġéap naca,
hladen here-wǽdum   hringed-stefna
méarum ond máðmum.   Mǽst hlífade
ofer Hróðgáres   hord-ġestréonum.
1900   Hé þǽm bát-wearde,   bunden golde
swurd ġesealde,   þæt hé syðþan wæs,
on meodu-benċe   máþm(e) þý weorþr(a),
yrfe-láfe.

Chapter XIV
The hero's homecoming

                    Homeward bound,
they drove o'er deep waters   and left Danemark.
1905 From the mast was hung   a huge sea-cloth,
a firm sail;   the sea-wood thundered.
The floater   was not frustrated
in its journey   by the wind and waves.

The foam-flecked prow   went forth o'er the sea,
1910 bound fast   across the brine,
'til they could see   the cliffs of Geatland*,
those well-known nesses.   The keel rushed up,
weather-beaten,   so that it stood on the strand.

Quickly was the coast-guard   in the water,
1915 he had awaited the belovèd men   for a long while;
he had watched   the water from afar.
By an anchor,   the deep-bosomed ship was bound,
fast to the sand,   lest the sea's strength
might carry off   the winsome wood.
1920 The atheling bade them   to bear forth
the gems and gold.

                    'Twas not far hence,
to the hall   of the gold-giver.
Hygelac Hrethling   dwelt there at home
by the sea-cliffs   with his companions.
1925 Beautiful was the building   and bold was the king,
high the hall,   and Hygd* was very young,
wise and well-thriven,   though few in winters
in the wallèd burg   had she abided.
Hæreth's daughter   was not overly humble,
1930 nor did she grudge gifts   to the Geatish people.

        Ġewát him on nac(a);
    dréfan déop wæter,   Dena land ofġeaf.
1905 Þá wæs be mæste   mere-hræġla sum,
    seġl sále fæst;   sund-wudu þunede.
    Nó þǽr wéġ-flotan   wind ofer ýðum
    síðes ġetwǽfde,   sǽ-genga fór.

    Fléat fámiġ-heals   forð ofer ýðe,
1910 bunden-stefna   ofer brim-stréamas,
    þæt híe Ġéata clifu   onġitan meahton,
    cúþe næssas.   Ċéol up ġeþrang,
    lyft-ġeswenċed,   on lande stód.

    Hraþe wæs æt holme   hýð-weard ġeara,
1915 sé þe ǽr lange tíd,   léofra manna
    fús æt faroðe   feor wlátode.
    Sǽlde tó sande,   síd-fæþme scip,
    onc(e)r-bendum fæst,   þý lǽs hym ýþa ðrym
    wudu wynsuman   forwrecan meahte.
1920 Hét þá up beran   æþelinga ġestréon,
    frætwe ond fǽt-gold.

            Næs him feor þanon,
    tó ġeséċanne   sinces bryttan.
    Hiġelác Hréþling   þǽr æt hám wunað
    selfa mid ġesíðum   sǽ-wealle néah.
1925 Bold wæs betliċ,   brego-róf cyning,
    héa(h on) healle,   Hyġd swíðe ġeong,
    wís wél-þungen,   þéah ðe wintra lýt
    under burh-locan   ġebiden hæbbe,
    Hæreþes dóhtor,   næs hío hnáh swá þéah,
1930 né tó gnéað ġifa   Ġéata léodum
    máþm-ġestréona.

She showed not   the malicious mind of Thryth*,
the haughty folk-queen,   who did dreadful deeds.
Of the dauntless,   none dared risk,
of the belovèd companions,   except her lord,
1935 to look at her   in the light of day,
for him deathly bonds,   bent by hand
were cruelly appointed!   Quickly then
after being grasped,   she gave them death;
a shadow-marked sword   made* known
1940 the baleful slaughter.   'Twas not a seemly way
for a lady to practice,   peerless though she be,
that a peace-weaver*,   a belovèd warrior
in feigned anger,   end their life.
However, she was humbled   by Hemming's kinsman.

1945 O'er their ale drinking,   men also told
that she practiced on the people   less evil
and spite,   since first she was
given gold-decked   to the young champion,
the glorious atheling   in Offa's hall
1950 o'er the fallow flood   at the urging of her father.
She sought that path,   where she afterwards prospered
on the gift-stool;   her goodness was famed.
She was fain of the life   that fate had given her,
and held high-love   for the chieftain of heroes;
1955 of all Mankind,   I have heard,
he was the best   between the two seas,
of the Human race.   Hence Offa was
in gifts and in the ways of war,   a spear-keen man,
widely famed;   in wisdom he ruled
1960 his estate,   'til Eomer awoke,
a help to heroes,   kinsman of Hemming,
Garmund's grandson,   skilled in battle.

Then the hardy warrior   with his henchmen departed
o'er the sand,   they treaded the sea-shore,
1965 the broad strand.   Bright was the world-candle,
the eager sun from the south.   They their journey had survived,
and strode with hasty steps   to the shield of earls,
to Ongentheow's bane   in his burg,
where the young   and bold battle-king
1970 dwelt,   and doled out rings.

128

Mód( )Þrýðo wæ ġ
fremu folces cwén,   firen ondrysne.
Nǽniġ þæt dorste   déor ġenéþan
swǽsra ġesíða,   nefne sin-fréa,
1935 þæt hire an dæġes   éagum starede,
ac him wæl-bende   weotode tealde
hand-ġewriþene!   Hraþe seoþðan wæs
æfter mund-gripe   méċe ġeþinged,
þæt hit sceáden-mǽl   scýran móste,
1940 cwealm-bealu cýðan.   Ne bið swylċ cwénlic þéaw
idese tó efnanne   þéah ðe hío ǽnlicu sý,
þætte freoðu-webbe,   féores onsǽċe
æfter líġe-torne   léofne mannan.
Húru þæt on hóhsnod(e)   Hem(m)inges mǽġ.

1945 Ealo drincende,   óðer sǽdan
þæt hío léod-bealewa   lǽs ġefremede,
inwit-níða,   syððan ǽrest wearð
ġyfen gold-hroden   ġeongum cempan,
ǽðelum díore   syððan hío Offan flet
1950 ofer fealone flód   be fæder láre.
Síðe ġesóhte,   ðǽr hío syððan well
in gum-stóle;   góde mǽre.
Líf-ġesceafta   lifiġende bréac,
híold héah-lufan   wið hæleþa brego;
1955 ealles Mon-cynnes   míne ġefrǽġe,
þ(one) sélestan   bí sǽm twéonum,
eormen-cynnes.   Forðám Offa wæs
ġeofum ond gúðum,   gár-céne man,
wíde ġeweorðod;   wísdóme héold
1960 éðel sínne,   þonon (Ēo)m(e)r wóc
hæleðum tó helpe,   Hem(m)inges mǽġ,
nefa Gármundes,   níða cræftiġ.

XXVIII
Ġewát him ðá se hearda   mid his hond-scole
sylf æfter sande,   sǽ-wong tredan,
1965 wíde waroðas.   Woruld-candel scán,
siġel súðan fús.   Hí síð drugon,
elne ġeéodon   tó ðæs ðe eorla hléo,
bonan Ongenþéoes   burgum in innan,
ġeongne gúð-cyning   gódne ġefrúnon
1970 hringas dǽlan.

129

To Hygelac was Beowulf's   travel told.
There in the stead,   the warden of warriors
learned how the shield-bearers   came back safe
still after the battle-play,   hale down the hall trode.
1975 The king bid   for the court to be cleared,
the guests were   given room.
Then he sat   by he who survived the battle,
kinsman by kinsman.   His lord
he greeted   with grace,
1980 with winsome words.   Mead-cups
passed through the hall.   Hæreth's daughter,
loved by the warriors,   bore the wine-cup
to the hands   of the heroes.

Hygelac stood then   in the high hall.
1985 He courteously questioned   the companions,
he was curious   about the Sea-Geats' sojourn.
"How fared you,   belovèd Beowulf,
when you went forth   far away,
seeking strife   o'er the salt water,
1990 to battle in Heorot?   And did you Hrothgar's
widely-known   woes lessen,
the famèd king?   I cared deeply in mine heart,
my soul seethed,   for I trusted not the venture
of my loved one.   Long did I beseech you
1995 not to face   the fell gast;
let the South-Danes   settle their own
feud with Grendel!   To God I give thanks
that I may   see you sound!"

Beowulf spake,   the son of Ecgtheow,
2000 "'Tis no mystery,   my lord Hygelac,
that meeting   to many men,
that I waged war   on Grendel
in the hall,   where a hoard of hardships
he showed   the victorious Scyldings,
2005 everlasting evils,   these I avenged.
There is no need   to boast of Grendel's kin
to any on Earth   for that uproar at dawn,
from the longest-lived   of that loathly race,
wrapped in faithlessness.   When first I came there
2010 to greet Hrothgar   in the ring-hall,
soon to me the splendid   son of Healfdene,
after my purpose   was made plain to him,

                        Hiġeláce wæs
síð Béowulfes   snúde ġecýðed,
þæt ðǽr on worðiġ   wíġendra hléo,
lind-ġestealla,   lifiġende cwóm
heaðo-láces hál,   tó hofe gongan.
1975 Hraðe wæs ġerýmed   swá se ríca bebéad,
féðe-ġestum   flet innan-weard.
Ġesæt þá wið sylfne   sé ðá sæċċe ġenæs,
mǽġ wið mǽġe.   Syððan man-dryhten
þurh hléoðor-cwyde   holdne ġegrétte,
1980 méaglum wordum.   Meodu-scenċum
hwearf, ġeond þæt side reċed.   Hæreðes dóhtor,
lufode ðá léode,   líð-wǽġe bær
hǽ(l)um tó handa.
                        Hiġelác ongan
sínne ġeseldan   in sele þám héan
1985 fæġre fricgean.   Hyne fyrwet bræc,
hwylċe Sǽ-Ġéata   síðas wǽron.
"Hú lomp éow on láde,   léofa Bíowulf,
þá ðú fǽringa   feorr ġehogodest
sæċċe séċean   ofer sealt wæter,
1990 hilde tó Hiorote?   Ac ðú Hróðgáre
wí(d)cúðne wéan   wihte ġebéttest,
mǽrum ðéodne?   Iċ ðæs mód-ċeare
sorh-wylmum séað,   síðe ne truwode
léofes mannes;   iċ ðé lange bæd,
1995 þæt ðú þone wæl-gǽst   wihte ne grétte;
léte Súð-Dene   sylfe ġeweorðan
gúðe wið Grendel!   Gode iċ þanc secge
þæs ðe iċ ðé ġesundne   ġeséon móste!"

Bíowulf maðelode,   bearn Ecgðíoes,
2000 "Þæt is undyrne,   dryhten Hiġelác,
(mǽru) ġeméting   monegum fíra,
hwylċ orleġ-hwíl   uncer Grendles
wearð on ðám wange,   þǽr hé worna fela
Siġe-Scyldingum   sorge ġefremede,
2005 yrmðe tó aldre,   iċ ðæt eal ġewræc,
swá (ne) beġylpan þearf   Grendeles mága
(ǽniġ) ofer Eorðan   úht-hlem þone,
sé ðe lengest leofað   láðan cynnes,
f(ǽcne) bifongen.   Iċ ðǽr furðum cwóm
2010 tó ðám hring-sele   Hróðgár grétan,
sóna mé se mǽra   mago Healfdenes,
syððan hé mód-sefan   mínne cúðe,

he gave me a seat   by his sons.
The company was joyous;   ne'er had I known
2015   under the vault of heaven   a hall-sitter's
mead-rejoicing greater.   The glorious queen,
the people's peace-weaver   would pass through the hall,
urged the youths   and gave gold-twisted rings
to the warriors,   ere she sought her seat.
2020   Sometimes to the youths,   Hrothgar's daughter
bore the ale-cup   to the earls.
Freawaru   the warriors called her,
when she   the golden goblet
gave to the proud heroes.   She is promised,
2025   young and adornèd with gold,   to the glad son of Froda;
the Scyldings' friend believes   that this will end the feud,
the realm's warden,   and the Witan deem it wise,
that with his wife   the war will end,
settle the slaughter.   However, seldom anywhere
2030   after the fall of folk,   even for a little while,
is the slaughter-spear put down,   though the bride is good!*

"Unhappy will be   the Heathobard lord
and all of the thegns   from that folk,
when he leads the lady   o'er the hall floor
2035   where noble Danes   dine at the tables.
On them,   ancient gold glistens,
ring-adornèd and hard   with the Heathobard's treasure,
carrying weapons   they once had wielded.

"'Til they had lost,   in the linden-play
2040   their belovèd companions   and their own lives.
Then, while drinking beer,   one speaks who sees a ringèd sword,
an old ash-wielder*   mindful of
the spear-death of warriors.   Stark of spirit,
he begins to question,   a young companion,
2045   tests his heart   and tries his mind,
awakens war-bale   with words like these,
'Do you, my dear friend,   recognize the blade
that your father   bore to battle
'neath his war-mask   in his final fight,
2050   dear iron,   where the Danes slew him
and held the battlefield,   where Withergyld* fell,
after the doom of heroes,   the hateful Scyldings?
Now the son,   of one of his slayers,,
boasting of his gold   goes across the hall,

wið his sylfes sunu   setl ġetǽhte.
Weorod wæs on wynne;   ne seah iċ wídan feorh
2015 under heofenes hwealf   heal-sittendra
medu-dréam máran.   Hwílum mǽru cwén,
friðu-sibb folca   flet eall ġeond-hwearf,
bǽdde byre ġeonge,   oft hío béah-wriðan
secge (sealde),   ǽr híe tó setle ġéong.
2020 Hwílum for (d)uguðe,   dóhtor Hróðgáres
eorlum on ende   ealu-wǽġe bær.
Þá iċ Fréaware   flet-sittende
nemnan hýrde,   þǽr hío næġled sinc
hæleðum sealde.   Sío ġeháten (is),
2025 ġeong gold-hroden,   gladum suna Fródan;
(h)afað þæs ġeworden   wine Scyldinga,
ríċes hyrde,   ond þæt rǽd talað,
þæt hé mid þý wífe   wæl-fǽhða dǽl,
sæċċa ġesette.   Oft nó seldan hwǽr
2030 æfter léod-hryre,   lýtle hwíle.
bon-gár búgeð,   þéah séo brýd duge!

"Mæġ þæs þonne ofþynċan   ðéoden Heaðo-Beardna
ond þeġna ġehwám   þára léoda,
þonne hé mid fǽmnan   on flett gǽð
2035 dryht-bearn Dena   duguða biwenede.
On him gladiað   gomelra láfe,
heard ond hring-mǽl   Heaðo-Beardna ġestréon,
þenden híe ðám wǽpnum   wealdan móston.

XXIX
"Oð ðæt híe forlǽddan   tó ðám lind-plegan
2040 swǽse ġesíðas   ond hyra sylfra feorh.
Þonne cwið æt béore   sé ðe béah ġesyhð,
eald æsc-wiga,   sé ðe eall ġeman,
gár-cwealm gumena   -him bið grim sefa-
onġinneð ġéomor-mód   ġeong(ne) cempan,
2045 þurh hreðra ġehyġd   hiġes cunnian,
wíġ-bealu weċċean   ond þæt word ácwyð,
'Meaht ðú, mín wine,   méċe ġecnáwan
þone þín fæder   tó ġefeohte bær
under here-gríman   hindeman síðe,
2050 dýre íren,   þǽr hyne Dene slógon,
wéoldon wæl-stówe,   syððan Wiðergyld lǽġ,
æfter hæleþa hryre,   hwate Scyldungas?
Nú hér þára banena   byre nát-hwylċes
frætwum hrémiġ   on flet gǽð,

133

2055　joyful of murder,　displaying the mathoms
　　　that by right　belong to you!'

　　　"Thus, he urges　every time
　　　with provoking words,　'til the time comes
　　　that the thegn of Freawaru,　for his father's deeds,
2060　from the bite of a blade,　must sleep in blood,
　　　lose his life　whilst the other
　　　escapes alive　to the land he knows.
　　　They are broken　on both sides,
　　　the oaths sworn by the earls.　Then in Ingeld
2065　deathly hatred wells within him,　and love for his wife,
　　　after surges of care,　grow cool.
　　　Thus I hold　the Heathobard's loyalty
　　　due to the Dane's　treacherous,
　　　a failed friendship.

　　　　　　　　　　　"I should speak further
2070　again of Grendel,　O giver of treasure,
　　　so that you might fully know　how the fight went,
　　　the hand-battle of heroes.　When Heaven's gem
　　　glided o'er the ground,　the wrathful gast came,
　　　the terrible night-stalker　to seek us out,
2075　where we held the hall,　unhurt.
　　　That was, for Hondscio　a hasty death,
　　　a baleful fate;　he was the first to fall,
　　　girded champion.　Grendel slew
　　　that mighty thegn　with his murderous maw,
2080　the belovèd man's　body was all devoured.
　　　Yet none the earlier,　he, empty-handed,
　　　the bloody-toothed bane,　mindful of bale,
　　　wished to walk　from the golden hall.
　　　He who was famed for ferocity,　attacked me,
2085　gripped in his grim grasp.　A sack hung there,
　　　deep and strange,　held fast with cunning clasps,
　　　by wile wrought,　it was all made
　　　by devilish craft　of Dragon hide.
　　　There inside,　innocent men were.
2090　The deathly doer　wished to devour
　　　many others,　only he could not do so,
　　　when I, in ire　upright stood.
　　　'Tis too long to recount　how I that ravager of the folk
　　　made pay for each　of his evils,
2095　where I was, my lord,　by the people
　　　honored for my works.　Away he fled,

　134　

2055   morðres ġylpe(ð),   ond þone máðþum byreð
        þone þe ðú mid rihte   rǽdan sceoldest!'

        "Manað swá ond myndgað   mǽla ġehwylċe
        sárum wordum,   oð ðæt sǽl cymeð
        þæt se fǽmnan þeġn   fore fæder dǽdum,
2060   æfter billes bite,   blód-fág swefeð,
        ealdres scyldiġ   him se óðer þonan
        losað (l)ifiġende   con him land ġeare.
        Þonne bíoð (b)rocene   on bá healfe,
        áð-sweor(d) eorla.   Syð(ðan) Ingelde
2065   weallað wæl-níðas,   ond him wíf-lufan.
        æfter ċear-wælmum   cólran weorðað.
        Þý iċ Heaðo-Bear(d)na   hyldo ne telġe
        dryht-sibbe dǽl   Denum unfǽcne,
        fréond-scipe fæstne.

                      "Iċ sceal forð sprecan
2070   ġén ymbe Grendel,   þæt ðú ġeare cunne,
        sinces brytta,   tó hwan syððan wearð
        hond-rǽs hæleða.   Syððan Heofones ġim
        glád ofer grundas,   gæst yrre cwóm,
        eatol ǽfen-grom   úser néosan,
2075   ðǽr wé ġesunde   sǽl weardodon.
        Þǽr wæs Hondsció   hil(d) onsǽġe,
        feorh-bealu fǽġum;   hé fyrmest læġ,
        gyrded cempa.   Him Grendel wearð,
        mǽrum mag(u)þeġne   tó múð-bonan;
2080   léofes mannes   líċ eall forswealg.
        Nó ðý ǽr út ðá ġén   ídel-hende,
        bona blódiġ-tóð,   bealewa ġemyndiġ,
        of ðám gold-sele   gongan wolde,
        ac hé mæġnes róf   mín costode,
2085   grápode ġear(o)folm.   Glóf hangode,
        síd ond syllíċ,   searo-bendum fæst;
        sío wæs orðoncum   eall ġeġyrwed
        déofles cræftum   ond Dracan fellum.
        Hé meċ þǽr on innan   unsynniġne.
2090   Díor dǽd-fruma   ġedón wolde
        maniġra sumne,   hyt ne mihte swá,
        syððan iċ on yrre   upp-riht ástód.
        Tó lang ys tó reċċenne   hú i(ċ ð)ám léod-sceaðan
        yfla ġehwylċes   (o)nd-léan forġeald,
2095   þǽr iċ, þéoden mín,   þíne léode
        weorðode weorcum.   Hé on weġ losade,

to enjoy his life   for a little while,
but behind him   he left the stronger
hand in Heorot.   Heartsick thence,
2100 the pitiful one fell   to the floor of the mere.

"For my fight   the Scylding's friend
rewarded me plentifully   with plated gold,
many mathoms   when morning came
and we had   sat at symbel.
2105 There was music and mirth.   The old Scylding
told many tales   of ages long past,
while the battle-bold one   played the harp,
old glee-wood,   and sung songs,
true and sorrowful,   or sellic spells*,
2110 rightly related   to the open-hearted king.
At times he began,   bound with his age,
the old warrior   to lament his lost youth,
his battle-strength;   his breast welled up,
when he wise in winters,   was mindful of his deeds.

2115 "So we were in the hall   the whole of the day
and were fain   'til fell
another night.   Then came swiftly
Grendel's mother   ready for revenge,
set forth sorrowfully.   Death had taken her son,
2120 through the war-hate of the Weders.   The fearsome woman
avenged her bairn   when a battle-man she
savagely slew.   From Æschere was,
wise old counselor,   life lost.
Nor could they,   when morning came,
2125 death-weary,   the Danish people,
burn his body   on a bale-fire,
belovèd man,   for she bore away his body
in the fiend's embrace   under the mountain stream.
'Twas a bitter hurt   for Hrothgar
2130 which the people's lord   long received.
Then the leader,   by your life implored, with troubled mind,
that I would   in the welling waters
fight the foe   and risk my life
by achieving glory;   he said he would grant me gold.
2135 Then I, in the welling waters,   as is widely known,
found the grim and ghastly   guardian of the deep.
There we grappled   hand-to-hand for a while,
and blood billowed   in the flood.
I hewed off her head   in the underwater hall

lýtle hwíle   líf-wynna br(éa)c,
hwæþre him sío swíðre   swaðe weardade
hand on Hiorte,   ond hé héan ðonan,
2100   módes ġeómor   mere-grund ġeféoll.

"Mé þone wæl-ræs   wine Scildunga
fǽttan golde   fela léanode,
manegum máðmum   syððan merġen cóm
ond wé tó symble   ġeseten hæfdon.
2105   Þǽr wæs ġidd ond gléo.   Gomela Scilding
fela-fricġende   feorran rehte,
hwílum hilde-déor   hearpan wynne,
gomelwudu grétte,   hwílum ġyd áwræc,
sóð ond sárlíċ,   hwílum syllíċ spell,
2110   rehte æfter rihte   rúm-heort cyning.
Hwílum eft ongan,   eldo ġebunden,
gomel gúð-wiga   ġioguðe cwíðan,
hilde-strengo;   hreðer inne wéoll
þonne hé wintrum fród,   worn ġemunde.

2115   "Swá wé þǽr inne   andlangne dæġ
níode náman,   oð ðæt niht becwóm
óðer tó yldum.   Þá wæs eft hraðe
ġearo gyrn-wræc   Grendeles módor,
síðode sorh-full.   Sunu déað fornam,
2120   wíġ-hete Wedra.   Wíf unhýre
hyre bearn ġewræc   beorn ácwealde
ellenlíċe;   þǽr wæs Æschere,
fródan fyrn-witan,   feorh úðgenge.
Nóðer hý hine ne móston,   syððan merġen cwóm,
2125   déað-wériġne   Denia léode
bronde forbærnan,   né on bǽl hladan
léofne mannan,   hío þæt líċ ætbær
féondes fæð(me)   under firġen-stréam.
Þæt wæs Hróðgáre   hréowa tornost
2130   þára þe léod-fruman   lange beġeáte.
Þá se ðéoden meċ   ðíne lífe
healsode hréoh-mód   þæt iċ on holma ġeþring
eorl-scipe efnde,   ealdre ġenéðde,
mǽrðo fremede,   hé mé méde ġehét.
2135   Iċ ðá ðæs wælmes,   þé is wíde cúð,
grimne gryrelícne   grund-hyrde fond;
þǽr unc hwíle wæs   hand ġemǽne,
holm heolfre wéoll,   ond iċ héafde beċearf
in ðám grundsele   Grendeles módor

137

2140   with the greedy edge   of a Giant's sword,
    and retained my life.   I was not yet doomed to die.
    Afterwards, the earl's defense   gave to me
    many mathoms,   the son of Healfdene.

    "Thus, the people's king   lived according to custom,
2145   and I was   rightfully rewarded,
    meed for my might;   he gave me mathoms,
    the son of Healfdene   for mine own holding.
    Now, these, warrior-king,   I wish to bring
    and gladly give to you.   Still, in you alone
2150   can I find favor,   as I have few
    closer kin than you,   Hygelac!"

    Then he bade his men   bring in the boar standard,
    the war-steep helm,   the hoary byrnie,
    and the excellent battle-sword.   Afterwards, he spake thus,
2155   'To me, Hrothgar   gave this war-gear,
    wise lord,   and with words bade me
    first to tell you   its tale.
    He told me that once   it was held by Heorogar,
    the Scylding lord,   for a long while.
2160   No sooner did he to his son   wish to leave it,
    to fierce Heoroweard*,   for he was faithful to him,
    the battle-byrnie.   Use it well!'"

    Then I've been told that four horses   followed the treasure,
    eager and swift   steeds all,
2165   apple-fallow*;   he gave those gifts,
    mares and mathoms.   So should kin be;
    they should not weave   a web of malice
    or by cunning craft,   fashion death
    of hand-companions.   Hygelac,
2170   his nephew held   in hard strife,
    and each was mindful   of the other's well-being.

    I then heard that to Hygd   he gave the neck-ring,
    the wondrous mathom   that Wealhtheow had given him,
    atheling's daughter,   and three steeds also,
2175   supple and saddle-bright.   Afterwards,
    that glittering torc   graced her neck.

    Bold was the bairn   of Ecgtheow,
    a man known   for mighty war-deeds,

2140　éacnum ecgum,　　unsófte þonan
　　　　feorh oðferede.　　Næs iċ fǽġe þá ġýt.
　　　　Ac mé eorla hléo　　eft ġesealde
　　　　máðma meniġeo,　　maga Healfdenes.

　　　　　　　　　XXX
　　　　"Swá se ðéod-kyning　　þéawum lyfde,
2145　nealles iċ ðám léanum　　forloren hæfde,
　　　　mæġnes méde,　　ac hé mé (máðma)s ġeaf,
　　　　sunu Healfdenes　　on (mín)ne sylfes dóm;
　　　　ðá iċ ðé, beorn-cyning,　　bringan wylle,
　　　　éstum ġeýwan.　　Ġén is eall æt ðé
2150　lissa ġelong,　　iċ lýt hafo
　　　　héafod-mága　　nefne, Hyġelác ðeċ!"

　　　　Hét ðá in beran　　eafor héafod-seġn,
　　　　heaðo-stéapne helm,　　háre byrnan,
　　　　gúð-sweord ġeatoliċ,　　ġyd æfter wræc:
2155　'Mé ðis hilde-sceorp　　Hróðgár sealde,
　　　　snotra fengel;　　sume worde hét,
　　　　þæt iċ his ǽrest ðe　　est ġesæġde:
　　　　cwæð þæt hyt hæfde　　Hiorogár cyning,
　　　　léod Scyldunga　　lange hwíle.
2160　Nó ðý ǽr suna sínum　　syllan wolde,
　　　　hwatum Heorowearde,　　þéah hé him hold wǽre,
　　　　bréost-ġewǽdu.　　Brúc ealles well!'

　　　　Hýrde iċ þæt þám frætwum　　féower méaras
　　　　lungre ġelíċe　　lást weardode,
2165　æppel-fealuwe;　　hé him ést ġetéah
　　　　méara ond máðma.　　Swá sceal mǽġ dón;
　　　　nealles inwit-net　　óðrum breġdon
　　　　dyrnum cræfte,　　déað rén(ian)
　　　　hond-ġesteallan.　　Hyġeláce wæs
2170　níða heardum,　　nefa swýðe hold,
　　　　ond ġehwæðer óðrum　　hróþra ġemyndiġ.

　　　　Hýrde iċ þæt hé ðone heals-béah　　Hyġde ġesealde,
　　　　wrǽtlícne wundur-máððum,　　ðone þe him Wealhðéo ġeaf,
　　　　ðéod(nes) dohtor,　　þrío wicg somod
2175　swancor ond sadol-beorht;　　hyre syððan wæs
　　　　æfter béah-ðeġe　　bré(o)st ġeweorðod.

　　　　Swá bealdode　　bearn Ecgðéowes,
　　　　guma gúðum cúð,　　gódum dǽdum,

and honor.   At his ale, he slew not
2180 hearth-companions;   his heart was not troubled.
      Of Mankind,   his might was greatest,
      that gracious gift   that God had sent him,
      he held bravery.   Long was he low
      in the sight of the Geatish sons   and deemed worthless*.
2185 He was considered of no consequence   on the mead-bench,
      nor would the Weder lord   grant him much honor.
      Men said   that he was slack,
      an insignificant atheling,   but a turn-around came,
      to the glorious men   for each of their grievances.

2190 Then the protector of earls   bade be brought,
      the warrior king,   Hrethel's heirloom,
      garnished with gold.   Among the Geats there was not
      a more splendid treasure   in the shape of a sword
      than he on Beowulf's   lap laid.
2195 He gave him   seven thousand hides of land*,
      hold-fast and high seat.   Theirs was both together,
      lordship o'er the lands   of their ancestors,
      inheritors on the Earth,   but the other was greater,
      he who ruled   that wide realm.

dréah æfter dóme, nealles druncne slóg
2180 heorð-ġenéatas; næs him hréoh sefa,
ac hé Man-cynnes mǽste cræfte
ġin-fæstan ġife þé him God sealde
héold hilde-déor. Héan wæs lange,
swá hyne Ġéata bearn gódne ne tealdon.
2185 Né hyne on medo-benċe miċles wyrðne
drihten We(der)a ġedón wolde.
Swýðe oft (sǽġ)don, þæt hé sléac wǽre,
æðeling unfrom. Edwenden cwóm
tír-éadigum menn torna ġehwylċes.

2190 Hét ðá eorla hléo in ġefetian,
heaðo-róf cyning, Hréðles láfe
golde ġeġyrede. Næs mid Ġéatum ðá
sinc-máðþum sélra on sweordes hád
þæt hé on Bíowulfes bearm áleġde,
2195 ond him ġesealde seofan þúsendo,
bold ond brego-stól. Him wæs bám samod
on ðám léod-scipe lond ġecynde,
eard éðel-riht, óðrum swíðor
síde ríċe, þám ðǽr sélra wæs.

Part II
The Lord of Geatland

Chapter XV
The Wrath of the Wyrm

2200   Then it came   to lapse in later days
          that while harrying,   Hygelac fell
          and Heardred was   hewn to death
          by battle-blades   behind the shield-wall.
          They sought him   at the forefront of his folk,
2205   the hardy warriors   of the Heatho-Scylfings*,
          and evilly attacked   Hereric's nephew.
          Then to Beowulf   that broad realm
          passed.   Power he held,
          the wise king,   for fifty winters.
2210   Well did he   ward the folk!

          Until, one dark night,   a Dragon rose.
          On the high heath,   he watched his hoard,
          from a steep stone barrow*.   A path lay underneath,
          unknown to men,   but inside one went,
2215   I know not who,   and found
          the heathen hoard.   In his hand he took
          a golden goblet.   He did not give it back,
          but stole away   as he slept,
          When it woke,   it discovered it had fallen prey
2220   to the thieving ways of Men   and was filled with wrath.

          He wielded not   his own will,
          when he entered   the earthen hoard
          in his dire distress,   a thrall* who belonged
          to a son of heroes.   From hateful blows he fled,
2225   and seeking safety,   he entered the barrow.

          The sinful man   soon found
          the sleeper,   and he stood in terror.
          Yet the wretched one   [went on
          and claimed   a golden cup,

144

2200   Eft þæt ġeíode   ufaran dógrum
        hilde-hlæmmum,   syððan Hyġelác læġ
        ond Hear(dr)éde   hilde-méċeas
        under bord-hréoðan   tó bonan wurdon,
        ðá hyne ġesóhtan   on siġe-þéode,
2205   hearde hilde-frecan,   Heaðo-Scilfingas,
        níða ġenǽġdan   nefan Hereríċes.
        Syððan Béowulfe   bráde ríċe
        on hand ġehwearf.   Hé ġehéold tela
        fíftiġ wintra;   wæs ðá fród cyning,
2210   eald éþel-weard,

                     oð ðæt án ongan
        deorcum nihtum,   Draca rícs(i)an.
        Sé ðe on héa(um) h(æþ)e   hord beweotode,
        stán-beorh stéa(p)ne;   stíġ under læġ
        eldum uncúð.   Þǽr on innan ġíong
2215   níða nát-hwyl(ċ,   ond nea) ġeféng
        hǽðnum horde.   Hond (ġewriþenne)
        since fáhne,   hé þæt syððan (bemáð),
        þ(eah) ð(e hé) slæpende,   (be)syre(d hæf)de
        þéo(f)es cræfte;   þæt síe ðiod (onfand)
2220   búfolc beorna,   þæt hé ġebolge(n) wæs.

XXXI

        Nealles mid ġewéoldum   Wyrm-horda(n) cræft,
        sylfes willum,   sé ðe him sáre ġesceód,
        ac for þréa-nédlan   þé(ow) nát-hwylċes
        hæleða bearna.   Hete-swengeas fléoh,
2225   (ærnes) þea(rfe)   ond ðǽr inne (f)eal(h.)

        Secg syn-bysiġ   sóna o(nfunde),
        þæt (ġean) ðám ġyste   (gry)rebr(ó)g(a) stód.
        Hwæðre (fyren)sceapen   . . . .
        . . . .

2230   ere he escaped the barrow,]   out of fear.
    Of mathoms,   there were many,
    ancient gold   in the earth house.
    Long ago, an earl   of some forgotten race
    left there the legacy   of his people*,
2235   heedfully he had   hidden away there
    dear gold.   Death had taken them all
    in earlier times,   'til there was only one
    who still lived,   the last of that folk,
    he wept for his friends,   but wished to delay that much,
2240   that he could enjoy for a little while,   the long-held treasure.

    The barrow   had been built
    on the wold   near the water,
    new on the ness,   made fast by hard work;
    he bore inside   the earl's treasure,
2245   a hoard   of hand-twisted rings
    and fretted gold.   A few words he spoke,
    "Hold now, earth,   since heroes cannot
    now have what earls had owned!   Lo, erst from you
    good men had taken it,   but they fell in baleful battle;
2250   all were claimed   by cruel death,
    my people,   after they gave me all this.
    There are none now to know   the joys of the hall,
    none who can wield   a blade in battle-play,
    or cleanse the gilded cup;   the drinkers have gone.
2255   And the hard helm,   bright with gold,
    stripped of its plates;   the polishers are asleep,
    they who could   burnish the battle-masks.
    And the byrnies,   which had, in battle,
    withstood the iron bite   and the breaking of shields,
2260   decay with their bearers.   The ringèd byrnie
    fares not widely   with the war-chief
    by the hero's side!   Nor was there the harp's joy,
    the gladness of the glee-wood,   nor the good hawk
    that soars through the hall,   nor the swift steed
2265   that stamps in the burg!   Baleful death has
    sent forth   my kith and kin!"

    Sorrowful of mind.   he bemoaned his grief,
    all alone.   Unblithely, he watched o'er the howe,
    both day and night,   'til death's surge
2270   o'er-whelmed his heart.   Hoard-joy he had,
    the old evil-doer,   when erst he found,

2230   . . . . . .   se fǽr beġeat,
        sinc-fæt (sohte).   Þǽr wæs swylcra fela
        in ðám eorð(se)le   ǽr-ġestréona,
        Swá hý on ġeár-dagum   gumena nát-hwylċ
        eormen-láfe   æþelan cynnes,
2235   þanc-hycgende   þǽr ġehýdde,
        déore máðmas.   Ealle híe déað fornam
        ǽrran mǽlum,   ond sé án ðá ġén
        léoda duguðe,   sé ðǽr lengest hwearf,
        weard wine-ġéomor,   (w)énde þæs yldan,
2240   þæt hé lýtel fæc   long-ġestréona
        brúcan móste.

                      Beorh eal ġearo
        wunode on wonge   wæter-ýðum néah,
        níwe be næsse,   nearo-cræftum fæst;
        þǽr on innan bær   eorl-ġestréona,
2245   hringa hyrde   ha(n)dwyrðne dǽl,
        fǽttan goldes.   Féa worda cwæð,
        "Heald þú nú, hrúse,   nú hæleð ne m(ó)ston
        eorla ǽhte!   Hwæt, hyt ǽr on ðé
        góde beġeáton;   gúð-déað fornam,
2250   feorh-bealo frécne,   fýrena ġehwylċne
        léoda mínra,   þá (me) ðe þis (líf) ofġeaf.
        Ġesáwon sele-dréam,   náh hwá sweord weġe,
        oððe f(æ)ġ(rie)   fǽted wǽġe,
        drynċ-fæt déore;   dug(uð) ellor seóc.
2255   Sceal se hearda helm,   (hyr)stedgolde,
        fǽtum befeallen;   feormiend swefað,
        þá ðe beado-gríman   býwan sceoldon.
        Ġé swylċe séo here-pád,   sío æt hilde ġebád,
        ofer borda ġebræc   bite írena,
2260   brosnað æfter beorne.   Ne mæġ byrnan hring
        æfter wíġ-fruman   wíde féran
        hæleðum be healfe!   Næs hearpan wyn,
        gomen gléo-béames,   né gód hafoc
        ġeond sæl swingeð,   né se swifta mearh
2265   burh-stede béateð!,   Bealo-cwealm hafað
        fela feorh-cynna   f(orð) onsended!"

        Swá ġíomor-mód   giohðo mǽnde,
        án æfter eallum,   unblíðe hwé(arf)
        dæġes ond nihtes,   oð ðæt déaðes wylm
2270   hrán æt heortan.   Hord-wynne fond,
        eald úht-sceaða   opene standan,

scales burning,   the barrow standing open,
the fearsome Dragon   who flies at night,
enfolded by fire.   Earth-dwellers
2275 greatly dreaded him.   'Twas his doom to seek
the hidden hoard,   ward the heathen gold,
wise in winters;   by no whit was he better for that!

So, the Wyrm,   for three-hundred winters,
held the hoard   beneath the earth,
2280 very strong,   until one awoke him,
a man who in his pride,   bore to his liege lord
the adornèd cup,   in a plea for peace.
Thus was   the barrow broken
and the ring-hoard borne off.   A boon was granted
2285 to the pitiful man;   the lord looked at,
for the first time,   that which was fashioned long ago.

When the Wyrm awoke,   wrath was kindled.
He rose like smoke o'er the stone.   The stark-hearted one
found the thief's footprints;   he had stepped too far
2290 in his cunning craft   by the Dragon's head!
So, may one who is utterly doomed,   with the Wielder's grace,
easily survive   evil and exile!

Then went   the warden of the hoard,
eagerly o'er the ground   to find the man,
2295 the one who had sorely grieved him   whilst he slept.
Hot and fierce-minded,   he flew above the howe
all around,   but no man was there
in the wilderness,   yet 'twas war he craved;
he was eager for battle!   To the barrow he returned,
2300 seeking the costly cup.   There he found
that some man   had searched through his gold,
his high treasure.   The hoard-ward waited
anxiously   'til eventide came.
Wroth was   the warden of the barrow;
2305 he was fain   to repay them with flame
for the dear drinking-cup.   Then the day had fled,
as the Wyrm had wished.   By the wall he lay no more;
he did not wait,   but fared forth
spouting fire and flame.   'Twas a fearful beginning
2310 for the folk on the fold,   as it soon was
for the giver of gold,   a terrible end.

sé ðe byrnende   biorgas séċeð,
nacod níð-Draca,   nihtes fléogeð,
fýre befangen.   Hyne fold-búend
2275   . . . . nan.   Hé ġeseċian sceall
(hláw under h)rúsan,   þǽr hé hǽðen gold,
waráð wintrum fród;   ne byð him wihte ðý sél!

Swá se ðéod-sceaða   þréo-hund wintra
héold on hrúsa(n)   hord-ærna sum,
2280   éacen-cræftiġ,   oð ðæt hyne án ábealh,
mon on móde,   man-dryhtne bær
fǽted wǽġe,   frioðo-wǽre bæd
hláford sínne.   Ðá wæs hord rásod,
onboren béaga hord.   Béne ġetíðad
2285   féa-sceaftum men;   fréa scéawode
fíra fyrn-ġeweorc   forman síðe.

Þá Wyrm onwóc,   wróht wæs ġeníwad.
Stonc ðá æfter stáne,   stearc-heort onfand
féondes fót-lást;   hé tó forð ġestóp
2290   dyrnan cræfte   Dracan héafde néah!
Swá mæġ (a)nfǽġe   éaðe ġedíġan
wéan ond wræc-síð,   sé ðe Waldendes
hyldo ġehealdeþ!

         Hord-weard sóhte
ġeorne æfter grunde   wolde guman findan,
2295   þone þe him on sweofote   sáre ġetéode.
Hát ond hréoh-mód,   hl(ǽ)wum oft ymbe hwearf
ealne útan-weardne;   né ðǽr æniġ mon
on þám wéstenne,   hwæðre wíġes ġefeh;
bea(do) weorces!   Hwílum on beorh æthwearf,
2300   sinc-fæt sóhte;   hé þæt sóna onfand,
ðæt hæfde gumena sum   goldes ġefandod,
héah-ġestréona.   Hord-weard onbád
earfoðlíċe   oð ðæt ǽfen cwóm.
Wæs ðá ġebolgen   beorges hyrde;
2305   wolde (s)e láða   líġe forġyldan
drinċ-fæt dýre.   Þá wæs dæġ sceacen,
Wyrme on willan.   Nó on wealle læġ;
bídan wolde,   ac mid bǽle fór,
fýre ġefýsed.   Wæs se fruma eġeslíċ
2310   léodum on lande,   swá hyt lungre wearð
on hyra sinc-ġifan,   sáre ġeendod.

Then the fiend   spewed fire
and bright homes burned.   The blaze rose up
and engulfed the land.   No living thing
2315   did the loathly flier   leave in its wake.
Widely was the Wyrm's   warring seen,
the fiend's fury,   near and far,
how the guileful scather   of the Geatish people
hated and hindered.   Then he shot back to his hoard,
2320   to the hidden hall   ere break of day.
The men of the land   had been licked by flame,
with blazing bale-fire.   In the barrow he trusted,
his war-skill and his walls,   but he was deluded in his belief!

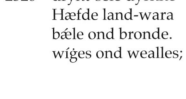

XXXII

    Ðá se gæst ongan   glédum spíwan,
beorht hofu bærnan.   Bryne-léoma stód
eldum on andan.   Nó ðǽr áht cwices
2315 láð lyft-floga   lǽfan wolde.
    Wæs þæs Wyrmes wíg   wíde ġesýne,
nearo-fáges níð   néan ond feorran,
hú se gúð-sceaða   Ġéata léode
hatode ond hýnde.   Hord eft gescéat,
2320 dryht-sele dyrnne   ǽr dæġes hwíle.
    Hæfde land-wara   líġe befangen,
bǽle ond bronde.   Beorges ġetruwode,
wíġes ond wealles;   him séo wén ġeléah!

Chapter XVI
Tales of Times Past

          To Beowulf was   this bale made known,
2325   suddenly in sooth,   that his own home,
          the best of buildings,   melted in burning waves,
          the Geatish gift-stool.   That gave to the good old king
          a heavy heart,   the greatest of mind-sorrows.
          The wise one   thought that the Wielder
2330   he embittered   by breaking the Old Laws,
          the everlasting Lord.   In his breast
          welled dark thoughts;   such was not his wont!
          The stronghold of the folk,   the fire-Drake had
          destroyed with flame,   the fortress
2235   down by the waves.   Then the war-king,
          wielder of the Weder-folk   plotted revenge.
          His smiths,   the protector of warriors bade work
          a shield all of iron*,   the lord of earls,
          a wondrous war-board,   for well did he know
2240   that wood worked not   against fire,
          linden would not help.   The old atheling
          must abide the end   of his loaned days,
          of life in this world   and the Wyrm together,
          though he had long   held that hoard!

2345   The ring lord   reckoned it shameful
          that he should follow the wide-flier   with a host,
          a broad army;   battle he feared not,
          nor did he dread   the Wyrm's warring,
          boldness and brawn.   Before that
2350   many evils   had he endured
          and hand-struggles,   since he Hrothgar's,
          the heroic king,   hall had cleansed,
          when he grappled   with Grendel
          and his loathly mother.   Not the least was
2355   the hand-battle   where Hygelac was slain,
          where the Geatish king was killed   in the clash of battle,

       Þá wæs Bíowulfe   bróga ġecýðed
2325 snúde tó sóðe,   þæt his sylfes h(á)m,
       bolda sélest,   bryne-wylmum mealt,
       ġif-stól Ġéata.   Þæt ðám gódan wæs
       hréow on hreðre,   hyġe-sorga mǽst.
       Wénde se wísa   þæt hé Wealdende
2330 ofer Ealde Riht,   Éċean Dryhtne,
       bitre ġebulge.   Bréost innan wéoll
       þéostrum ġeþoncum;   swá him ġeþýwe ne wæs!
       Hæfde líġ-Draca   léoda fæsten,
       éa-lond útan,   eorð-weard ðone
2335 glédum forgrunden.   Him ðæs gúð-cyning,
       Wedera þíoden   wræce leornode.
       Heht him þá ġewyrċean   wíġendra hléo
       eall-írenne,   eorla dryhten,
       wíġ-bord wrǽtlíċ;   wisse hé ġearwe
2340 þæt him holt-wudu   he(lpan) ne meahte,
       lind wið líġe.   Sceolde (lǽn)daga,
       æþeling ǽr-gód   ende ġebídan,
       worulde lífes,   ond se Wyrm somod,
       þéah ðe hord-welan   héolde lange!

2345 Oferhogode ðá   hringa fengel
       þæt hé þone wíd-flogan   weorode ġesóhte,
       sídan herġe;   nó hé him þá sæċċe ondréd,
       né him þæs Wyrmes wíġ   for wiht dyde,
       eafoð ond ellen.   Forðon hé ǽr fela
2350 nearo néðende   níða ġedíġde,
       hilde-hlemma,   syððan hé Hróðgáres,
       sigor-éadiġ secg,   sele fǽlsode,
       ond æt gúðe forgráp   Grendeles mǽgum
       láðan cynnes.   Nó þæt lǽsest wæs
2355 hond-ġemot(a),   þǽr mon Hyġelác slóh,
       syððan Ġéata cyning   gúðe rǽsum,

the lord and friend of the folk;   in Frisia
Hrethel's son   in the sword-play died,
beaten by blades.   Thence Beowulf escaped*,
2360   by his skill alone,   he made the sea voyage.
He held in his arms   thirty iron swords,
battle-gear of earls,   when he braved the waters!
The Hetware* had no reason   to boast
of the fight   where they fared against him,
2365   bearing linden boards,   for few survived,
when the hero   sought out his home!

Then he sailed o'er the seal's path,   the son of Ecgtheow,
wretched and alone,   back to his land.
There Hygd offered him   hoard and realm,
2370   rings and treasure-seat,   for she trusted not
that her son   could stand against
foreign foes,   now that Hygelac was dead.
Yet by no means   could that meager nation
urge the atheling   to agree
2375   to become   Heardred's liege lord,
and claim the kingdom   of the Geats;
yet, he, of the folk,   offered him friendly counsel,
and showed him honor,   'til he grew older,
and wielded the Weder-Geats.   To him, wretches
2380   sought across the sea.   The sons of Ohthere*
had rebelled against the rule   of the Scylfing's helm,
the most splendid   of sea-kings,
who dealt out riches   in the Swedish realm,
bright lord.   Thus it became Heardred's end.
2385   For his hospitality,   he was hewn to death
by the swing of a sword,   Hygelac's son,
but he went back,   the bairn of Ongentheow,
to seek his home   after Heardred fell,
and left Beowulf   as the lord of the Geats,
2390   to hold the gift seat.   That was a good king!*

He for the fall of his lord,   retribution remembered
in after days.   To Eadgils he became
a fast friend,   and sent forces
over the water   to the son of Ohthere,
2395   with warriors and weapons.   He had vengeance then
from that bitter battle,   when he took the king's life.

154

fréa-wine folca;   Fréslondum on
Hréðles eafora   hioro-drynċum swealt,
bille ġebéaten.   Þonan Bíowulf cóm
2360   sylfes cræfte,   sund-nytte dréah;
hæfde him on earme   (ecgas) þrítiġ
hilde-ġeatwa,   þá hé tó holme (stá)g.
Nealles Hetware   hrémġe þorf(t)on
féðe-wíġes   þé him foran onġéan,
2365   linde bǽron;   lýt eft becwóm
fram þám hild-frecan   hámes níosan!

Oferswam þá sioleða bigong,   sunu Ecgðéowes,
earm án-haga   eft tó léodum;
þǽr him Hyġd ġebéad   hord ond ríċe,
2370   béagas ond brego-stól,   bearne ne truwode
þæt hé wið æl-fylċum   éþel-stólas
healdan cúðe,   ðá wæs Hyġelác déad.
Nó ðý ǽr féa-sceafte   findan meahton
æt ðám æðelinge   æniġe ðinga
2375   þæt hé Heardréde   hláford wǽre,
oððe þone cyne-dóm   ċíosan wolde;
hwæðre hé him on folce,   fréond-lárum héold,
éstum mid áre,   oð ðæt hé yldra wearð,
Weder-Ġéatum wéold.   Hyne wræc-mæcgas
2380   ofer sǽ sóhtan.   Suna Óhteres
hæfdon hý forhealden   helm Scylfinga,
þone sélestan   sǽ-cyninga
þára (ðe) in Swío-ríċe   sinc brytnade,
mǽrne þéoden.   Him þæt tó mearce wearð.
2385   Hé þǽr (f)or feorme   feorh-wunde hléat,
sweordes swengum,   sunu Hyġeláces,
ond him eft ġewát   Ongenðíowes bearn
hámes níosan   syððan Heardréd læġ,
lét ðone brego-stól   Bíowulf healdan,
2390   Ġéatum wealdan.   Þæt wæs gód cyning!

XXXIII

Sé ðæs léod-hryres,   léan ġemunde
uferan dógrum,   Éadġilse wearð
féa-sceaftum féond;   folce ġestepte
ofer sǽ síde   sunu Óhteres,
2395   wigum ond wǽpnum.   Hé ġewræc syððan
ċealdum ċear-síðum,   cyning ealdre binéat.

Thus he had survived   each of these struggles,
cruel clashes,   the son of Ecgtheow,
with valorous deeds,   'til one day
2400   when he must   wrestle with the Wyrm.

Then went he, one of twelve,   seething with anger,
the lord of the Geats   to seek the Serpent.
He heard   how this feud arose,
bale for the men,   when the bright cup
2405   was laid on his lap   by the thief's hand.
Beowulf was in that band   the thirteenth member*,
for he who started this strife,   was brought as a captive.
Mournful in mind,   he was bade hence,
reluctantly to lead them   o'er the land
2410   to the earth-hall   that he alone knew,
the deep howe   near the surging sea,
the whelming waves.   Inside, 'twas full
of gems and twisted gold.   A grim warden,
war-keen,   kept those golden mathoms,
2415   old under the Earth.   That was no easy task,
to get the gold,   for any man!

The battle-hard king   sat on the headland
and bid his hearth-companions   be hale,
gold-friend of the Geats.   Gloom he felt in his heart,
2420   wavering and death-bound.   His doom was near,
ready to embrace   the old one,
seeking his soul-hoard   to tear asunder,
life from his lich.   Not for long
would his spirit   be bound by flesh.

2425   Beowulf spake,   the son of Ecgtheow,
"Many struggles have I survived   in my youth,
and all of those battles   I remember.
I was but seven winters old,   when the wielder of treasure,
the friend of the folk,   took me from my father,
2430   for Hrethel King   to have and to hold;
he gave me gold and feasts,   remembered kinship.
Nor did he find me lower,   whilst I lived there,
a bairn in the burg,   than his own sons,
Herebeald, Hæthcyn   and Hygelac.
2435   The eldest one,   unfittingly,
by his brother's act,   was his death-bed was laid*,
when Hæthcyn   with a horn-bow
his lord and friend   felled with an arrow;

Swá hé níða ġehwane ġenesen hæfde,
slíðra ġeslyhta, sunu Ecgðíowes,
ellen-weorca, oð ðone ánne dæġ
2400 þé hé wið þám Wyrme ġewegan sceolde.

Ġewát þá twelfa sum, torne ġebolgen,
dryhten Ġéata Dracan scéawian.
Hæfde þá ġefrúnen hwanan sío fǽhð árás,
bealo-níð biorna, him tó bearme cwóm
2405 máðþum-fæt mǽre þurh ðæs meldan hond.
Sé wæs on ðám ðréate þreottéoða secg,
sé ðæs orleġes ór onstealde.
Hæft hyġe-ġiómor, sceolde héan ðonon,
wong wísian. Hé ofer willan ġíong
2410 tó ðæs ðe hé eorð-sele ánne wisse,
hlǽw under hrúsan holm-wylme néh,
ýð-ġewinne. Sé wæs innan full
wrǽtta ond wíra. Weard unhíore,
ġearo gúð-freca gold-máðmas héold,
2415 eald under eorðan. Næs þæt ýðe ċéap.
tó ġegangenne, gumena ǽnigum!

Ġesæt ðá on næsse níð-heard cyning
þenden hǽlo ábéad heorð-ġenéatum,
gold-wine Ġéata. Him wæs ġeómor sefa,
2420 wǽfre ond wæl-fús, Wyrd unġemete néah,
sé ðone gomelan grétan sceolde,
seċean sáwle hord sundur ġedǽlan,
líf wið líċe. Nó þon lange wæs
feorh æþelinges flǽsce bewunden.

2425 Bíowulf maþelade, bearn Ecgðéowes,
"Fela iċ on ġiogoðe guð-rǽsa ġenæs,
orleġ-hwíla, iċ þæt eall ġemon.
Iċ wæs syfan-wintre, þá meċ sinca baldor,
fréa-wine folca, æt mínum fæder ġenam,
2430 héold meċ ond hæfde Hréðel cyning;
ġeaf mé sinc ond symbel, sibbe ġemunde.
Næs iċ him tó lífe, láðra ówihte,
beorn in burgum, þonne his bearna hwylċ,
Herebeald ond Hæðcyn oððe Hyġelác mín.
2435 Wæs þám yldestan, unġedéfelíċe,
mǽġes dǽdum morþor-bed stréd,
syððan hyne Hæðcyn of horn-bogan,
his fréa-wine fláne ġeswencte;

he missed his mark,   and shot his kinsman dead,
2440   the younger brother the other,   with a blood-stained bolt.

"That was a fee-less fight   and a frightful sin,
heart-wrenching in Hrethel's breast,   yet he must
let the atheling   die unavenged!
Anguish it is   for an old man
2445   to bear,   when his bairn rides
young to the gallows.   He gives a lament*,
a sorrowful song   for his hanged son,
for the sport of ravens.   No rescue
can he give,   old and grey-haired!
2450   He is reminded   when morn breaks
of his offspring's journey elsewhere,   and no longer
does he wish   to bide within the burg
as the warden of his wealth,   when the one
he held most dear   had suffered death.
2455   Sorrowfully,   he looks to his son's burg,
the wasted wine-hall   and the windswept house,
bereft of revels.   The riders sleep,
the heroes are buried   and the harp does not sound;
there is no joy in the courts,   where there once was.

2460   "Then he goes to his bed   and utters a song of sorrow,
one after another;   it seems all too roomy,
the fields and the homestead.   Thus the Helm of the Weders
endured heart's sorrow   for Herebeald,
o'er-whelming woe.   Not a whit could he
2465   on that life-bane   better the feud;
nor could he hurl   hatred at his heir
with loathly deeds,   though he loved him not.
He then with that sorrow,   which he sorely endured,
gave up men's gladness,   and chose God's light;
2470   left lands and the folk-burg   to his heir,
as was well,   when he went from this life.

"Then was there suffering and strife   betwixt Swedes and Geats;
o'er the wide waters,   war came,
hard battle-hostilities,   when Hrethel died.
2475   To him, Ongentheow's   offspring were
bold and firm;   they wished not for friendship
to hold beyond the water,   but at Hreosnaburg*
committed   savage slaughter.
We avenged that feud,   my friends!

158

                miste merċelses   ond his mǽġ ofscét,
2440   bróðor óðerne,   blódigan gáre.

            "Þæt wæs feoh-léas ġefeoht,   fyrenum ġesyngad,
            hreðre hyġe-méðe,   sceolde hwæðre swá þéah
            æðeling unwrecen   ealdres linnan!
            Swá bið ġeómorlíċ   gomelum ċeorle
2445   tó ġebídanne,   þæt his byre ríde
            ġiong on galgan.   Þonne hé ġyd wrece,
            sáriġne sang   þonne his sunu hangað
            hrefne tó hróðre   ond hé him helpan ne mæġ
            eald ond in-fród   æniġe ġefremman!
2450   Symble bið ġemyndgad   morna ġehwylċe
            eaforan ellor-síð;   óðres ne ġýmeð
            tó ġebídanne   burgum on innan
            yrfe-weardes,   þonne se án hafað
            þurh déaðes nýd   dǽda ġefondad.
2455   Ġesyhð sorh-ċeariġ   on his suna búre,
            wín-sele wéstne,   windġe reste,
            réote berofene.   Rídend swefað,
            hæleð in hoðman,   nis þǽr hearpan swéġ;
            gomen in ġeardum,   swylċe ðǽr iú wǽron.

                                    XXXIV
2460   "Ġewíteð þonne on sealman,   sorh-léoð gæleð,
            án æfter ánum;   þúhte him eall tó rúm,
            wongas ond wíċ-stede.   Swá Wedra Helm
            æfter Herebealde   heortan sorge
            weallende wæġ.   Wihte ne meahte,
2465   on ðám feorh-bonan   fǽghðe ġebétan;
            nó ðý ǽr hé þone heaðo-rinc   hatian ne meahte
            láðum dǽdum,   þéah him léof ne wæs.
            Hé ðá mid þǽre sorhge,   þé him sío sár belamp,
            gum-dréam ofġeaf,   Godes léoht ġeċéas;
2470   eaferum lǽfde,   swá déð éadiġ mon,
            lond ond léod-byriġ,   þá hé of lífe ġewát.

            Þá wæs synn ond sacu   Swéona ond Ġéata;
            ofer (w)íd wæter   wróht ġemǽne,
            here-níð hearda,   syððan Hréðel swealt.
2475   Oð ðe him Ongenðéowes   eaferan wǽran
            frome fyrd-hwate;   fréode ne woldon
            ofer heafo healdan,,   ac ymb Hréosnabeorh
            eatolne inwit-scear   oft (ġe)fremedon.
            Þæt mǽġ-wine,   míne ġewrǽcan!

2480 That war   was widely known,
     but the elder one   paid with his life.
     For Hæthcyn   that was a hard purchase,
     'twas a fateful fight   for the Geatish lord.
     In the morn I heard,   his kin on the killer
2485 was avenged   by the edge of a blade,
     when Ongentheow   fought Eofor.
     His war-helm was hewn   and the agéd Scylding
     fell corpse-fallow.   Death is mindful
     of many feuds;   the final blow was withheld not.

2490 "Many mathoms   he gave me,
     for the war repaid me   with gifts of gold,
     a splendent sword   and swaths of land he gave me,
     an estate, a joy on this Earth.   He hadn't need
     to search   among the Gifthas*,
2495 or seek the Swedes   or Spear-Danes,
     and weaker warriors   buy with wealth!
     Ever was I in   the front of the fyrd,
     and thus shall I always   be foremost in the fight,
     whilst I draw breath   and my blade endures,
2500 that later or sooner   has oft served me.
     Since I in my daring,   Dæghrefn* slew
     by mine hand,   the Hugas' champion.
     Nor could   the Frisian king claim
     the Brisingamen   from his breast,
2505 but rather was   the standard-bearer slain.
     The brave atheling,   the blade was not his bane,
     but in my battle-gripe,   his heart burst
     and the bone-house was broken.   Now, with the blade's edge,
     hand and hard sword,   I must fight for the hoard!"

2480   Fǽhðe ond fyrene   swá hyt ġefrǽġe wæs,
        þéah ðe óðer hit   ealdre ġebohte,
        heardan ċéape,   Hæðcynne wearð,
        Ġéata dryhtne   gúð onsǽġe.
        Þá iċ on morgne ġefrǽġn,   mǽġ óðerne
2485   billes ecgum   on bonan stǽlan,
        þǽr Ongenþéow   Eofores níosað.
        Gúð-helm tóglád,   gomela Scylfing
        hréas (heaþo)blác.   Hond ġemunde
        fǽhðo ġenóge;   feorh-sweng ne oftéah.

2490   "Iċ him þá máðmas   þé hé mé sealde,
        ġeald æt gúðe   swá mé ġifeðe wæs,
        léohtan sweorde,   hé mé lond forġeaf,
        eard éðel-wyn.   Næs him ǽniġ þearf
        þæt hé tó Ġifðum   oððe tó Gár-Denum
2495   oððe in Swíoríċe   séċean þurfe
        wyrsan wíġ-frecan   weorðe ġeċýpan!
        Symle iċ him on féðan   beforan wolde,
        ána on orde,   ond swá tó aldre sceall
        sæċċe fremman,   þenden þis sweord þolað,
2500   þæt meċ ǽr ond síð   oft ġelǽste.
        Syððan iċ for duġeðum,   Dæġhrefne wearð
        tó hand-bonan,   Húga cempan.
        Nalles hé ðá frætwe   Frés-cyning(e)
        bréost-weorðunge   bringan móste,
2505   ac in cempan ġecrong   cumbles hyrde.
        Æþeling on elne,   ne wæs ecg bona,
        ac him hilde-gráp,   heortan wylmas,
        bán-hús ġebræc.   Nú sceall billes ecg,
        hond ond heard sweord,   ymb hord wígan."

Chapter XVII
The Battle at the Barrow

2510 Beowulf gave a battle-speech
 for the final time. "I have fought many
 wars in my youth, yet I wish now,
 old warden of the folk, to seek this feud
 and do great deeds, if that destroyer of men
2515 will come out of his earth-hall!"

 He then hailed each helm-bearer
 and addressed them one last time,
 "Dear brethren, I would not bear a blade,
 a weapon 'gainst the Wyrm, if I knew how
2520 else to best the fierce fiend, else I would
 grapple for glory as I erst did with Grendel,
 but I must fear the flames of war
 and his poisonous breath. Therefore I bear
 board and byrnie. Nor shall I from the barrow's warden
2525 flee a foot, but we must fight
 this war at the wall, as Wyrd allots,
 the Maker of all Men. I am firm in mind,
 that I, against the war-flier refrain from boasting.

 "Now you must abide by the barrow dressed in byrnies,
2530 warriors in war-gear, and see who can
 during the war-rush, survive wounds better,
 of either of us. 'Tis not your adventure,
 nor in the mastery of any man, save mine alone.
 My strength I shall deal out on the Dragon
2535 and achieve glory. I must with my might
 gain the gold or war shall take me,
 loathly life-bale, your lord!"

 Up then stood the stout warrior, leaning on his shield,
 hard under his helm, dressed in his war-harness
2540 under the stony cliffs; he trusted in the strength

2510   Béowulf maðelode,   béot-wordum spræc
          níehstan síðe,   "Ić ġenéðde fela
          gúða on ġeogoðe,   ġýt ić wylle,
          fród folces weard,   fǽhðe séċan,
          mǽrðum fremman,   ġif meċ se mán-sceaða
2515   of eorð-sele   út ġeséċeð!"

          Ġegrétte ðá   gumena ġehwylcne,
          hwate helm-berend   hindeman síðe
          swǽse ġesíðas,   "Nolde ić sweord beran,
          wǽpen tó Wyrme,   ġif ić wiste hú
2520   wið ðám áglǽcean,   elles meahte
          ġylpe wiðgrípan   swá ić gió wið Grendle dyde,
          ac ić ðǽr heaðu-fýres   hátes wéne,
          réðes ond háttres.   Forðon ić mé on hafu
          bord ond byrnan.   Nelle ić beorges weard
2525   oferfléon fótes trem,   ac unc (feohte) sceal
          weorðan æt wealle,   swá unc Wyrd ġetéoð,
          Metod Manna ġehwæs.   Ić eom on móde from,
          þæt ić wið þone gúð-flogan   ġylp ofersitte.

          "Ġebíde ġé on beorge   byrnum werede,
2530   secgas on searwum,   hwæðer sél mǽġe
          æfter wæl-rǽse,   wunde ġedýġan
          uncer twéġa.   Nis þæt éower síð,
          né ġemet mannes,   nefn(e) mín ánes;
          (þæ)t hé wið áglǽcean   eofoðo dǽle
2535   eorl-scype efne.   Ić mid elne sceall
          gold ġegangan   oððe gúð nimeð,
          feorh-bealu frécne,   fréan éowerne!"

          Árás ðá bí ronde   róf óretta,
          heard under helm,   hioro-serċean bær
2540   under stán-cleofu;   strengo ġetruwode

of himself alone.   'Tis not an unmanly action!
Then he went the wall,   that worthy lord,
he who had won   many wars,
when the armies collided   in the battle-clash.
2545   There stood an arch of stone   and within a stream
that broke from the barrow;   the bourn's whelm
was hot with harmful fire.   He could not get near the hoard
unburned   for any length of time
or endure the deeps,   for the Dragon's flames.

2550   Then he let out a bellow,   his anger burst from his breast,
the Weder lord   a word cried out,
and the stark-hearted one's   roar rang back,
a clear battle-cry   'neath the hoary stone.

Hate was enkindled   when the hoard-ward heard
2555   a man's voice;   there was no more time
to pledge for peace.   Then came forth
the breath of the Serpent   out of the stone,
a hot battle-reek;   the earth resounded.
Beneath the barrow,   Beowulf swung his shield,
2560   the lord of the Geats,   at the grim beast;
then was the heart   of the ring-coiled one compelled
to seek strife.   His sword he drew,
the good war-king,   that heirloom of old,
a keen edge.   Each of the two
2565   foes was afeared   of the other.
The stout-minded one stood   with his shield raised high,
the friend of warriors,   then the Wyrm coiled
together suddenly;   in his war-gear he waited.
Then the burning fiend   went forth,
2570   hurrying toward his doom.   The shield defended well
the body and life   of the famèd lord
for a shorter time   than he sought.
For the first time   then he his sword
wielded,   but Wyrd denied him
2575   glory in battle.   His blade he raised,
the lord of the Geats,   and the grim one smote.
The heirloom's edge   was weakened,
brown on bone   and bit more weakly
than the clan's king   had need,
2580   driven in distress.   Then the barrow's ward was,
after the war-blow,   in a wild mood.
He spewed slaughter-flames;   widely spread
that blazing light.   He boasted not of that battle,

ánes mannes.   Ne bið swylċ earges síð!
Ġeseah ðá be wealle,   sé ðe worna fela,
gum-cystum gód   gúða ġedígde,
hilde-hlemma,   þonne hnitan féðan,
2545   stó(n)dan stán-bogan,   stréam út þonan
brecan of beorge;   wæs þǽre burnan wælm
heaðo-fýrum hát.   Ne meahte horde néah
unbyrnende   ǽniġe hwíle
déo(p) ġedýġan,   for Dracan léġe.

2550   Lét ðá of bréostum,   ðá hé ġebolgen wæs,
Weder-Ġéata léod   word út faran,
stearc-heort styrmde   stefn in becóm,
heaðo-torht hlynnan   under hárne stán.

Hete wæs onhréred,   hord-weard oncníow
2555   mannes reorde;   næs ðǽr mára fyrst
fréode tó friclan.   From ǽrest cwóm
oruð áglǽcean   út of stáne,
hát hilde-swát;   hrúse dynede.
Biorn under beorge,   bord-rand onswáf
2560   wið ðám gryre-ġieste,   Ġéata dryhten;
ðá wæs hring-bogan   heorte ġefýsed
sæċċe tó séċeanne.   Sweord ǽr ġebrǽd,
gód gúð-cyning,   gomele láfe,
ecgum un(s)láw.   Ǽġhwæðrum wæs
2565   bealo-hycgendra   bróga fram óðrum.
Stíð-mód ġestód   wið stéapne rond,
winia bealdor,   ðá se Wyrm ġebéah
snúde tósomne;   hé on searwum bád.
Ġewát ðá byrnende   ġebogen scríðan,
2570   tó ġescipe scyndan.   Scyld wél ġebearg
lífe ond líċe   lǽssan hwíle,
mǽrum þéodne,   þonne his myne sóhte;
ðǽr hé þý fyrste   forman dógore
wealdan móste,   swá him Wyrd ne ġescráf
2575   hréð æt hilde.   Hond up ábrǽd.
Ġéata dryhten,   gryre-fáhne slóh
incgeláfe;   þæt sío ecg ġewác,
brún on báne,   bát unswíðor
þonne his ðíod-cyning   þearfe hæfde,
2580   bysigum ġebǽded.   Þá wæs beorges weard
æfter heaðu-swenge,   on hréoum móde.
Wearp wæl-fýre;   wíde sprungon
hilde-léoman.   Hréð-sigora ne ġealp,

the gold-friend of the Geats,   for his war-blade failed,
2585 stark in the strife,   as it should not have,
that ancient iron.   'Twas no easy thing
for the famèd   heir of Ecgtheow
on this Earth   to endure,
for he must oblige,   against his will,
2590 dwell elsewhere,   as must every man
leave these loaned days!

              'Twas not long then
before the foes   met each other again.
The hoard-ward hardened his heart   and his breast swelled
once more.   He cruelly suffered again,
2595 enfolded with fire,   he who ruled the folk!
Nor yet did   his company of comrades,
atheling's bairns,   about him stand
in war valor,   but had fled to the forest
to save their lives.   The heart of one alone
2600 surged with sorrows,   for kinship will never
wend for he who   thinks well!

Wiglaf was he named,   Weohstan's son*,
belovéd linden-bearer   of the Scylfing lord,
kinsman of Ælfhere.   His king he saw,
2605 suffering the heat   'neath his maskèd helm.
He was mindful then   of the gifts he had ere been given,
the wealthy hall   of the Wægmundings
and the folk-rights   his father had;
no longer could he wait.   He held his shield high,
2610 the yellow linden,   and seized his ancient sword.
'Twas known to Men   as an heirloom of Eanmund,
Ohthere's son.   A friendless exile he was,
slain by sword-edge   in battle
by Weohstan,   who won for his kin
2615 the bright helm   and ringèd byrnie,
and an old sword of Ettins,   a gift from Onela.
Weohstan ever held   his kinsman's war-gear,
the famèd corselet.   Of that feud Onela spoke not,
though his brother's bairn   had been killed.
2620 For many winters,   Weohstan held that hoard,
blade and byrnie,   'till his bairn could
earn an earlship   like his ancestors.
Then, among the Geats,   he gave him that war-gear,
a great many,   ere he left this life,

gold-wine Ġéata;   gúð-bill ġeswác,
2585 nacod æt níðe,   swá hyt nó sceolde,
íren ǽr-gód.   Ne wæs þæt éðe síð
þæt se mǽra   maga Ecgðéowes
grund-wong þone   ofġyfan wolde;
sceolde willan,   wíċ eardian
2590 elles hwerġen,   swá sceal ǽġhwylċ mon
álǽtan lǽn-dagas!

                    Næs ðá long tó ðon
þæt ðá áglǽcean   hý eft ġemétton.
Hyrte hyne hord-weard,   hreðer ǽðme wéoll
níwan stefne.   Nearo ðrowode
2595 fýre befongen   sé ðe ǽr folce wéold!
Nealles him on héape   h(a)nd-ġesteallan,
æðelinga bearn,   ymbe ġestódon
hilde-cystum,   ac hý on holt bugon,
ealdre burgan.   Hiora in ánum wéoll
2600 sefa wið sorgum;   sibb ǽfre ne mæġ
wiht onwendan   þám ðe wél þenċeð!

XXXV

Wíġláf wæs háten,   Wéoxstánes sunu,
léoflíċ lind-wiġa   léod Scylfinga.
mǽġ Ælfheres.   Ġeseah his mon-dryhten,
2605 under here-gríman   hát þrówian.
Ġemunde ðá ðá áre   þé hé him ǽr forġeaf,
wíċ-stede weliġne   Wǽġmundinga,
folc-rihta ġehwylċ,   swá his fæder áhte;
ne mihte ðá forhabban.   Hond rond ġeféng,
2610 ġeolwe linde,   gomel swyrd ġetéah;
þæt wæs mid eldum   Ēanmundes láf,
suna Óhtere(s).   Þám æt sæċċe wearð,
wræċċan wine-léasum   Wéohstánes bana
méċes ecgum,   ond his mágum ætbær
2615 brún-fágne helm,   hringde byrnan,
eald sweord Eotonisc;   þæt him Onela forġeaf,
his gædelinges   gúð-ġewǽdu,
fyrd-searo fúslíċ.   Nó ymbe ðá fǽhðe spræc,
þéah ðe hé his bróðor   bearn ábredwade.
2620 Hé frætwe ġehéold   fela misséra,
bill ond byrnan,   oð ðæt his byre mihte
eorl-scipe efnan   swá his ǽr-fæder;
ġeaf him ðá mid Ġéatum,   gúð-ġewǽda,
ǽġhwæs unrím,   þá hé of ealdre ġewát,

2625 wise when he fared forth.   That was the first time
that the young champion,   with his liege lord
should brave   the rush of battle.
His courage did not melt,   nor did his might
weaken in the war.   Thus the Wyrm found out,
2630 when the two   together clashed!

Wiglaf spake   in commanding words;
sad was his heart   as he said to his companions,
"I am mindful of the time   when mead we drank
and we made oaths   to our lord
2635 in the beer-hall,   to he who bestowed rings,
that we would repay him   for our war-gear,
for our helms and hard swords,   if the need ever arose.
He chose us from his army   to accompany him
and aid him   on this adventure!
2640 He deemed us worthy of glory   and gave us these gifts,
because he considered us   keen spear-warriors,
bold helm-bearers,   though our lord for us
this hero-work,   intended alone,
to finish,   the folk protector,
2645 because he of men   the most glory has won
for daring deeds!   Now has the day come
that your liege lord   has need of the might
of good warriors!   Let us go
to help our hero-king   while there is heat still,
2650 the fearsome fire!   God knows
that to me it is far more lief   that my life,
along with my gold-giver's,   be consumed by flame.
It is unseemly   that we should bear shields
homeward hence,   lest we first may
2655 fell the foe   and defend the life
of the Weder lord.   Well I know
that his past deeds are not such   that he alone should,
of the Geat war-band,   suffer sorrow
and sink in the strife.   My sword and helm,
2660 byrnie and battle-shield   will serve us both!"

Then he strode though the smoke   to support his lord,
his battle-helm he bore.   A few words he quoth,
"Dear Beowulf,   do all well,
as you in your youth   once said
2665 that you would not let,   while you had life still,
your glory fail!   Now you must, in daring deeds,

2625   fród on forð-weġ.   Þá wæs forma síð
        ġeongan cempan,   þæt hé gúðe ræs
        mid his fréo-dryhtne   fremman sceolde.
        Ne ġemealt him se mód-sefa,   né his mæġenes láf
        ġewác æt wíġe;   þa se Wyrm onfand,
2630   syððan híe tóġædre   ġegán hæfdon!

        Wíġláf maðelode   word-rihta fela;
        sæġde ġesíðum   him wæs sefa ġeómor,
        "Iċ ðæt mæl ġeman   þǽr wé medu þéġun,
        þonne wé ġehéton   ússum hláforde
2635   in bíor-sele,   ðé ús ðás béagas ġeaf,
        þæt wé him ðá gúð-geatwa   ġyldan woldon
        ġif him þyslicu   þearf ġelumpe,
        helmas ond heard sweord.   Ðé hé úsiċ on herġe ġeċéas
        tó ðyssum síð-fate   sylfes willum!
2640   Onmunde úsiċ mærða   ond mé þás máðmas ġeaf,
        þé hé úsiċ gár-wíġend   góde tealde,
        hwate helm-berend,   þéah ðe hláford ús
        þis ellen-weorc   ána áðóhte
        tó ġefremmanne,   folces hyrde,
2645   forðám hé manna mǽst   mærða ġefremede,
        dǽda dollicra!   Nú is se dæġ cumen
        þæt úre man-dryhten   mæġenes behófað
        gódra gúð-rinca!   Wutun gangan tó
        helpan hild-fruman   þenden hyt sý,
2650   gléd-eġesa grim!   God wát on meċ
        þæt mé is miċle léofre   þæt mínne líċ-haman,
        mid mínne gold-ġyfan,   gléd fæðmie.
        Ne þynċeð mé ġerysne   þæt wé rondas beren
        eft tó earde,   nemne wé ǽror mæġen
2655   fáne ġefyllan,   feorh ealgian
        Wedra ðéodnes.   Iċ wát ġeare,
        þæt nǽron eald-ġewyrht   þæt hé ána scyle
        Ġéata duguðe   gnorn þrówian,
        ġesíġan æt sæċċe;   úrum sceal sweord ond helm,
2660   byrne ond b(ea)du-scrúd   bám ġemǽne!"

        Wód þá þurh þone wæl-réċ   wíġ-heafolan bær.
        fréan on fultum.   Féa worda cwæð,
        "Léofa Bíowulf,   lǽst eall tela,
        swá ðú on ġeoguð-féore   ġeára ġecwǽde
2665   þæt ðú ne álǽte,   be ðé lifiġendum,
        dóm ġedréosan!   Scealt nú dǽdum róf,

169

steadfast atheling,   with all your might
save your life!   I will support you!"

After these words,   the Wyrm came again,
2670   the awful Serpent,   a second time
in a flood of fire   to seek his foes,
the hated fiends.   Waves of flame
burned the board,   and the byrnie could not,
to the young spear-warrior,   give support,
2675   but the young man,   quickly under his kinsman's shield
went forth eagerly,   when his own was
all burned by the blaze.   Then the war-king
remembered glory   and with all his strength struck
his battle-blade down   upon the Wyrm's head,
2680   a baleful blow,   but Nægling* burst asunder!

Beowulf's sword   shattered in the struggle,
old and grey-hued.   'Twas not granted to him
that the iron   edge could
help in battle;   his hand was so strong
2685   that each of his blades,   I have been told,
he overstrained his stroke   when he used in the fight
a wound-hardened weapon*;   'twas no better for him.

Once more   the folk-scourge struck,
the fierce Fire-Drake   was mindful of the feud
2690   and rushed the stout one,   where room allowed,
hot and battle-grim,   bit into Beowulf's neck,
clamping it   between his teeth.
His life-blood   flowed forth.

170

æðeling án-hýdiġ,   ealle mæġene
feorh ealgian!   Iċ ðé fullæstu!"

Æfter ðám wordum,   Wyrm yrre cwóm,
2670 atol inwit-gæst,   óðre síðe
fýr-wylmum fáh   fíonda níosan,
láðra manna.   Líġ ýðum fór
born bord wið rond,   byrne ne meahte
ġeongum gár-wigan   ġéoce ġefremman,
2675 ac se maga ġeonga,   under his mǽġes scyld
elne ġéeode,   þá his ágen (wæs)
glédum forgrunden.   Þá ġén gúð-cyning
m(ærða) ġemunde,   mæġen-strengo slóh
hilde-bille,   þæt hyt on heafolan stód
2680 níþe ġenýded;   Næġling forbærst!

Ġeswác æt sæċċe   sweord Bíowulfes,
gomol ond grǽġ-mǽl.   Him þæt ġifeðe ne wæs
þæt him írenna   ecge mihton
helpan æt hilde;   wæs sío hond tó strong,
2685 sé ðe méċa ġehwane,   míne ġefrǽġe,
swenge ofersóhte   þonne hé tó sæċċe bær
wǽpen wundum heard;   næs him wihte ðé sél.

Þá wæs þéod-sceaða   þriddan síðe,
frécne fýr-Draca   fǽhða ġemyndiġ,
2690 rǽsde on ðone rófan,   þá him rúm áġeald,
hát ond heaðo-grim,   heals ealne ymbeféng,
biteran bánum.   Hé ġeblódegod wearð
sáwul-dríore;   swát ýðum wéoll.

Chapter XVIII
Beowulf's Bane

I heard then that   at the folk-king's need,
2695   the earl alongside him   showed his worth,
his craft and his cunning,   as he was wont.
He heeded not the Wyrm's head,   though his hand was burned,
the hearty man   helped his kinsman.
A little lower he struck   the evil-doer,
2700   his sword   he drove in deep,
blazing bright,   so that the fire began
to wane.   Then again the war-king
wielded his wits   and drew his war-seax,
bitter and battle-sharp   that he wore on his belt
2705   and the Helm of the Weders   cleaved the Wyrm in twain!
They had felled the fiend;   his life was finished.

So the kinsmen   had killed him,
the two athelings;   so ought a man to be,
a noble in need!   By his own deeds,
2710   that was the lord's   last victory
in this world's works.   Then his wound began,
which the earth-Drake   had erst made,
to swelter and swell;   soon he found that
bale welled   in his breast,
2715   a perilous poison.   Then the atheling went,
so that he, by the wall,   wise in thought.
sat on a seat   and looked upon the work of Giants;
the stone arches stood fast   on mighty pillars
and held up that   everlasting earth-house within.
2720   Then Wiglaf,   the hands of the hero,
the reknownèd king,   wet with sword-sweat,
his lord and friend,   washed with water,
weary from war   and unfastened his helm.

Beowulf spake   in spite of the pain
2725   from his grievous wound.   Well he knew

XXXVI

Ðá iċ æt þearfe (ġefræġn)   þéod-cyninges,
2695 and-longne eorl   ellen cýðan,
cræft ond cénðu,   swá him ġecynde wæs.
Ne hédde hé þæs heafolan,   ac sío hand ġebarn,
módiġes mannes   þǽr hé his mæġ(e)s healp;
þæt hé þone níð-gæst   nioðor hwéne slóh,
2700 secg on searwum   þæt ðæt sweord ġedéaf
fáh ond fǽted,   þæt ðæt fýr ongon
sweðrian syððan.   Þá ġén sylf cyning
ġewéold his ġewitte,   wæll-seaxe ġebrǽd,
biter ond beadu-scearp,   þæt hé on byrnan wæġ;
2705 forwrát Wedra Helm   Wyrm on middan!
Féond ġefyldan;   ferh ellen wræc

ond hí hyne þá béġen   ábroten hæfdon,
sib-æðelingas;   swylċ sceolde secg wesan,
þeġn æt ðearfe!   Þæt ðám þéodne wæs
2710 síðas síġe-hwíle   sylfes dǽdum,
worlde ġeweorces.   Ðá sío wund ongon,
þé him se eorð-Draca   ǽr ġeworhte,
swelan ond swellan;   hé þæt sóna onfand
þæt him on bréostum   bealo-níð wéoll
2715 attor on innan.   Ðá se æðeling ġíong,
þæt hé bí wealle,   wís-hycgende,
ġesæt on sesse,   seah on Enta ġeweorc;
hú ðá stán-bogan   stapulum fæste
éċe eorð-reċed   innan healden.
2720 Hyne þá mid handa   heoro-dréoriġne,
þéoden mǽrne,   þeġn unġemete till,
wine-dryhten his   wætere ġelafede,
hilde-sædne   ond his hel(m) onspéon.

Bíowulf maþelode,   hé ofer benne spræc,
2725 wunde wæl-bléate.   Wisse hé ġearwe

173

that this was the last   of his life-days,
joys on the Earth;   ended were
his count of days   -death was near,-
"Now I might bestow   on a son of mine
2730 this war-gear,   if it were granted to me
that there was   any heir of mine
own blood.   The burg I've held
for fifty winters.   No folk-king was there ever
from any   of the neighboring nations
2735 who dared   to wage war on me,
threaten with horror.   At home I abided
my Wyrd,   and wielded mine own;
I sought not subtle crafts,   nor did I swear
a false oath ever.   Of all these things,
2740 though weak with wounds,   I am glad;
he will have no need to rebuke me,   the Ruler-of-All
for the baleful killing of kin,   when departs my
life from my lich.   Now, go quickly,
and gather the hoard   from beneath the hoary stone,
2745 belovèd Wiglaf,   where the Wyrm now lies,
sleeps sore-wounded,   bereaved of his treasure.
Be now in haste,   so I may behold
that ancient treasure   and gaze upon the gold
and shining gems,   so that I can more gladly,
2750 by the sight of that   splendid hoard, leave my
life and lands   I long have held!"

Then I have been told   that swiftly the son of Weohstan,
after he had heard   those words from the wounded king,
the war-weary one,   bore away his ring-net,
2755 the woven battle-sark   beneath the barrow's roof.
Victorious,   he saw as he sat down
many costly gems,   the keen thegn,
and glittering gold   upon the ground,
wonders on the wall,   and bright cups stood there
2760 in the Dragon's den,   the old dawn-flyer,
unburnished beakers   of bygone days,
stripped of their riches,   and rusted helms
of ages past;   arm-rings there were,
cleverly crafted.   Easily may treasure,
2765 gold in the ground,   overreach
any man,   hide it he who will!
Saw he then a standard hanging,   all of gold,
high o'er the hoard,   the greatest of hand-wonders,

þæt hé dæg-hwíla   ġedrogen hæfde,
Eorðan wyn(ne);   ðá wæs eall sceacen
dógor-ġerímes   -déað unġemete néah,-
"Nú iċ suna mínum   syllan wolde
2730   gúð-ġewǽdu,   þǽr mé ġifeðe swá
ǽniġ yrfe-weard   æfter wurde
líċe ġelenge.   Iċ ðás léode héold
fíftiġ wintra.   Næs sé folc-cyning
ymbe-sittendra   ǽniġ ðára
2735   þé meċ gúð-winum   grétan dorste,
eġesan ðéon.   Iċ on earde bád
mǽl-ġesceafta,   héold mín tela;
ne sóhte searo-níðas,   né mé swór fela
áða on unriht.   Iċ ðæs ealles mæġ,
2740   feorh-bennum séoc,   ġeféan habban;
forðám mé wítan ne ðearf,   Waldend Fíra
morðor-bealo mága,   þonne mín sceaceð
líf of líċe.   Nú ðú lungre ġeong
hord scéawian   under hárne stán,
2745   Wíġláf léofa,   nú se Wyrm liġeð,
swefeð sáre wund,   sinċe beréafod.
Bío nú on ofoste,   þæt iċ ǽr-welan
gold-ǽht onġite,   ġearo scéawiġe.
sweġle searo-ġimmas,   þæt iċ ðý séft mǽge
2750   æfter máððum-welan   mín álǽtan
líf ond léod-scipe,   þone iċ longe héold!"

XXXVII

Ðá iċ snúde ġefræġn   sunu Wíhstánes
æfter word-cwydum   wundum dryhtne
hýran heaðo-síocum,   hring-net beran,
2755   brogdne beadu-serċean   u(n)der beorges hróf.
Ġeseah ðá siġe-hréðiġ,   þá hé bí sesse ġéong
mago-þeġn módiġ   máððum-siġla fealo,
gold glitinian   grunde ġetenge,
wundur on wealle,   ond þæs Wyrmes denn,
2760   ealdes úht-flogan,   orcas stondan,
fyrn-manna fatu   feormend-léase,
hyrstum behrorene;   þǽr wæs helm moniġ
eald ond ómiġ,   earm-béaga fela,
searwum ġesǽled.   Sinċ éaðe mæġ,
2765   gold on grunde,   gumena cynnes ġehwone
ofer-hígian,   hýde sé ðe wylle!
Swylċe hé siomian ġeseah,   seġn eall-ġylden,
héah ofer horde,   hond-wundra mǽst,

woven with words;   a light shone forth,
2770   so that he might see   on the stony ground
the treasures that lay there.   No sign of the Serpent
was seen, for the sword   had taken him.

I heard then that the hill   was looted of its hoard,
the old work of Giants   by one alone;
2775   he bore beakers and bowls   in his arms,
and of his own will,   he also took the banner,
the brightest of beacons.   His old lord's blade,
-its edge was of iron-   had already wounded
he who guarded   the gold
2780   for a long time;   those furious flames
spread hot 'round the hoard   in horror-billows
at midnight,   'til he met his death.
The herald hastened forth,   urged by the hoard,
eager to get back;   curiosity burst in him,
2785   whether he would find   the bold atheling alive still
where he left   the lord of the Weders,
the war-ravaged king   weak by the wall.

He took those treasures   to his lord,
and found the   famèd chieftain bleeding;
2790   his life was almost at its end.   Again the thegn
washed him with water,   'til the point of a word
broke through his breast-hoard.   Beowulf spake,
old and grim,   he gazed at the gold,
"For this gold,   I give thanks to the God of All,
2795   the King of Wonders,   and these words say
to the Eternal Lord,   which I look on here,
that I could   gain this gold
for my people,   ere my death-day.
Now I for this treasure,   I have traded
2800   the length of my life!   Look now
to the needs of the nation;   I must not wait longer.
Bid war-famèd men   to build me a barrow*,
bright after the bale-fire   by the water's edge;
a reminder   among the folk,
2805   towering high   on Hronesness,
so that wanderers from across the waves   will call it
Beowulf's Barrow,   they whose ships
drive o'er   the dark flood."

Then he took the torc of gold   from his neck,
2810   the bold lord,   and bestowed it on his thegn,

176

ġelocen leoðo-cræftum;   of ðám léoma stód,
2770 þæt hé þone grund-wong   onġitan meahte
wrǽ(t)e ġiond-wlítan.   Næs ðæs Wyrmes þǽr
onsýn æniġ,   ac hyne ecg fornam.

Ðá iċ on hlǽwe ġefræġn   hord réafian,
eald Enta ġeweorc   ánne mannan;
2775 him on bearm hl(a)dan   bunan ond discas
sylfes dóme,   seġn éac ġenóm,
béacna beorhtost.   Bill ǽr-ġescód
-ecg wæs íren-   eald-hláfordes
þám ðára máðma   mund-bora wæs
2780 longe hwíle;   líġ-eġesan wæġ
hátne for horde,   hioro-weallende
middel-nihtum,   oð þæt hé morðre swealt.
Ár wæs on ofoste   eft-síðes ġeorn,
frætwum ġefyrðred;   hyne fyrwet bræc,
2785 hwæðer collen-ferð   cwicne ġemétte
in ðám wong-stede,   Wedra þéoden,
ellen-síocne,   þǽr hé hine ǽr forlét.

Hé ðá mid þám máðmum   mærne þíoden,
dryhten sínne   dríoriġne fand;
2790 ealdres æt ende.   Hé hine eft ongon
wæteres weorpan,   oð þæt wordes ord
bréost-hord þurhbræc.   (Béowulf maðelode;)
gomel on ġiogoðe   gold scéawode,
"Iċ ðára frætwa,   Fréan Ealles ðanc,
2795 Wuldur-Cyninge,   wordum secge,
Éċum Dryhtne,   þé iċ hér on starie,
þæs ðe iċ móste   mínum léodum
ǽr swylt-dæġe   swylċ ġestrýnan.
Nú iċ on máðma hord,   mí(n)e bebohte
2800 fróde feorh-leġe!   Fremmað ġéna
léoda þearfe;   ne mæġ iċ hér leng wesan.
Hátað heaðo-mære   hlǽw ġewyrċean,
beorhtne æfter bǽle   æt brimes nósan;
sé scel tó ġemyndum   mínum léodum,
2805 héah hlífian   on Hrones-næsse,
þæt hit sǽ-líðend   syððan hátan
Bíowulfes biorh,   ðá ðe brentingas
ofer flóda ġenipu   feorran drífað."

Dyde him of healse   hring ġyldenne,
2810 þíoden þríst-hýdiġ,   þeġne ġesealde;

177

his helm of burnished gold,   byrnie and ring,
and bade Wiglaf   to use them well,
"You are the last remnant   of our race,
of the Wægmundings*.   Wyrd has swept away
2815 the rest of my kin   to their destined doom,
earls in their might.   Now, I must now follow them."

Those were the last words   of that wizened man,
the thoughts of his heart,   after the hot flames he chose,
the blazing bale-fire.   Then from him went
2820 his soul to seek   his final judgement.

ġeongum gár-wigan,   gold-fáhne helm,
béah ond byrnan,   hét hyne brúcan well,
"Þú eart ende-láf   ússes cynnes,
Wǽġmundinga;   ealle Wyrd fors(w)éo(p)
2815 míne mágas   tó metod-sceafte,
eorlas on elne.   Iċ him æfter sceal."

Þæt wæs þám gomelan   ġinġeste word,
bréost-ġehyġdum,   ǽr hé bǽl cure,
háte heaðo-wylmas.   Him of hweðre ġewát
2820 sáwol séċean   sóð-fæstra dóm.

Chapter XIX
Shadow of the Scylfings

'Twas painful   for the proud young thegn
when he saw   his dear lord dead,
his life on this Earth   at an end,
a bitter burden.   His bane lay there too,
2825   the dreadful earth-Drake   bereaved of life,
balefully beaten down.   No longer the ring-hoard
could it wield,   the winding Wyrm,
for the iron-edge   had destroyed him,
battle-sharp and hard,   the leavings of hammers;
2830   the wide-flyer   fell to the ground,
by wounds stilled   near the hoard-store.

No longer could it fly far   through the air
in the middle of the night,   proud in its possessions,
delighting in destruction,   when it fell to the earth
2835   by the work   of the war-lord.
Few of the folk   could succeed,
though they were mighty men,   or so I've heard,
ones who were daring   in every deed,
against the poisonous breath   of the perilous beast
2840   rush on   the ring-hoard,
if he found its   warden watching,
abiding in the barrow.   Beowulf paid
for those lordly mathoms   with his life;
each arrived at their ends.

2845   'Twas not much later,
that those who shunned the war   left the woods,
the craven troth-breakers,   ten together.
With darts   they dared not fight
in their liege-lord's   great need,
2850   but in shame,   bore shields,
battle-armor,   to where the old one lay,
and looked to Wiglaf.   Weary he sat,

(XXXVIII)

Ðá wæs ġegongen   gum(an) unfródum
earfoðlíċe,   þæt hé on Eorðan ġeseah
þone léofestan   lífes æt ende
bléate ġebǽran.   Bona swylċe læġ,
2825   eġeslíċ eorð-Draca   ealdre beréafod,
bealwe ġebǽded.   Béah-hordum leng
Wyrm wóh-boġen   wealdan ne móste,
ac him írenna   ecga fornámon,
hearde heaðo-scearpe,   homera láfe;
2830   þæt se wíd-floga   wundum stille,
hréas on hrúsan   hord-ærne néah.

Nalles æfter lyfte   lácende hwearf
middel-nihtum,   máðm-ǽhta wlonc,
ansýn ýwde,   ac hé eorðan ġeféoll
2835   for þæs hild-fruman   hond-ġeweorce.
Húru þæt on lande   lýt manna ðáh,
mæġen-áġendra   míne ġefrǽġe,
þéah ðe hé dǽda ġehwæs   dyrstiġ wǽre,
þæt hé wið attor-sceaðan   oreðe ġerǽsde
2840   oððe hring-sele   hondum styrede,
ġif hé wæċċende   weard onfunde,
búon on beorge.   Bíowulfe wearð
dryht-máðma dǽl   déaðe forgolden;
hæfde ǽġhwæð(er)   ende ġeféred
2845   lǽnan lífes.
            Næs ðá lang tó ðon,
þæt ðá hild-latan   holt ofġéfan,
týdre tréow-logan,   týne ætsomne;
ðá ne dorston ǽr   dareðum lácan
on hyra man-dryhtnes   miċlan þearfe,
2850   ac hý scamiende   scyldas bǽran,
gúð-ġewǽdu   þǽr se gomela læġ,
wlitan on Wí(ġ)láf.   Hé ġewérġad sæt,

the foot-soldier   by the side of his lord;
he tried to rouse him with water,   but it worked not a whit.

2855 He could not in this world,   though he wished well,
preserve the life   of his patriarch,
nor the Wielder's will   turn a bit;
God's doom will rule   o'er the deeds
of every man,   as it always has.

2860 A grim answer   gave he,
the youth to they   who yielded their courage.
Wiglaf spake,   Weohstan's son;
full of grief,   he looked upon the unloved men,
"Indeed he will say,   he who speaks sooth,
2865 that our lord   who gave us gifts
and the byrnies   which you bear,
when oft he gave   on the ale-bench,
swords and helms   to the hall-sitters,
the lord to his thegns,   the greatest of gear
2870 which he could   find near or far,
he who cast off   his corselet
in his wroth,   when the battle began.
Not at all did the folk-king   or his fyrd,
have need to boast,   but God gave him,
2875 the Giver of Victory,   vengeance on the Wyrm
alone with the edge,   when he had need.
Little life-defense   could I
offer in the battle,   but I began
to hopelessly help   my kinsman.
2880 It's strength was less   when I struck it with my sword,
the deadly foe,   the fire less fiercely
surged from its head.   Too few helpers
thronged about him   in the throes of battle.

"Now shall the giving of gifts,
2885 all happiness and hope for your kin,
shall fail for our folk.   All land-rights
of everybody in the burg
will be lost, when lords
from afar   hear of your flight,
2890 inglorious deeds.   Death is better
than a long life   of shame!"

He bade that the battle-work   be announced at the burg
up o'er the cliffs,   where the earls sat
all morning long,   sorrowful in spirit,

féðe-cempa   fréan eaxlum néah;
wehte hyne wætre,   him wiht ne spéo(w).

2855   Ne meahte hé on Eorðan,   ðéah hé úðe wél,
on ðám frum-gáre   feorh ġehealdan,
né ðæs Wealdendes   wiht onċirran;
wolde dóm Godes   dædum rædan
gumena ġehwylcum,   swá hé nú ġén déð.

2860   Þá wæs æt ðám ġeong(an)   grim andswaru,
éð-beġéte   þám ðe ǽr his elne forléas.
Wíġláf maðelode,   Wéohstánes sunu;
sec(g) sáriġ-ferð   seah on unléofe,
"Þæt lá mæġ secgan   se ðe wyle sóð sprecan,

2865   þæt se mon-dryhten,   se éow þá máðmas ġeaf,
éored-ġeatwe   þe ġé þǽr on standað,
þonne hé on ealu-benċe   oft ġesealde,
heal-sittendum   helm ond byrnan,
þéoden his þeġnum,   swylċe hé þrýðlícost

2870   ówer feor oððe néah   findan meahte,
þæt hé ġénunga   gúð-ġewǽdu
wráðe forwurpe   ðá hyne wíġ beġet.
Nealles folc-cyning,   fyrd-ġesteallum
ġylpan þorfte,   hwæðre him God úðe,

2875   Sigora Waldend,   þæt hé hyne sylfne ġewræc
ána mid ecge,   þá him wæs elnes þearf.
Iċ him líf-wraðe   lýtle meahte
ætġifan æt gúðe   ond ongan swá þéah
ofer mín ġemet   mǽġes helpan.

2880   Symle wæs þý sǽmra   þonne iċ sweorde drep
ferhð-ġeníðlan,   fýr unswíðor
wéoll of ġewitte.   (W)erġendra tó lýt
þrong ymbe þéoden,   þá hyne sío þrág becwóm.

"(N)ú sceal sinċ-þego   ond swyrd-ġifu,
2885   eall éðel-wyn   éowrum cynne,
lufen álicgean.   Lond-rihtes mót
þǽre mǽġ-burge   monna ǽġhwylċ
ídel hweorfan,   syðða æðelingas
feorran ġefricgean   fléam éowerne,
2890   dóm-léasan dæd.   Déað bið sélla
eorla ġehwylcum   þonne edwít-líf!"

XXXIX

Heht ðá þæt heaðo-weorc   tó hagan bíodan
up ofer egc-clif,   þǽr þæt eorl-weorod
morgen-longne dæġ,   mód-ġiómor sæt,

2895   the shield-bearers,   sure of one of two things.
    Would this be the   day of his death
    or would their   belovèd lord return?

    Of little was he silent   of that new story,
    the herald that rode o'er the headland,   but spoke truly of all,
2900   "Now is the wish-giver   of the Weder folk,
    the Geat lord,   lying fast on his death-bed,
    in slaughter-sleep   by the Serpent's deeds.
    Besides him lies   his life-scourge,
    sick with seax-wounds;   his sword he could not
2905   on that fell-foe   in any way
    work wounds.   Wiglaf sits
    o'er Beowulf,   the bairn of Weohstan,
    the earl   by the unliving one;
    he holds with reverence   in his heart a head-watch
2910   o'er both the loved and the loathed.

                 "Now must the land
    wage war,   when unhidden
    to the Franks and Frisians   the fall of the king
    widely becomes.   These woes were first wrought
    hard with the Hugas   when Hyglelac came,
2915   faring the fleet   to Frisian lands.
    There the Hewaras   humbled him in battle,
    fought stoutheartedly   and with great strength,
    that the byrnie-clad one   bowed down,
    fell among the foot-warriors;   to his fyrd
2920   the earl could not give out rings!   Afterwards,
    the Merovingians*   showed us no mercy.

    "But, I expect   no truce or troth
    from the Swedes.   'Tis spoken from afar
    of how Ongentheow   ended the life
2925   of Hæthcyn Hretheling   at Hrefnesholt*,
    when the Geatish folk   first sought out
    the Battle-Scylfings   in their bluster.
    Soon the old father   of Ohthere,
    agèd and awful,   returned the onslaught,
2930   slew the sea-king   and rescued his wife,
    the old lady   though left without gold,
    mother of both   Onela and Ohthere.
    He then followed   his mortal foes,
    until they escaped   without ease,

2895   bord-hæbbende,   béga on wénum.
    Ende-dógores   ond eft-cymes
    léofes monnes.
                "Lýt swígode
    níwra spella   sé ðe næs ġerád,
    ac hé sóðlíċe   sæġde ofer ealle,
2900   Nú is wil-ġeofa   Wedra léoda,
    dryhten Ġéata,   déað-bedde fæst,
    wunað wæl-reste   Wyrmes dædum.
    Him on efn liġeð   ealdor-ġewinna,
    s(e)x-bennum séoc;   sweorde ne meahte
2905   on ðám áglæċean   æniġe þinga
    wunde ġewyrċean.   Wíġláf siteð
    ofer Bíowulfe,   byre Wíhstánes,
    eorl ofer óðrum   unlifiġendum;
    healdeð hiġe-mæðum   héafod-wearde
2910   léofes ond láðes.
                "Nú ys léodum wén
    orleġ-hwíle,   syððan und(y)r(ne)
    Froncum ond Frýsum   fyll cyninges
    wíde weorðeð.   Wæs sío wróht scepen
    heard wið Húgas   syððan Hiġelác cwóm,
2915   faran flot-herġe   on Frésna land;
    þǽr hyne Hetware   hilde ġe(n)ǽġdon,
    elne ġééodon   mid ofer-mæġene,
    þæt se byrn-wiga   búgan sceolde,
    féoll on féðan,   -nalles frætwe ġeaf
2920   ealdor dugoðe!   Ús wæs á syððan,
    Merewíoingas   milts unġyfeðe.

        "Né iċ tó Swéo-ðéode   sibbe oððe tréowe
    wihte ne wéne.   Ac wæs wíde cúð
    þætte Ongenðío   ealdre besnyðede
2925   Hæðcen Hréþling   wið Hrefnawudu,
    þá for on-médlan   ǽrest ġesóhton
    Ġéata léode   Gúð-Scilfingas.
    Sóna him se fróda   fæder Óhtheres,
    eald ond eġes-full;   hondslyht áġeaf,
2930   ábréot brim-wísan,   brýd (á)h(red)de,
    gomela ío-meowlan   golde berofene,
    Onelan módor   ond Óhtheres,
    ond ðá folgode   feorh-ġeníðlan
    oð ðæt hí oðéodon   earfoðlíċe
2935   in Hrefnesholt,   hláford-léase.

2935 lordless   into Hrefnesholt.
He beset the sword-survivors   at the great harrow*,
weary with wounds   and oft threatening woes
to that wretched throng,   through the long night.
Quoth he, that on the morrow,   he would slay with the sword
2940 and give them   to the gallows-tree*,
for the rapture of ravens.   But relief came
to those destitute men   when the day dawned,
with the sounding   of Hygelac's horns
and they heard the battle-cry   of their bright lord,
2945 the land's champions,   as they charged their foe.

"The bloody swathe   of Swedes and Geats
and their war-rush   was widely seen,
how the folk   that feud awoke.
Then went the Swedish king   with his companions,
2950 the sorrowful warriors   sought their own stronghold
and the atheling Ongentheow   retreated to the heights;
he had heard   of Hygelac's might,
the proud one's war-craft.   He trusted not in resistance,
that he could strive   against the sea-men
2955 or hold his hoard   against the harriers,
his bairn and bride;   he fell back thence,
old behind the earth-wall.   They came after
the Swedish folk,   the standards of Hygelac
o'er-ran   the peaceful plain,
2960 when the Hrethelings   breached the burg.

"Then was Ongentheow   with the edge of a sword,
the hoary one,   made to halt,
the folk-king   forced to surrender
to the doom of Eofor.   In his ire
2965 Wulf Wonreding stuck   with his weapon,
and from the blow   sprang blood
forth from under his hair.   No fear felt he,
the old Swede,   but straightaway repaid
with a worse stroke   for that wicked wound,
2970 the folk-king   turned on his foe.
He could not,   the stout son of Wonred,
give onslaught   to the agèd atheling,
for the helm on his head   was sheared.
Bloody,   he bowed down,
2975 fell on the field,   but his fate had not come yet,
and he roused himself,   though his wounds weakened him.
Then Hygelac's   hardy thegn

Besæt ðá sin-herġe   sweorda láfe,
wundum wérġe,   wéan oft ġehét
earmre teohhe   ondlonge niht.
Cwæð, hé on merġenne   méċes ecgum
2940 ġetan wolde,   sum(e) on galgtréowu(m),
(fuglum) tó gamene.   Frófor eft ġelamp
sáriġ-módum   somod ǽr-dæġe,
syððan híe Hyġeláces   horn ond býman,
ġealdor onġeáton,   þá se góda cóm
2945 léoda dugoðe,   on lást faran.
XL

    "Wæs sío swát-swaðu   Sw(é)ona ond Ġéata,
wæl-rǽs weora   wíde ġesýne,
hú ðá folc mid him   fǽhðe tówehton.
Ġewát him ðá se góda   mid his ġædelingum,
2950 fród fela-ġeómor   fæsten séċean,
eorl Ongenþío   ufor onċirde;
hæfde Hiġeláces   hilde ġefrúnen,
wlonces wíġ-cræft.   Wiðres ne truwode,
þæt hé sǽ-mannum   onsacan mihte,
2955 heaðo-líðendum   hord forstandan,
bearn ond brýde;   béah eft þonan,
eald under eorð-weall.   Þá wæs ǽht boden
Swéona léodum,   seġn Hiġeláce(s)
freoðo-wong þone   for(ð) oféréodon,
2960 syððan Hréðlingas   tó hagan þrungon.

    "Þǽr wearð Ongenðío   ecgum sweord(an),
blonden-fexa   on bid wrecen,
þæt se þéod-cyning   ðafian sceolde
E(o)fores ánne dóm.   Hyne yrringa
2965 Wulf Wonréding   wǽpne ġerǽhte,
þæt him for swenge   swát ǽdrum sprong
forð under fexe.   Næs hé forht swá ðéh,
gomela Scilfing,   ac forġeald hraðe
wyrsan wrixle   wæl-hlem þone,
2970 syððan ðéod-cyning   þyder onċirde.
Ne meahte se snella,   sunu Wonrédes,
ealdum ċeorle   hondslyht ġiofan,
ac hé him on héafde   helm ǽr ġescer;
þæt hé blóde fáh   búgan sceolde,
2975 féoll on foldan,   næs hé fǽġe þá ġít,
ac hé hyne ġewyrpte,   þéah ðe him wund hríne,
Lét se hearda   Hiġeláces þeġn
bráde méċe,   þá his bróðor læġ,

187

brandished his blade   where his brother lay,
the old blade of Ettins,   through his helm
2980   broke o'er the board-wall.   The king bowed,
the folk's warden   dropped in death.

"There were many   who bound his brother's wounds,
rose him up   and made room for them,
so that they might   wield the war-field
2985   and look   about for loot.
He took from Ongentheow   his iron byrnie,
his hard-hilted sword   and helm too,
and bore the hoary one's   harness to Hygelac.
He took these treasures,   and fairly pledged
2990   rewards for his retainers,   and he did so.
He repaid that war-rush,   the Geatish lord;
Hrethel's heir,   when he came home
he gave to Eofor and Wulf*   a wealth of mathoms.
Each of them had   a hundred-thousand hides
2995   of land and lockèd rings   -no need to scorn them
had any man on Middle-Earth,   for they earned them with might-
and then he gave to Eofor   his only daughter,
an honor for his home,   to affirm their friendship.

"Such is the feud   and our foe's hatred,
3000   the deathly loathing of men;   'tis likely I think,
that the Swedish nation   shall seek us at home
when they   learn that our lord
lies lifeless,   he who once held
hoard and realm   against ravagers,
3005   after the fall of heroes*,   the haughty Scylfings;
he had furthered   the folk's ambitions
and accomplished daring deeds.

"Now, haste is best,
that we look upon   the lord of the Geats,
the one who gave us gifts,   and bear him away
3010   to his pyre.   Nor must one part
melt with the manly king,   but a hoard of mathoms,
gold unnumbered   and grimly gained
that was last bought   with his life;
all of the treasure shall   be taken by the blaze
3015   -fire shall eat it.   No earl must wear
these mathoms as a a memorial,   nor a fair maiden
put a precious ring   about her neck,
but must sorrowfully   give up their gold

eald sweord Eotonisc,   entiscne helm
2980 brecan ofer bord-weall;   ðá ġebéah cyning,
folces hyrde   wæs in feorh dropen.

"Ðá wǽron moniġe   þe his mǽġ wriðon,
ricone árǽrdon,   ðá him ġerýmed wearð,
þæt híe wæl-stówe   wealdan móston.
2985 Þenden réafode   rinc óðerne,
nam on Ongenðío   íren-byrnan,
heard swyrd hilted   ond his helm somod,
háres hyrste   Hiġeláce bær.
Hé (ðám) frætwum féng   ond him fǽġre ġehét
2990 léana (mid) léodum,   ond ġelǽst(e) swá;
ġeald þone gúð-ræs   Ġéata dryhten,
Hréðles eafora,   þá hé tó hám becóm,
Iofore ond Wulfe   mid ofer-máðmum.
Sealde hiora ġehwæðrum   hund þúsenda
2995 landes ond locenra béaga-   ne ðorfte him ðá léan oðwítan
mon on Middan-Ġearde,   syðða(n) híe ðá mǽrða ġeslógon-
ond ðá Iofore forġeaf   ángan dóhtor,
hám-weorðunge,   hyldo tó wedde.

"Þæt ys sío fǽhðo   ond se féond-scipe,
3000 wæl-níð wera;   ðæs ðe iċ (wén) hafo,
þé ús séċeað tó   Swéona léode
syððan híe ġefricgeað   fréan úserne
ealdor-léasne,   þone ðe ǽr ġehéold
wið hettendum   hord ond ríċe
3005 æfter hæleða hryre,   hwate Scil(f)ingas;
folc-réd fremede   oððe furður ġén
eorl-scipe efnde.

        "(Nú) is ofost betost,
þæt wé þéod-cyning   þǽr scéawian
ond þone ġebringan,   þé ús béagas ġeaf
3010 on ád-fære.   Ne scel ánes hwæt
meltan mid þám módigan,   ac þǽr is máðma hord,
gold unríme   grimme ġeċéa(po)d
ond nú æt síðestan   sylfes féore
béagas (ġeboh)te;   þá sceal brond fretan,
3015 -ǽled þeċċean.   Nalles eorl weġan
máððum tó ġemyndum,   né mæġð scýne
habban on healse   hring-weorðunge,
ac sceall ġeómor-mód   golde beréafod
oft nalles ǽne   elland tredan,

and oft tread   the trail of wanderers,
3020 now that our war-leader   has laid aside laughter,
games and glee.   Many spears shall,
morning-cold,   be clasped in fists,
hefted in hand,   nor shall the sound of the harp
awaken the warriors,   but the dark wingèd raven,
3025 fain of the fallen,   speaks of many things,
boasts to the eagle   of how it eats,
when he and the wolf   waste the slain."

Thus, did he speak   that loathly spell,
nor did the   loyal one lie
3030 in works or words.   The warriors all arose
and unblithely   went to Earnaness*
with welling tears   to see that wonder.
They found him lying   lifeless on the sand,
ruling his rest-bed,   he who once gave rings
3035 in earlier times;   that was his end-day,
the battle-king   who searched for bold men.
A wondrous death   the Weder lord suffered.

They saw there too   a strange creature,
the unfurled fire-Drake   upon the ground,
3040 the loathsome one lying dead;   the Wyrm was
a grim and fearful fiend,   burnt by flame.
They reckoned that   fifty foot-spans
long it lay;   aloft it ruled
the night time,   'til it turned back again
3045 to seek its den.   It was fast in death,
it's joys in the earth-house   had ended.
By it stood   bowls and beakers,
dishes lay there   and dear swords,
eaten with rust   in the earth's embrace,
3050 and for a thousand   winters waited.
Then was that   mighty monument,
the mathoms cursed   by men of old*
that none could   touch that treasure
of Mankind,   unless the Maker,
3055 the True King,   kenned him worthy,
Man's Helper,   for the hoard to open,
even so to every man   as seemed meet to Him.

<pre>
3020   nú se here-wísa   hleahtor áleġde,
        gamen ond gléo-dréam.   Forðon sceall gár wesan
        moniġ morgen-ċeald,   mundum bewunden,
        hæfen on handa,   nalles hearpan swéġ
        wíġend weċċean,   ac se wonna hrefn,
3025   fús ofer fǽġum   fela reordian,
        earne secgan   hú him æt ǽte spéow,
        þenden hé wið wulf   wæl réafode."

        Swá se secg hwata   secgende wæs
        láðra spella,   hé ne léaġ fela
3030   wyrda né worda.   Weorod eall árás
        éodon unblíðe   under Earnanæs
        wollen-téare   wundur scéawian.
        Fundon ðá on sande   sáwul-léasne,
        hlim-bed healdan,   þone þe him hringas ġeaf
3035   ǽrran mǽlum;   þá wæs ende-dæġ
        gódum ġegongen,   þæt se gúð-cyning,
        Wedra þéoden   wundor-déaðe swealt.

        Ǽr hí þǽr ġeséġan   syllicran wiht,
        Wyrm on wonge   wiðer-ræhtes þǽr
3040   láðne licgean;   wæs se léġ-Draca
        grimlíċ gry(re-gæst),   glédum beswǽled.
        Sé wæs fíftiġes   fót-ġemearces
        lang on leġere;   lyft-wynne héold
        nihtes hwílum,   nyðer eft ġewát
3045   dennes niosian.   Wæs ðá déaðe fæst,
        hæfde eorð-scrafa   ende ġenyttod.
        Him biġ stódan   bunan ond orcas,
        discas lágon   ond dýre swyrd,
        ómiġe þurh-etone   swá híe wið eorðan fæðm
3050   þúsend wintra   þǽr eardodon;
        þonne wæs þæt yrfe   éacen-cræftiġ,
        iú-monna gold   galdre bewunden,
        þæt ðám hring-sele   hrínan ne móste
        gumena ǽniġ,   nefne God sylfa,
3055   siġora Sóð-Cyning   sealde þám ðe hé wolde
        -Hé is Manna Ġehyld-   hord openian,
        efne swá hwylcum manna   swá Him ġemet ðúhte.
</pre>

Chapter XX
The Balefire of Beowulf

Then it was seen   that his adventure did not aid
he who unrightly   hid in the hall,
3060   wrath under the wall!   The warden had already slain
one of the few;   then was the feud
revenged with rage.   'Tis a wonder when
a man of might   should meet the end
of his doomed life,   when he no longer can
3065   man the mead-hall   with his kinsmen.
So it was with Beowulf,   when he the barrow's guardian
sought that struggle;   he did not know
what his leaving this life   would bring about.
Thus 'til Doomsday   deeply named
3070   the ancient athelings   who put it there,
that the man would stand   accused of sins,
held from the harrow,   in Hell-bonds fast,
punished his crimes,   he who plundered that place.
He was not greedy for gold,   nor had he
3075   fully seen the favor   of its owner.

Wiglaf spake,   Weohstan's son,
"Oft must many men,   for the will of one
endure exile,   as we must.
Our belovèd king   did not care,
3080   the herder of the realm,   for any rede
to greet not   the gold-ward
and let it lie,   where long it had been,
endure in the earth-house   'til the ending of the world;
hold it under the heavens.   The hoard is now our's,
3085   grimly gained;   that was given him,
which pushed forth   our people-king.
I was there inside,   and all I saw,
riches in the hall,   when room was made,
though 'twas not   a pleasant path I took
3090   under the earth-wall!   Eagerly I took

XLI

Þá wæs ġesýne   þæt se síð ne ðáh
þám ðe unrihte   inne ġehýdde,
3060   wræce under wealle!   Weard ǽr ofslóh
féara sumne;   þá sío fǽhð ġewearð
ġewrecen wráðlíċe.   Wundur hwár þonne
eorl ellen-róf   ende ġefére
líf-ġesceafta,   þonne leng ne mæġ
3065   mon mid his m(æ)ġum   medu-seld búan.
Swá wæs Bíowulfe,   þá hé biorges weard
sóhte, searo-níða;   seolfa ne cúðe
þurh hwæt his worulde ġedál   weorðan sceolde.
Swá hit oð Dómesdæġ   díope benemdon
3070   þéodnas mære   þá ðæt þǽr dydon,
þæt se secg wǽre   synnum scildiġ,
hergum ġeheaðerod,   Hell-bendum fæst,
wommum ġewítnad,   sé ðone wong str(u)de.
Næs hé gold-hwæte   ġearwor hæfde
3075   áġendes ést   ǽr ġescéawod.

Wíġláf maðelode,   Wíhstánes sunu,
"Oft sceall eorl moniġ   ánes willan
wræc ádréog(an),   swá ús ġeworden is.
Ne meahton wé ġelǽran   léofne þéoden,
3080   ríċes hyrde,   rǽd æniġne,
þæt hé ne grétte   gold-weard þone,
léte hyne licgean,   þǽr hé longe wæs,
wícum wunian   oð woruld-ende;
héoldon héah-ġesceap.   Hord ys ġescéawod,
3085   grimme ġegongen;   þæt ġifeðe (wæs),
to swið þé ðone (þéod-cyning)   þyder ontyhte.
Iċ wæs þǽr inne   ond þæt eall ġeond-seh,
reċedes ġeatwa,   þá mé ġerýmed wæs,
nealles swǽslíċe   síð álýfed
3090   inn under eorð-weall!   Iċ on ofoste ġeféng

193

from the hoard   with mine hands,
a great burden   and bore it hither out.
My king   was quick still,
wise and witty,   and he spoke of many things;
3095 old in his grief,   he sent his greetings,
and bade us build   in his honor
a high barrow   o'er his balefire,
mickle and mighty.   Of men he was
the worthiest of warriors   o'er this wide Earth,
3100 whilst he still found bliss   in the burg.
Let us hasten out now,   once again,
to see and to seek   that stow of treasure,
a wonder under the walls!   I will show the way,
so that you may   see stored there
3105 rings and broad gold.   Let the bier be prepared,
made quickly   when out we come,
and then carry   our king,
the belovèd man,   where long he shall
abide in the watch   of the Wielder."

3110 Then he bade,   the bairn of Weohstan,
the hardy hero,   that many warriors,
who held homes,   wood for the bale-fire
fetch from afar,   they who owned the folk
for that faméd king.   "Now shall fire consume,
3115 the wan flames wax   on the strengthener of warriors,
he who oft endured   the iron-shower,
when an arrow-storm   sent from his bow-string
shot o'er the shield-wall,   and the shaft held true,
the fervent feather-trappings   followed the barb."

3120 So, the   wise son of Weohstan
called from the company   of king's thegns
seven of the best   from that band.
He went, one of eight,   beneath that evil roof
whilst one hardy warrior   stood in front,
3125 bearing a burning brand   in his hand.
They did not cast lots   for who should loot the hoard,
when they saw the gold   was unguarded,
abiding   in the barrow,
lying without a lord;   little did any mourn
3130 when they   quickly carried it out,
the dear mathoms!   The Dragon they shoved,
the Wyrm o'er the cliff-walls   and let the waves take him,
the flood grasp   the guardian of the gold.

194

miċle mid mundum   mæġen-byrðenne,
hord-ġestréona,   hider út ætbær.
Cyninge mínum   cwico wæs þá ġéna,
wís ond ġewittiġ,   worn eall ġespræc;
3095   gomol on ġehðo   ond éowiċ grétan hét,
bæd þæt ġé ġeworhton   æfter wines dædum
in bæl-stede   beorh þone héan,
miċelne ond mærne.   Swá hé manna wæs
wíġend weorð-fullost   wíde ġeond Eorðan,
3100   þenden hé burh-welan   brúcan móste.
Uton nú efstan   óðre (síðe),
séon ond séċean   searo-ġeþræc,
wundur under wealle!   Iċ éow wísiġe,
þæt ġé ġenóge   néon scéawiað
3105   béagas ond brád gold.   Síe sío bær ġearo,
ædre ġeæfned   þonne wé út cymen,
ond þonne ġeferian   fréan úserne,
léofne mannan   þær hé longe sceal
on þæs waldendes   wære ġeþolian."

3110   Hét ðá ġebéodan,   byre Wíhstánes,
hæle hilde-díor,   hæleða monegum,
bold-ágendra,   þæt híe bæl-wudu
feorran feredon,   folc-áġende
gódum tóġénes,   "Nú sceal gléd fretan,
3115   weaxan wonna léġ   wiġena strengel,
þone ðe oft ġebád   ísern-scúre,
þonne stræla storm   strengum ġebæded
scóc ofer scild-weall,   sceft nytte héold,
fæ(ð)erġearwum fús   fláne full-éode."

3120   Húru se snotra   sunu Wíhstánes
áċígde of corðre   cyninges þeġnas
syfone (tósom)ne   þá sélestan.
Éode eahta sum,   under inwit-hróf
hilde-rinc(a)   sum on handa bær
3125   æled-léoman,   sé ðe on orde ġéong.
Næs ðá on hlytme   hwá þæt hord strude,
syððan or-wearde   æniġne dæl.
secgas ġeségon   on sele wunian,
læne licgan;   lýt æniġ mearn
3130   þæt hí ofostliċ(e)   út ġeferedon,
dýre máðmas!   Dracan éc scufun,
Wyrm ofer weall-clif,   léton wéġ niman,
flód fæðmian   frætwa hyrde.

Then was the wound gold   on a wain laid,
3135   countless kinds of mathoms;   the king they bore,
the hoary hero   to Hronesness.

Then they for him prepared,   the Geatish people,
a funeral fire   upon the earth;
they hung it with helms   and battle-shields
3140   and bright byrnies,   as he bade,
and laid amid it   their mighty king-
heroes wept   for their belovèd wielder.
They began on the barrow   the greatest of bale-fires,
the warriors to awaken;   wood-smoke arose,
3145   black o'er the blaze and the burning roared,
wound with weeping,   -the wind was still-
'til the bone-house   was broken,
hot at the heart.   Heavy were their moods,
they bemoaned their misery   for their lord's demise.
3150   A lone Geatish widow*   a death-wail
braided for Beowulf,   bound hard;
she sang sorrowfully   of how she in full
dreaded the dark days   that soon would come,
a flock of the slain,   the fear of the folk,
3155   thralldom and shame.   Heaven swallowed the smoke.

Then wrought   the Weder folk
a howe on the headland,   high and broad,
to wave-farers   widely seen;
they toiled on it   for ten days,
3160   the battle-chieftain's beacon.   They placed brands around it
and built a wall,   the worthiest ever
that the wisest of men   could make.
In the barrow   they put brooches and rings,
all the treasures   they had taken,
3165   those hardy men   from the hoard;
the wealth of earls   they let the earth hold,
gold in the grit,   where still it lies
as useless to Men   as ever it was.

About the barrow rode   the battle-stout ones*,
3170   the sons of athelings,   twelve in all;
they cried out their cares   and mourned their king,
sang dirges   and spake of their lord.
They praised his earldom   and acts of courage
they deemed worthy;   well it is
3175   that men laud their lord and friend   with words

196

Þ(á) wæs wunden gold   on wǽn hladen,
3135   ǽġhwæs unrím;   æþelin(g) boren,
      hár hilde(rinc)   tó Hronesnæsse.

XLII

      Him ðá ġeġiredan   Ġéata léode
      ád on eorðan   un-wáclícne;
      helm(um) behongen,   hilde-bordum,
3140   beorhtum byrnum,   swá hé béna wæs,
      áleġdon ðá tó-middes   mǽrne þéoden-
      hæleð híofende,   hláford léofne.
      Ongunnon þá on beorge   bǽl-fýra mǽst,
      wíġend weċċan;   wud(u)réċ ástáh
3145   sweart ofer swi(o)ðole,   swógende lé(ġ,)
      wópe bewunden,   -wind-blond ġelæġ-
      oð þæt hé ðá bán-hús   ġebrocen hæfde,
      hát on hreðre.   Hiġum unróte,
      mód-ċeare mǽndon,   mon-dryhtnes cw(e)alm.
3150   Swylċe ġiómor-ġyd   (Ġé)at(isc) anmeowle
      (Biowulf bræġd,)   bundenheorde;
      s(a)ng sorgċeariġ   sǽlde ġeneah(he)
      þæt hío hyre (hearmda)gas   hearde ond(r)ede,
      wælfylla worn,   werudes eġesan,
3155   hyðo ond hæf(t)nyd.   Heofon réċe swealg.

      Ġeworhton ðá   Wedra léode
      hlǽ(w) on h(líð)e,   sé wæs héah ond brád,
      (w)ǽġlíðendum   wíde ġesýne
      ond beti(m)bredon   on týn dagum.
3160   beadu-rófes bécn.   Bronda láfe
      wealle beworhton,   swá hyt weorðlícost
      fore-snotre men   findan mihton.
      Hí on beorg dydon   béġ ond siġlu,
      eall swylce hyrsta   swylċe on horde ǽr,
3165   níð-hédiġe men   ġenumen hæfdon;
      forléton eorla ġestréon   eorðan healdan,
      gold on gréote,   þǽr hit nú ġén lifað
      eldum swá unnyt   swá hit (ǽre)r wæs.

      Þá ymbe hlǽw riodan   hilde-déore,
3170   æþelinga bearn,   ealra twelfa;
      woldon (cearġe) cwíðan   (ond) kyning mǽnan,
      word-ġyd wrecan   ond ymb we(r) sprecan.
      Eahtodan eorl-scipe   ond his ellen-weorc
      duguðum démdon;   swá hit ġed(éfe) bið
3175   þæt mon his wine-dryhten   wordum herġe,

197

and harbor love in their heart,   when hence
from his lich,   his life is led.

So mourned   the men of the Geats,
his hearth-companions   for the loss of their lord.
3180 Quoth they,   that of all this world's kings,
he was of men the mildest   and most generous,
the kindest to his people,   and the most eager for praise.*

ferhðum fréoġe,   þonne hé forð scile
of líċhaman,   (lǽded) weorðan.

Swá begnornodon   Ġéata léode,
hláfordes (hry)re,   heorð-ġenéatas.
3180   Cwǽdon þæt hé wǽre   wyruldcyning,
manna mildust   ond mon(ðw)ǽrust,
léodum líðost   ond lofġeornost.

COMMENTARY

This commentary is far from comprehensive, something which I, in fact do not think is feasible. It would take thousands of pages to cover the entirety of *Beowulf* studies, and would soon be out-of-date. Therefore, I did not even attempt to make it comprehensive. In general, I use a historical/cultural focus, which is my expertise, rather than a literary/linguistic focus, though I do occasionally delve into topics such as linguistics or poetics. I also do not typically spend much time on scholarly theories that I find unlikely. There are plenty of books out there that focus on these areas that my commentary are deficient in. I encourage any reader interested in other areas of *Beowulf* studies to look up the sources in my *Bibliography*.

The poem is hedged about with so many uncertainties… that even the simplest and most strait forward statements can provoke a battle royal among scholars… Thus the analysis of the poem is endless. (Earl, 1994)

Note on quotations: Old English translations are my own. Bible verses use the *Douay–Rheims Bible* translation, an English translation of the Latin *Vulgate, St. Jerome's Bible* translation from 382 AD. The Vulgate and the DRV are rarely used nowadays, but as the Latin *Vulgate* would have been the Bible translation used in Anglo-Saxon England, I have opted to use this.

Line 1a- How we have heard…

Traditionally, *hwæt*, in this line, has been translated as an exclamation (e.g. Lo, Listen, So, Hark, etc). It was believed that this was to capture the attention of the audience in a hall. However, George Walkden, a professor at the University of Manchester, believes that here *hwæt* rather than being a command, was meant to inform the reader of the wider exclamatory nature of the sentence. Thus, the line should be read like "How we have heard of the glory of the Spear-Danes", rather than "Lo! We have heard of the glory of the Spear-Danes" (Walkden, 2011).

Line 1b- Spear Danes

The Danes were a North Germanic tribe, who ruled the southern tip of Sweden (Skåneland), the Danish islands and small areas of the Jutland peninsula, including Schleswig (the Danish Marches, from which Denmark gets its name, now part of Germany) in the Nordic Iron Age. They probably originated in what is now Sweden.

Due to the alliterative style of *Beowulf*, the Danes are referred to under multiple epithets (e.g. Spear Danes, Sword Danes, East Danes, South Danes, etc).. These epithets are not meant to differentiate them from other groups of Danes. The Danes are also sometimes referred to as Scyldings (descendants of Scyld, the name of the royal family). even when it is referring to the people rather than the royal family. In the Finnesburg Episode (Lines 1066-159) and a few other places, it even refers to pre-Scylding (or at least non-Scylding) Danish dynasties as Scyldings.

Line 3b- Athelings

An atheling (Old English: *æþeling*) was a member of the royal family. It is often translated as 'prince,' but 'atheling' had a broader meaning. An atheling could be fairly distant from being in line to the throne. In fact, in early Old English, the word 'atheling' needn't apply to a royal at all, and could refer to any member of the nobility. Thus, an atheling could be a king, a prince or an earl. In poetry, the meaning was even broader; an atheling simply meant 'a good and noble man,' and could equally apply to Christ, a saint or a hero as to a member of royalty (Lapidge, 2003).

Line 4-11- Scyld Scefing

Scyld Scefing is the eponymous founder of the Scyldings, the Danish royal house,

corresponding to the Skjöldr of Norse legends. The -*ing* ending is an Anglo-Saxon patronymic, but can also have meanings such as 'of' or 'with', so the original meaning may have been 'Scyld (Shield) of the Sheaf' (as in a sheaf of corn), rather than 'Scyld, son of Sceaf.'

There are various Germanic legends of a Lombard king named Sceafa. Later legends seem to confuse Scyld and Sceafa, by attributing Scyld's origin story to Sceafa. However, as Scyld is discovered as a foundling, 'Scyld of the Sheaf' is more likely than 'Son of Sceafa.' In fact, according to some Anglo-Saxon genealogies, Scyld was the fourth son of Noah, born on the Ark (Chambers, 1959).

Line 6a- the Eorlas

The original line said *eorl* and is traditionally emended to *eorlas*, earls. However, Charles Leslie Wrenn emends it to *Eorle*, or the Heruli, a fearsome tribe from the Danish islands during the Roman era, who spread terror across Europe. According to Jordanes, the Danes overthrew the Heruli as the rulers of the Danish islands, and Wrenn believes the *Beowulf* poet was attributing that Danish victory to Scyld (Slade, 2005).

Line 10a- Whale Road

'Whale road' is a *kenning* for 'the sea.' A kenning is when a word is replaced with another word or phrase with the same meaning, common in Germanic poetry. Typically, these are simple, like 'sea-stead' for 'ship,' but especially in Norse poetry, can be quite long, like 'fire-slingers of the storm of the giantess of the shelter-moon of the steeds of ship-sheds,' meaning 'warriors' in the *Hafgerðingadrápa*.

Professor Tolkien notes that translating *hron-rád* as 'whale road' is incorrect. 'Whale' in Old English is *hwæl*, not *hron*. He mentions an Anglo-Saxon gloss that said, "Seven seals are plenty for a *hron*, and seven *hron* are plenty for a *hwæl*." (Bosworth, 1921), which suggests a dolphin, porpoise or orca, rather than a whale. He also notes that while *rád* is the ancestor of the modern English 'road', the meaning is closer to the word 'ride,' as in 'riding on a horse.' His biggest aversion to 'whale road,' however seems to be that it sounds too much like 'railroad.' While I do agree with Tolkien on the etymology of *hronrád*, I still opted to use 'whale road' in this translation. As trains are not in as common use for travel in the 21st Century as in the late 1920s, I do not feel that most readers will notice the similarity in sound. I also think "whale road" has a nice ring to it, and even if it doesn't have quite the same meaning as it does in Old English, it works equally well as a kenning (Tolkien, 2014).

Line 14b-6a— …that great distress that they had ere endured…

This is probably a reference to the reign of Heremod before the rise of the Scyldings. See more in the Commentary for Line 901.

Line 18- Bedwig

In the West Saxon genealogies, Scyld's son is named Beow. However, in the manuscript, he is called Beowulf. John Mitchell Kemble believed that the manuscript's copyist mistook Beow as an abbreviation of Beowulf, in anticipation of the main character of the same name.

Beow is called Bedwig in other Anglo-Saxon traditions and Bedvig in Norse tradition, so I have opted to name him Bedwig in my translation to further differentiate him.(Chambers. 1959).

Lines 19b- Scandian Lands

Scandia is an old name for Scandinavia, derived from the Proto-Germanic name *Skaðinaujô*.

Greek and Roman writers thought of Scandia as a great island north of Germania, the homeland of the Goths (Tolkien, 2014).

Lines 26-52- Scyld's Ship-Burial

Scyld Scefing is almost a sort of Germanic Moses. Both of them were fosterlings, set out on the water as infants, but discovered, and who grew up to lead their people to greatness. While Moses was not placed in a ship at death, there is another parallel. The poem describes how Scyld is pushed out into the unknown, and how *men cannot truly say… who collected that cargo.* Deuteronomy 34:6 says that God *…buried him [Moses] in the valley of the land of Moab over against Phogor: and no man hath known of his sepulchre until this present day.* Thus, both Scyld and Moses's final resting place is a mystery to Men; both were left in God's hands (Arner, et al, 2013).

Ship burials, while not exceptionally common, were certainly not unheard of in Germanic cultures, especially in Scandinavia. However the description of Scyld Scefing's funeral seems to be unique among the Germanic peoples, though it does bear some resemblance to some Celtic Christian practices, in which they set themselves adrift in the North Atlantic in oarless coracles to let God bring them to whatever shores He willed (which led to the founding of monastic settlements in the Faeroe Islands and Iceland, and possibly even the European discovery of North America). In the Rhuys *Life of Saint Gildas*, when Gildas died, he asked for his unburnt body to be set adrift in a boat. Most Germanic ship burials involved cremation, such as the famous example in the account of Ahmad ibn Fadlan that he saw in 922 along the Volga River or the account in the *Ynglinga saga* of the sea-king Haki (likely the same character as Hoc, the father of Hildeburh, mentioned in Line 1076) when he ordered that his body be laid on his longship alongside his slain men, and be set adrift while the ship burned. Other times, the ship, containing their cremated remains were buried, such as the ship burials at Oseberg and Gokstad in Norway. However, the ship buried in Mound 1 at Sutton Hoo in Suffolk perhaps sheds the most light on *Beowulf*, especially toward the funeral of Scyld Scefing.

The Sutton Hoo ship burial was most likely for Rædwald, king of East Anglia and *Bretwalda*, the Anglo-Saxon high king, who died in about 625, only a few generations before *Beowulf* was most likely developed. (and perhaps a descendant of Wiglaf, Beowulf's successor) Curiously, the ship, contains no evidence of a body. Some believe this was a cenotaph, but most now believe that any trace of a body would have decomposed in the highly acidic soil. Whatever the case, the space where the body would have been laid was in the center of the ship, surrounded by armor, weapons and treasure, just like Scyld (Owen-Crocker, 2010).

Lines 35a- Ring Givers

One of the expectations of a Germanic king was to show generosity to his followers. A good king was supposed to reward his men with treasure, and the most common treasure given out were arm-rings. There was no form of currency in Iron Age Scandinavia, so the rings could be cut up for their silver, but this would be an act of desperation; arm-rings were viewed with pride and the number of arm-rings a man wore showed his prowess in battle.

Line 36b- Mathoms

Mathom is a direct translation of the Old English word *máþum*, meaning a treasure or a gift. The word survived into Middle English, as *mathem* or *madme*, but became obsolete during the shift to Early Modern English. However, with the spelling mathom, it was reintroduced into Modern English by J.R.R. Tolkien in The Lord of the Rings, where it referred to a Hobbitish term for an item of no

immediate use, a trinket. I am using the word in its original meaning (Gilliver, et al, 2009).

Line 40a- Byrnies

The Anglo-Saxons, and Germanic peoples in general, used chain-mail armor. In Old English, chain-mail shirts were known as *byrnes*, and this is where the word 'byrnie' comes from. Only one complete Anglo-Saxon byrnie has ever been found, one from Mound 1 of Sutton Hoo that is severely corroded. It seems to have been at least thigh length and in alternating rows of welded iron links and links held together with copper rivets. A 4th-5th Century byrnie in much better condition was discovered in Vimose, Denmark, of much the same description as the Sutton Hoo byrnie; this byrnie has over 20,000 links, and would thus have taken a substantial period of time to make (Mortimer, 2011).

Line 52b-3a- Fitts

Beowulf is divided into 43 'fitts', with Fitt I beginning at Line 53. A 'fitt' is a sectional division, based on an Old English word meaning 'song,' (though in this case, 'reading or passage' is closer to its meaning) basically the equivalent of the Latin 'canto'. All but three of the fitts in *Beowulf* are headed by the Roman numeral denoting the fitt number, but all of the fitts begin with an initial, thus a new fitt can be deduced even when it lacks a number. (Orchard, 2003)

It can't be known whether the original poem was divided into fitts, or if, like the chapters in the books of the Bible, these divisions were made later for the ease of those reading the manuscript (Arner, et al, 2013).

I left the fitts in the Old English text, but I decided to break the modern English text into 20 chapters and a prologue. I feel that, while the 43 fitts provide ease of reading short passages of the poem, I feel that they sometimes end abruptly and can feel disjointed. I think that the chapter divisions feels more natural. I gave the chapters alliterative titles to match the style of the poetry.

Line 53b- Burgs

A burg or *burh* in Old English was a fortified settlement, that had a degree of autonomy. Burgs were common in Scandinavia during the Migration Era, built near rivers in order to defend those living nearby. In England, burgs were often repurposed Celtic hillforts and Roman forts. In the 9th Century, Alfred the Great, developed a network of burgs across England to fend off Vikings. Many former burgs have names ending in *-bury* or *-burgh* (Lapidge, 2003).

Lines 57-62- Healfdene and his Children

The name Healfdene, meaning "half Dane", only occurs in *Beowulf*, but is a direct translation of the common Norse name, Halfdan. While this name typically denotes mixed heritage, (a man with one Danish parent and one non-Danish parent) Tolkien believed that his name instead referred to the Half-Danes, the people ruled by Hnæf from the Finnesburg episode (see Commentary for Lines 1066-59) and specifically Hoc, the father of Hnæf and Hildeburh. He believed that Half-Dane was actually the title of Hoc, and the name was later applied to the dynasty, and eventually the people, like how the Danes are sometimes called the Scyldings, even though the Scyldings technically only referred to the ruling family. Tolkien proposed a third sibling to Hnæf and Hildeburh: an unnamed sister who married Beow (or Bedwig in my translation), king of the Danes. Tolkien notes that it was a common Germanic practice to name a boy after the maternal grandfather, and proposes that is why Beow's son was named Healfdene, in honor of his grandfather, Hoc 'Half-Dane.' (Tolkien, 1983)

In the Norse sources, Heorogar does not appear. However, his son, Heoroweard (Hjörvarðr) does appear. Hjörvarðr is the husband of Skuld, the half-Elven half-sister of Hrólfr Kraki (Hrothulf) who talks her husband into rebelling against Hrólfr (and killing him), in order to claim the throne for himself, before being killed himself. While Hjörvarðr's parentage is not given, if we follow the lineage presented in *Beowulf*, this would explain how Skuld was able to convince Hjörvarðr that he had as much right (or possibly more) to the Danish throne than her half-brother. It's very likely then that Heorogar existed in earlier legends, but was forgotten by the point the Norse sagas were written down. See also commentary for Line 2161a.

Halga (Helgi) is another major character in the Norse sources. As explained above, Helgi was the father of Hrólfr Kraki, perhaps the most famous Danish king in the Legendary Sagas. Before Hrólf's birth. Halga and his elder brother, Hróarr (Hrothgar) reclaimed the Danish throne from their evil uncle Fróði (this legend is one of the sources of *Hamlet*). When the two reclaimed the throne, they agreed to co-rule; Hróarr ruled the land, while Helgi ruled the sea (Gammonsway, et al, 1971).

In the Norse sources, Hrothgar and Halga's sister was named Signy. Due to a textual crux in the *Beowulf* manuscript, Hrothgar's sister is unnamed. The manuscript reads: *…hȳrde iċ, þæt elan cwén* (and, I have heard -ela's queen). Friedrich Kluge amended it to *…hȳrde iċ, þæt Siġeneow wæs Sǣwelan cwén* (and, I have heard, Sigeneow, who was Sǣwela's queen). The name Signy in Old English would have been Sigeneow, and her husband in *Hrólfs saga kraka* was named Sævil (Sǣwela). Most scholars believe however, that *-elan* most likely should have been *Onelan* (Onela is a Swedish king mentioned later in the poem). With the rules of alliteration, the name of *Onela's queen* would have to also start with a vowel. Most scholars believe that this name would have been Yrse. In the Norse sources, Yrsa is the name of Helgi's daughter, who unwittingly married Helgi and gave birth to Hrólfr Kraki and who later married Aðils (Eadgils). Eadgils is the nephew of Onela in the poem. Therefore, the English and the Norse traditions evolved quite differently. (Slade, 2005).

Shippey thinks that Yrsa was actually Halga's daughter, and thus both ealfdene's daughter-in-law and granddaughter. The poet simply said that she was Healfdene's daughter so he could avoid talking about incest (Shippey, 2015).

Line 75b- Middle-Earth

The word *Middanġeard* is translated in modern English as Middle-Earth. Middanġeard corresponds with the Old Norse *Miðgarðr*, the world of Men. It is the "Middle-Earth" because it is the center-point of the Nine Worlds on *Yggdrasil*, the World Tree. *Middanġeard* was the inspiration for Middle-Earth, the common name for Arda in Tolkien's *Legendarium* (Gilliver, et al, 2009).

Line 78b- Heorot he named it…

The mead-hall was at center stage of the life of a Germanic kingdom. Many people think of mead-halls almost like pubs; a fancy building where people went to drink alcohol, especially mead (a sort of wine, made of honey, rather than grapes). Mead-halls were, in fact, much more than that. They were a king's (or lord's) residence, a barracks, a war-room, an assembly hall, and a social meet all rolled into one. Michael Swanton said, "…it was the practical and emotional center of heroic society, all that a man could wish; and its destruction therefore represented the negation of all that society stood for" (Swanton, 1978). This is why early in the poem, it said that *Scyld Scefing seize{d} the mead-benches of frightened foes*; tearing down an enemy's mead-hall was taking away the center-point of theirs, and was the ultimate symbol of their lost independence (Shippey, 2015).

Mead-halls were massive wooden buildings, usually consisting of a single, long room with a

fire-pit running its length and high roofs with holes to let out the smoke. The heath lay in-between long tables and benches, that could seat hundreds of men. Along the center of one of the long walls were double-doors that were guarded at all times, and on the far wall was the king's throne.

In the Norse sources, the royal seat of the Danes in the Iron Age, was Lejre (*Hleiðr* in Old Norse) on the Danish island of Zealand. Beginning in the 1980s, the nearby Roskilde University began excavations in Gammel Lejre and discovered signs that this was indeed an important site in the pre-Viking Iron Age. In the summers of 2004-5, the remains of a hall was found, about 50 meters long (over half the length of a football field), nearly twice the size of the Northumbrian royal hall at Yeavering, the largest Anglo-Saxon building ever made. This hall was built in the 6th Century- the same time as *Beowulf*. This may have been the real Heorot (Christensen, 2010).

Heorot in Old English means "hart" or "stag." The Anglo-Saxons saw the stag as the "King of the Forest" and used the stag as a symbol of kingship by the Anglo-Saxons. This can be seen in the Sutton Hoo whetstone/scepter (Newton, 1999).

Line 82b-85- Enmity 'twixt in-laws

In the poem *Widsith*, it mentions an attack on Heorot. Lines 45-49 say:

Hróþwulf ond Hróðgár héoldon lengest
sibbe ætsomne suhtorfædran,
siþþan hý forwræcon Wícinga cynn
ond Ingeldes ord forbígdan,
forhéowan æt Heorote Heaðobeardna þrym.

Hrothulf and Hrothgar, uncle and nephew, held
peace with each other, for a long time,
after they repelled the race of Vikings
and hewed down Ingeld with the edge of a sword,
utterly defeated the Heathobard host at Heorot.

It can be assumed that this *Widsith* passage is referring to the same lost legend that these lines in *Beowulf* is. The Danes and the Bards were in a feud, which Hrothgar intended to end by marrying his daughter, Freawaru to Ingeld, the Bardish king. During the nuptials, the feud was reborn. The Bards burnt down Heorot, and Hrothgar and Hrothulf led the Danes in a battle where Ingeld was slain (Gammonsway, et al, 1971). See more in the commentary for Lines 2025-2079.

(NOTE: The word *Heaðo* means 'War', and when these types of prefixes are added to a tribal name, it seems to have only been done for alliterative purposes. From now on I'll be omitting the *Heaðo* prefix when referring to tribal names, except when used in quotes).

Lines 90-8- Scops and the Song of Creation

Court poets in Anglo-Saxon culture were known a scops. The scop would both compose and recite poems. During feasts, they might be asked to tell a tale of the heroes of old at a feast, or create a new poem in honor of their patron. A poem in someone's honor was the surest way that they'd be remembered after their death, so a scop could be very richly rewarded. Anglo-Saxon poetry uses alliteration rather than rhyme as its poetic device, making it easier to memorize. *Beowulf* was almost certainly an oral poem told by scops that was written down later.

207

These eight verses are often known as the "Song of Creation". These lines are modeled on Genesis 1:16: *And God made two great lights: a greater light to rule the day; and a lesser light to rule the night: and the stars.* (Slade, 2005). It is interesting that it is a scop who sings the Song of Creation. The word *scóp* derives from *sceapen* 'to shape or form' and the word *frumsceaft* 'Creation' also derives from *sceapen*.

Some scholars have argued that the Song of Creation is connected with various Germanic pagan lays, most notably the Norse *Völuspá*, though I believe that it was probably more inspired by the 7th Century Old English *Cædmon's Hymn*, a Christian poem about God's creation of the Earth (Arner, et al, 2013).

Line 100b- Fiend from Hell

The word *feond* is Old English for 'enemy'- this connects him with the Hebrew שָׂטָן or Satan (which literally means 'the Adversary') (Arner, et al, 2013).

Line 102a- Gast

Often in *Beowulf*, it is ambiguous whether the word *gæst* means 'guest' or 'ghost.' The word *ġest* means either 'guest' or 'stranger' and *gást* means either 'spirit' or 'ghost' (this is why many older sources say the Holy Ghost, rather than the Holy Spirit; in Old English, He is called the *Hálga Gást*, even though He is not a ghost in the modern sense). Because spelling was not standardized in Old English, both of these words were often spelled *gæst*, leading to confusion. Sometimes, it is clear which word was meant, but often it is uncertain (Klaeber, 2008).

Line 102b- Grendel

The etymology of the name Grendel is uncertain, but is perhaps derived from the Old English *grindan* meaning "to grind" or from *grund* meaning "ground, bottom" (as in the mere bottom from where he lives; other suggestions include a connection with Old Norse *grindill* meaning "storm" or Middle English *gryndel* meaning "angry." The name Grendel also appears in several English place names, such as Grendelsmere and Grendeles Pytt (Cardew, 2005).

Grendel is hardly described at all. About the only descriptions he's given is that he is huge and has a humanoid shape, claws and glowing eyes. Therefore, he's been interpreted in myriad ways: from hairy beasts to deformed giants to Neanderthals and even dinosaurs! Most likely, his description is intentionally vague, so as to create suspense and allow the audience to use their imagination (Lapidge, 1993).

Grendel is thought to be related to the Grindylow of Yorkshire folklore, a creature said to live in meres, who drowns people. Shippey, who believes that *Beowulf* was written somewhere in the vicinity of Hartlepool, believes that Grendel was also an inspiration for the Hart Hall Hob, a creature that haunts Heorot, the hall of the hart (Shippey, 2015).

Line 103b-4- Fens: Realm of Monsters

In Old English, the words for marshes, moors and fens are interchangeable, all referring to barren wetlands (Bosworth, 1921). The Anglo-Saxons feared wetlands, which at the time made up much of England. It was this fear that Alfred the Great took advantage of, when he hid from the Great Heathen Army in Sedgemoor, which at that time was a moor, hence its name. Fens were rightly feared, as dangerous animals and outlaws lived there. But to the Anglo-Saxons what was feared most about fens, were that monsters lived there. *Maxims II* says, *Þyrs sceal on fenne ġewunian ana innan*

lande "A Troll shall dwell in the fens, alone in his own lands" (Slade, 2005). According to the early 8th Century *Life of St. Guthlac*, while living as a hermit in the Lincolnshire Fens, Guthlac has multiple battles with Demons (Newton, 1993). See also Commentary for Lines 1357-76.

Lines 106-14- Clan of Cain

In Medieval theology, Cain, Adam's son and the first murderer, was the ancestor of many types of monsters. According to Genesis 6:2-4:

> *The sons of God seeing the daughters of men, that they were fair, took themselves wives of all which they chose…Now giants were upon the earth in those days. For after the sons of God went in to the daughters of men and they brought forth children, these are the mighty men of old, men of renown.*

Gigantes, or Giants is a translation of the original Hebrew נְפִילִים, the Nephilim, meaning the "Fallen Ones." There has been much debate about who these "Sons of God" refer to, but early interpretations almost exclusively agree that these were Fallen Angels. The pseudepigraphical *Book of Enoch*, which was popular in Anglo-Saxon England, also took this view. A group of Fallen Angels known as the Watchers mated with Human women (specifically the sinful offspring of Cain) and they gave birth to gigantic, monstrous children, the Nephilim. They *devoured one another's flesh, and drank the blood.*

All of this would have been familiar to the monks who wrote down *Beowulf*, so it is reasonable to assume that by calling Grendel a descendant of Cain, they were connecting him with the Nephilim tradition (Orchard, 2014).

The manuscript also mentions: *Eotenas, Ylfe* and *Orc-néas*. These three creatures are deeply rooted in Germanic mythology. *Eoten* is the Old English form of the Norse *Jötunn*, a species that dwelt in Jötunheim, consisting of Trolls and Frost Giants. *Ettin*, a three-headed giant in Northumbrian folklore is a direct descendant of *Eoten*. This is the word I chose for my translation.

Ylfe means Elves. Tolkien did not like this, due to his appreciation of all things Elven, so he just ignored it altogether and translated it as 'goblins' (Tolkien, 2014). But the fact remains that the Anglo-Saxons had a mistrust of Elves. Some were mostly good-natured, but temperamental and mischievous, while others were downright wicked. In Norse myth, Elves are divided into two types, the *Ljósálfar*, or Light Elves and the *Dökkálfar*, or Dark Elves. Some scholars believe that Dark Elves are just an alternative name for Dwarves, but I think that Dark Elves are evil Elves.

Orc-néas seems to come from *Orc*, 'Demon' and *né*, corpse, a 'demonic corpse'. This brings to mind the Norse *Draugr* or Tolkien's barrow-wights, perhaps even Vampires or Zombies (Gilliver, et al, 2009).

Lines 119a- Symbel

The term *symbel* (or *sumbl* in Old Norse) is often translated to 'feast,' but it should be realized that a symbel was more than simply a feast. While feasting was almost certainly part of symbel, the symbel was first and foremost a drinking ritual. Another misconception is that the symbel was a pagan custom. Many Germanic neo-pagans believe that symbels were about creating a link between humans. In fact, many of the poems with references to symbels are explicitly Christian in nature, such as *The Dream of the Rood* or *Genesis A*. Symbels seem to have actually been social rituals.

The earliest record of what is probably a symbel is by Tacitus in the First Century AD, in a description of the Anglii, the ancestors of the Angles, in his *Germania*:

> *To pass an entire day and night in drinking disgraces no one … Yet it is at their feasts that they generally consult on the reconciliation of enemies, on the forming of matrimonial alliances, on the choice of chiefs,*

finally even on peace and war, for they think that at no time is the mind more open to simplicity of purpose or more warmed to noble aspirations.

According to the Norse *Hymiskviða*, symbels occurred at least once a year, at harvest, but in most literature,, it seems that symbels occurred fairly often, probably whenever important visitors came to a mead-hall. It seems that symbels might have been the same as the Passing of the Mead. See also the Commentary for Line 614-30 (Wills, 2012).

Line 123a- Thegns

Thegns (deriving from the word *þegnian*, meaning 'one who serves') were members of a a social class just below an earl or king, comparable to the nobility or aristocracy. A thegn owned substantial tracts of land and was a lord in his own right. However, he was still expected to serve the king. A thegn could be promoted to an earl for showing exemplary service to the king (Lapidge, 1999).

Lines 130b- Un Prefix

The Germanic prefix *un-*, meaning 'not' derives from the reconstructed Indo-European *ŋ-*, from which we also get the Greek *à-* and Latin *in-*. The Old English corpus has about 1,250 words with the prefix *un-*, but only around one-eighth of these survive in Old English (Shuman, 1960).

Lines 126-63- Feuds

Feuds were extremely common among the various Germanic peoples and could last for several generations, to the point where families might have forgotten why the feud had started in the first place (such as the feud between the Montegues and Capulets in Shakespeare's *Romeo & Juliet*). Often, feuds only ended after one of the families were completely destroyed; the Norse sometimes accomplished this with a *heim-sókn* or 'home visit'- in other words, when a family all gathered at their hall, the feuding family would bar the doors and set the hall on fire, letting them all burn to death (such as in the famous Icelandic *Njál's saga*).

Obviously, this soon became a problem in Germanic societies, especially after they were Christianized. So, a system called the *weregild*, meaning 'Man-Price' in Old English was developed. Every Freeman had a certain price that the killer was obligated to pay the other's family (or lord if they had no living kin,) unless they were killed in battle, in self-defense or during a theft. Even foreigners had weregilds (though these were significantly lower than the weregild of an Anglo-Saxon of the same rank). A Freeman who owned no land was worth 200 shillings and the weregild went up the higher they were in rank. If a pregnant woman was killed, the killer had to pay both her weregild and her husband's weregild, for the unborn child. While slaves legally had no weregild, it was common practice that the killer would pay the master what ever they paid for the slave.(Lapidge 1999).

Weregilds also applied to different body parts; if someone cut off or damaged a body part of someone else, they had to pay certain fractions of their full weregild to them, a higher fraction depending on how important it was.

Lines 157a- The Witan

The *Witan*, literally 'Wise Men' or *Witenaġemót* 'Moot' or 'Meeting of Wise Men,'was an Anglo-Saxon king's council. The Witan, which was made up of nobles and bishops, had no set number of members. would advise the king in any matter the king wished to be counseled on. This included

210

approving new laws and royal proclamations, attesting to land grants and advising them in dealing in rebellions and matters of war. They also would elect a new king and could dismiss an unjust king (Lapidge, 1999).

Line 163a- Necromancers

Necromancers is the translation of the Old English *helrúnan*: a compound word meaning "Consulters of Hell." This word is apparently related to *haliurunnas* appears in Jordanes' *Getica*, a history of the Goths from the 6th Century, as a Gothic word meaning *magas mulieres* meaning "witches" and is likely a Latinization of the Gothic *ᚻᚨᚨᚷᚱᚾᚾᚨ, *haljōrūna.* (Tolkien, 2014).

Lines 168- The Gift-Seat

These lines are somewhat obscure and have been much debated. A 'gift-seat' refers to a throne, the seat where a king gives gifts to his retainers. But whose throne is being spoken of here? At first glance, it seemingly refers to Hrothgar's throne, but then, in Tolkien's words, "Why could Grendel not approach the throne, when he was in sole control of Heorot?…no doubt Grendel could have sat in the king's throne and gnawed bones there" (Tolkien, 2014).

He and other scholars believe that the 'gift-seat' is in fact referring to the Throne of God. Thus, the poem is saying that Grendel would not humble himself before God and ask for His mercy. This is perhaps the simplest explanation, and I altered capitalizations to reflect this. However, I'm not completely convinced that this is the only correct reading.

I think the poet wrote these lines to be deliberately vague. I think the 'gift-seat' refers to both God's Throne *and* Hrothgar's throne. I believe that the reason Grendel did not approach Hrothgar's throne, was the poet's way of showing that Grendel did not have have the motivations that Men would have for raiding the hall. He was not after the throne's wealth and power; he only cared about causing death and destruction. It also has been suggested that whatever reason Grendel had for not approaching the throne, is meant to be taken as a glimmer of hope to the Danes. God had not abandoned the Danes, and even if the Danes could not see it, the audience could (Chickering, 1977).

Lines 175-88- The Idolatry of the Danes

Most *Beowulf* scholars find this passage inconsistent with the rest of the poem. Characters throughout the poem praise and acknowledge God, yet here they are called heathens who "knew not the Lord God." Some scholars use this passage as evidence that *Beowulf* was originally a pagan poem, but as I explained in the Introduction, this is unlikely the case.

It should be noted that while God is mentioned quite often, there is no mention of Christ, the saints or anything that is explicitly Christian. This is fairly common of pagans in Medieval literature, such as in Chaucer's *Troilus and Criseyde*, where a Greek pagan acknowledges both God and Venus in the same sentence. Brodeur theorized that the meaning of this passage was to confirm that the characters were indeed pagan, even though they spoke of God at times; this was very much how people spoke at the time the poem was written, and so making references to God was expected (Brodeur, 1959).

Brodeur believed that the poet also wanted to emphasize that while the characters may be pagans, they were noble pagans. If they recognized no greater power than themselves, they'd be seen as arrogant, but if they recognized pagan gods as the power greater than themselves, they'd be seen as devil worshippers, for all false gods were considered demons. Therefore, referring to a generic "God" would give the impression of a noble monotheistic mindset, but not necessarily of a devout Christian.

211

Rev. Douglas Hill agrees that the poet intended to show noble pagans, but rather than trying to excuse paganism, this was to promote the Gospels. The poet was

> *...not showing us this paganism to say, 'See, pagans can be noble too—even without Jesus!'...Instead of saying that nobility is possible without Christ, the poet shows that such nobility does not keep a people from being utterly and completely lost...Our poet shows us this pagan hopelessness in a period of history just before their conversion to the Christian faith. He is recounting the testimony of his people, and, just as with modern testimonies, the sin is highlighted. But it is art to conceal art, and he leaves us hanging just before the explicit moment of conversion. His original listeners knew exactly what was going to happen next* (Wilson, 2007).

The nobility of these pagans was meant to make them sympathetic to the audience and to "...show that they are in need of Christ and salvation—that that which makes them sympathetic does not in any way earn them salvation" (Wilson, 2007).

Tolkien theorized that the poet wanted to connect *Beowulf* with the Old Testament, especially with the Books of Kings and Chronicles.

> *I think that he attempted to equate the noble figures of his own northern antiquity with the noble figures, sages, judges, and kings of Israel – before Christ... The leading idea (in the work) is that noble pagans of the past who had not heard the Gospel, knew of the existence of Almighty God, recognized him as 'good' and the giver of all good things; but were (by the Fall) still cut off from Him so that in time of woe they became filled with despair and doubt -- that was the hour when they were specially open to the snares of the Devil: they prayed to idols and false gods for help* (Tolkien, 2014).

Similarly, Martin Camargo said,

> *By linking that past to Old Testament history, by making clear that the hero is the best of men acting in strict accordance with the best rules of conduct then available to him, and finally by showing how far even this exemplary pagan's beliefs fall short of the Christian ideal, the poet instead forces his audience to recognize, and thence to abhor, the lingering vestiges of paganism in their own hearts* (Wilson, 2007).

The characters in *Beowulf* actually resemble the Jews of the Old Testament more than they did the pagans of Scandinavia. They worship God, yet they do not know of Jesus. They follow the *ealde riht*, the Old Laws (see Line 2330b,) but have no priests and they are prone, in times of distress, to backslide into idolatry. In this sense, they are more like the Free Peoples of Middle Earth in J.R.R. Tolkien's Legendarium

But, they are not Jews. The *ealde riht* is not the *Torah* given by God to Moses at Mount Sinai, but rather 'Natural Law,'... The Danes seem to be 'Noachites,' that is, gentiles who weren't quite Christians, but not pagans either; monotheists who worshiped the God of Japheth (Hill, 1994).

Line 195b- The Geats

The Geats (Old Norse Gautar) were a people living in Götaland, today an area of southern Sweden. In the 19th Century, the Geats were generally thought to refer to the Jutes, but that theory has been mostly dismissed. Tolkien was vehemently against the Jutish hypothesis, or as he termed it, 'the Jutish lunacy.' He said, "Once you admit that queen-bee into your bonnet it will lay a hive of maggots there" (Tolkien, 2014).

It appears that the Geats in *Beowulf* are more specifically the Western Geats, that is the people of Västergötaland. The Geats are often referred to as the Weder-Geats or simply, Weders and Geatland was sometimes referred to as Wedermark. *Weder* means 'storm' or 'wind' and is the ancestor of the modern English word 'weather.' It seems likely that the Väderöarna, an archipelago in the Skaggerak off of the coast of Västergötaland is a folk memory of this alternate name of the Geats and

should be read as the Weder Islands, rather than the Weather Islands. (Overing, 1988)

Line 202-3a- Litotes

Arthur Sedgewick said that the usual meaning of irony is conscious inadequacy of speech. Irony is the main sense of humor in *Beowulf* and litotes are probably the most noticeable form of irony in the poem. Litotes are essentially massive understatements or negation of opposites. There are 94 examples of litotes in *Beowulf* or approximately once every 34 lines. (Shuman, 1960)

While the litotes found here is not the first in the poem, this is perhaps the most famous one. This is what Tolkien had to say about it:

"Of his journey, mindful men found little fault…" is not the first litotes found in the poem, but the first that a general reader would perhaps notice. About this line, Tolkien said, "Here, all that is required for one engaged in reading the text is to realize that the literal 'found very little fault with that journey' does not mean "that their objections were not important, though they had some; it does not even mean they had nothing to say against it… and said, 'Very well, go if you wish.' It means they applauded the project." (Tolkien, 2014)

Line 204b- Omens

The various Germanic people believed that certain phenomena could have positive or negative effects on a situation. Pagan Germanic priests engaged in various divination practices, like rune-reading and astrology, but none were as common as reading and interpreting behavior of birds, especially ravens. Perhaps derivative of the Roman 'augurs,' this seems to be what the poem is describing here.

There is a legend that around 500 AD, Hermigisel, king of the Warini, saw a raven in a tree that prophesied that he would die within four months, which he did. Over a century later, Edwin, the newly converted king of Northumbria was riding to church one Sunday, when the whole company stood frozen in fear in the middle of the street when they saw and heard a raven who 'sang with an evil omen.' Thinking quickly, Bishop Paulinus, who was with Edwin, ordered a servant to shoot the raven. Afterwards, Paulinus brought the raven impaled on the arrow and showed it to Edwin's still-Pagan followers and told them, "that they should know by so clear a sign the ancient evil of idolatry was worthless to anybody," that the raven "did not know that it sang of death for itself" and therefore had no power to prophecy. (Chaney, 1970)

While augury fell out of favor after the Anglo-Saxon became Christian, belief in omens continued. Even though the Bible speaks against it, such as in Jeremiah 10:2- "Thus saith the Lord, Learn not according to the ways of the Gentiles: and be not afraid of the signs of heaven, which the heathens fear,'" astrology became common-place. The zodiac came to England from the Greco-Roman world, so the Anglo-Saxons would not have known about it before Christianization. Christian Anglo-Saxons also were known to look for omens in the sky. In 793 AD, *The Anglo-Saxon Chronicles* reported that "…excessive whirlwinds, lightning, and fiery dragons… flying in the sky," were believed to have predicted the first Viking raid on Lindisfarne, and in 1066 the appearance of Hailey's Comet was believed to have predicted Harold II's defeat at the Battle of Hastings.

Line 263b- Ecgtheow

The name 'Ecgtheow' meaning 'servant (or slave) of the (sword) edge' is only recorded elsewhere in the *Völulspá*, a poem in the Old Norse *Poetic Edda* as Eggþér, a Giant who sits on a mound, playing a harp. Tolkien believes that there must have once been legends surrounding the

character of Ecgtheow that have now been lost (Tolkien, 2014).

Line 303-6a- Helms

The helmet was an important piece of armor to the Anglo-Saxons, however they were expensive and not available to most. Because of the rarity of helmets, only four Early Anglo-Saxon complete helmets have been uncovered, with eight complete contemporary helmets of similar style discovered in Sweden, and numerous helmet fragments across England and Scandinavia, In the Late Anglo-Saxon period, helms became simpler and more cost-effective, so helms became more common, but before the 9th Century, since only the wealthy could afford them, the helmet was also a status symbol, typically fitted with silvered or tinned bronze decorative foils and gold animal heads. While dragon, raven or horse images were often used, no animal featured on helms more than the wild boar.

The wild boar was a symbol of courage to the Anglo-Saxons and other Germanic peoples. Small boar figures often graced the tops of helms, such as on the Benty Grange and Pioneer helms. The word *bárhelm* ('boar-helm,' found only in the Finnesburh Fragment) probably refers to these. Boar images or of men wearing boar helms also often appeared on these foils or brow terminals of these helms, as seen on the Sutton Hoo and Coppergate helms.

In Norse tradition, Áli (Onela) had a helm named *Hildisvíni*, meaning 'Battle Swine', suggesting a boar helm. After Áli died at the Battle on the Ice at Lake Vänern (see commentary for Line 2390,) After the battle, Aðils (Eadgils) took the helm for his own. (Gammonsway, et al, 1971).

The various references to *grímhelmas* or 'masked helms' in *Beowulf* were originally thought to be a fiction, or at least a poetic metaphor. However, after the discovery at Sutton Hoo, these form of helms were proved to have been in use during this period. Partial masks for helms have also been found elsewhere (Mortimer, 2011).

Line 330a- Grey-tipped ash-wood

The spear is perhaps the oldest human weapon, being so simple to make. Essentially a pole with a sharp point, they could be used as a stabbing weapon or a projectile. The Anglo-Saxons used spears both ways, however javelins were typically referred to as 'darts' rather than 'spears.' The spears wielded by the infantry were heavy wood poles with iron heads, standing taller than a man. It would inflict devastating damage on an enemy, but while very effective at a distance, was rendered almost useless in close combat. Darts were lighter and shorter, letting one hold perhaps three of them in their hand behind their shield. They could then rapidly launch them at an approaching enemy with their main hand and then move into a shield-wall (see Line 2337-41) before they reached them.

The best spears and darts had ash-wood shafts, therefore spears are often simply referred to as ash-wood; this went so far that 'forest of ashes' is a kenning for 'an army' (Mortimer, 2011).

Line 343b- Beowulf is my name

The name Beowulf is an extremely uncommon Anglo-Saxon name. The only record of the name before the Norman Conquest outside of this poem, is a mention in the 7th Century Northumbrian *Liber Vitae* of a monk from Durham named Biuuulf, the Northumbrian spelling of Beowulf (Gammonsway, et al, 1971). The name Beowulf is usually thought to mean 'bee-wolf', a kenning for 'bear,' which greatly compliments the character of the bear-like Beowulf.

The character of Beowulf is thought to be closely related to the character of Bödvarr Bjárki of Norse sources. Bjárki, which means 'little bear' and Beowulf are both names associated with bears,

214

nd both characters have similarities in their stories. Bjárki is a Norwegian rather than a Gaut, but his
brother was the king of the Gautar.

While visiting his brother in Gautland, Bjárki heard that the hall of Hrólf Kraki (Hrothulf),
king of the Danes, has been attacked for two winters by "the greatest of monsters." When he arrives
at Lejre, he encounters some men pelting a boy named Hott with bones, and Bjárki goes to Hott's
defense, but rather than in a flyting as in *Beowulf* (see Commentary for Lines 499-606), Bjárki flings the
bone back at the man, and kills him. That night, Bjárki kills the monster, (who is described more like
a Dragon than a Troll) but sets it up, so that Hrólf will think Hott killed it. Hrólf renames Hott, Hjalti
and makes them both one of his twelve champions (Olson, 1916).

Line 348b- The Wendels

The Wendels were most likely the people living around the Limfjord in the modern-day
Vendsyssel region of Jutland, possibly under Danish control at this time. Interestingly, according to
the *Heimskringla*, Ohthere was killed on a raid in this region, which was also called Wendel by the
Anglo-Saxons and Vendill by the Norse, by the jarl of Vendel. Could this jarl have developed from the
same proto-legend that Wulfgar derived from? (Gammonsway, et al, 1971).

Another possibility is that they were from Vendel in Sweden. This is supported by the
possibility that Hrothgar's sister was married to Onela. This would suggest that the Danes and
Swedes were allies, making a Swede at the Danish court not out of place (Newton, 1993).

Line 379b-80- Strength of thirty men

Tolkien notes that while thirty men appears at first glance to just be a random number, that
it is to be compared with the statement that Grendel could carry off thirty corpses. In other words,
Beowulf and Grendel are of equal strength (Tolkien, 2014).

Line 405-55- Boasting

Béot was the Old English term for a ritual boast. While in many cultures, boasting is seen as a
sign of arrogance, boasting was seen in a positive light in Germanic cultures, but only if it was true.
When one boasted that they would do something, they were expected to carry it out or die trying.
Drunkenness was no excuse. As explained in the commentary for Lines 506-606, an honorable person
was not supposed to lie. So, boasting of something, but not carrying it out (or trying) made one a
nithing (see commentary for Line 683).

It seems that most boasts were made in a hall, before a large audience. The Anglo-Saxon
practice seems to be related to the Norse *Bragarfull* or 'Promise Cup,' where a cup of mead or ale was
passed around the hall and each man, when he got the cup, could make a boast about something he
did or would do. This is the origin of the modern English 'brag' (Einarsson, 1934).

Line 407a- Be thou, Hrothgar, hail!

Wishing someone health, by saying *Wæs hál!*, or "Be hale!" is a common Anglo-Saxon greeting.
The Norse version of this, *Ves heil*, as used especially in drinking culture, and so is the origin of the
English *Wassail*.

Line 422a- Nicors

The *Nicor* was an Anglo-Saxon water demon. The Nicor exists in many Germanic folklores,
such as the English *Neck*, German *Nix* and Dano-Norwegian *Nøkk*. The description of these changes

215

drastically between different cultures and is often thought to be a shape-shifter, changing its form to better lure people into the water, in order to drown them. The oldest Scandinavian sources portray them as horse-like, and while it seems likely that the Anglo-Saxons also sometimes imagined them like this, they do not seem so here. It is possible that the poet imagined these Nicors to be more akin to Knuckers, a type of water-dragon in English folklore also descended from this word.

Line 445a- Hrethmen

The manuscript uses the words *hréðmanna*, which Tolkien believes is connected with *Hreiðgotar*, the Old Norse name for the Ostrogoths, and the *Hréðgotum* mentioned in *Widsith*. The Geats, two lines above are referred to as *Geotena*. Tolkien believe that this is actually a corruption of the word *Gotena*, or Goths, and the scribe, being unfamiliar with this term, wrote *Geotena*, blending the words *Gotena* and *Ġeata*. The Geats were likely originally a branch of the Goths, a fact that was probably not remembered by the time the manuscript was written down. (Tolkien, 2014).

Line 451b- Liches

The word 'lich' is an archaic word, meaning 'corpse,' that derives from the Old English word *líċ*, occurring most often in the term 'lich gate,' the gate at a churchyard, where the coffin is carried through. The word 'lich' is now also used in roleplaying games, starting with *Dungeons & Dragons* to refer to undead wizards.

Line 455a- Weyland

Weland (or Völundr in Old Norse) was a Giant smith from Germanic heroic legend, who forged some of the best weapons and armor ever made. English folklore says he lives in Wayland's Smithy, a long barrow in Oxfordshire (Davidson, 1958).

Line 455b- Wyrd

Wyrd is the Germanic concept of fate. In Norse myth, the fate of every person was woven by three women called the Norns. In Anglo-Saxon paganism, they called them the Wyrd Sisters, which eventually became the Weird Sisters, most famously used in Shakespeare's *Macbeth*. In Anglo-Saxon Christianity, Wyrd was actually seen as the will of God. "In his translation of Boethius… King Alfred reasons from a Christian viewpoint that wyrd is the accomplishment of God's providence." (Robinson, 1984)

Shippey says that the word *wyrd* ultimately comes from the Proto-Germanic **werþana*, "to become", while *fate* comes from Latin *fatus*, "to speak." He says that while the Classical cultures thought of fate as something that the gods decreed, the Anglo-Saxons thought of wyrd just as what happened or will happen to a person; while God is ultimately in control, He shouldn't be thought of as necessarily decreeing everything that happens. Shippey thinks that the Anglo-Saxons' concept of wyrd was closer to the modern conception of luck or chance, more than fate. Thus, Lines 572-3 shouldn't be read as *…Fate oft saves a man not doomed to die, when his courage is good!* This would be a very illogical statement. But if it's read as *…chance oft saves a man not doomed to die, when his courage is good*, makes more sense. (Shippey, 2015)

Line 461a- The Wulfings

The Wulfings seem to have been the same clan as the Norse *Ylfings*, whom the sagas say came from Östergötaland, or eastern Geatland, and were possibly the ancestors of the East Anglian Wuffings

ynasty (see commentary for Lines 2999-3005). Heatholaf is a Wulfing warrior (presumably their champion,) who was killed by Ecgtheow, during a feud.

The Wulfings demanded an exorbitant weregild (see commentary Line 156) from Ecgtheow, hat his people refused to pay. According to the manuscript, Ecgtheow's people are the *Gara cyn*, he 'Spear clan.' However, this reading poses an issue; it does not alliterate. Obviously, *Gara cyn* s a scribal error. Most translators have emended *gara* to *Wederas*, the 'Weder-folk' meaning that Ecgtheow's people were Geats. This emendation also presents issues. How would the scribe have mistakenly written *gara* instead *Wederas*? And why would Hrothgar, while trying to show gratitude o Beowulf, rudely remind him that his grandfather was too cheap to pay his own son-in-law's weregild? And why would Ecgtheow be banished from Geatland, and not just from Wulfing lands?

It seems that *gara* should actually be emended to *[Wul]gara*, the Old English form of the name *Vulgares*, a people mentioned by Paul the Deacon, whom Kemp Malone believed were the same people as the Wulfings. If this is correct, then this would mean that the Ecgtheow was a Wulfing, and his feud with Heatholaf was an inter-tribal feud. Thus, it was the Wulfings who banished Ecgtheow.

Ecgtheow then sought the succor of Hrothgar, who paid his weregild. Some readers have wondered why Ecgtheow asked the Danish king for help. The answer to this is probably found in the Anglo-Saxon poem *Widsith*. In this poem, Helm is listed as the Wulfing king. In *Beowulf*, Wealhtheow s said to be a Helming lady, thus it seems that she was a daughter of the Wulfing king. This perhaps xplains why Hrothgar would be willing to help Ecgtheow. He was of the same clan as Hrothgar's wife, erhaps even a relative, making Hrothgar inclined to aid his wife's kinsman in his plight (Farrell, 1972).

ine 499a- Unferth

In the manuscript, Unferth is spelled *Hunferð*, however the line's alliteration suggests that he name should start with a vowel. The scribe likely added an *H* to Unferth, as *Un-* was not an Anglo-Saxon naming convention, but *Hun-* was relatively common. Unferth has, traditionally, been hought to be made up of *un*, "not" (see Commentary for Line 130b) and *frið*, "peace," which would e a fitting name for the character who starts the quarrel with Beowulf. However, Fulk believed that *erth* was not derived from *frið* at all, but from *ferhð*, "soul, mind, spirit or life." In many Germanic anguages, names beginning with a long vowel could interchangeably be spelled with an H. Thus, *Un-* could have derived from *Hun-*, while still being spelled *Unferth* rather than *Hunferth*, (Fulk, 1987).

Tom Shippey suggested that, due to various sound shifts, *Unferð* is the Old English form of Old Norse *Húnrøðr*. *Húnrøðr* is usually thought to be made up from *húnn*, "bear cub" and *friðr*, "peace," ut he believes it derives from *Hún*, "a member of the Hunnish tribe" and *fjǫr*, "life, spirit, or vigor." f this is a correct etymology, then *Húnrøðr* would mean "Hunnish spirit," and thus, *Húnferhð* or *Inferð* would mean the same.(Shippey, 2015).

ines 499-606- The Flyting of Unferth

This section of the poem is often referred to as the "Flyting of Unferth," though the term *flyting* s never used in text. A flyting consists of a formulaic exchange of insults that is common in Germanic nd Celtic poetry, and is possibly the precursor of modern African-American rap battles (Holmes, 016). The word flyting; derives from Old English *flítan* meaning 'quarrel.' Flytings typically occur etween two men in a hall, but sometimes between a man and woman or between a group of men nd rarely between two women. Sometimes, a flyting will end in violence or the threat of violence. Other times, the loser takes it graciously and will agree to share a cup of mead with the winner.

The nature of flytings have been misunderstood by many readers. *Two misapprehensions in*

particular concerning the Norse flyting have impeded identification of the traditional nature of the Unferþ-Beowulf exchange. The first, that the flytings are mere games and that their charges are 'whopping lies'… In Germanic literature, heroes can always be relied on to tell the truth. If they say something, no matter how unlikely it may seem, you can know what they are saying is true; thus Beowulf's words can be trusted as true (in the context of the story,) this fact is not changed just because he's involved in a flyting. *The second [misapprehension], that they consist only of crude insults from a 'ruder age,' is similarly inaccurate.* This is probably said, because often the insults in flytings are sexual in nature, as can be seen in the Norse *Lokasenna*, However, the "Flyting of Unferth" contains no innuendo (Clover, 1980).

Lines 506-86- The Swimming Contest

Some scholars have argued that Beowulf and Breca's contest should not be read as a swimming contest. While the word *sund* often means 'swimming,' it can also be read as 'sea,' and they argue that this should be read as a 'sea voyage' i.e. boating contest rather than a swimming contest. However, I find this interpretation unlikely. Swimming contests seem to have been quite common among the Germanic peoples, with both Roman sources and later Norse sagas depicting them engaging in swimming contests in full armor. Rowing however was seen as a mundane activity; thus rowing contests were not depicted in Germanic literature; they probably happened in real life, but were too ordinary to talk about in their literature. Thus, I find it probable that Beowulf and Breca's contest was indeed a swimming contest (though the distance swam is problematic, if one does not interpret the two boys as superhuman. However, a few theories have been formed that help make this contest more plausible; these are explained in the commentaries for Line 519 and Line 580).

It seems that the object of this contest was to see which of them could swim the fastest to the Reamish coast (see commentary for Line 519) while armed and armored. While Beowulf does admit to losing the contest, he explains that it is because he was driven far off course and was attacked by nine *Nicors* (see commentary for Line 422), and not because he was a slower swimmer. He says that what happened was actually much more manly than Breca winning the contest. (Klaeber, 2008)

Beowulf's battle with the nine Nicors has been compared to the Norse myth of the god, Thor fishing for Jörmungandr, the Midgard-Serpent, told in the *Hymiskviða* in the *Elder Edda*. In fact, Beowulf has, in general been compared to Thor, with scholars pointing out that Beowulf's final battle with the Dragon echoes Thor's final battle with Jörmungandr at Ragnarök (Bjork, 1998).

Line 519b- The Reamas

The Reamas (Old Norse: Raumar) seem to be the people of Raumaríki (modern Romerike), then a Norwegian petty-kingdom based around the Oslofjord. *By the land of the Heaðo-Ræmas (519) is meant the region of the modern Romerike (to the north of [Oslo]) called in ON: Raumariki, and cited as a tribal name Raumaricii by Jordanes…*

Another explanation is that the Reamas refers instead to the people of Raumsdalr (modern Romsdal), suggesting they were swimming along the west coast of Norway. *The enormous distances separating the landing places of Beowulf and Breca would be lessened if we assume that the term Heaðo-Ræmas refers to Romsdalen (ON Raumsdalr) on the west coast of Norway.* (Osborn, 1989)

Line 521b- Breca and the Brondings

In the 19th Century, many scholars thought of Breca and the Brondings as wholly mythologica creations. Breca was often thought of as a personification of the sea, or even as a minor Germanic sea god, pointing out that the name 'Breca' might be related to the word 'breaker,' (Oglivy, 1983) but this

218

theory has been all but dismissed.

The Brondings seem to have been a real people. They are mentioned in *Widsith*, where Breca is listed as their king (Chambers, 1912). It is thought that Brondings were the people of the island Brandey, which is mentioned in the poem *Helgakviða Hundingsbana I*. Brandey is suggested to be Brännö, an island off of Västergötland (Rydberg, 1889).

Line 572b-3- one utterly doomed…

The manuscript here uses the word *unfǽġne*, which appears to mean 'undoomed.' This word appears twice in the Old English corpus, both instances in *Beowulf*, here and in Lines 2291. The thing is, neither instance makes much sense if *unfǽġne* has this meaning; why would an undoomed man need saving?

Tolkien said it this way, *This as it stands is about as completely an 'illogical' reference to Fate as could be devised. Fate often preserves (from Fate?) a man not at the time fated to die when his courage does not fail-preserved him from what- death (already fated)!* (Tolkien, 2014)

Some scholars take *unfǽġne* to mean 'brave' (or rather 'uncowardly,') related to German *feig* 'timid' and Danish *ufej* and Swedish *ofeg* 'bold or fearless.'. This sounds plausible, but this would make the line redundant; it would be saying, in other words,'Wyrd oft saves a brave man, when he is brave.'

Another explanation is that *unfǽġne* is a scribal error for *anfǽġne*. While the prefix *un-* means 'not,' the prefix *an-* means 'very.' The letter *a* is often confused with *u* in the *Beowulf* text. In fact, *an-* has probably been mistaken for *un-* elsewhere in the text; Line 357a says that Hrothgar is *unhár*, 'unhoary,' while the scribe almost certainly misspelled *anhár*, 'very hoary.' If *anfǽġne* is indeed meant in place of *unfǽġne*, then rather than saying, 'Wyrd oft saves an undoomed man, when his courage is good,' it should say 'Wyrd oft saves an utterly doomed man, when his courage is good,' thus a person who shows bravery can often save themselves in a situation where they would have been killed otherwise. Thus, Beowulf's proverb mimics the modern maxim, 'Fortune favors the bold' (Porck, 2020).

580b- Finnmark

In the manuscript, it says that after Beowulf's battle with the Nicors, he came ashore to *Finna Land*. Many readers are left asking, *How could Beowulf, in his swimming match with Breca, be borne by the sea to Finland* (Bosworth, 1921)? If this was a swimming contest in the Skaggerak, how is it that Beowulf got so off course as to swim all the way around Sweden and into the north Baltic?

Finna Land was in fact, not the modern Finland. Finn was the old Germanic name for a member of the Sámi, the indigenous people from northern Fennoscandia. I reflect this in translating *Finna Land* to 'Finnmark,' the 'Finn Marches' meaning the Sámi borderlands, a term still used for the northernmost county in Norway.

This still does not solve the problem of how Beowulf came to the land of the Sámi if they swam the Skaggerak. The typical explanation is that the poet did not realize that this did not make sense; he did not have maps to consult, and only knew this took place 'far North' (Lawrence, 1928). But this seems to be wishful thinking. *Beowulf* was written down by learned men, most likely clergy, who had access to various works on Scandinavia, including *The Voyages of Ohthere of Hålogaland*. Even though they would not know specifics about Scandinavian geography (e.g. Denmark is said to have mountains in the poem, whilst in reality, Denmark's highest natural point, Millehøj in central Jutland is only 170.86 meters [561 feet]!) they would probably have not made such a grievous error as this.

Perhaps then, they meant this to be read differently.

In the commentary for Line 519, I put forth a suggestion that this swimming contest actually took place on the western coast of Norway. This would make it plausible for Beowulf to end up among the Sámi on the northern coast while Breca came ashore in Romsdalen on the central coast. Another possibility is that *Finn* does not refer to the Sámi at all. Osborn points out that *fín* means 'a heap of wood' (and by extension, driftwood) in Old English. She suggests that *Finna Land*, rather than meaning the 'land of the Sámi' meant 'Driftwood Land,' comparing it to 'Markland,' the name Leif Eiriksson gave part of the North American coast, that was probably Labrador. 'Driftwood Land' is an apt description of many areas along the Skaggerak coast. Klaeber suggested it could be referring to modern Finnved in Småland, Sweden (Osborn, 1989).

Line 587-9- Unferth's Brothers

Beowulf claims that Unferth murdered his brothers. We can assume that what Beowulf says is true (see commentary for Lines 506-606), but this might not be the whole truth. Some have speculated that Unferth is from another tribe, where he was outlawed for kinslaying, but Hrothgar took him in, much like he did with Ecgtheow (Arner, et al, 2013). This is possible, but doesn't seem very convincing; as I've already shown, kinslaying was one of the greatest crimes one could commit in Anglo-Saxon and Norse societies, so even if Hrothgar did forgive Unferth for these murders, which would be far from certain even if it occurred before he knew him, it seems unlikely that he would promote him to a thyle (see commentary for Line 1165), which seems to have been a high rank in the king's court. It seems more likely that Unferth was forced to kill his brothers in some conflict between his family and Hrothgar. In the words of Professor Shippey: *Unferth has committed a breach of the loyalty-to-family code... it's a common feature of Germanic stories, loyalty to kin, loyalty to lord, who do you pick?*

The edge of this page has been damaged, but Thorkelín emended this line, so that it said *Þæs þú in (helle) scealt werhðo dréogan, þéah þín wit duge*, "For that, in Hell you shall suffer damnation, though your wit is good." This has almost always been the accepted emendation, but perhaps this is wrong. Perhaps rather than *helle*, the manuscript really said *healle*, 'the hall'. *If the word was "hell", then werhðo would mean damnation. But if it's "hall", then it could mean "reproach, condemnation", which I think suits the context better.* It seems out of character of Beowulf to condemn a man to Hell; that would be overstepping his bounds. And why would he add "though your wit is good"? Why would anyone think he'd go to Heaven just because he's clever? We can assume that the author of *Beowulf*, who was likely a cleric, understood about the grace of God. He would not condemn a sinful believer to Hell, just as He would not let a righteous pagan into Heaven. Kinslaying, though a heinous crime was not enough in of itself to become damned. If he died a pagan, (which would be almost certain if *Beowulf* was historical) he would be damned, but if he was a Christian, he would have gone to Heaven. So, saying that Unferth would suffer damnation would pose several problems, but it would make sense if Beowulf told Unferth people reproached him in the hall because of his kinslaying (Shippey, 2015).

Line 605-6b- Sun Shining from the South

In the far north, the sun can appear to rise in the south, rather than the east. T.M. Pearce suggests that since 'Hell' in Germanic thought is often associated with cold and the North, the sun in the South could be a metaphor for God's favor (Arner, et al, 2013).

Line 612b- Wealhtheow

The most common etymology proposed for the name Wealtheow is a contraction of *Wealh* (meaning 'foreign', but especially used when referring to people of British Celtic descent. from where the word 'Welsh' comes from) and *þéow* (meaning 'servant' or 'slave'). This is a highly unlikely name to give a Geatish noblewoman. Instead, it actually seems to come from *wala* meaning 'chosen' or 'beloved'. Thus Wealhtheow would mean 'beloved servant.' *Þéow* could also mean 'devotee', probably to a certain god. If Wealtheow indeed has this etymology, then it would make it the feminine form of the Norse name *Valthjófr* (Farrell, 1972).

Wealhtheow may also have been associated with Anglo-Saxon England. The Norse sources say that Hrothgar's wife was an English princess, and the *Hrólfs saga Kraka* gave even more detail, by naming her Ögn and saying she was the daughter of Norðri, the king of Northumbria (Gammonsway, et al, 1971).

Line 614-30a- Passing of the Mead

The passing of the mead cup was one of the most important rituals between war-bands in Germanic cultures. Mead was a very precious drink, being both expensive and exclusive, so mead had much greater symbolism than ale, or even wine, so not just anyone could serve the mead. At a feast, the first round of mead was passed by the highest ranking lady present, typically either the lord's wife or daughter. She would pass a richly adorned cup or horn, full of mead to every man in the hall, starting with he of the highest rank and going down. She would say a few words to each of them as she offered them the cup and the men were allowed to make a boast before they took a drink. The lord of the hall was not just cementing his war-band by honoring his men, buts also establishing his right to be their lord and comrade (Enright, 2013).

Line 683a- Nithing

In Anglo-Saxon society, a *niðing* (Old Norse *niðingr*) was a person without honor. The word *nið* is cognate with modern English 'beneath' (as in 'one beneath honor') and 'nether.' In honor-societies, being thought of as a nithing was often worse than death. A man accused of being a nithing was honor-bound to challenge the accuser to a duel; to not do so was an admission of guilt, however if the accuser lost the duel, then *he* would be considered a nithing, because he falsely accused the winner of being a nithing. There were multiple ways to be considered a nithing ranging from oathbreaking, disability, outlawry, practicing passive homosexuality, practicing magic and cowardice (Jákobsson, 2017).

Line 739-43a- Hondscio

It strikes many readers as odd that Beowulf lets Grendel eat his thegn; whose name is later in the poem revealed to be the thegn named Hondscio. Hondscio is an odd name for a person, as the name literally means 'hand shoe,' or glove (compare modern German *Handschuh*).

Most scholars now believe that this scene played out somewhat differently in the proto-*Beowulf* legend. In many faerie-stories, the hero competes against rivals. Often, he is the youngest of three brothers and seems the unlikeliest to succeed, but details are sometimes different. The contest can be anything from cutting down the most wood to wooing a princess (or killing a monster). The rivals are the most likely to succeed and are first to compete, but fail miserably. Then it's the hero's turn to try, but though he's mocked for thinking he has any chance, he succeeds. It is thought that in the original legend, the Bear's Son comes to the King's hall, hoping to rid him of the Monster; perhaps the King

221

offers the killer his daughter's hand in marriage and half the kingdom to the killer, as the deal goes in many faerie-stories. The Bear's Son has two rivals, Mar-peace (Unferth) and Hand-shoe (Unferth might not have been a rival in the original; it just makes sense that there would be a second rival). Mar-peace publicly taunts the Bear's Son that he has no chance, and that night he faces the Monster, but is killed. The next night, Hand-shoe faces the Monster and is also killed. The Bear's Son faces the Monster on the third night, and kills it. As the legend evolved, this rivalry was forgotten, but Hand-shoe being killed by the Monster was remembered, and so an odd half forgotten tradition remained (Tolkien, 2014).

Grendel usually takes any remains of his victims back to his lair in his sack presumably to eat later, a hideous version of a take-away. This is comparable to the sacks used by Giants and Trolls in folk-tales. Strangely though, Grendel's giant Dragon-skin 'sack' is actually referred to as a *glof*, a 'glove.' No one is completely sure why the sack is referred to as a glove, though many scholars suggest a connection to the Norse myth of Thor and his companions sleeping inside the Giant Skrymir's mitten. As I said above, Hondscio means 'glove, suggesting yet another connection to Grendel's glove.

The author's exclamation that Grendel ate Hondscio's hands and feet has sometimes been connected to Jezebel being eaten by dogs in *2 Kings 9:35*; *And when they went to bury her, they found nothing but the skull, and the feet, and the extremities of her hands.* Many animals will not eat the flesh from the heads, hands and feet (or at least eat it last), due to their boniness and also, perhaps for their supposed bitterness. That Grendel would eat these parts without hesitation shows his gluttony (Orchard, 2014).

Line 769a- ...frozen with fear...

The word used here is *ealuscerwen*, a word only recorded here. There has been much debate about the exact meaning of this word, but it is agreed that its general meaning is 'caused terror.' *Ealu* is Old English for 'ale' and the word *meoduscerwen* appears in the Anglo-Saxon poem *Andreas*, the same word, but substituting 'mead' for 'ale'. Klaeber believed that this meant 'the pouring of (bitter) ale,'as the word *bescerwen* means 'deprive', that **scerwen* could possibly mean 'allot' (Klaeber, 2008). However, it has been noted that the prefix *be-* is not a negation. Tolkien also says that ale (or, indeed alcohol in general) is always used as a symbol for good in Anglo-Saxon sources, so 'bitter ale' would be a foreign concept to the Anglo-Saxons. Thus, he and several other scholars believe that the word means 'deprived of ale'. Tolkien further believes that this word has more meaning than simply being denied alcohol, but that 'ale' is symbolic of peace and order, so that being 'deprived of ale' would mean being 'deprived of peace and order.' He compares this to Line 4-5, where "Scyld Scefing seize(d) the mead-benches of frightened foes..." (Tolkien, 2014).

Lines 785-7- Grendel's Deathsong

Grendel is said to utter a *gryreléoð*, a 'horrible song.' Usually this is glossed as a 'wail,' but this does not seem to be the full picture. While Grendel's 'weeping' indeed terrifies the men, it is undoubtedly described as a song or a 'lay' of mourning. *Grendel's sound is thereby intimately connected to some of the poem's most moving moments of loss, memorialization, and elegy.* As Grendel is a monster and his deathsong is in a language unknown to man, they can only hear a terrible sound. It is a common motif for a person to sing just before their death. This is the origin of the phrase 'swan song,' due to the Ancient Greek belief that swans remain silent throughout their lives, only to sing a mournful song just before death. This motif is especially common in Norse legend, with the most famous example

being the deathsong of Ragnar Lodbrok, the *Krákumál* (Cohen, 2012).

Lines 874-97- Sigemund

Sigemund the Wælsing is the same character as Sigmund the Völsung of Norse myth. In the Norse sources, it is Sigmund's son, Sigurd who slays a Dragon Fafnir, rather than Sigemund, aided by his nephew, Fitela (or Sinfjötli, his son by his sister in the Norse sources) (Gammonsway, et al, 1971).

Lines 901a- Heremod

Heremod was probably the predecessor of Scyld as king of the Danes. Heremod can perhaps be identified with the figure of Lotherus of Saxo Grammaticus. He said that Lotherus was the son of Dan, the first king of the Danes, and namesake of Denmark, and the predecessor of Skioldus. Lotherus was also a wicked king who was driven into exile. Tolkien noted that the 17th Century Swedish historian, Johannes Messenius wrote … *therefore Lotherus, King of the Danes, bereft of his wealth because of his excessive tyranny, and defeated, fled into Jutia.* As this was long before *Beowulf* was known about, Tolkien believe that it was a tradition that he fled to the Jutes (Tolkien, 1983).

Lines 929a- Shucks

The manuscript here used the word *Scuccum*, a word which survives as the mythic 'Black Shuck'. The Black Shuck is a demonic Black Dog that dwells in East Anglia (Slade, 2005).

Lines 1018b-9- …Treason

These lines foreshadow a time of discord among the Scyldings. Typically, this is thought to refer to Hrothulf killing Hrethric (see commentary for Line 1189), an event recorded by Saxo Grammaticus. However, Saxo does not say that 'Rørik' is in any way related to Hrólf, and it actually goes against how Hrólf is portrayed in the Norse sources if he did kill his cousin to usurp the throne.

> Here we have the elements of a fiction, constructed from scattered sources, that has been repeated so often that it has come to take on the semblance of fact… the notion of Hrothulf's blood guilt and usurpation has remained unaffected by the Beowulf's poet's failure to provide information about such crimes. Nor does any other source mention Hrothulf's guilt; it is a product of critical extrapolation from a few lines of text that can just as well be taken to refer to something completely other than Hrothulf' supposed usurpation (Bjork, 1998).

Cooke thinks this line actually refers to Heoroweard's killing of Hrothulf. *As for Hrothulf, in the only two places where he appears in* Beowulf *the poet gives him nothing but praise, so we have no secure grounds for doubting that the poet shared his northern counterparts' esteem for him* (Cooke, 2007).

Line 1044b- Ingwines

In *Beowulf*, Hrothgar is called 'the lord of the Ingwines.' *Ingwines* (friends of Ing) is used here as another moniker for the Danes, though the term has a deeper meaning. Ing is the Anglo-Saxon form of the Norse fertility god, Yngvi-Freyr.

The Roman historian, Tacitus, in his book *Germania* tells of a people called the *Ingaevones*, who lived along the North Sea, who believed they were descended from a great Northern king, named Ing, (he was not considered a god at this point, and may not have been until the Viking Age). The Ingaevones seemed to have been a confederation of tribes rather than a tribe itself, and included the Frisians, Angles, Saxons and Jutes. Like their ancestors, the Anglo-Saxons also considered themselves descended from Ing. Scandinavians are not typically considered Ingaevones, but as the *Yngling*

223

dynasty, originally from Sweden and later from Norway (see commentary for Line 2205) also claimed descent from Yngvi, it would not be a stretch to consider Scandinavia Ingaevonic. (Grimm, 1882)

In the Anglo-Saxon sources, Ing has a close relationship to Denmark. In the stanza for the Ing rune (ᛜ, the rune that gives the 'ng' [ŋ] sound) in the *Anglo-Saxon Rune Poem*, it tells a tale very similar to that of Scyld Scefing…

ᛜ *Ing wæs ærest mid Eástdenum*
ġesewn secgum, oð he síððan eást
ofer wæġ ġewát. Wæn æfter ran.
þus Heardingas þone hæle nemdon.

ᛜ *Ing was first among the East Danes*
seen by men, 'til eastward he went
over the waves. His wain ran after him.
Thus the Hardings named that hero.

While the rune poem says that Ing was a king of the Danes, it appears that he was not a native of Denmark. In fact, as he is said that he 'was first among the East Danes seen by men,' that he was not originally of this world. When his time came, he sailed off eastward into the unknown, presumably to return from whence he came. It would seem that this episode about Ing is derived from the same tradition as Scyld (Olrik, 1919).

Lines 1066b-159a- The Finnesburg Episode

The Finnesburg Episode is not known only from *Beowulf*. The *Finnesburg Fragment* is a short section of an Anglo-Saxon poem about 50 lines long; part of once a longer epic poem. The original manuscript is lost, but the words survive in an 18th Century transcript. The Finnesburg Episode however, is difficult to interpret, but Tolkien believed that he worked out this 'lost tale' and most scholars agree with his reconstruction. Tolkien believed the story's original title was *Freswæl*, "the Frisian Slaughter." He thinks it's a rather better title than the modern "Fight at Finnesburg". I agree with Tolkien that it was likely called *Freswæl* by the Anglo-Saxons, but I opted to us its modern name to be consistent in giving alliterative titles for each chapter.

Hnæf, king of the "Half-Danes" (probably a sub-group of Danes, who have conquered and settled the northern part of the Jutland peninsula) was in a feud with Finn, king of Frisia, but they decide to make a truce. Hnæf gives Finn his sister, Hildeburh's hand in marriage, and Hnæf fosters their son, who Tolkien believed was called Frithiwulf (he came to this conclusion by comparing the Anglo-Saxon Royal genealogies. He also surmised that Finn and Hildeburh had a second son named Frealaf, who continued Finn's line). I'll refer to this son as Frithuwulf from now on.

During the autumn, years later, Hnæf sails to Frisia, to return Finn and Hildeburh's son, and to spend the winter in Finnesburg (Finn's Burg [Fort]). He brings a band of 60 thegns, mostly Jutes, led by a Jute named Hengest. When they arrive at Finnesburg, they find that many of Finn's thanes are also Jutes, and bitter against Hengest's Jutes who had sided with the Danes when they conquered northern Jutland.

Finn separates the Half-Danes and Frisians to avoid trouble with the Jutes on both sides, by giving Hnæf and his men a separate hall to sleep in. However, the Frisian Jutes make a pre-dawn attack on the Half-Danes' hall, thinking to surprise them. But, Hengest expected that, so he had set

224

a watchman. For four days, the Half-Danes held the hall, without losing a single man, but on the morning of the fifth day, the Frisians break into the hall, and slay both Hnæf and Frithiwulf.

Finn then calls for a truce, and both sides are so depleted, they must agree to set aside their weapons, and wait in Frisia until spring, for they could not sail home during winter. After they all agree to the truce, Hnæf and Frithiwulf are burned on the same pyre.

Over the winter, Hengest broods over whether to honor the peace-treaty with Finn, or to honor his duty to avenge Hnæf. When winter is almost over, one of Hengest's men, known only as 'the son of Hunlaf' (but likely Guthlaf or Oslaf,) takes a sword called *Hildeleoma*, ('Battle-Light', which most scholars just assume is just a kenning for a sword, but I take as the name of the sword) which was probably Hnæf's sword, and lays it in Hengest's lap. Hengest then decides that his loyalty to Hnæf outweighed his oaths to Finn. When winter ends, Hengest sends Guthlaf and Oslaf home to gather the army while he stays at Finnesburg.

When they return, Hengest opens the gates to the Half-Danes. They kill Finn and his men, loot and burn down Finnesburg, before returning home, taking Hildeburh with them.

It seems most likely that this Hengest is the same Hengist who together with his brother Horsa, invaded England in 453, likely only a few years later.

As I said earlier, Tolkien believed that Hoc, Hnæf and Hildeburh's father, was the grandfather of Healfdene, Hrothgar's father. Thus, not only would the *Freswæl* be a Danish nationalistic tale, but one about Hrothgar's family; a fitting tale to be told in Heorot (Tolkien, 1997).

Line 1165b- Thyle

The exact role of the Þyle (or Þulr in Old Norse) is debated, but it is likely they were advisors and spokesmen. In some older sources, they are thought to be something akin to jesters, though this theory has been mostly dismissed (Shippey, 2015) .

It seems likely that it was the job of the Thyle to challenge bold statements made in the hall. This way, the king could dispute an unlikely boast made by a guest, but did not have to call them out. This is perhaps the reason behind the Flyting of Unferth (Lines 505-605). Unferth wasn't simply mocking Beowulf, but testing Beowulf, to see if he really intended to face Grendel, or if he was letting the mead go to his head. Whether or not this was a true concern of Hrothgar's, this was expected of Unferth. This would also be why Hrothgar did not intervene or apologize to Beowulf (Pollington, 2012).

Lines 1175-87- Wealhtheow's Warning

Wealhtheow advises Hrothgar not to adopt Beowulf, but to remember his own kinsmen, specifically Hrothulf, whom they both have aided in his youth. She says that she trusts Hrothulf to take care of her sons once Hrothgar dies, so that the rule of the kingdom may be passed on in time to her own sons. It is typically believed that this is meant to show irony that Wealhtheow trusts the lives of her sons to the man who will one day kill the eldest and usurp the throne (see commentary for Lines 1018-9).

As I stated earlier, Cooke argues that Hrothulf never usurped the throne and was rather elected as the new king when Hrothgar died. He thinks that Wealhtheow knew that Hrothulf would become king next, and rather than thinking that Beowulf would inherit if Hrothgar adopted him (that wasn't Hrothgar's choice to make), she was voicing her concern for her children's rights. She hinted at trouble, and tried to plead with Beowulf to aid her sons. In the commentary for Lines 1835-9, I explain how I believe that Beowulf took these words to heart, and how he responded to her (Cooke, 2007).

Line 1189a- Hrethric and Hrothmund

Hrethric and Hrothmund are the two sons of Hrothgar. In Norse traditions, there are several characters by the name of Rørik, the Old East Norse form of Hrethric. Saxo records that Hrólf Kraki (Hrothulf) killed (or at least deposed of) a certain king named 'Rørik, son of the covetous Baug.' 'Son of the covetous Baug' seems to be a mistranslation of *Hnøggvanbaugi*, meaning 'Ring-Stingy'. After the death of Hrólf Kraki, he is succeeded as King of the Danes by Rørik *Slyngebond* or 'Ringslinger' (who is most famous as the grandfather of Amleth, the inspiration for Shakespeare's Hamlet), who the writer of the *Skjöldunga Saga* said was Hrólf Kraki's kinsman.

I believe that Hrethric is the same person as the two Rørik characters, with ring-related nicknames (Olrik, 1919). I believe that after Hrothgar died, Hrothulf took the throne, and after Hrothulf's death, Hrethric returned to be king of the Danes. Perhaps Hrethric took up Beowulf's offer to stay in Geatland (see commentary for Lines 1835-9,) and this explains Saxo's confusion regarding Rørik being Swedish (Cooke, 2007).

The name 'Hrothmund' appears in the East Anglian royal genealogies. While this could be purely coincidence, it also could show that the East Anglian kings thought they had a connection with the Scyldings. The fact that Hrothmund is shown to be the son of Trygils, rather than Hrothgar, is not enough to show that he cannot actually have been Hrothgar's son. The genealogies were very careful in giving the king's family fourteen generations to connect them with the fourteen generations of Jesus in the Book of Matthew, while also connecting them with historical and mythical characters. An example from the same genealogy is that Woden (or Odin, the Germanic god) is the father of (Julius) Caesar! Hrothmund also possibly corresponds with 'Hrómund the Hard', one of Hrólf Kraki's champions in Norse tradition (Newton, 1993).

Line 1198b-1201- Theft of the Brisingamen

Hama, known as Heime in Middle High German and Heimir in Old Norse, is a character in the German Dietrich von Bern (Theodoric) cycle of legends and the Norse *Þiðrekssaga*.

In the *Þiðrekssaga*, Heimir is one of Erminrík's (Eormenric) men, but ends up betraying him and fleeing with Erminrík's treasure, which he gives to a monastery and retires there. Perhaps the Brisingamen was one of the treasures Hama stole from Eormenric? When *Beowulf* says that *[Hama] chose eternal reward*, this is likely referring to the tradition of Hama joining the monastery.

In Norse myth, the *Brísingamen* is the necklace of Freyja, the goddess of love and beauty. *Brísing* is an Old Norse poetic term for 'fire', so *Brísingamen* would mean 'the fiery necklace'. In the *Beowulf* manuscript, the necklace is referred to as the *Brósinga mene*, which could either have the same meaning as *Brísingamen*, or mean 'the necklace of the (people known as the) Brosings'. However, no people group called the Brosings are known of.

Eormenric was an East Gothic king from the 4th Century. Eormenric was indeed a real king, who is spoken of in Roman records, as ruling the area around the Black Sea. He became a very popular character in the Germanic heroic tradition, as a tyrant, who had Svanhild (Sigurd the Völsung's daughter and Eormenric's wife) trampled to death by horses, because he suspected her of having an affair, and of murdering his nephews. In Germanic legends, he is often portrayed as Theodoric the Great's uncle and enemy (though Eormenric lived about one and a half centuries before Theodoric in real life) (Gammonsway, et al, 1971).

Line 1202b- Swerting

In the *Beowulf* manuscript, Swertng is said to be the *nefa* of Hygelac. *Nefa* has several meanings

226

such as nephew, father-in-law, stepson, or grandson. As this name does not alliterate with the names of the Hrethelings, Swerting is thought to be Hrethel's father-in-law, and therefore the grandfather of Hygelac. Swerting appears as a Saxon king or earl in various traditions, often in connection with the Bardish feud (See Commentary for Lines 2025-2079) (Olson, 1916).

Lines 1203-13a- Hygelac's Last Raid

Hygelac's Last Raid is the only event in *Beowulf* that has an historical record, so it can be accurately dated to somewhere between 516 and 522 AD, with a date around 521 being most likely. The 6th Century Gregory of Tours wrote that a 'Chlochilaichus, King of the Danes' was killed in battle, by Theudebert, the son of Theuderic, King of the Franks, while he was returning from a raid in northern Gaul. Chlochilaicus is believed to be a Latinization of *Hugilaikaz*, his Proto-Germanic name, and the mistaken identity, of him being a Dane seems to be due to the Franks not realizing the difference between the various Scandinavian tribes, a bit like how many people nowadays often can't tell the difference between Norway, Sweden and Denmark. The *Liber Historiae Francorum* gives the same basic story, but adds that Hygelac's raid was on an area inhabited by the *Attoarii* tribe, a Latinization of *Hetware*, one of the tribes said to have fought against Hygelac on his last raid in the poem (See more on Commentary for Line 2363).

The final record of Hygelac besides *Beowulf* is the Anglo-Saxon *Liber Monstrorum*, or Book of Monsters. It agrees with *Beowulf* in that Hygelac is King of the Geats, and with all of them in that he was killed by Franks while returning home, but it adds to them by saying he was a giant of a man, who could not ride a horse by the time he was 12. The Franks were so impressed by the king's height that and as a Pagan he could not be buried in consecrated ground, his bones were kept on the island where he fell, and "travelers from afar" came to the island to see them (Gammonsway, et al, 1971).

Using all four sources, the place that this battle took place seems to have been on an island in the Rhine estuary lose to the North Sea. The scholar, Francis P. Magoun suggested that this may have been the western part of the island, Goeree Overflakke. However, recent excavations suggest the island may have been Oegstgeest in the Netherlands, near Rotterdam might be the place of Hygelac's last battle. While Oegstgeest may not appear to match the description of where he fell, evidence shows that the town was once an island. The excavations have uncovered artifacts such as an ornate silver bowl, an Anglo-Saxon belt buckle, wine barrels and imported pottery, all from the Migration Era, suggesting that this was a site of international activity in the 6th and 7th Centuries, which may have been due to a gigantic skeleton kept there, like in *Liber Monsgorum* (Porck, 2017).

Line 1208a- Arkenstone

Arkenstone is a direct translation of the Old English word *eorclanstán*, meaning a great and precious gem, especially a pearl or topaz. However, with the spelling *arkenstone*, it was reintroduced into Modern English by J.R.R. Tolkien in *The Hobbit*, where it referred to as a great gem that is revered by the Dwarves of Erebor (Parker, 2014).

Lines 1258-309- The Mere-Wife's Revenge

For the first time in 12 years, the men in Heorot are able to sleep in the hall without fear; Grendel is dead and they are safe. Little did they know that a new terror would come for them that very night while they slept. Grendel's mother came up out of the mere where Grendel and she lived, seeking revenge. Grendel's mother goes into the hall, takes back her son's arm and kills one of Hrothgar's retainers, Æschere, before fleeing.

Feuds were very common in all Germanic cultures (see commentary for Line 156). Of course, a parent may legally kill their child's murderer, but she took revenge on the wrong person.

Beowulf is said to have been sleeping in a guest-house that night, so was not in the hall when she attacked. She took one man to compensate for the loss of one son, rather than killing everyone, showing that this was thought out and that it was meant to be within the boundaries of a feud. It is not explained why she singled out Æschere, who had nothing to do with the death of Grendel, but perhaps since Beowulf was not in the hall, Æschere, being Hrothgar's right-hand man, was the best-dressed and equipped man in the room and Grendel's Mother mistook him for Grendel's killer?

Grendel's mother is reminiscent of various water hags in English folklore, especially Peg Powler, who is said to haunt the River Tees, near Hartlepool (which I argue in the commentary for Line 1372 has a connection with Grendel's Mere). If Hartlepool does have a *Beowulf* connection, it is possible that Peg Powler is a folk-memory of Grendel's Mother (Shippey, 2015).

Lines 1316-20- He asked if it had been a pleasant night

This is an attempt at humor, and likely a glimpse at the *Beowulf* proto-legend. Throughout the poem, Beowulf is shown to be wise and tactful. This is to fit him into the courtly mood of the poem. However, in the proto-legend, Beowulf was most likely a simple and tactless strongman, who was more apt to kill first and ask questions later. This has been mostly covered up, but shines through in a few places; perhaps nowhere more so than here, where Beowulf walks into the hall and stupidly asks the weeping Hrothgar if he slept well. Hrothgar is frustrated by Beowulf's obtuseness, and snaps at him, "Ask not of my pleasure!"

Line 1324- Yrmenlaf's elder brother

Yrmenlaf, Æschere's younger brother, is only mentioned here; this name appears nowhere else in any Germanic corpus. However, it seems unlikely that the poet would simply invent a name for a character who is of no importance to the narrative. It seems probable that Yrmenlaf was a character who was known in folklore (Shippey, 2014).

Lines 1357b-76a- Grendel's Mere & it's surroundings

It seems likely that Grendel's lair was a cave behind a waterfall in the *Beowulf* proto-legend, rather than in a mere. The word *fyrgen-stréam*, 'mountain stream' used in Line 1359 might actually be the way that a person who doesn't know a waterfall would describe one (Lawrence, 1912). In many Norse legends and sagas (for an example, see commentary for Lines 1492-1622). Trolls and other creatures often live behind waterfalls; a belief that has survived in the Norwegian *Fossegrim*. However, England, or for that matter, Denmark, does not have waterfalls of a comparable size as that of Norway or Iceland. They do however have many meres, fens and marshes. Many Germanic stories do take artistic license, but while an Icelandic tale might speak of a huge Danish waterfall, or an English tale speak of Danish mountains (Denmark's highest natural peak, Møllehøj, is only 170.86 meters [561 feet] tall,) it seems unlikely that an Anglo-Saxon would write about a geographical feature that was foreign to England.

It is also curious to note that the fictional description of Grendel's borderlands also closely matches the real-life borderlands of where Heorot would have stood. A fifteen minute walk from Gammel Lejre is a region called the 'Dead Ice Zone.' At the end of the Ice Age, the melting ice sheet there left behind vast quantities of rubble, creating a hilly region riddled with lakes and tarns. This area used to be heavily wooded and has always been a hinterland (Christensen, 2010).

It has also been noted that the description of the mere bears great similarity to the description of Hell given in the Anglo-Saxon *Blickling Homily* XVI:

Swa Sanctus Paulus wæs ġeseonde on norðanweardne þisne Middanġeard, þær ealle wæteru niðer ġewítað, and he þær ġeseah ofer ðam wætere sumne hárne stán. Wæron norð of ðam stáne, aweaxene swiðe hrimiġe bearwas, and ðær wæron þiestru ġenipu, and under þam stáne wæs Nicra eardung and Wearga. He ġeseah þæt on ðam clife, hangodon on ðam ísiġean bearwum, maniġe swearte sawla be heora handum ġebundne and þa fynd þara on Nicra onlicnesse heora gripende wæron, swa swa grǽdiġ wulf. And þæt wæter wæs sweart under þam clife neoðan, and betweox þam clife on ðam wætere wæron swelċe twelf míla, and ðonne ða twigu forburston, þonne ġewiton þa sawla niðer þa þe on ðam twigum hangodon, and him onfengon ða Nicras. Ðis ðonne wæron ða sawla þa ðe her on worulde mid únrihte ġefirenode wæron and ðæs noldon ġeswican ær heora lifes ende…

'As St. Paul was looking towards the northern part of this Middle-Earth, from whence all waters pass down, he saw there above the water a hoary grey stone. North of the stone, grew a very rimy grove, and there were dark mists, and under that stone was the dwelling place of Nicors and Wargs. He also saw that on that cliff, hanging in that icy wood, many swarthy souls with bound hands; there fiends in the likeness of Nicors were gripping them like greedy wolves. The water was black beneath the cliff, and betwixt the cliff and the water there were about twelve miles, and when the twigs broke, then the souls who were hanging on the twigs went down, and the Nicors seized them. These were the souls who here in this world were sinful with crimes and would not cease them ere their lives ended… (Orchard, 2003).

Line 1372a- A Hart with its head raised high

Scribe A accidentally omitted a word in this passage:

Nó þæs fród leofað
ġumena bearna þæt þone grund wite.
Ðéah þe hǽð-stapa hundum ġeswenċed,
heorot hornum trum holt-wudu séċe,
feorran ġeflýmed, ǽr hé feorh seleð,
aldor on ófre, ǽr hé in wille,
hafelan … Nis þæt héoru stów!

Even when the heath-stepper is harassed by hounds,
the stout hornèd hart seeks the holt,
thus far driven, will first give up his life,
ere he will leap into those loathly waters,
its head… 'Tis not a happy place!

Usually, this has been emended to *hýdan*, 'hide.' Thus, the translation would say, *… ere he [the hart] will leap into those loathly waters to hide his head. Beorgan, helan* and *hafenian* have also been suggested, but all of these emendations present various problems. However Thijs Porck suggests that the emendation should be *hafene*, 'to raise,' making it say *… ere he [the hart] will leap into those loathly waters, with its head raised high.* This poses no metrical problems and actually describes how deer swim, holding their head above the waterline. Then rather than imagining the hart hiding beneath

the water, it shows that, at any other body of water, the hart would dive in and swim across to escape the hounds, a common tactic of hunted deer. (Porck, 2019)

There might be a sign of a Northumbrian authorship of *Beowulf* in the form of the town of Hartlepool. Hartlepool, indeed means 'the pool of the hart,' named for a mere there that was said to be bottomless, and has been called this since the 7th Century. Since the 12th Century, the Hartlepool coat-of-arms has depicted a stag standing at the edge of the water, who is being attacked by a hound. This was likely already an old image associated with the Hartlepool mere when it became the coat-of-arms and likely started not much later than the founding of the settlement. It seems less and less likely that Hartlepool and this passage of the poem is simply a coincidence (Shippey, 2015).

Line 1457-64- *Hrunting* and other Swords

Swords are the most commonly mentioned type of weapon in *Beowulf* and perhaps in all of World Literature. However, despite how often they appear in Germanic sources, they were the least common weapon; a sword was much more expensive than axes, spears or bow and arrows, so only a wealthy person could own a sword. Swords were so valuable, they were passed from father to son, often being used for hundreds of years. When they were finally buried with their master, they were in risk of grave-robbers. Sometimes, a sword would be bent or broken before being buried, so as to make it useless to grave-robbers.

Swords were often thought of as having a soul. They were thought of as having a personality, having a literal hunger or thirst that was sated when it shed blood and were sometimes 'ceremonially killed' when they were no longer of use. While this was downplayed when the Anglo-Saxons converted to Christianity, the custom of naming swords continued. Two swords in *Beowulf* are named: Unferth's sword *Hrunting* and Beowulf's sword *Nægling* (for more on this sword, see the commentary for Line 2680).

Hrunting, like many Germanic swords, is pattern welded. Pattern welding is when two or more rods of metal (in this case, typically iron of differing qualities) are heated up, twisted and hammered together. A blade made in this way was incredibly strong and flexible, a technique that would not be improved until the introduction of crucible steel in the mid-9th Century. Not only were pattern-welded swords more powerful, they were beautiful as well. Pattern-welding gave the blade a blue-black color and produced intricate patterns on the blade, such as herringbone or waves, 'the serpents' that the poem mentions. The 6th Century Roman scholar, Cassiodorus quoted a letter from Theoderic the Great to the Vandal king, thanking him for the gift of a pattern-welded sword:

…In the middle of the blade are beautiful incisions like winding worms and there are shadows numberless so you believe the bright metal had been interwoven with many different colors (Mortimer, 2011).

The etymology of Unferth's sword, *Hrunting*, is obscure. Theories on the name meaning have ranged from 'Resounding' to 'Thrusting.' Kemp Malone believed that the *Hrunt-* prefix is the Old English form of *Hrotti*, a sword in Fafnir the Dragon's hoard in Norse mythology (Malone, 1943).

Hrunting is described as a *hæft-méce*, a hapax legomanon (a word only recorded in one source), that presumably means a 'long-handled sword.' This also appears to directly correspond to the Norse *hepti-sax*, also a hapax legomanon from the *Grettis Saga*. Aside from the similarities of this word, the *Grettis Saga* has many comparisons with *Beowulf*, see Commentary for Lines 1497-1622.

Line 1497-1617- The Battle in Grendel's Mere

Many read this passage as saying that Beowulf swam for a whole day, but is this really what the text was saying? Even supposing he could hold his breath for many hours, if the mere took that

230

long to swim down, it'd mean it was impossibly deep for an inland body of water. Most humans can only hold their breath underwater for two minutes, but some have been known to hold it for close to 12 minutes (though Aleix Segura held his breath for over 24 minutes, after breathing pure oxygen in 2016). Not even marine mammals can stay submerged for a whole day; the record for holding breath goes to a Cuvier's beaked whale off the coast of California who stayed submerged for 2 hours and seventeen minutes. A human also cannot go so deep underwater and survive. The deepest a human has ever dived without scuba gear is 253 meters (830 feet) done by Herbert Nitsch in 2012, although he suffered extreme decompression sickness and had to spend several months in rehabilitation (MacDonald, 2017). So if someone reads this that way and knowing that Beowulf is being honest, one must assume that he is using magic, has invented scuba gear, is not fully human or that this is a miracle.

But, is this really what the poet was saying? The Old English text actually says that the sun had risen by the time Beowulf reached the bottom of the mere. If they do mean this, then it means they went to the mere while it was dark. It might just mean the sun was at its highest.

Some scholars have suggested that Beowulf's descent into the mere is symbolic of the Harrowing of Hell, the Catholic doctrine that Jesus descended into Hell after the crucifixion to free the righteous dead. These scholars suggest that symbolically the waters are death and the cave Hell; they claim that Beowulf is a Messiah figure, who defeats "Death" and returns to life victorious, the waters cleansed. Others suggest that the descent is rather meant to symbolize baptism. But, it must be remembered that *Beowulf* is not an allegory. There can be Christian echoes in a work, without it being wholly symbolic (Chickering, 1977).

When Beowulf reached the bottom of the mere, Grendel's Mother seizes him and drags him to a dry underwater cave. Although unusual, this is, in fact, possible because underwater caves sometimes have air-pockets, where one can breathe, until the air is used up. One such cave system is found under the Bjurälven, a river in Jämtland in northern Sweden. The underwater cave in *Beowulf* is like a twisted, mirror-image of a mead-hall, complete with a fire pit. It gives the disturbing realization that Evil has a structure that mimics what is Good, though it is a mockery.

Hrunting is said to have never failed in a fight, but the blade proved useless against the hide of Grendel's Mother, just as weapons could not be used against her son. Beowulf tossed away the useless blade and intends to fight her with his bare hands. In the text, Beowulf seized Grendel's Mother by her *eaxle*, her 'shoulder' to throw her down onto the floor to wrestle her. Klaeber thought it likely that *eaxle* likely a corruption of *feaxe*, her 'hair.' This might actually make more sense, but it is possible the change was actually deliberate; the scribe may have thought it unfitting for a hero to pull on a woman's hair, albeit a monstrous woman (Klaeber, 2008).

The poet tells us that Grendel's Mother would have killed Beowulf, if it were not for Weland's byrnie (see Commentary for Line 455a). Beowulf was losing his fight with the Mere-Wife, when suddenly he sees, hanging on the wall (presumably, God directed his gaze toward it), an *eald sweord eotenisc*, an 'old sword of Ettins' with the power to hew the hides of Cain's kin (see Commentary for Lines 1687-98 for more on this sword) and he smites off her head. It is not explained why this sword could cut the Grendelkin; perhaps it was because it was not forged by Men, or maybe it was fashioned with a metal that was stronger or more magical than iron, or maybe Grendel could only be harmed by his own weapon.

After Grendel's Mother is dead, a beam of light appears (see Commentary for Lines 1571-3a,) leading Beowulf to the body of Grendel. He beheads the corpse and Grendel's acidic blood eats the blade. Beowulf eschews the piles of gold in the cave, and taking only Grendel's head and the hilt of

the Giant's Sword, he returns to the surface of the mere.

This scene, and *Beowulf* in general, has much in common with the Icelandic *Grettis Saga*. Grettir Ásmundarsson, while based on a real 11th Century Icelandic outlaw, has a life that appears to be more folktale than reality. Despite having an inglorious youth, he grows up to be the strongest man in Iceland. Every Yule, a Troll woman attacks a farm called Sandhaugar and kills everyone. One Yule, Grettir waits at the farm for her, where he wrestled her and cut her arm off. She flees, so Grettir and a priest named Steinn follow her blood to a waterfall. Steinn lowers a rope for Grettir to use to come back from a cave behind the waterfall, but cuts the rope and flees after he enters the cave. In the cave, a Troll man (presumably the Troll woman's mate) attacks him, armed with a *hepti-sax* (which seems to be a related to the word, *hæft-méċe*; see Commentary for Lines 1457-64). Grettir's sword breaks against the Troll in the fight, but he sees a sword hanging on the wall, which he uses to kill the Troll, and climbs out of the cave by himself (Gammonsway, et al, 1971).

There are too many coincidences to have been accidental, though it's highly doubtful that the saga's writer would have even known about *Beowulf*. Rather it seems to have derived from the same proto-legend that *Beowulf* derived from; a literary cousin rather than a brother or child. For more on the proto-legend, see Commentary for Line 343.

Line 1545b- Seax

The *seax* (or *sax*) is a type of one-edged blade used by the Anglo-Saxons and other Germanic cultures. Seaxes were very common; all freemen owned one. In fact, they were so widely distributed that the Saxons named themselves after the seax. Seaxes were often used simply as knives, but were sometimes used in battle. Typically, the seax has a short blade, around the size of a dagger, but can be nearly as long as a sword. The poem suggests that Grendel's Mother's seax is of the dagger-variety (Mortimer, 2011).

Line 1570-2a- Brightness blazed forth...

This beam of light seems to be a holy light, rather than from the fire or the sword itself, as Martin Puhvel suggests. The Giant's Sword is not holy in itself, rather the opposite in fact, as the sword is said to have been forged by antediluvian Giants. But, Grendel and his mother are said to be enemies of God, so when *Hrunting* fails against the Mere-Wife, God shows him the one weapon that can harm her and after he kills her, God sends a holy light in the darkness of the cave to lead him to the body of Grendel (Chickering, 1977).

Line 1591b- The "clever" companions...

I added the apostrophes around 'clever' to humorously emphasize the irony of the statement; that the men assume that the blood in the water must be Beowulf's, when they knew that Beowulf intended to kill Grendel's Mother, and known that the blood could be either of theirs. The word 'clever' in the manuscript, *snottre* seems to not be intentionally ironic.

Really though, their abandonment probably has more to do with cowardice than dimwittedness. Grendel's Mere is obviously an unnerving place and the watchers probably took any opportunity to leave, though they did not want to lose honor by abandoning the watch without a good reason.

I translated *ċeorlas* as 'companions,' which is intentionally a mistranslation. *Ċeorlas* in fact means 'churls or peasants,' which was not the intended connotation.

232

Line 1600a- The Ninth Hour

This passage seems to be a Biblical reference. The Danes abandoned Beowulf at the mere on the ninth hour, or 'Nones', 3 PM. This is the same hour that Jesus died on the cross, abandoned by all but a faithful few (Chickering, 1977). Luke 24:44-46 says:

And it was almost the sixth hour: and there was darkness over all the earth until the ninth hour. And the sun was darkened, and the veil of the temple was rent in the midst. And Jesus crying with a loud voice, said: "Father, into thy hands I commend my spirit." And saying this, he gave up the ghost.

Line 1687-98- The Old Sword of Ettins

The Giant's Sword has Biblical origins. The hilt is said to depict the destruction of the Giants during the Flood, likely in pictographs on the sword's foils. This is an obvious reference to the Flood account in Genesis, which was at least partly used by God to destroy the Nephilim. In the Commentary for Lines 106-114, I suggest that Grendel was one of the Nephilim; this would explain why Grendel had this sword in his lair. One of Cain's descendants, Tubal-Cain was said to be *a hammerer and artificer in every work of brass and iron* according to Genesis 4:22 (Orchard, 2014).

It has been argued that the Giant's Sword is somehow related to *Gullinhjalti* (Goldenhilt,) the sword that Hrólf Kraki (Hrothulf) gave to his retainer, Hött in *Hrólfs saga Kraka*. Perhaps Hrothgar had a new blade forged for the golden hilt? Not knowing the original name of the Giant's Sword, they just named it *Gyldenhilt*, a sword that only the strongest of warriors could wield (Olrik, 1919).

Line 1700-84- Hrothgar's "Sermon"

This section is often called 'Hrothgar's Sermon,' because of the moralistic content, but it is really more of a moral exhortation than a sermon. Hrothgar warns Beowulf about becoming too prideful, and while it does have a Christian feel, Hrothgar does not make any references to Scripture. However, there are some places where the wording of the speech are reminiscent of various Bible passages; Hrothgar's list of things that may overcome Men resemble Psalm 91 and Romans 8, when they speaks of things believers need not fear and Ecclesiastes 12, when it speaks of old age and death. It is quite possible that the poet realized these similarities, but as Hrothgar does not know Scripture and is not purposely referencing them, this speech should not be thought of as a sermon (Staver, 2005).

Line 1745- ...his heart 'neath his harness

In the manuscript this line reads "... the heart beneath the helm." This is an odd line, as saying 'beneath the helm' implies that it is referring to the head, and the heart is most certainly not in the head. The poet may have meant, "... his heart, very far below his helm, in his breast," but it is still an awkward phrase. I changed the word 'helm' to 'harness as in 'mail harness', which both made more sense and works with the original alliteration.

Line 1769a- Half a Hundred Years

Hrothgar claims to have ruled the Danes for fifty years; this is also said to be the length of Beowulf's reign. This is clearly not literal seemingly just a poetic figure of speech to indicate 'a long time.' If Hrothgar had ruled for fifty years, this would mean that Heoroweard must be nearly that age, at the youngest, and so would have been approaching 80 when he rebelled against Hrothulf. More likely, Hrothgar became king a few years before the birth of his own children, while some have even suggested he began construction of Heorot soon after becoming king, making his reign only a

233

bit more than twelve years.

Similarly, a 50 year reign is very unlikely. Klaeber estimated that Beowulf fought the Dragon in 583 AD at the age of 88. While it can be argued that Beowulf is a legendary character capable of supernatural feats, I still believe it is unlikely that he fought the Dragon when he was nearly ninety. I suggest rather that Beowulf had a reign between 30 and 40 years, fighting the Dragon in his mid to late 60s, still an impressive age, but more plausible (Klaeber, 2008).

Lines 1835-9- If Hrethric should ever come to… the Geats

Beowulf's offer of welcoming Hrethric to Hygelac's court is perhaps more than a mere courtesy, but a offer of safety, directed at Wealhtheow. In Lines 1175-87, Wealhtheow hinted that she feared trouble between her sons and Hrothulf after the death of Hrothgar, (a fear that I, in the commentary for those lines, suggest was unfounded,) and hoped that Beowulf would be clever enough to pick up on her plead for help. I believe that this was his reply to her. He may have been reassuring Wealhtheow, telling her. "If you believe your sons are in danger, send them to the Geatish court. We'll protect them." If Rørik Ringslayer, who becomes King of the Danes after Hrólf Kraki in the Norse sources is indeed the same character as Hrethric, then Wealhtheow may well have taken up Beowulf's offer when Hrothgar died (Cooke, 2007).

Lines 1876b-80a- A Secret Longing

It is becoming a trend to say that all love must be sexual or, at least romantic; so any strong friendships between members of the same sex is, by necessity homosexual. This is especially common in recent academia, when speaking of people in fiction or historical sources. Thus people like David and Jonathan, are claimed to be homosexual. This is not to say that friendships can never have a sexual element to them, but this is an exception, rather than a rule, and is especially true in historical contexts.

Beowulf has not escaped this homosexual revision. While it is still a minority view, the interpretation that Hrothgar was in love with Beowulf is a growing view. This passage is the main source of these claims; that Hrothgar's 'secret longing' is a repressed sexual desire for Beowulf. This is completely taking the passage out of context; while Hrothgar does indeed love Beowulf, the poem shows it to be like the love of a father for his son. Lines 1175-80 show that Hrothgar was considering adopting Beowulf as a son, until Wealhtheow warned him against the notion. He relents, but it still a desire of his to have Beowulf as a son, though he must keep his wish secret. Hrothgar also knows he will most likely die before he'll be able to see him again.

Lines 1903-2199- Homecoming of Beowulf

Beowulf can be split into two parts, the young Beowulf's adventures in Denmark being Part I and the old Beowulf as King of the Geats as Part II. Some scholars in the past thought that these were originally two separate poems about Beowulf, but while it is indeed possible that there were once multiple folktales concerning Beowulf, the modern consensus is that this was always a unified poem. However, because of the significant length of the poem, it is doubtful that the poem was recited all in one session. Likely, the scop would recite the first 1902 lines, and finish the poem the next day. The homecoming scene was perhaps a recap of Part I. Many readers of *Beowulf* are left wondering why the Homecoming is repeating the same things they just read, but the thing is that there is some new information presented; just as I and II Chronicles seems to be a mirror of I and II Kings in the Bible, it is in fact a retelling of the story from a different point of view and adds new details (Staver, 2005).

 234

Line 1926b- Hygd

Hygd is the wife of Hygelac and the mother of Heardred. She is said to be very young, probably closer in age to Beowulf. It thus seems quite unlikely that Hygd is the mother of the daughter of Hygelac who married Eofor. She was probably from Hygelac's first marriage, and was perhaps only slightly younger than Hygd.

The names *Hygd* and *Hygelác* are both related. *Hygd* means 'thought or mind' and *Hygelác* traditionally means 'mind play,' but its also been theorized as meaning 'lack of thought' i.e. 'reckless,' referencing his rash raid in Frisia Lines (see Commentary for Lines 2200-2) as a direct contrast to his wife. (Bjork, 1998)

Tolkien theorized that the name of Hygd's father, *Hæreþ*, perhaps suggests that he was the King of the *Hæreða* (known as the *Hörðar* in Old Norse) the people of Hordaland in western Norway, based around the Hardangerfjord, which at the time was a petty kingdom. (Tolkien, 2014)

Lines 1931-62- Thryth and Offa

The manuscript says *Módþrýðo*, not *Þrýð*. Therefore, many translate the name of Offa's wife as Modthryth. However, it seems that the manuscript should have said *Mód Þrýðo*, or "the mind of Thryth." Indeed, the Anglo-Saxon name *Þrýð* and Norse *Þrúðr*, meaning 'power' seem to have been relatively common names, but *Módþrýð* is not recorded. Fulk suggests that Fremu is her name as Lines 1931B to 1932A reads *Módþrýðo wæg fremu folces cwén*, taking Fremu as a proper noun (Fulk, 2005). The etymology of the name *Offa* is uncertain, but is possibly a hypocorism (shortened form) of the name *Osfrið*.

The Thryth digression is reminiscent of *The Taming of the Shrew*. Thryth is a princess who has any man who gives her the wrong look put to death. She is everything a queen should *not* be, until she is married off to Offa who is able to 'humble' her. However, the poet does not say she was humbled. It says she was hamstrung. The word *hóhsnode* means 'hamstring' and is a cognate to Modern English 'hock,' thus, *Húru þæt on hóhsnod(e) Hem(m)inges mæg* literally means *However, her hamstring was cut by Hemming's kinsman*. Severing one's hamstring causes severe pain and cripples them for life. Thus, most scholars consider this hamstringing to be metaphorical. (Shippey, 2015)

There were two Offas in history. the 4th or 5th Century Offa of Angeln, a king of the Continental Angles, and his descendant, the 8th Century Offa of Mercia. Offa of `Angeln is obviously the Offa spoken of here, though some scholars believe that *Beowulf* was first written down during the reign of Offa of Mercia, and this passage was meant as a commentary on the Mercian monarchy. Purporters of this theory note that Offa of Mercia's wife was named Cynethryth. Indeed, the 12th Century *Life of Two Offas* presents quite a similar tale about 'Quendrida', Offa II's wife. It tells how Drida' was a Frankish princess, who was set to sea in a rudderless boat to die, as punishment for some wicked deed. Her boat landed in England and she was brought to Offa of Mercia, who was stricken by her beauty and married her. She afterward changed her name from Drida to Quendrida. However, unlike the Thryth of Offa I, Quendrida was never "tamed", and continued her wicked ways until her death. (Gammonsway, et al, 1971)

While this tale was attributed to Offa II, the *Life of Two Offas* attributed several legends of Offa to Offa II. The tale of Quendrida is therefore thought to have originally been told of Thryth, not Cynethryth. Cynethryth was in fact, supposedly a kind and pious woman, who became a nun in her life in most sources (Klaeber, 2008). Tolkien noted that if this was meant as a not-so-subtle disguising of the current monarchs, the poet would likely be banished, if not downright killed by Offa (who was supposedly the real tyrant, rather than Cynethryth). (Tolkien, 2014)

Three other Angles are mentioned here, Offa's son, Eomer, Offa's father, Garmund and a kinsman named Hemming, of unknown relationship. The scribe apparently did not recognize *Éomer* as a proper noun and hyper-corrected it to *onġeómor* meaning something like 'the sad one.' Eomer appears in the Mercian genealogies, but he is listed as the son of Angeltheow, the son of Offa of Angeln. Eomer is best known as the father of Icel, the founder of the Mercian royal family, who was involved in the Anglo-Saxon Invasion of Britain, and also as the namesake of Éomer of Rohan in Tolkien's *Lord of the Rings*. *Gármund* is not found in the Anglo-Saxon Genealogies and is most likely a scribal error of *Wǽrmund* (Newton, 1993).

Line 1939- Scribe B

It appears that the scribe who had been writing the Nowell Codex ended abruptly at the word *scýran* with a different hand picking up at the word *móste*. The first hand, known as Scribe A, appears to have been the younger of the two, as his Rounded Insular Minuscule is a more modern handwriting than Scribe B's more conservative, yet crude, Late Square Minuscule. While Scribe A's handwriting is characteristic of the early 11th Century, Scribe B's handwriting is more characteristic of the late 10th Century, thus suggesting a generational age gap. Scribe B also made a number of corrections to Scribe A's work, suggesting he was Scribe B's student (Orchard, 2003).

Line 1942- Peace-weaving

The term *freoðuwebba* or peace-weaver is often thought to refer to a woman who is married off into an enemy people with the intent of forming a peace. While this was a relatively common Germanic practice, it seems that this term does not apply exclusively to this. The term 'peace-weaver' occurs only three times in the Old English corpus, twice for queens who might or might not have been given in marriage to an enemy and once referring to an Angel (who were always portrayed as male). It seems to refer rather to someone who is supposed to ensure peace among the people. Thus, Thryth was perhaps not given in marriage by an enemy of the Angles (Porter, 2001).

Lines 2024b-69a- The Bardish Feud

Using both *Beowulf* and *Widsith*, the legend behind this passage can be reconstructed. The Danes and the Bards agreed to end a feud between them by marrying Hrothgar's daughter, Freawaru to Ingeld, Froda's son. The wedding is held at Heorot, and during the wedding feast, an old Bardish warrior (see more about him on the commentary for Line 2037) sees one of the Danes carrying a sword that had once belonged to a Bardish warrior. He then begins to egg one of the younger Bards into killing him and reclaiming the sword. Thus, the feud begins anew. Ingeld leads the Bardish, who burn Heorot to the ground, but are finally defeated by the Danes, led by Hrothgar and Hrothulf (Gammonsway, et al, 1971).

The Bards were likely a branch of the Langobards, who lived in the modern region of Lower Saxony in Germany. The municipality of Bardowick in this region was possibly named for them. It has also been theorized that the Bards could refer to the Heruli (see commentary for Line 6). The Bards were forgotten in Scandinavia, so in the Norse sources they were also Danes. Frodi (Froda) was the younger brother of Halfdan (Healfdene), and started the feud by slaying Halfdan. Halfdan's sons Hróarr and Helgi (Hrothgar and Halga) eventually took revenge by killing Fródi and taking back the kingdom. R.W. Chambers believes that the Bards were also remembered by Saxo as the character, Hothbrodd, a king of Södermanland in Sweden, is also in a feud with the Scyldings.

Ingeld seems to have been a popular character in Anglo-Saxon legendary tradition. Alcuin.

the Northumbrian clergyman and scholar wrote a letter to the bishop of Lindisfarne, rebuking the monks for listening to heathen songs and legends of pagan kings. The letter includes the famous question: *Quid enim Hinieldus cum Christo?* "What has Ingeld got to do with Christ?" (Chambers, 1959).

Line 2039-2062- …an old ash warrior…

The word actually used was *grim*, rather than *stark*. This was a linguistic pun on my part. The "old ash-warrior" is thought to be a reference to the figure of Starkaðr (Gammonsway, et al, 1971). The name Starkad comes from Old Norse *starkr hòðr* meaning 'stark battle,' though Sophus Bugge believed it meant 'the stark Heath(obard,) though this is unlikely.

Starkad is a hero in Norse tradition. This episode about the unnamed warrior rebuking Ingeld, corresponds to an episode in the *Gesta Danorum* where Starkad urges Ingellus, the Danish king to avenge his father, Frotho against the Saxons who murdered his father, when Ingellus married the daughter of Swertingus, the Saxon king (Olrik, 1919).

Line 2051b- Withergyld

Withergyld appears to be the name of the young Bardish warriors's father. This figure also appears near the end of the Anglo-Saxon poem *Widsith*, mentioned along with other Germanic heroes.

Rædhere sóhte iċ ond Rondhere, Rumstán ond Ġíslhere,
Wiþergield ond Freoþeríċ, Wudgan ond Haman;
ne wǽran þæt ġesíþa þa sǽmestan…

I sought Rædhere and Rondhere, Rumstan and Gislhere,
Withergyld and Freotheric, Wudga and Hama;
They were by no means the least of companions…

The name Withergyld (or any variation on the name) does not appear anywhere else, so it can be assumed they both are the same character. Withergyld must have been a famous figure in Anglo-Saxon legend, who played a major role in the Danish-Bardish feud.(Chambers, 1912).

Line 2109- Sellic spells

The words used here in the original Old English are *syllíċ spell*. *Spell* in Old English means 'a story, news or an account' (from where the word 'Gospel' comes from- *Gódspel* meaning 'Good News') and *syllíċ* or *sellíċ* means 'strange or wonderful (Bosworth, 1921). One reason why I opted to use the translation 'sellic spells' rather than, say, 'strange stories' was to give a sense of the old age of the poem and of 'otherness'. I considered changing *syllíċ* to a Modern English word. However, the only Modern English descendant of *sellíċ* is 'selly' an Archaic word, usually encountered in Scots, and has an unfortunate resemblance to the word 'silly,' which gave the phrase the wrong impression. The other reason for this translation, and, I confess, the bigger reason, is because *Sellic Spell* is the title of a story by Tolkien telling a hypothetical folktale that inspired *Beowulf* (Tolkien, 2014).

Line 2161a- Heoroweard

While Heorogar, Hrothgar's elder brother does not appear in any of the Norse accounts, his

son, Heoroweard does appear. Hjörvard rebelled against and killed Hrólf (Hrothulf) who becomes King of the Danes after Hróarr (Hrothgar). Hjörvard is not mentioned as being related to Hrólf by blood, but as the husband of Skuld, Hrólf's half-, Elven half-sister, he would be his brother-in-law. He is a jarl in Denmark, so it is possible that he could be related. Hjörvard did not enjoy his victory for long, as he is slain soon after by one of Hrólf's retainers, Vöggr. According to Saxo Grammaticus, Vöggr agreed to be Hjörvard's retainer, so offered him the blade of Hrólf's sword, *Skofnung*, to swear on. Vöggr insists on swearing by the hilt, and when Hjörvard turns *Skofnung* around, Vöggr stabbed him through the heart, thus avenging Hrólf with his own sword (Gammonsway, et al, 1971). See also commentary for Lines 57-62.

In Germanic cultures, it was not enough to simply be the king's son to inherit the throne; all freemen in the society were allowed to vote for who would be king. While, the previous king's son did typically get chosen, it was not a guarantee. The strongest and most capable leader was almost always chosen, so if the king's son was a child, he'd typically just be passed over, rather than have a reagent until they were of age (as was the case of Æthelwold, the nephew of Alfred the Great. This makes Beowulf passing over the kingship of the Geats and being advisor to Heardred even more unusual). Heoroweard was most likely a child when Heorogar died, thus his uncle Hrothgar became king instead, but could compete with Hrethric, Hrothmund and Hrothulf as the next king after Hrothgar died.

Heoroweard thus had no legal right to vengeance regarding being passed over as king. But, Heoroweard did have a right to vengeance in that Hrothgar gave away his father, Heorogar's armor to Beowulf. A man's armor and weapons were always inherited by the son; in the case of the son being a child, a guardian might hold onto them, but he was honor-bound to give it to him when he came of age. Withholding a man's weapons and armor from his son was a serious offense and was enough to justify a killing. This mention of Hrothgar giving Beowulf Heorogar's sword and armor was likely meant to foreshadow that Heoroweard betray Hrothgar- perhaps the *fácen-stafas* mentioned in Lines 1018-9 (Shippey, 2015).

Line 2165a- Apple-fallow

The horses that Beowulf gave Hygelac are said to be fallow-colored. *Fealuwe* is a somewhat difficult word to translate. Technically the word means 'fallow,' but early Germanic color names are much less specific than modern color names, tending not to recognize different hues, (the Norse *Prose Edda* says that the rainbow is made of three colors, red, blue, and green, unlike the seven shades that are recognized today,) so rather than 'fallow' referring just to a sandy brown, it can refer to a variety of hues ranging from reds to yellows to grey. The word used here is more specific: *æppel-fealuwe*, 'apple-fallow.' Bosworth-Toller defines *æppel-fealuwe*, as 'the color of apples, a reddish yellow' (Bosworth, 1921). Jennifer Neville however, suggests that *æppel*, as used here refers to a round shape, like an apple, rather than the fruit itself. She takes this as referring to the round markings found on a dappled horse, and translates *æppel-fealuwe* as 'dapple dun.' It is impossible to know exactly what color the poet had in mind when he mentioned the colors of these horses, so I just opted to leave my translation vague, and let the reader decide (Neville, 2006).

Line 2183b-9- Beowulf's Inglorious Youth

This passage briefly mentions that there was a time while Beowulf was growing up that he was 'low in the sights' of the Geats. This would appear to be a contradiction to the rest of the poem, where he appears to have always been a promising youth. Scholars feel that 'Beowulf's inglorious

238

youth' is probably an element of the original folktale, comparable to Askeladden or Jack the Giant-Killer, who were lazy and useless, before they began to do heroic feats.

Line 2195b- Seven-Thousand Hides of Land

The original text simply says that Hygelac gave Beowulf 'seven-thousand', leaving whatever it is unstated. Some translators have believed that this gift refers to money, saying that Hygelac gave Beowulf "seven-thousand coins." However, the most likely reading is the one given, '"even thousand hides of land." According to Bede, North Mercia was the same size - so the land holding would be roughly the size of a large county. A hide simply referred to the amount of land required to support a freehold, so the amount varied, however typically a hide was about 120 acres, so 7,000 hides is 840,000 acres, or about 1312 square miles (3400 square kilometers,) roughly the size of Rhode Island or slightly smaller than modern Sussex (Staver, 2005).

Line 2205b- The Scylfings

The Scylfings are the Swedish royal family, thus the Swedes in general. Scylfing is the Old English form of the Norse *Skilfingar*. This name seems to have originally meant "men of the (rocky) shelf" (Slade, 2005), though Snorri Sturluson in the *Prose Edda* attributes the name to their first king, Skelfir. The Skilfings are usually called the *Ynglingar*, named for Yngvi, the human form of the god, Freyr, who they claimed as an ancestor. The Ynglings were originally kings in Sweden, but shortly after the events of *Beowulf*, they migrated west into Norway and became kings. Centuries later, Harald Fairhair, a member of the Ynglings became the first king of a united Norway, where his descendants still rule (Gammonsway, et al, 1971).

Line 2213a- The Dragon's Barrow

The description of the Dragon's Barrow is of a prehistoric passage grave. While the poem describes the barrow as over three hundred years old, it would actually be significantly older. Megalithic tombs were built throughout Sweden between 4000 and 1700 BC. It is likely that this barrow was built by the Battle Axe culture, a Bronze Age people who were famous for building huge and elaborate barrows.

Various Germanic cultures did make barrows, but these were relatively small and made with wood supports, if they indeed had any; however old prehistoric barrows were often reused, especially by the Anglo-Saxons, for their own burials. Prehistoric barrows were typically large and built of stone (sometimes with pillars and arches, like the Dragon's Barrow) that were covered with earth. This barrow is large even for a prehistoric barrow, large enough to house a fifty-foot long Dragon, and like any monolith, was thought to be the work of Giants. (Owen-Crocker, 2010)

It is uncertain where the tradition of Dragons guarding something came from, but it might have been a proto-Indo-European tradition, as it is seen in not only Germanic legends, but also Greek, Slavic, Celtic and Vedic legends. In Germanic legends, Dragons usually hoard gold. The gold would be useless to the Dragon, but it would lay atop the mounded gold, sleeping and brooding, becoming enraged if someone stole even the smallest piece of the treasure. A Dragon's lair was typically in a cave, but the Anglo-Saxons had a tradition of Dragons living in barrows. The Anglo-Saxon *Maxims II* says, *Draca sceal on hlæwe, fród, frætwum wlanc*, "A Dragon shall dwell in a barrow, old and proud of his treasures" (Klaeber, 2008).

Line 2223b- Thrall, Thegn or Thief?

The second half of Line 2223 contains a textual crux. The half-line reads *þe- nathwylces*, "a the-, I know not who." The *þe* appears to be the first two letters of a word describing the man who took the cup from the Dragon's hoard, and there is room for two more letters. Three suggestions have been made for the word meant: *þéow, þegn* or *þéof*, thrall, thegn or thief.

'Thegn' seems a rather unlikely emendation. Why would a lesser noble be on the run from a 'son of heroes' and attempt to buy back his favor with a stolen cup? I suppose its possible, but without more information, it seems safe to dismiss. 'Thief' seems more likely, though it seems a bit redundant to say that he is a thief, right after he steals a cup; his actions already showed that he's a thief, why do they have to explain again? 'Thrall' seems the most likely explanation.

Slavery was common in both Iron Age Scandinavia and Anglo-Saxon England. Slaves had no rights, and their owner could punish or kill them on a whim. This could explain why he was running from his master and why he'd offer a golden cup as a ransom for his life (de Roo, 1982).

Lines 2231-66- The Lay of the Last Survivor

This section of the poem is often called 'The Lay of the Last Survivor,' as it tells of how the last member of an ancient and forgotten race stores the remnants of his people's treasure in the barrow that the Dragon later inhabits. It is a vast and magnificent hoard, but the Last Survivor knows it is all useless without anyone to use them. After the gold is stored away, the Last Survivor dies, having no more purpose in life.

As I mentioned earlier, the barrow is prehistoric. If the Last Survivor's people indeed were the builders, then this was probably the Bronze Age, rather than Neolithic, as metal objects are in the hoard.

Some scholars have made an intriguing suggestion; that the Last Survivor and the Dragon are all one in the same. In Germanic legends, sometimes people buried themselves alive with their gold in order to eternally guard it, but their greed over time, transformed them from a man into a Dragon. This most notable example of this tradition is in the Icelandic *Völsunga Saga*, where the Dwarf Fafnir becomes obsessed with the ring, *Andvaranaut* and becomes the Dragon that Sigurd faces, (Gammonsway, et al, 1971,) and was popularized by C.S. Lewis in *The Voyage of the Dawn Treader*.

I think this is a very likely explanation about the Dragon. If this is not the case, then this passage seems random; why do the audience need to know why there is gold in the barrow? It would just be assumed to be grave goods. It is also hard to believe that gold left unguarded in a barrow for hundreds of years, would remain intact, until a Dragon just happened to discover it. I believe it is a reasonable conclusion that, after storing the treasure in the barrow, the Last Survivor entered the barrow to guard it and eventually transformed into the Dragon (Klaeber, 2008).

Line 2337-41a- The Iron Shield

The most important piece of armor to the Anglo-Saxons was the round shield. Many poor Anglo-Saxon warriors, such as members of the *Fyrd* (see Commentary for Line 2497,) would not be able to afford a helm and only the wealthy could afford chainmail. Besides the cost, these would only protect a localized area of the body. But a shield was cheap and extremely efficient.

Shields were constructed of multiple planks of wood, preferably linden (lime) wood (which would not split easily,) and held together by glue in a round frame between about 1.5 to 4 feet (45 to 120 cm) in diameter, and had a central iron boss to protect the hand and perhaps to jab into an opponent (the bosses were often pointed, especially in older shields). For maximum efficiency, the

Anglo-Saxons often employed a shield-wall formation, where the warriors would stand next to each other with their shields held before them, thus forming a continuous wall of shields. A shield-wall would consist of at least two, but usually more, layers. If someone was killed, the men next to him could step in to close the gap. The shield-wall was an extremely effective tactic, and was employed in almost every battle (Mortimer, 2011).

Of course, Beowulf could not use a regular shield. Dragon fire would burn away a wooden shield, Beowulf has his smith make him a shield that is unlike any ever used by the Germanic peoples, one made all of iron and large enough to protect his whole body.

This would be an extremely heavy shield, especially compared to the light wooden shields used by everyone else. Despite his advanced age, everyone would be reminded of his great strength and the heroism of his youth, but it may not have occurred to him that, while a wood shield would burn and be useless in a Dragon fight, an iron shield would be less than useless. The fire would make the shield (and his byrnie too,) become red-hot, covering him in third-degree. Even if he defeated the Dragon, without being bitten, he would most likely die from the burns.

But perhaps he did realize that the iron would burn him. Beowulf knew that he would die in this battle, so perhaps he wore it to show-off his strength rather than to help him. He mourns that he cannot fight the Dragon unarmed like he fought Grendel. Perhaps he is just using this Dragon incident to relive his glory days and die in a blaze of glory.

Lines 2359b-66- The Flight from Frisia

The traditional way that this section of the poem is read is that Beowulf, being the only surviving Geat from the raid on Frisia escapes Frisia by swimming home. It would be improbable that Beowulf cold swim this vast distance, especially considering the rough waters north of the Skaggerak, but not impossible for Beowulf. However, the traditional interpretation is that he swam to Geatland, while carrying thirty coats of mail. This interpretation defies belief. But, this is probably not what the poet meant.

First of all, the poem does not say he carried thirty byrnies. The word used is not *byrne*, but *hilde-ġeatwa*, meaning 'battle-gear,' which could refer to helms, shields or swords just as easily. Beowulf is said to have taken Hygelac's and Dæghrefen's swords, so it seems likely that swords were meant when it used *hilde-ġeatwa*. It is also possible that the lacuna in the next line that Klaeber emended as *eorla*, 'earls' originally said either *ecgas* 'edges' or *irens* 'irons,' both alternate words for swords.

While thirty swords weigh less than thirty byrnies, it would still be impossible to swim so far with them. But, the Old English word *swimman* does not have an identical meaning to modern 'swimming.' Rather, the word refers to any kind of movement in water, including by ship; this can be seen in one of Ælfric's *Homilies*, when Noah's Ark is referred to as *se swymmenda arc*, literally 'the swimming ark.' This usage of the word 'swim' continued into Middle English, only changing to its modern definition after the advent of Modern English. Therefore, it is quite possible that the poet intended that Beowulf actually single-handedly sailed from Frisia to Geatland (Wentersdorf, 1971).

Line 2363a- The Hetware

The *Hetware* were a Frankish tribe on the Lower Rhine, closely associated with the West Frisians in the Merovingian empire. The *Liber Histiriae Francorum* says the raid by Chlochaicus (Hygelac) was in *Atuarii* land, suggesting that the Hetware are identical to the *Chattuari*, a Frankish tribe living around the Rhine, who were first mentioned by the Romans. Tolkien says that the Frisians

were split into two groups, the Greater Frisians, living in the marshlands of the northern Low Countries and the Lesser Frisians, living in the southern Low Countries. While Finn was king of the Greater Frisians, the Hugas and the Hetware were related to the Lesser Frisians, and as they were within the former Roman Empire, were under Frankish territory. (Tolkien, 1983)

The *Hugas* are possibly the same people as the *Chauci*, a tribe neighboring the Frisians, in the land between the Rivers Ems and Elbe, closely related to the Saxons (Chambers, 1912).

Line 2379b-90- Ohthere & Sons

Ohthere is the son of the Swedish King Ongentheow. His sons are Eadgils and Eanmund - who are apparently exiled by their uncle King Onela for a failed attempt at rebellion. Headred , now King of the Geats, harbors them; for which act Onela invades Geatland and slays Headred, after which Beowulf ascends to the throne.

In the Norse sources, Ohthere corresponds to Óttar and his son, Eadgils corresponds to Aðils, but Eanmund only appears in *Beowulf*. Snorri Sturlusson gives Óttar the nickname 'Vendelcrow,' explaining that he was killed on a raid in Vendsyssel (formerly called Vendel) in Jutland, where his corpse was laid out on a barrow to be eaten by birds and wild animals. Other sources attribute the nickname Vendelcrow to Óttar's father, Egill (or Ongentheow). However, the 'Vendel' mentioned here, most likely refers to the Vendel in Sweden rather than Vendsyssel. Since the 17th Century, a barrow in Vendel has been called Ottarshögen, or Óttar's Barrow, showing that there was at least a tradition linking Ohthere with Vendel.

After Óttar died, his son, Aðils ascended to the throne. At some point, he got into a war with a certain Áli, the Norse version of Onela. However, he is not the brother of Óttar in Norse tradition. Rather Áli is said to be the King of Oppland in Norway. This likely stems from a confusion between Oppland and Uppland, the core region of the Swedes, both called *Úppland* in Old Norse. Eventually, Aðils defeated Áli at the Battle on the Ice at Lake Vänern.

Rather than Onela being married to Yrse, Aðils is married to Yrsa (see Commentary for Lines 57-62). Aðils has a villainous role in the Norse sources, usually portrayed as the nemesis of his stepson, Hrólf Kraki (Gammonsway, et al, 1971).

Snorri Sturluson said that one of the three Royal Grave Mounds in Uppsala held the remains of Eadgils. Birger Nerman suggested the Western Mound. Indeed, an elaborate burial of a man was found here, dated to around 575, a probable date of death for Eadgils (Nerman, 1925).

Line 2390b- That was a good king!

The king here seems to refer to Onela, rather than Beowulf. While many scholars believe that Onela is a villainous character, the *Beowulf* poet holds Onela in high praise, making that interpretation questionable. The language used to describe Eanmund and Eadgils is generally negative, and the *Beowulf* poet seems to disprove of their rebellion against Onela. Heardred seems to have been well-intentioned, but unwise in supporting Ohthere's sons. Beowulf, as Heardred's advisor, probably warned him not to support Ohthere's son, but he ignored Beowulf's counsel, and was eventually killed because of this (Farrell, 1973). As Onela was most likely married to Hrothgar's sister, Beowulf likely felt conflicted in fighting against Onela, who was not only kin to his allies, but also an honorable king, but was duty-bound to avenge Heardred (Newton, 1993). The poet called this a *ċeald ċear-síð* ('woeful quest', or in my translation a 'bitter battle'). Sophus Bugge suggests *ċeald ċear-síð* may also be a play on words, referring to the battle on the Ice of Lake Vänern. A cold quest indeed (Klæber, 2008).

Line 2406- The thirteenth member

One might notice that Beowulf leading twelve men to the barrow resembles Jesus and his twelve disciples. This is probably an intentional parallel on the poet's part. Thirteen eventually became an unlucky number because of this; Judas, who betrayed Jesus, was the thirteenth member.

No one betrayed Beowulf, however there is another connection with Jesus' disciples. All but one abandons their leader in both accounts, Wiglaf in *Beowulf* and John in the Gospels. Here, eleven of Beowulf's men were afraid of the Dragon and fled into the woods, while Wiglaf alone stood by Beowulf. In the Gospels, after Jesus' arrest, all the disciples but Peter and John, scattered, and Peter that night denies knowing Jesus, thus John is the only one not to abandon Him.

Lines 2435-40- The Death of Herebeald

The killing of Herebeald by Hæthcyn may relate to the story of the death of Baldr by Hödr in Norse myth. Klaeber even noted the similarities in names; *Hæð-* and *Höðr* and *-beald* and *Baldr* are etymologically the same (Klaeber, 2008).

In the *Prose Edda*, it tells of how the god, Baldr had a dream of himself being killed. He told his mother, Frigg about his dream, so she decided to go to everything in existence that could hurt him, and make them swear not to harm him. After this, the other gods began to play a game where they would throw things at Baldr, and see them bounce harmlessly off of him. But Loki, the god of mischief, discovered that a certain sprig of mistletoe had been overlooked by Frigg when she was making all things swear not to harm Baldr. Loki took the mistletoe and fashioned a dart from it. He offered to help Baldr's blind brother, Hödr aim the dart at Baldr, so he could join in the other gods' games. The dart hit Baldr's heart and killed him (Gammonsway, et al, 1971).

This incident might remind one of the death of William II by Henry I in 1100; during a hunt in the New Forest, Henry killed William by shooting him with a bow and arrow, which he claimed was accidental, but is often believed to have been deliberate. This is a coincidence however, for this happened about 100 years after the *Beowulf* manuscript, and perhaps about 400 years after the poem was composed. This does however bring up an intriguing thought. Was Hæthcyn's killing of Herebeald really accidental? It doesn't seem to have mattered much to the poet, nor to the Anglo-Saxons in general. Kin-slaying was a heinous crime, whether intentional or not (compare with Unferth's kin-slaying in Lines 587-9). This passage (along with the Unferth passage mentioned above) invokes the Cain motif seen earlier in the poem (see Commentary for Lines 106-14), perhaps deliberately. Though Beowulf's words have been softened in the translation, in the original Old-English, Beowulf refers to the killing as a murder and a wicked deed, seemingly condemning Hæthcyn (Georgianna, 1987).

Lines 2441-71- The Father's Lament

Many readers mistakenly interpret the passage of Hrethel's mourning as the execution of Hæthcyn. In fact, Hæthcyn is *not* hanged; this passage only compares Hrethel's grief with a father whose son has been hanged. Since, this hypothetical son did some heinous crime, he has been judiciously sentenced to hang, his family has no right to vengeance. The family's right to avenge a wrongdoing was taken for granted by the Anglo-Saxons (though the system of Weregild was soon developed to limit the amount of blood-feuds; see Commentary for Line 156), so having that right revoked was seen as nearly as bad as the wrongdoing itself. The father of a hanged son not only grieved for his dead son, he also knew he could do nothing about it. Likewise, Hrethel could not avenge Herebeald on Hæthcyn, because he was also his son. Thus Hrethel has no more reason to live.

So he "chose God's light," meaning that he died of grief, and being a righteous man, God took his soul to Heaven, one of the few characters in the poem whose salvation is assured (Georgianna, 1987).

Line 2477- Hreosnaberg
Hreosnaberg, the 'Ruined Hill', is a hill (probably a hillfort) in Geatland that Onela and Ohthere attacked at some point after the death of Hrethel, leading to the First Swedish-Geatish War.

Most scholars view this as a wholly fictional hill, but there's some evidence that this is a real place. *Hreosnabeorh* in Modern Swedish would be *Ryssberg*, and indeed there is a Ryssberg in the county of Uddevalla in Bohuslän, which was likely part of Geatish territory at that time, but this seems unlikely to have been this Hreosnaburg. Ryssberg does not appear to have ever been a hillfort, and is also on the Norwegian border, which would make a Swedish attack unlikely. It is more likely that Hreosnaburg is the plateau of Halleberg in Vänersborg county of Västergötaland. Halleberg is the largest hillfort in Scandinavia, and was in use during the period of *Beowulf*. Halleberg is known to have been a strategic location, and was likely an inspiration for Valhalla in Norse myth. It is also on the Geatish side of the Swedish border, making it a logical place for the Swedes to attack. Halleberg appears as a crumbling hill, much eroded and with many rockslides, making 'Ruined Hill' a fitting name (Wadbring, 2008).

Line 2494b- The Gifthas
The *Gifthas*, or the *Gepids* were an East Germanic tribe related to the Goths. They originally lived in what is now modern-day Poland, but by the third century, they carved out a kingdom in modern-day Hungary and Romania, which fell to the Lombards in the sixth century. *Beowulf* likely is speaking of a remnant of the tribe still living on the Baltic (Slade, 2005).

Line 2497- Fyrd
It should be noted that the word *fyrd* is not used here in the Old English. The word in question is actually *féðan*. *Féðan* means 'a troop of foot-soldiers,' which has a very similar meaning to *fyrd*, thus I opted to translate *féðan* as *fyrd*, to keep the alliteration.

The words *fyrd* and *here* both meant 'army' in Old English, but had different connotations, especially in early Old English. *Here* meant an invading army, especially a Viking army (e.g. the *mycel hæþen here*, the 'Great Heathen Army'). Before the Viking Age, the core of the fyrd was made-up of a king's retinue and sometimes supplemented by a levy of able freemen, led by a thegn. Fyrds in the 6-7th Centuries were generally small, usually consisting of several hundred men; in the laws of Ine, King of Wessex a fyrd could be made-up of as few as 35 men (Lapidge, 2001).

Lines 2501-8a- Dæghrefen
Dæghrefen was the leader of the Húgas (see Commentary for Line 2363,) who probably killed Hygelac, before being crushed to death by Beowulf. Beowulf killed him with his bare hands, his preferred method of killing, most likely in a bear hug, which plays with Beowulf's bear kenning name (Shippey, 2015). The ring he took from Dæghrefen is likely the neck ring Wealhtheow gave Beowulf (Arner, et al, 2013).

Dæghrefen literally means 'Day Raven'. *Day* names are fairly common in Old English, but *Raven* names are extremely rare. Thus the name *Dæghrefen* in Old English is only recorded in *Beowulf*. *Raven* names however, are common in Frankish. Two Carolingian manuscripts record the name *Dagohramnus*, with this same meaning (Shippey, 2014).

244

Lines 2602-04a Wiglaf

Wíglāf (whose name literally means 'War remains,' a name he certainly lives up to, as he survives the battle with the Dragon) is the son of *Wéohstán* and a kinsman to Beowulf.

Weohstan corresponds to a certain Vésteinn, who appears in the Norse *Kálfsvísa*, where he is mentioned as riding a stallion named Valr (whose name would have been Wæl in Old English) at the Battle on the Ice at Lake Vänern (see commentary for Line 2390). Weohstan fought for Onela against the Geats, and was the one who slew Eanmund. This would make sense if the Wægmundings were Swedes, but could still work if they were Geats. Weohstan could have married into the Scylfing royal family. Either way, this would explain why Weohstan fought for the Swedes against the Geats, and why Wiglaf is described as a Scylfing, yet fights for the Geats; Wiglaf would be a Swede by birth, but accepted by the Geats, because of his relationship to Beowulf.

Ælfhere is said to be a kinsman of Wiglaf. Some scholars believe that Ælfhere was Beowulf's true name, with Beowulf being a nickname (Klaeber, 2008). However, I believe that the two were separate characters, both familiar to Anglo-Saxon audiences.

Line 2680b- *Nægling*

Nægling (probably meaning 'Nailer') is perhaps the name of Hrethel's sword, which Hygelac gave to Beowulf in Lines 2190-4. *Nægling* may have a connection with *Nagelring*, the sword of Theodoric in *Þiðreks Saga*. (Klaeber, 2008)

Line 2687a- A wound-hardened weapon

Often this is emended to *wundrum heard* or "wondrously hard." However, I use the original wording, "wound-hardened." In pagan Germanic tradition, people believed that swords gained strength and power from the blood it spilled (Slade, 2005).

Line 2802-8- Beowulf's Barrow

Swedish archeologist, Birger Nerman believed that the barrow at Skalunda in Västergötland is the most likely place of Beowulf's barrow. Skalunda was a very important place in Iron Age Geatland, and close to Skalunda, the Geatish capital. It is also close to Årnäs, the place where Beowulf might have been killed (see commentary for Line 3031). Skalunda Barrow is one of the larger barrows in Scandinavia, and though it is still unexcavated, it is thought to have been built sometime around 600 AD, the approximate time of Beowulf's death. The Skalunda barrow is built on a major promontory along Lake Vänern; almost exactly like the description of Beowulf's Barrow (while the barrow is not visible from sea, the Old English *sǣ* can refer to any large body of water) (Nerman, 1956).

Lines 2813-14a- You are the last… of the Wægmundings

The *Wægmundings* were a clan descended from someone named *Wægmund*. Many scholars believe that the Wægmundings were a Swedish clan, but in the Commentary for Line 460, I explained that the Wægmundings may have been a sub-tribe of the Wulfings. Hrethel, the king of the Geats likely gave his daughter in marriage to Ecgtheow to make an alliance with the Wulfings. As Wiglaf is Beowulf's only male relative, he is the only candidate for king.

Line 2921a- The Merovingians

The *Merovingians* were the royal family of the Franks from around 450 till 750. They were named for their ancestor, Merovech (Wood, 1994). This is possibly evidence that *Beowulf* was written

before 750, when the *Carolingians* came into power.

Line 2923b-7- Hrefnesholt

Hrefnesholt, or Ravenswood, seems to correspond to modern-day Ramshult, on the island of Orust, off of Västergötaland. There is a Migration Era hill-fort here (Meijer, 1919).

Line 2936b- The Great Harrow

Sinherge is usually translated as 'with a great host,' taking *herge* as *here*, 'army.' While this does make sense, Raymond P. Tripp Jr. theorizes that *herge* could in fact mean *hearg*, 'a temple, altar, or grove.' This would mean that *sinherge* would have the meaning 'at the great harrow' (Slade, 2005).

Line 2940- ...he would give them to the gallows-tree...

As the battle is in a forest called 'Raven's Wood', and especially if *sinherge* does in fact mean 'at the great harrow', then this passage may be a reference to sacrifices to the heathen god, Woden (North, 1997). In Norse myth, Odin sacrifices himself by hanging himself from a branch of Yggdrasil, pierced with his spear, in order to learn the runes. This seems to have been the way human sacrifices were made to Odin.

Line 2961-98- Eofor & Wulf

Eofor and Wulf, both sons of Wonred, were two Geatish thegns. Ongentheow fought against Wulf during the battle of Hrefnesholt, and severely wounded him, so Eofor came to Wulf's aid and killed Ongentheow. Afterwards, Hygelac rewarded the both richly, and gave Eofor his daughter's hand in marriage.

Ongentheow corresponds with Egil the Yngling in Norse legend. According to Snorri Sturluson, Egil was gored to death by a bull he was trying to sacrifice. While this doesn't appear to correspond with Ongentheow's death in *Beowulf*, when one looks at the original Old Norse text, a different picture emerges (Gammonsway, et al, 1971).

Trónju farra, which means 'weapons of the bull (i.e. horns)', can also mean 'snout of the pig (i.e. tusks)'. Eofor is Old English for 'boar', so using boar kennings for Egil's killer would make sense. Probably, over time, the identity of Egil's killer was forgotten and these kennings were mistaken as descriptions of an animal (Vickerey, 2009).

Line 2999-3005a- The Fall of the Geats

The Geats were a people who lived in Götaland, south of Svealand and north of Skåne (historically part of Denmark). For a long time, scholars have taken the messenger's words in *Beowulf* as foreshadowing the conquest of the Geatish nation by the Swedes. But is this truly what the poet meant?

> In a classic example of the tragic fallacy... Beowulf's death is taken to be the prelude of the extinction of the Geats as a people... Entranced by the lure of high tragedy, and giving literal value to dire prophecies made by several speakers near the end of the poem, scholars too numerous to mention have taken these prophecies as relating to history and have dated the actual destruction of the Geats to one or another period before the poem was composed (Bjork, 1998).

Might not the messenger's words have just foreshadowed the Geats defeat in the Geatish-Swedish Wars and the loss of Geatish supremacy rather than their collapse?

Götaland was, in reality, independent from Sweden until the late Middle Ages and until 1973,

the kings of Sweden were called *Sveriges, Götes och Vendes Konung*, the King of the Swedes, Geats and Wends.

There is also some evidence that some Geats might have settled in England. While the majority of the Anglo-Saxon migrants were Angles, Saxons and Jutes, there were also groups of Frisians and Franks, and most scholars believe other tribes, most notably Scandinavians. Newton theorizes that the East Anglian royal dynasty, the Wuffings may have been descended from the Wulfings, an East Geatish tribe (see commentary for Lines 460-1). Furthermore, he believes that Wuffa, the founder of the Wuffing dynasty was a Geat, who was the inspiration for Wiglaf. Wuffa was said to be son of Wehha, which is believed to be a shortened form of the name Weohstan. Newton's greatest evidence for a Geatish origin of the Wuffings, however, is the Sutton Hoo ship burial, which bears great resemblance to the Vendel burials from Sweden (Newton, 1999) and the armor, especially the helm, which seems identical to Swedish craftsmanship, and was most likely crafted in the same workshop as the Vendel helms (Mortimer, 2011).

It has been suggested that some Geats might also have settled in Richmondshire in North Yorkshire. Richmondshire was formerly called Gillingshire, named for the Anglo-Saxon tribe that lived in the region, which the Venerable Bede referred to in his *Ecclesiastical History of the English People* as the *Getlingum* which seems to be a Latinization of the Old English *Ġeátlings* meaning the 'little Geats' (Shippey, 2015).

Line 3031b- Earnaness

Earnanæs, the "Eagle's Headland", is the name given to the site of Beowulf's death. Earnaness corresponds to Årnäs, a fortress which stood by the shore of Lake Vänern, near Skara in Västergötland, the Geatish capital. The first mention of Årnäs was that a castle existed there in 1283, but it is likely much older, and legends tell of fortifications existing there during the Migration Era (Wickberg, 1914).

Lines 3052-3057- Cursed by men of old

The poem says that the Last Survivor cursed the gold in the barrow, dooming anyone who possessed it, reminiscent of Andvari's ring from the *Völsunga Saga*. The Dragon (assuming it is not the transformed Last Survivor- see commentary for Lines 2231-66) was eventually killed for the gold, Beowulf died before getting a chance to enjoy it and the Gears are warned of their impending downfall. Thus everyone who possessed the gold, even briefly, met their downfall.

However, the Christian poet found this passage problematic- implying that the heathen gods had no power to curse on anyone. So, he explains that the curse was only effective if God allowed it.

Line 3150-51a- A lone Geatish widow…

Much speculation has been made about the woman who sings at Beowulf's funeral. Who is she and what is her relationship with Beowulf? Some have thought that she is just a random Geat woman, but I find this hard to believe. Others suggest she may have been Beowulf's personal wise woman or augur, something like the Norse *völva*. This is a possibility, and does fit in well with pre-Christian Germanic kingship, but I still feel like there's more to her than a wise-woman. It's also been proposed that this woman might have been Beowulf's wife. I think this is likely.

Some have wondered why, if this was indeed Beowulf's wife, why didn't they have children? There are a few possibilities; they may have been unable to have children, had only daughters (who would not have been considered heirs) or that he had a son or sons who had already died. Perhaps

this all had been explained in a legend about him now lost to us.

Readers have often assumed that since the hero has no heir and since no wife is mentioned we are to understand that he remained solitary and celibate throughout his life. It is quite possible, however, that the poet simply felt that Beowulf's marital status was of insufficient interest to warrant mention in the poem (Robinson, 1984).

The other question about this, would be who was Beowulf's wife? It could have just been an unnamed noblewoman, but there's a possibility she was in the poem. In *Hrólfs saga Kraki*, the daughter of Hrólf Kraki, Hrút was betrothed to Agnar, Ingeld's son to make peace, but Agnar betrays Hrólf at the wedding, where Bödvarr Bjarki kills Agnar and later marries Hrút (Olrik, 1919). This seems to be a misremembered version of Freawaru and Ingeld's marriage. Hrút is thought by some to have been the original name of Freawaru (which alliterates with the other Scylding names) and Bjarki, who I've explained earlier probably derived from the *Beowulf* proto-legend. It then would make sense if Beowulf was originally married to Freawaru (Turville-Petre, 1976).

The most popular theory about Beowulf's widow was given by Sophus Bugge, who suggested she was Hygd, the former wife of Hygelac. In heathen times, a new king would often marry the wife of the former king to strengthen their claim to the throne, sometimes even marrying their stepmother. Hygd, being an aunt by marriage, could marry Beowulf without it being incest. Hygd is also described as very young, making it most likely that the two were very close in age. When Hygelac died, Hygd offered the throne to Beowulf. The only way he could claim kingship would have been to marry her. Therefore, Hygd effectively proposed to him. While Beowulf rejected her offer, according to this theory they did marry after the death of Heardred (Bugge, 1899).

Lines 3169-77- The Funeral Procession

At the conclusion of Beowulf's funeral, Beowulf's men ride about his barrow, singing laments for their dead lord. This resembles funeral customs recorded by Vergil and Homer in Classical literature, but the most striking parallel to this passage from *Beowulf* is found in Jordanes' *Getica*. Before Attila the Hun's burial, his men ride in circles about the corpse, singing dirges for their lord. This is believed to reflect a Gothic funeral custom rather than a Hunnish one, and as the Goths were a Germanic people, it makes sense that this was also a funeral custom among their Scandinavian cousins (Klaeber, 1927).

The funeral procession consists of twelve of Beowulf's men riding about his barrow, but are these the same men who abandoned Beowulf in his last battle? It's entirely possible, but I can't help but think they are not. In the commentary for Line 1401, I explained that these twelve men seem to be a parallel to Jesus' twelve disciples. Only one of the disciples did not abandon Jesus, the same as Wiglaf. Of course, all the disciples (with the exception of Judas, who hanged himself) returned to Jesus' side after He rose again and began to spread the Gospel throughout the Known World; however, I do not imagine that Wiglaf would be so forgiving of these men. Desertion was seen by the Anglo-Saxons as one of the most heinous acts a follower of a lord could commit. Outlawry was the typical punishment for deserters. Therefore, I do not think these were the same twelve who followed Beowulf to the barrow. I believe these were loyal men of Beowulf's who rode about his barrow. I feel that if Wiglaf had not already outlawed or executed them, they would have been too disgraced to even consider participating in his funeral.

Line 3182b- ...most eager for praise.

The last word of *Beowulf, lofgeornost* (meaning 'eager for praise'), generally is a negative word

248

in Old English literature, having a connotation of 'overeagerness', comparable with *ofermód*. (Tolkien, 1953) However, Owen-Crocker points out that the Old Norse cognate, *lofgjarn* is not a critical word. *Only in the final words of the poem, does an elegy take on a Christian tone, but even here the final word lofġeornost is double-edged, and may mean one thing to the dramatized Geats and another to the Christian audience* (Owen-Crocker, 2000).

The Anglo-Saxons did not see anything wrong with pride. While they saw *ofermód* as problematic, pride was seen as a good thing. In fact, the Anglo-Saxons originally had no word for humility, and had to coin a word after Christianity was introduced. (Shippey, 2015)

But, whether or not the poet was being critical of Beowulf's pride, he was still making a theological point; Man without God, no matter how exemplary their life, is doomed. The tales of the Nordic Heroic Age were all about extraordinary men who do glorious deeds. But, the *Beowulf* poet laments that these heroes do not know God, so that when they die, they are not saved. Beowulf may be a just and good-hearted man, but he is still a man. And a heathen man. He is not a Christ figure, though some have argued it. He did not die for his people, he died for gold, and ultimately his death led to the fall of the kingdom. He wants to believe that men like Beowulf might find Salvation, but he doesn't believe that he will. Thus, he finds the end of the poem truly tragic, he has not only died in this world, but there is little hope that he will enter the Afterlife.

It is thus reasonable to regard Beowulf as a just man who has fought the good fight during his lifetime, but who was in the end brought to death by the flaws in his human nature, the legacy of Adam's sin, in trying to fight the dragon alone. He acts as a moral example in his early life, but in his last days he presents to the Christian audience the tragedy of fallen man… (Goldsmith, 1970).

Potential Beowulf Timeline

As most scholars are quick to point out, *Beowulf* is not a historical record, and because the events are (for the most part) fictional, the story elements cannot be accurately dated. This is only partially true. As Hygelac's Frisian raid is a true event that can be accurately dated, a tentative dating system for *Beowulf* can be deduced.

The most famous *Beowulf* chronology was created by Klaeber, who relied upon the work of Andreas Heusler. Additional use was made of studies done by George Clark and Marijane Osborn. These were taken as the basis of a further scrutiny of the poem by the author, who made extensive use of secondary source documents, along with much inference and extrapolation, to develop the sequence of events. All dating must be taken as highly conjectural, and only relatively accurate, as the single piece of datable-historical evidence comes from the sketchy reference to Hygelac's raid on Frisia, as given by Gregory of Tours in his *Historia Francorum*, and this can only be confined reliably to a period roughly between 516-531 AD, with 521 generally accepted as the best guess.

275- The Dragon discovers the hoard in the Earnaness Barrow
340- Heremod, king of the Danes is exiled to Jutland
345- Scyld Scefing washes up as a baby in a boat in Denmark
360- Scyld becomes king of the Danes
375- Hama steals from Eormenric
　　　　Death of Eormenric
385- Beow, son of Scyld Scefing, is born
405- Death of Scyld Scefing
420- Healfdene born
435- Hrethel born
　　　　Froda born
440- Offa, king of the Angles marries Thryth
　　　　Ongentheow born
　　　　Death of Beow
448- The Battle of Finnesburg
450- Heorogar born
452- Hrothgar born
454- Halga born
460- Ohthere born
462- Onela born
465- Froda kills Healfdene

470- Herebeald born

472- Hæthcyn born

474- Hrethel's daughter born

475- Hygelac born

479- Yrse born

485- Ingeld born

Healfdene's sons kill Froda

490- Heoroweard born

492- Death of Heorogar

Hrothgar becomes king of the Danes

493- Hrothgar marries Wealhtheow

494- Hygelac marries his first wife

Hygd born

495- Ecgtheow marries Hrethel's daughter

Hygelac's daughter born

Hrothulf born

497- Beowulf born

498- Hrethric and Hrothmund born

500- Freawaru born

Ecgtheow slays Heatholaf

Ecgtheow is banished from Geatland and seeks refuge with Danes

503- Beowulf begins his fosterage with Hrethel

Herebeald accidentally killed while hunting by Hæthcyn

Hrethel dies of grief

Hæthcyn becomes king of the Geats

Heorot is finished being built

Grendel begins his nightly raids

Ecgtheow killed by Grendel?

504- Death of Halga

505- Battle of Hreosneburg

508- Yrse marries Onela

Eadmund born

510- Eadgils born

Battle of Hrefnesholt

Hæthcyn killed by Ongentheow

Ongentheow killed by Eofor

Hygelac betroths his daughter to Eofor

Hygelac becomes king of the Geats

Ohthere becomes king of the Swedes

512- Beowulf's swimming contest with Breca

Hygelac maries Hygd

Eadgils born

513- Heardred born
515- Beowulf's adventures in Denmark
516- Ingeld marries Freawaru
    The Bards attack and burn Heorot
    Ingeld slain
521- Geat raid on Frisia
    Death of Hygelac
    Heredred becomes king of the Geats
525- Death of Hrothgar
    Hrothulf becomes king of the Danes
528- Death of Ohthere
    Onela becomes king
    Eanmund and Eadgils rebel against Onela and lose
    Eanmund and Onela seek refuge in Geatland
530- Heardred and Eanmund are killed
    Beowulf becomes king of the Geats
535- Battle on the Ice of Lake Vänern
    Onela is killed
    Eadgils becomes king of the Swedes
540- Wiglaf is born
545- Hrothulf is killed by Heoroweard
    Heoroweard is killed
    Hrethric returns from exile?
560- The Dragon awakens
    Death of Beowulf
    Wiglaf becomes king of the Geats
565- Eadgils conquers Geatland
    Wiglaf leads an exodus to England?
575- Death of Eadgils

Bibliography

LANGUAGE RESOURCES:

Bosworth, Joseph, and T. Northcote Toller. *An Anglo-Saxon Dictionary: Based on the Manuscript Collection of J. Bosworth with Supplement.* Oxford University Press, 1921.

Hall, John R. Clark, and Herbert Dean Meritt. *A Concise Anglo-Saxon Dictionary.* 4th ed. Cambridge University Press, 1962.

Kiernan, Kevin *Electronic Beowulf,* 4th online ed. University of Kentucky / The British Library, 2015

Klaeber, Fr, R. D. Fulk, Robert E. Bjork, and John D. Niles. *Klaeber's Beowulf; and the Fight at Finnsburg.* 4th ed. University of Toronto, 2008.

USEFUL SOURCES:

Arner, Timothy D., et al. *The Grinnell Beowulf- A Translation with Notes.* Grinnell College, 2013.

Bjork, Robert E., and John D. Niles. *A Beowulf Handbook.* University of Exeter Press, 1998.

Chambers, R. W., and C. L. Wrenn. *Beowulf; an Introduction to the Study of the Poem with a Discussion of the Stories of Offa and Finn.* 3rd ed. Cambridge University Press, 1959.

Chickering, Howell D. *Beowulf: A Dual-Language Edition: Translated with an Introduction and Commentary.* Anchor, 1977.

Garmonsway, G.N, et al. *Beowulf and Its Analogues.* E.P. Dutton & Co. Inc, 1971.

Lapidge, Michael. *The Blackwell Encyclopaedia of Anglo-Saxon England.* Blackwell, 2003.

Lawrence, William. *Beowulf and Epic Tradition.* 2nd ed., Harvard University Press, 1928.

Orchard, Andy. *A Critical Companion to Beowulf.* DS Brewer, 2003.

Shippey, Tom. *Beowulf* through Tolkien." Spring 2015, Signum University. Online Class (Anytime Audit).

Slade, Benjamin. *"Beowulf with New Modern English Facing Translation." Beowulf on Steorarume [Beowulf in Cyberspace],* 2005.

Tolkien, J. R. R., and Christopher Tolkien. *The Monsters and the Critics, and Other Essays.* HarperCollins, 1997.

Tolkien, J. R. R., and Christopher Tolkien. *Beowulf: A Translation and Commentary: Together with Sellic Spell.* Houghton Mifflin Harcourt, 2014.

OTHER SOURCES:

Benson, Larry D. "The Pagan Coloring of *Beowulf." Old English Poetry: Fifteen Essays.* Brown University Press, 1967.

Brodeur, Arthur Gilchrist. *The Art of Beowulf.* University of California Press, 1959

Bugge, Sophus. *The Home of the Eddic Poems; with Especial Reference to the Helgi-Lays.* Translated by William Henry Schofield, Revised ed., vol. 11, David Nutt in the Strand, 1899.

Cardew, Philip. "Grendel: Bordering on the Monstrous." *The Shadow-Walkers: Jacob Grimm's Mythology of the Monstrous.* Arizona Center for Medieval and Renaissance Studies, 2005.

Chaney, William A. *The Cult of Kingship in Anglo-Saxon England.* University of California Press, 1970.

Clover, Carol J. "The Germanic Context of the Unferþ Episode." *Speculum*, vol. 55, no. 3, pp. 444-68, 1980.

Chambers, R. W. *Widsith: A Study in Old English Heroic Legend*. Cambridge University Press, 1912.

Christensen, Tom. "Lejre Beyond Legend- The Archaeological Evidence." *Journal of Danish Archaeology*, 2010.

Cohen, Jeffrey Jerome. "The Promise of Monsters." *The Ashgate Research Companion to Monsters and the Monstrous*, 2012.

Cooke, William. "Hrothulf: A Richard III, or an Alfred the Great?" *Studies in Philology*, vol. 104, no. 2, 2007.

Davidson, H. R. Ellis. "Weland the Smith." *Folklore*, vol. 69, no. 3, pp. 145-59. 1958

de Roo, Harvey. "*Beowulf* 2223b: A Thief by Any Other Name?" *Modern Philology*, vol. 79, no. 3, pp. 297-304. 1982.

Drout, Michael D.C. "'*Beowulf*: The Monsters and the Critics': The Brilliant Essay that Broke Beowulf Studies", *The Lord of the Rings Fanatics Plaza*, April 25, 2010.

Earl, James W. *Thinking about Beowulf*. Stanford University Press, 1994.

Einarsson, Stefán. "Old English Beot and Old Icelandic Heitstrenging." *Pmla*, vol. 49, no. 4, pp. 975-93. Dec. 1934.

Enright, Michael J. *Lady with a Mead Cup: Ritual, Prophecy, and Lordship in the European Warband from La Tène to the Viking Age*. Four Courts, 2013.

Farrell, Robert T. *Beowulf: Swedes and Geats*. Viking Society for Northern Research, 1972.

Fulk, R. D. "Unferth and His Name." *Modern Philology*, vol. 85, no. 2, 1987, pp. 113–127.

Fulk, R.D. "The Name of Offa's Queen: Beowulf 1931–2." *Anglia*, vol. 122, no. 4, 2005, pp. 614-39.

Georgianna, Linda. "King Hrethel's Sorrow and the Limits of Heroic Action in Beowulf." *Speculum*, vol. 62, no. 4, 1987, pp. 829-50.

Gilliver, Peter, et al. The Ring of Words: Tolkien and the Oxford English Dictionary. Oxford University Press, 2009

Goldsmith, Margaret E. *The Mode and Meaning of Beowulf*. The Athlone Press of the University of London, 1970.

Grimm, Jacob Ludwig Karl. *Teutonic Mythology*. Trans. James Steven Stallybrass. 3rd ed. Vol. 1. George Bell & Sons, 1882.

Hill, Thomas D. "The Christian Language and Theme of *Beowulf*." *Companion to Old English Poetry*. VU University Press. 1994.

Holmes, Tao Tao. "Flyting Was Medieval England's Version of an Insult-Trading Rap Battle." Atlas Obscura. 31 July 2019.

Jakobsson, Ármann, and Sverrir Jakobsson. *The Routledge Research Companion to the Medieval Icelandic Sagas*. Routledge, 2017.

Klaeber, Frederick. "Attila's and Beowulf's Funeral." *Publications of the Modern Language Association of America*, vol. 42, no. 2, pp. 255-267. Jun. 1927.

Lapidge, Michael. "*Beowulf* and the Psychology of Terror." *Heroic Poetry in the Anglo-Saxon Period: Studies in Honor of Jess B. Bessinger, Jr.* pp. 373-402. 1993.

Lawrence, William Witherle. "The Haunted Mere in *Beowulf*." PMLA, vol. 27, no. 2, pp. 208-45. 1912.

MacDonald, Jessica. "Diving Records: Humans vs. Animals." DeeperBlue.com, 13 Nov. 2017.

Malone, Kemp. "The Tale of Ingeld." *Studies in Heroic Legend and in Current Speech*, Rosenkilde og Bagger, pp. 1-62. 1959.

Meijer, Bernhard, and Theodor Westrin. "Ramshult" *Nordisk Familjebok: Konversationslexikon och Realencyklopedi: Tidsekvation - Trompe*. 2nd ed. Vol. 29. Nordisk Familjeboks Förlags Aktiebolag, 1919.

Meyer, Thomas. *Beowulf: A Translation*. Punctum Books, 2012.

Mortimer, Paul. *Woden's Warriors: Warfare, Beliefs, Arms and Armour in Northern Europe during the 6th and 7th Centuries*. Anglo-Saxon Books, 2011.

Neidorf, Leonard, et al. "Large-Scale Quantitative Profiling of the Old English Verse Tradition." *Nature Human Behaviour*, vol. 3, no. 6, 2019, pp. 560–567.

Nerman, Birger. *Det Svenska Rikets Uppkomst*. Generalstabens Litografiska Anstalt, 1925.

Nerman, Birger. "När kom Västergötland under svearnas välde?" Västergötlands Fornminnesförening, 1956.

Neville, Jennifer. "Hrothgar's Horses: Feral or Thoroughbred?" *Anglo-Saxon England*, vol. 35, pp. 131-157. 2006

Newton, Sam. *The Origins of Beowulf and the Pre-Viking Kingdom of East Anglia*. D.S. Brewer, 1999.

North, Richard. *Heathen Gods in Old English Literature*. Cambridge Studies in Anglo-Saxon England. Cambridge University Press, 1997.

Ogilvy, J. D.A., and Donald C. Baker. *Reading Beowulf*. University of Oklahoma, 1983.

Olrik, Axel. *The Heroic Legends of Denmark*. American-Scandinavian Foundation, 1919.

Olson, Oscar Ludvig. *The Relation of the Hrólfs Saga Kraka and the Bjarkarímur to Beowulf: A Contribution to the History of Saga Development in England and the Scandinavian Countries* . University of Chicago Press, 1916.

Orchard, Andy. *Pride and Prodigies: Studies in the Monsters of the Beowulf Manuscript*. University of Toronto Press, 2014.

Osborn, Marijane. "Beowulf's Landfall in "Finna Land"." *Neuphilologische Mitteilungen*, vol. 90, no. 2, pp. 137-42. 1989.

Overing, Gillian R."Reinventing Beowulf's Voyage to Denmark." *Old English Newsletter*, vol. 21, no. 2, pp. 30-9. Spring 1988.

Owen-Crocker, Gale R. *The Four Funerals in Beowulf and the Structure of the Poem*. Manchester University Press, 2010.

Parker, Eleanor. "Christ the Arkenstone and *The Hobbit*." *A Clerk of Oxford*. Blogspot, 18 Dec. 2014.

Porck, Thijs. "A Medieval Giant on Display: Last Resting Place of *Beowulf*'s Hygelac Discovered?" Dutch Anglo-Saxonist, WordPress, 7 July 2017.

Porck, Thijs, and Berber Bossenbroek. "A Hart with Its Head Held High: A New Emendation for *Beowulf*, Line 1372a." *ANQ: A Quarterly Journal of Short Articles, Notes and Reviews*, pp. 1-5. 2019.

Porck, Thijs. "Undoomed Men Do Not Need Saving. A Note on Beowulf , LL. 572B-3 and 2291-3A." *OUP Academic*, Oxford University Press, 10 Apr. 2020.

Porter, Dorothy Carr. "The Social Centrality of Women in *Beowulf*: A New Context" *The Heroic Age*, vol. 5, 2001.

Pollington, Stephen. *The Meadhall: The Feasting Tradition in Anglo-Saxon England*. Anglo-Saxon Books, 2012.

Robinson, Fred C. "History, Religion, Culture." *Approaches to Teaching Beowulf*. The Modern Language Association of America, 1984.

Rydberg, Viktor. *Teutonic Mythology*. Trans. Rasmus B. Anderson. Swan Sonnenschein & Co, 1889.

Shuman, R. Baird, and H. Charles Hutchings. "The Un- Prefix: A Means of Germanic Irony in 'Beowulf.'" *Modern Philology*, vol. 57, no. 4, pp. 217-222. 1960.

Shippey, Tom. "Names in *Beowulf* and Anglo-Saxon England" *The Dating of Beowulf: A Reassessment.* D.S. Brewer, 2014.

Staver, Ruth Johnston. *A Companion to Beowulf.* Greenway Press, 2005.

Swanton, Michael. *Beowulf.* Manchester University Press, 1978.

Tolkien, J.R.R. "Ofermod." *Essays and Studies.* Vol. 6. John Murray Ltd. 1953.

Tolkien, J. R. R., and Alan Bliss. *Finn and Hengest: The Fragment and the Episode.* Harper Collins, 2006.

Turville-Petre, Edward Oswald Gabriel. *The Heroic Age of Scandinavia.* Greenwood Press, 1976.

Wadbring, Bengt. "Fornborgen Halleberg." *Bengans Historiasidor.* 14 May 2008.

Walkden, George. "The Status of *hwæt* in Old English." *English Language and Linguistics,* vol. 17, no. 3, pp. 465-88. 30 Aug. 2011,

Wentersdorf, Karl P. "Beowulf's Withdrawal from Frisia: A Reconsideration." *Studies in Philology,* vol. 68, no.4, pp. 395-415. Oct. 1971.

Wickberg, Rudolf. *Beowulf- En Fornengelsk Hjeltedikt.* 2nd ed. Ekblad, 1914.

Wills, John. "Symbel: The Heathen Drinking Ritual?" *Oðrærir,* vol. 2, 2012.

Wilson, Douglas. "The Anglo-Saxon Evangel." *Touchstone,* 2007.

Wood, Ian. *The Merovingian Kingdoms, 450-751.* Longman Group, 1994.

About the Author

Andrew P. Boynton was born in Beverly, Massachusetts, but has lived most of his life in Central California, where he loves spending time in the old Sequoia forests of the Sierras or on the rocky shorelines of Cambria and Pebble Beach. He grew up reading fantasy and historical novels about medieval Europe. He has a passion for ancient cultures and languages and has studied Old English, Old Norse and Hebrew. He is presently working on *Guthbrand's Saga*, an historical fantasy trilogy that is a prequel to *Beowulf* (in prose, not alliterative poetry). He is also translating the Old Testament from its original Hebrew into English.

Printed in Great Britain
by Amazon